EARTH
2020

EARTH
2020

THE EXTINCTION OF HUMANITY

WILLIAM WALTER

Book Ordering Information

Phone Number: 347-901-4929 or 347-901-4920
Email: info@globalsummithouse.com
Global Summit House
www.globalsummithouse.com

Printed in the United States of America

Contents

2020

PART 1

2021

PART 2

PART 3

2023

PART 4

INTRODUCTION

———•●❋●•———

Planet Earth, the jewel of the galaxy. A beautiful perfect pearl in an endless black sea. The inhabitants of this world live their lives engrossed in their pursuit of wealth and power, living meaningless, self-centered lives. It's part of human nature to strive for more, but through this quest for more, we kill and take what we want with the strength of our warriors and abilities of our weapons. With the greed and careless ways of these inhabitants, the world has been on a path of self-destruction for the past ten thousand years. As the millennia tick by, the greed of man and the killing abilities of his armies and weapons increase to the point of self-destruction. Now we are capable of planetwide destruction.

The reasons for killing have never changed, just the technology. We kill to make our kingdoms larger and wealthier, or to make others conform to our laws, or we simply kill in the name of our gods. We would assume that after thousands of years, the inhabitants of Earth would learn to live as one group on one planet. We would hope they would learn to make the lives of their fellow human beings better, as well as realize the damage they are causing to their beautiful pearl. We would also assume they would realize that their destructive path could not continue for the sake of all the inhabitants of the planet.

Imagine what would happen if beings more advanced than ourselves spotted our pearl and decided to take it for their own. It is inevitable that one day this will happen, but the question is would the inhabitants of Earth finally pull together as one to save it? Only time will tell.

PART 1

CHAPTER 1

Parachute, Colorado
October 12, 2020, 04:00

Bill wanders through the dark house trying to avoid the obstructions that may be in his path. It's a morning just like any other morning, filled with the same rituals. He makes a pot of strong coffee and heads to the bathroom to get ready to begin his day. By six o'clock he's headed for the door and knows someone will be waiting for him as always. His dog, Sassy, likes her human (he can't say master because he knows it's not true). She is a creature of habit, and to her this is a morning just like any other. They are absolutely two of a kind.

As they leave the house into the clutches of a cool Colorado morning, half of the pair goes on her way to make her morning ritual stops, and the other half heads to his studio for the creation of beautiful, as well as strange works of art. Bill turns on the lights, lights a fire in the woodstove, and then, the most important thing on the list, turns on the rock and roll real loud. It's the same thing every morning. He truly is a creature of habit. Speaking of habits, there is one part of his morning ritual yet to be taken care of. He walks over to his bench where his pipe is waiting and fills it with his "Special Blend." This part of the ritual is what helps him forget the cruel world he strives so hard to escape from.

Bill absolutely loves his life and does exactly what he wants, when he wants, with nobody to bother him. That's why he bought his piece of a valley and quit the rat race to enjoy his art. With his son Willis, the youngest of five children, they have created a very profitable business that involves the creation of art, by carving it from concrete.

Several projects are under way in the large studio, but most of their work is custom ordered by the wealthy residents of the Vail and Aspen Ski Mecca. When the two aren't working on custom orders, they have time to create whatever they want to sell in the galleries. Bill is currently working on an eight-foot-tall Celtic cross for the Donahues, and on the other side of the studio, Willis is sculpting a nude statue of Dr. Dean's wife.

The father and son enjoy their privacy so much that the house and studio, as well as numerous other buildings, are nestled in a valley four miles out of town on fifty acres of land. The house and other buildings are all nestled into the side of a mountain, and virtually invisible because of their talents. If you didn't know they were there, you would walk right by without noticing them.

Fresh water runs in the stream that runs off the mountain for the entire length of the valley, and there is plenty of wild game in the mountains. They have a greenhouse for growing vegetables, solar panels for power and hot water, a huge root cellar for storage, and fruit trees planted among the pine and aspen trees. With a hundred cases of Corona in the root cellar and his "special crop" growing in the greenhouse, Bill has no reason to leave the valley. "Life is good."

Bill is in the studio working when Willis finally wanders in. He is still half asleep with an energy drink in his hand.

"What's up? Besides you finally?" Bill asks as he sits at his work smoking his pipe.

"Not much," Willis said as he fanned the smoke away from him as he made his way through the sweet-smelling cloud.

"How's Mrs. Dean coming along?" Bill asked as he put down his "tool," as he called it, on the bench and walked over to examine the statue.

"Almost finished. I'm just finishing her nipples."

"That's incredible work," his father said as he walked around the statue admiring it.

"Thanks."

Dr. Dean, who is a pharmaceutical researcher, hired Willis to do the nude statue of his wife. The good doctor is quite proud of his wife's body, and he should be with the alarming amount of money he has invested in it.

Bill is jealous of his son's ability to recreate the human body, as the sculptures he creates would make the masters of ancient Greece green with envy. Bill on the other hand is more of a master of reproductions and abstract art. He can create anything from stone to dragons.

"Did you get some breakfast?"

"No, not yet. I wanted to get Mrs. Dean finished first. Then I need to go into town for some new guitar strings. We have a show tonight in Aspen. You should come."

"I wish I could but I really need to get this cross finished for the Donahues. They expect it by the eighteenth, and that's only six days from now. I also have a date with Monica tonight, and we all have our priorities," Bill said with a grin.

Bill always takes Monica out on Thursday nights. It's been a ritual since he met her at one of Willis's concerts. She brings a bit a humanity into his hermit lifestyle.

"Oh, that's right, it's Thursday night. You two have fun tonight. I know you old guys need to enjoy life while there's still time," he said with a smile. "I'm going to put the finishing touch on these double Ds," he said with a huge concrete breast in each hand. "Then I'm going to hit the road."

"Okay. Drive safe."

"I will, Dad."

Bill returned to his project and repacked his pipe, then turned the music up "real loud" and went back to work. "Life is good," he thinks to himself.

CHAPTER 2

Kabult Station
October 12, 2020, 08:00

The Kabult Station commander, Corisk, is on the command deck reviewing the plans for the assault on planet S-3. The world below has been the object of interest of the Corisole planet for almost one hundred years, and after twenty years of preparation it's now time to attack.

"What's the status of our assault force, Captain Misk?"

Captain Misk approaches his commander and old friend. "Final preparations are almost complete, sir. We are fueling and arming the assault vehicles as we speak and will be ready to launch in thirty-six hours as planned."

The commander rises from his seat and begins pacing the deck of the orbital station. "Are the mines ready for launch?"

"Yes, sir. There are five thousand mines armed and ready for launch at your command. With their boosters they should be able to reach the planet surface two hours after they are launched."

"Well done, Captain. We will launch in twenty-four hours to coincide with the meteor showers this planet experiences, in order to conceal their approach. The planet's inhabitants lack the defense capabilities to fend off our attack, and once they realize they are under attack, it will be too late to do anything about it. By disguising the mines as meteors they will have no warning until the first city is destroyed. With each mine capable of destroying a major city, by 0200 hours virtually every major city on the planet should be in ruins along with their military installations."

The commander continues to pace, going over the plan in his head. "Are the second wave of attack ships being fueled now?"

"Yes, sir. A total of two thousand ships will be ready for the final assault. We also have twenty refueling towers ready to depart and assume their positions on the planet when needed."

Is the fleet still scheduled to arrive in orbit on time?"

"They're scheduled arrival is in forty-eight hours, sir, and I have been assured by Captain Korg that they are on schedule and will be here at the designated time."

"Excellent, Captain. We should be well into our final sweep of the planet when they arrive. The Supreme Leader will be quite pleased with our progress."

The commander returned to his chair and continued contemplating the attack as he looked around the now busy control room. "Commence the attack in twenty-four hours as planned, Captain."

"Yes, sir," Misk replied as he saluted his commander.

The commander sits in his seat considering the outcome of their attack. This attack will break almost every galactic law dealing with evolving planets, but the Corisole has no choice. The S-3 planet is absolutely necessary to the survival of their race since their own planet is now near death. There are other planets that are compatible, but they are either out of reach with their short time frame, or it will take too long to terraform the atmospheres for their needs.

Meanwhile on the planet Corisole, which is located in the Almitack star system of the Orion sector, the Supreme Leader waits for word from the Kabult Station. He sits contemplating the repercussions of his decision to invade S-3. The consequences will be quite serious, but his people have no other alternative. Their planet and their people are running out of time.

The Alliance has had a research facility on the S-3 moon for several decades until the Galactic Alliance banned all intrusions into the S-3 system. At one time, every planet in the Alliance had its eye on S-3, but it was obvious that it would be absolutely unethical to interfere with the planet's natural evolution, so the station was deemed off limits from then on. The Galactic Alliance then created the 12:7:141 Treaty to protect the planet and its inhabitants. An incoming message interrupted his thoughts.

"Your Majesty. We have received a communication from the Kabult Station. All preparations for the invasion of S-3 are complete, and Commander Corisk assures you that the attack will start on schedule."

"Understood."

Twenty years of preparation have passed, and the planet Corisole will finally reap the fruits of its labors. The planet's inhabitants are on the verge of extinction. They are constantly at war with each other and have created weapons that are capable of destroying not only each other but the entire planet. With these facts facing them, the Corisole have decided that they cannot prolong the operation any longer. They absolutely must have the S-3 planet to ensure the survival of their race, and as soon as the planet is cleansed, they will proceed with the colonization of the new world with their own people.

Leader Mirosh activated his comms. "Send Advisor Nalen to my office," he ordered.

"Yes, Your Majesty," his secretary replied.

After a few minutes had passed, his advisor entered his office. "You called for me, Your Majesty?" Nalen asked.

"Yes, Mr. Nalen. What is the overall plan for the colonization of the planet S-3?"

His advisor walked over and activated a large monitor, and a map of the S-3 planet appeared. "The fleet vessels currently en route to the planet are carrying a complement of atmospheric processors. Unfortunately, the atmosphere is so contaminated that it will take approximately two years to make the planet ready for colonization."

"Mr. Nalen, at the rate Corisole's environment is deteriorating, our planet will be scarcely able to support life in ten years, and absolutely uninhabitable in one hundred years. It will take at least five years to completely transfer our people to the new planet, and another five years to relocate our industries. We will have the fleet return after the situation is stabilized, and send more processers to the planet to speed up the process."

"I'm aware of the time frame, Your Majesty, but I do not see any way to speed up the process. The inhabitants of the planet are like a plague. They have polluted the waters to the point that isolated parts of the oceans are dying, and the atmosphere is on the verge of destruction. If the current inhabitants are allowed to proceed on their current path, S-3 will be uninhabitable in two hundred years. Of course that's if they don't destroy the planet with their weapons first."

Mirosh contemplates the information given to him by his trusted adviser. "Such beings don't deserve to inhabit this planet. Therefore, I will feel no guilt for removing them. Even if it is against galactic law and brings the wrath of the Alliance down on us, our race will benefit from it, so we must take the risk. I want to know the moment our fleet reaches the S-3 system."

"Yes, sir."

"That will be all, Mr. Nalen."

The Supreme Leader is relieved after hearing Nalen's report but is still concerned with the repercussions his planet will face because of his acts. The invasion of the S-3 planet will bring the wrath of the Alliance down on them with a vengeance. It is absolutely necessary that they establish themselves on the planet before the Alliance steps in to stop them.

CHAPTER 3

Parachute, Colorado
October 12, 2020, 12:00

Bill is sitting outside the studio enjoying a beautiful October day, the mountain air fills his lungs, and the warm Colorado sun shines on him, taking the bite out of the fall day. Willis has left for the day, and it gets lonely on the mountain. After a civilized divorce he decided he didn't want to leave Colorado or its beauty, so after a year of searching he found this valley and began to build his paradise. It took five long years of excavating, construction, and landscaping, but the valley is now back to its pristine state. Bill's valley is his best work of art, and he treasures every minute he spends in it.

The property is fifty acres of pine and aspen trees surrounded by a split rail fence. The dirt drive winds through the trees along the stream and ends at a huge stone fire pit, which is in front of the hidden house and next to the stream. If it wasn't for the No Trespassing sign at the gate, there would be campers fishing in the stream. The house and all the other buildings are buried in the mountain and landscaped to match the beautiful country side. If it wasn't for a few windows and the rustic-looking wooden doors, you would never know it was there. To Bill this place is as close as you can get to heaven.

As he sits next to his studio, the other female in his life, and actually the bossy one, comes running through the trees with a stick in her mouth. She's trying to tell him something, and he knows well what it is. It's time for a walk and a few tosses of the stick. Bill really tries to take her once a day, but some days there's just not time.

They walked up the trail that runs alongside the clear trout-filled stream. The stream runs from the top of the mountain to the bottom of the valley, then across the landscape until it finds its way into the Colorado River. The stream full of brook trout, the mountains full of game for hunting, it's an outdoorsman's paradise. Sassy, who has no care for hunting and fishing, has only one care on her little mind. Throw the stick in the stream so I can go for a swim. She lives only for her daily walks and swims, which is why he feels guilty when he can't take her.

After a long hour long walk, it's back to the studio, and back to work. Sassy plops down on her bed to chew on her stick, and Bill goes back to his work. Playtime's over, and he has a project to finish, so he cranks up the tunes and dances his way back to his work

After a few stops on the way and a two-hour drive, Willis pulls into the high mountain town of Aspen. It's a cool day to be driving the Jeep, but he enjoys the fresh mountain air blowing in his face. He pulled off the highway into the parking lot of his mother's property management business and parked in front of the office. He can't come to town without visiting his mom, they have a special relationship, and he misses her a lot, so he visits her every chance he gets.

"Hi, Mom," he said as he walked in the door, then went over and gave her a kiss and a big hug.

"Hi, sweetheart, what are you doing all the way up here?"

"We have a show to do in town tonight, so I thought I would stop and see if you felt like some lunch."

"That sounds great. There's a pizza place down the street. How's peperoni sound?" (Which she knows is a silly question because that's the only kind he eats.)

"You know the answer to that question."

Devona grabbed her coat off the rack, locked the door, and off they went walking down the streets of Aspen to the Pizza Pub. The Pub is a cozy place where you can sit by the window and watch people from all over the world walk by. Willis likes it for its scenery, which contains some of the most beautiful women in the world. The ski season will be starting in a few weeks, and the town is beginning to fill with the beautiful fur-wearing bunnies from around the world.

"So how's work going?"

"It's going good. I finished Dr. Dean's statue of his wife today. He's going to love it. It came out great."

"Well, if it looks anything like she does it'll be beautiful. She's a beautiful lady."

"You think she's beautiful, you should see her nude," he said with a huge grin. "I'm serious, there's a lot of Doc Dean's money invested in that body, it's perfect. I've got the pictures to prove it too. Too bad I have to give them back," he said, still grinning.

"Willis!" his mother said, then slapped him on the shoulder and laughed.

"So why don't you and Alex come to the show tonight? I'll save you a table up front."

"You know I love to watch you play, but you also know how I hate crowded bars, and it's a little loud for my taste. Also Alex is in Steamboat and I wouldn't want to go alone."

"That's okay. I'll stop by after the show if it's not too late."

"So how's your dad?"

"Oh, you know Dad, as long as he has his three ins he's happy. Smokin, drinkin, and workin." They both laughed, knowing exactly true of a statement it was. Bill is a hopeless workaholic who tends to have vices that he indulges in every chance he gets.

"Yea he'll never change, will he."

"Never. But he's happy, and enjoys his life just the way it is. No headaches and no stress."

They enjoyed their lunch and talked about all the new things in each other's lives. Their unique relationship allowed them to talk to each other about absolutely anything.

"Well, I've got to get back to work. Have to pay the bill's, you know," his mother said as she waved the waitress over and paid the bill.

They walked back up the street to her office, enjoying the cool mountain air and each other's company. They eventually ended up back at the office, where the mother and son said their good-byes, then hugged and kissed each other. Willis waited for her to go into her office. Then he jumped back in the Jeep and headed down the road toward the Lift House Pub. He has a show to get ready for tonight, and the rest of the band will be waiting for him to get in some rehearsal time in before the night's show.

Bill is in the studio as always, and Sublime is playing very loud on the stereo system as he dances and sings while he works. The dog is lying in her bed looking at him like he's retarded, when the phone rings, so he turns down the music and dances over to answer it.

"Yea," he said, irritated that someone has to interrupt his afternoon festivities. He doesn't like to call it work because he absolutely believes that if you enjoy what you do, you never work a day in your life.

"Why do you always answer the phone like that?" Devona asks.

"Sorry old habits are hard to break."

"Well, it's not very businesslike."

"Well, neither am I."

"Yea, that's the truth. I had lunch with our son today. He seems really happy with the Dean sculpture."

"You would be happy too if you saw it, it's beautiful. He'll be even happier when we deliver it tomorrow and he gets the eight thousand dollars in his hand. He's been saving his money so he can pay off his Jeep and move to Denver," he said with a tone of sorrow in his voice.

"Don't remind me. I don't know what I'm going to do without him around. The girls are grown and gone now, and he's all I've got left." You can hear the tears in her eyes as she says it. "I won't have anyone to come and see me after he leaves."

"Yea, I'll only have Sassy to keep me company after he's gone," he said, petting the dog, which has arrived at his feet after hearing her name.

"I thought that was Monica's job."

"Now, now, be nice."

"You know I'm just kidding. I like Monica, she's good for you. She keeps you out of trouble, and we all know what a full-time job that can be," she added with a chuckle.

"So how's Alex doing?" he asked, changing the subject.

"He's in Steamboat trying to round up some more clients. We're expanding the business this year and with the ski season beginning it's the perfect time to round up more work."

"You know what they say. All work and no play, makes life boring and miserable."

"Yea and I also know all too well your philosophy. All work and all play is the only option. Someday you'll grow up."

"You know it's a really tough job but somebody has to do it, and I volunteered for the job a long time ago. Oh and by the way that reminds me, I'm neglecting my duty. Hold on a minute." He strolls over to his fridge and grabs a beer. "It's Miller time."

"It's only one o'clock."

"You know quite well my answer to that one."

"Unfortunately I do. It's five o'clock somewhere."

"You got it." They both laugh as he pops the cap on a cold bottle of Corona and takes a long drink from the icy bottle.

"Hey, the meteor showers are tonight. Are you going to watch them?" she asked.

"Monica and I are going to dinner tonight. But after dinner we'll probably start a fire in the pit and watch the stars fall out of the sky. I should be working. I've got a lot of work to do and it's only gonna get worse after Willis leaves."

"Stop reminding me," she said sadly. "I know you hate having employees, but maybe you should hire on a couple of sculptors to help. There's a lot of college art students who would love to do it."

"Yea I know, but I really like my privacy. Plus, I couldn't handle the laughter when I dance while I'm working. They wouldn't get much work done if they are lying on the floor laughing."

"It is truly a pitiful sight. You would think you would get better at it as much as you do it."

"You would think so, huh."

"All right, I've got to go. I'll talk to ya later. Bye."

"Okay. Bye."

It's funny how two people who couldn't live together could be such good friends, he thinks to himself. But he is glad that they still are friends.

"Well, Sassy, back to work." Bill walked over to the stereo beer in hand, and cranked it up real loud, then danced his way back to his work. "Life is good, Sassy," he said to the dog as he took another drink of the frosty brew, then set the bottle on the bench. Sassy returned to her bed under the bench, where he could swear she was shaking her head and laughing. Everyone's a critic.

CHAPTER 4

---•◉•---

Kitt Peak Observatory, Arizona
October 12, 2020, 14:00

Ben Murphy is sitting at the base of his very large telescope gazing at the stars, when his assistant Allen Tosh walks into the building. Normally Ben would be staring at some faraway star at full power, but tonight he is set on low and looking to spot some large meteors.

"What's up, Ben?"

"Nothing but a bunch of stars, Allen," he said, looking at the sky. "You getting ready for the show tonight?"

"Yes, I'm taking my astronomy class to the top of the mountain tonight to view the showers. Should be quite a show," he replied as he climbed the stairs to the viewing platform. "What are you doing tonight?" he asked, noticing that Ben hasn't taken off the viewer since he entered.

"Well, I've been scanning the skies trying to spot some meteors, when I spotted something peculiar toward the Orion sector."

"What do you mean by peculiar?"

"I'm not sure. I've discovered six object where there shouldn't be any."

"Mind if I take a look?"

"Sure thing," Ben said as he moved from the chair.

Allen traded places with Ben at the viewer of the telescope. "Wow, that is strange, but it's really hard to see them through the filters. Why don't you call your buddy John at NASA and see if he can get a shot with the Hubble?"

"Great idea. Get me those coordinates and I'll give John a call and see what he can find out about our six little spots." He then headed down to his office on the main level of the observatory.

"Okay. Give me a minute and I'll have the coordinates." Allen calculated the coordinates and hurried down to Ben's office.

John Alistair is the director of operations at NASA, and his job keeps him quite busy these days. With the Mars rovers, the deep space probes, and now the always manned International Space Station, his day is full. With a Mars mission in the works now, it has gotten even busier.

He is sitting at his computer going over the data sent to him from his team leaders and trying to keep up with the steady flow of information. He sat back and was rubbing his eyes as his phone rang.

"Hello."

"John, Ben Murphy here, you got a few minutes?"

"Always for a friend, Ben. What's up?"

"Well, John, I have a big favor to ask. I've spotted six anomalies in an area where there shouldn't be any, and I wondered if you could point that big beautiful lady of yours at them and take a look?"

"Sure, Ben, send the coordinates to me and I'll see what she can see."

"I already e-mailed them to you."

"Pretty sure of yourself, aren't you, Ben?"

"I knew you wouldn't let me down, buddy. I'll be here all night, so let me know what you come up with. And thanks a million, John."

"You got it, Ben. I'll let you know as soon as I find out anything."

"Thanks, John. Good-bye."

"Good-bye, Ben."

John calls the command center to pass Ben's coordinates to his righthand man, Brad Meyer. "Brad, this is John."

"Yea, John, what can I do for you?"

"I'm sending you a set of coordinates from our friend Ben Murphy at Kitt Peak. See if you can get that pretty lady of ours to see anything."

"Any idea what I'm looking for."

"None whatsoever. Ben said that he spotted six unknowns at those coordinates."

"You got it, John. I'll let you know if we find anything."

"Thanks, Brad."

John hung up the phone and leaned back in his chair, speculating on what Ben's unknown spots are. Ben Murphy has been at the director at Kitt Peak for many years, so if he says it's something strange, you can count on it.

Chapter 5

————•●❋●•————

Planet Torani
October 12, 2020, 16:00

The planet Torani is a pristine ocean world of hundreds of very large islands scattered on the surface of a never-ending beautiful blue sea. The inhabitants are a peaceful race of beings, dedicated to maintaining the safety of the galaxy.

Fleet Commander Brydon is in his office at Torani Central Command, which is located in the Torani capital city of Carista. He is reviewing the Alliance fleet's monthly mission logs when Major Arden appears on his video screen.

"Commander Brydon. Our tracking systems have detected a fleet of six vessels carrying a Corisole signature. Sir, they appear to be en route to the Sol System."

"That's impossible, Major. The Sol System is deemed off limits to all Alliance systems. The Treaty of 12:7:141 has absolutely restricted that system to further incursion for the last thirty years. The S-3 planet is closed to all research until the inhabitants are capable of at least intersystem travel, which is not expected for at least another fifty years," he stated angrily. "Thank you, Major, for the report." He hit the call command on his console for his secretary. "Moroi. Get me the emperor immediately."

"Yes, Commander."

The commander sat stroking his spikey white beard, wondering how the Corisole planet actually believed they could so blatantly defy the treaty. For them to think the Alliance sensors wouldn't notice their actions was ludicrous, and the commander wasn't going to let them get away with it.

The Kabult Station is a massive complex with miles of tunnels, as well as millions of square feet of hangar space to accommodate the two thousand attack ships that are now ready for launch. With a full complement of highenergy laser cannons and crew quarters for three thousand crewmen, it's the most powerful single station in the galaxy.

Commander Corisk is in his quarters double- and triple-checking the invasion plans, when Ensign Myano appears on the video screen.

"Commander Corisk. We have received a transmission from Fleet Commander Salick. He has informed us that the Alliance sensors have discovered our fleet en route to us and have informed the Torani leaders of our movements. They have launched their fleet in pursuit of our fleet, but we do have a three-day lead on them."

"Thank you, Ensign. Inform Salick that since he has a three-day advantage on the Torani fleet, they should be of no consequence to our plan. But inform him that he needs to begin planning for their fleet's arrival at S-3. They will not take our actions lightly, and we cannot allow the Torani to interfere with our goal at any cost. Is that clear, Ensign?"

"Yes, sir."

"I assume the station is ready to launch the attack on planet S-3."

"Yes, sir. I have been informed that the mines are all alarmed and ready for launch, and the flight computers are programmed with the coordinates of the planet's major cities and military installations. Once the mine strike is complete, the planet will have no defensive capabilities remaining, which will leave our attack ship force virtually unstoppable."

The commander leaned toward the screen as if Misk was standing right in front of him. "This planet will not know what hit them. I want the attack ships launched two hours after the last mine is launched. I don't want to give them a chance to take a breath. Our ships will eradicate the remaining inhabitants with ease. Do we have an estimate on total planetwide eradication?"

"We estimate the planet will be cleared of all its inhabitants in ten days, sir."

"That's well within the initial estimates. And when is the fleet now scheduled to arrive in orbit."

"Three days after the secondary assault, sir."

"Inform Korg that I want the fleet set up in a defensive posture upon their arrival. With no prior knowledge of what we have created on this station, we will easily destroy them upon their arrival." He growled. "Inform me when we are ready to launch the attack."

"Yes, Commander."

The screen faded, and Corisk leans back in his chair. The commander returns to his battle plans; his huge black eyes take in every detail as he contemplates his victory, as well as the victory for his planet. It is all just a matter of time now.

After making his way through the crowded streets of Aspen, Willis pulled the Jeep into the parking lot of the Lift House Pub and made his way to the front door. As he entered the pub, he noticed that the crowd was already starting to gather two hours before the show. He made his way to the rear of the pub, where the stage was located and his friends were preparing for the show. They spotted him and his six-foot frame as he made his way to the stage.

"What's up, guys?" he asked.

"Nothing much, just tuning up. Glad you could make it. We were starting to worry," Scooter commented as he tuned his guitar.

"Good timing, bro, we're almost finished with all the work," Mark said, as he fingered the strings on his bass guitar.

"How does it look on your end, Alice?" he asked, as he looked at the light and sound boards.

"Looks absolutely perfect from here," Alice said as she looked him over from top to bottom. "Lights and sound are ready too," she said with a wink of one of her big blue eyes.

Willis and Alice have been dating for almost a year, but don't think that's how she got her job. She is one of the best light and sound technicians in the business, and she is also responsible for all of the female vocals for the group.

"You ready for some sound checks, Master Willis," Nick kids. He knows it drives Willis crazy when he calls him that, but he does it on a regular basis anyway.

"Yea. Not that you need any more practice beating on things," he jabs. Everyone else laughed heartily at the joke. "Very funny," Nick replied as he was twirling his sticks in his fingers.

Willis takes his place on the stage and grabs his guitar and played a few notes. "All right let's start with some Avenged Sevenfold and finish up with some Papa Roach."

They played three songs for the people in the pub, giving them a preview of tonight's show, and decided they were ready for the show.

"Sounds awesome, guys," Willis said. "Hey, what do you all say about grabbing some beers after the show, and go up to the top of Independence Pass to watch the meteor shower? You drink the beers, and I'll drive."

"Sounds awesome," Mark said, holding up a microbrew.

"I'm game," Nick said. "How about you, Scoot?"

"Sure, why not."

"What about me?" Alice asked with her bright red lip-glossed bottom lip pouting comically.

"Oh, I knew you would come along, you can't resist my male magnetism," he said as he pushed out his chest and smiled.

"You better hope that big magnetic head of yours doesn't attract one of those meteors," she said with a big smile.

"Hey, guys. What do you say we pick up some groupies and take them up on the mountain with us?" Nick said, grinning ear to ear.

"You mean you want us to pick up an extra one for you," Scoot ribbed.

"Very funny."

"We'll have to take your van, Mark. There's no way in hell we'll all fit in my Jeep."

"Sure you can handle something that big?" Mark teased.

"I do it at least four times a day, depending how much I drink," Willis said, smiling. "Sounds like we got a plan then. Alice and I are going to go get a bite to eat before the show. We'll be back before eight."

"Okay, master," Nick said in his best Igor voice.

"Very funny, Igor. Try not to drag any dead bodies in while were gone," he said as they headed for the door. "And take it easy on those brews, we've got a long night ahead of us."

The guys waved them out the door and headed for the bar. Willis and Alice are out the door and on their way to dinner. They all get ready for the show in their own way.

Meanwhile back in the valley, Bill is in the studio working as usual. After a few beers and a few bowls, he doesn't notice his visitor sneak through the door.

"Hey, baby, what's up?" Monica yells to get above the music. He doesn't hear her, so she walks over to the stereo and turns it down, which catches his attention as well as Sassy's.

"Hey, don't mess with my tunes, woman. People have been hurt for a lot less," he said with a fake mad look on his face.

"Do you ever quit working? Never mind, I already know the answer to that one."

"I just did," he said, setting down his tools and walking over to his refrigerator. He opened it and grabbed two frosty bottles of Corona. "Want a cold beer?"

"No. Actually I just want one of these," she said, as she planted a long kiss on his lips.

"Keep that up and you can have anything you want," Bill said as he did a Groucho Marx impression with his eyebrows.

"Dirty old man."

"That's why you love me."

Sassy comes over wondering where her kiss is, feeling jealous and left out. Like all girls she hates being left out, so Monica gave her a kiss on the nose and a good petting. After she finished with the dog, she looked around the studio and noticed the Dean statue standing over in Willis's area of the studio. She walked over to the statue and admired the work. "Wow, I want some of these," she said as she put one hand on each of Mrs. Dean's huge concrete breasts.

"I'll have to sell a lot of artwork to afford a set of those."

"Then you better get busy, mister," she joked.

"I'll get my mess cleaned up, you go start a fire, and I'll meet you at the pit in ten minutes."

"Deal. Come on, Sassy."

Monica headed out the door with the dog hot on her heels (traitor). Bill shut down the studio and grabbed a bucket of Coronas and his pipe, then headed out the door. The pit already had a roaring fire blazing in it, and Monica was lying on the lounge chair with a blanket over her legs with what was now "her shadow" lying next to her.

"Nice job," he said, pointing at the fire.

"I'm good at everything I do, especially lighting your fire."

"You got me there," he said as he bent over and gave her a kiss, then handed her a cold beer.

"Thank you," she said as she looked up at him lovingly.

"You're welcome."

"I love this place. I can never wait to be here by the fire with your arms around me."

"It's great, isn't it. Now you know why I built the place."

"How about we skip dinner tonight."

"I'm with you," he said as he slipped into the chair behind her and put his arms around her. Bill started a fire in the barbeque and cooked them a perfect steak dinner. He is also an artist when it comes to cooking, which Monica enjoys. After dinner they enjoyed what was left of the cool October day—and into the night as well. A roaring fire, his two best girls, and a cold beer in his hand. It just doesn't get any better than this. "Life is good."

CHAPTER 6

Aspen, Colorado
October 12, 2020, 23:00

It was eleven o'clock when the band finally quit playing, and now they all stood on the stage talking and getting ready to leave on the night's adventure.

"Let's leave everything here since we have a show tomorrow night," Willis said. "The bartender will watch it for us, and I'm ready to go see some stars."

"And we're ready to drink some serious beers," Scooter said, standing with his arm around one of the many beautiful girls that were ready to go party with the band.

The meteor showers have been something that Willis and his family have always enjoyed, weather permitting. It's a clear Colorado sky tonight, and you couldn't get any better conditions for watching the showers. They left the pub, and all piled into the van, then headed for the top of the pass to watch the show and relax.

John hurried through the halls of the Space Center on his way to the control room. He was curious to see what Brad had found out about Ben's strange discovery. As he walked across the floor of the control room, he could tell something was up by the excited mood of his people.

Brad Meyer was at the Hubble command center, so John headed in his direction. Brad noticed his entrance and waved him over with a very eager expression on his face. His team had spent the last nine hours repositioning the huge telescope at the coordinates to get the pictures.

"What is it, Brad? I can tell by your expression that you have news."

"Nothing yet, but the pictures are coming up now. It took us a while to find the anomalies but we finally have them dialed in."

"They are coming in now, sir," Brad's assistant said, as he put the pictures up on the big screen at the front of the control room. You can feel the anticipation as the screen lights up and the Hubble images appear. The first images are of six objects in a small cluster, clearly visible at the center of the screen.

"What's the magnification?" John asked.

"Ten times magnification, sir," the technician said to his director.

"Give me a shot at 50 percent of full power."

"Yes, sir, but it will take a minute for it to appear."

"So what do you make of it so far, Brad?"

"The pictures aren't clear enough to make any assessment yet, but Ben was right about one thing, there has never been anything recorded at these coordinates."

The screen image changed. On the screen are now six large white spots, but they are still not clear enough to identify.

"Well, that sucks," John said. "We still can't tell what they are."

Brad walked toward the screen, studying the image, scratching his now two-day-old beard. "They aren't clear, but do you see what I see? They are glowing, or maybe shining. If they were asteroids, they wouldn't shine like that. If we go any stronger, we'll only get an image that's even more distorted than it is already."

"All right, Brad. I want your best guys on this so we can determine exactly what those are," he said, pointing at the screen. "I also want to know if they are moving. And if they are moving, I want to know exactly where they are headed. I want an answer on this as soon as possible, gentlemen. Tweak whatever you have to, to clear that image. We should be able to see a dust mote on a flea's ass with this thing, so do whatever it takes, gentlemen. And, Brad?"

"Yes, sir?"

"I want an answer by 6:00 a.m. I'm going to my office and to catch a few zzz's. I'm exhausted."

"We all are, John."

"I know that, Brad, I'm sorry. You guys have put nine hard hours on top of a normal day. Thank your team for me."

"This is NASA, we're used to long hours, John."

"Wake me as soon as you have something."

"You got it. Go get some rest."

Brad stands back as the six men of the Hubble team hover over the controls, determined to give their boss exactly what he wants. That's why they get paid the big bucks.

On the planet Torani, we find the emperor in his luxurious office, sitting at his huge desk reviewing the reports from Fleet Command on the reported Corisole fleet movements. He reaches for the comms switch and pages his secretary. "Moroi. Get me Commander Brydon."

"Yes, Emperor." A few moments later, Commander Brydon appears on the big screen on the wall.

"Emperor, what can I do for you?"

"Commander, what news do you have on the Corisole situation?"

"As you already know, sir, the Corisole leadership has ignored the treaty, and their fleet is now en route to the Sol System."

"With six cruisers we can assume their intentions are not peaceful. Am I correct, Commander?"

"I would have to agree, sir. Also any attempts at contact with the Corisole Fleet Command have been ignored. I believe that task is up to you now, sir. You must make contact with the Leader Mirosh and get some answers."

"Leave that to me, Commander. Have you sent our fleet to peruse the Corisole fleet?"

"Yes, sir. I dispatched the fleet two hours ago, but the Corisole have a three-day head start on our fleet, so I don't know if we can catch them before they reach the Sol System."

"I want that fleet caught, Commander. If they won't turn back, I want our fleet to destroy them," he said, slamming his huge golden fist on his desk.

"Yes, Emperor."

"Contact all ship commanders and inform them that I expect them to run their engines at absolute maximum to catch that fleet. I don't care if we lose a vessel or two by doing so."

"Yes, Emperor. I will pass on your orders."

"Very good, Commander. Keep me informed. In the meantime, I will try to contact the Supreme Leader and demand an explanation for their actions, as well as the return of their fleet."

"Good day, sir."

The emperor relaxes back in his large throne-like chair and allows his conversation to soak in. He then leans forward and pages his secretary.

"Yes, Emperor."

"Put me through to the Corisole Supreme Leader, and insist that he reply."

"Yes, Emperor."

He leans back in his large chair and hopes for a response from the Corisole leadership. Commander Brydon is in his office at the fleet headquarters. He taps a comms button. "Major Arden."

"Yes, sir."

"Major, contact Commander Skoby aboard the vessel Jayden. I want you to inform him that the emperor wants that fleet caught, and I quote, 'at any cost.' I don't care if they have to melt their reactors to molten pools to do it. If the Corisole fleet will not retreat, I want them destroyed. I expect it done, and I won't accept failure. Is that absolutely understood, Major?"

"Yes, sir, clearly understood."

Brydon terminates the transmission. He wonders just exactly how his commander will be able to carry out his orders. With a three-day lead, they will need a miracle to catch the rogue fleet. Even with the greater speed capabilities of their vessels, the Corisole fleet will be almost impossible to overcome.

CHAPTER 7

---•◦✿◦•---

The bridge of the Jayden is in high gear and engaged in the pursuit of the Corisole fleet, which is in violation of all noninterference laws that the Alliance holds dear and must be stopped at all costs. Ensign Lyle is currently at the communication station and turns to his commander. "Commander Skoby. We have an incoming communication from Fleet Command."

"Put it through, Ensign."

"Commander Skoby."

"Major Arden. What can we do for you?"

"Commander. I have a message for you from Commander Brydon. The commander has directed me to inform you that you are to either catch and turn the Corisole fleet, or destroy them at any cost, and I quote, 'Even if we have to melt our engines to molten pools to do it.' That fleet is not to reach planet S-3, sir."

"Understood, Major, and thanks for the encouraging news. Inform the commander we will do everything in our power to succeed." Skoby ends the transmission and turns to his chief engineer.

"Mr. Mock!" he bellows.

"Yes, Commander."

"I assume you heard what the major just said."

"Yes, sir, but it's not going to be easy, sir."

"Nothing that's worth doing is ever easy, Mr. Mock."

"But, sir, we are already running at full power. And when that fleet figures out we're perusing them, it's only going to get harder. And I'm going to assume, sir, that they already know we are after them."

"I agree, Mr. Mock, so you will need to get your men to get every ounce of energy out of our engines and more. Is that clear?"

"Yes, sir. We'll get right on it."

Mock hits the comms button at his engineering station. "This is Chief Engineer Mock. I want all available personnel to report to the engineering section immediately. Mock out. Three days is an enormous lead. It will be a miracle if we catch them, sir."

"You have to catch them, Mr. Mock. And, Mr. Mock, I seem to remember you pulling off a miracle from time to time," his commander said, eyeing him confidently.

"Yes, sir," Mock replied as he rose and headed for engineering, shaking his head.

John is sound asleep on the leather couch in his office at Johnson, when a knock at the door wakes him from his slumber.

"Come in," he said groggily.

"I'm sorry to bother you, John, but you're going to want to see this."

The two men made their way through the corridors of NASA to the control room. As they entered, John couldn't help but notice the excitement, mixed with fear, in the atmosphere.

"What's going on, Brad?"

"See for yourself," he said, pointing at the screen.

On the screen was the unbelievable image of six alien vessels. John had to take a minute to let it sink in what he was actually seeing. It's every person at NASA's dream to discover alien life, but this was more of a nightmare.

"Is that what I think it is?"

"It absolutely is, sir."

"Brad, if that was only one ship I would be excited, but seeing how there's six of them, it kind of makes the hair stand up on the back of my neck. Do we know where they are headed?"

"They are on a beeline straight for us."

"What is their estimated arrival time?" he asked, walking closer to the screen to get a closer look.

"Not yet, sir. I have a team trying to determine just exactly that as we speak."

"Brad, let's drop the sir crap, we're friends. We have to determine how much time we've got before they arrive in Earth orbit. And since we aren't sure of their intentions, the rest of Earth needs to know too."

"As soon as I know, John, you'll know."

"Thanks, Brad. And, Brad?"

"Yes."

"Have someone in communications put a call through to the White House. Tell them to patch it through to my office. The president needs to know about this immediately."

Brad gave him a nod of agreement and walked away to take care of his tasks. John has to tear himself away from the screen, then heads for his office to wait for what will undoubtedly be the most important call of his career.

The president entered the briefing room, which is already filled with his cabinet members and several advisors. They are all concerned because of the early hour of this meeting and are waiting patiently for the reason. The president walks to his chair at the end of the long table without uttering a single word and sits down.

"Ladies and gentlemen," he begins, "I am sure you are quite curious as to why you've been called here at this late hour. Well, to answer that question. At two fifteen this morning I received a call from our friend John Alistair at NASA's Johnson Space Center. People, we have a big problem."

The occupants of the room looked at each other with curiosity, as well as worry on their faces.

"Elsa, could you please."

Elsa Ault, the secretary of state, reaches for the communication controls and turns on the wall-mounted video screen. John Alistair's image appears on the screen.

"Good morning, John."

"Good morning, Mr. President."

"Well, I'm not sure if I would consider this morning yet, and after what you've just told me, I doubt there's anything good about it. Why don't you show everyone here what you just showed me?"

John thinks about his next statement carefully for a few seconds, then begins.

"Ladies and gentlemen. At 1400 hours yesterday, a colleague of mine Ben Murphy at Kitt Peak Observatory called me with an unusual request. He asked me to point the Hubble at a part of the galaxy where there is normally nothing to be seen. He claimed to have spotted an unusual group of objects near the Orion sector of our galaxy. We set the Hubble to the coordinates, and discovered these six unknown objects."

The screen split to allow John to show the pictures.

"This shot was taken at 2300 hours last night."

"John, it's Horace Hunt. They don't look like much. What do you think they are?"

"Give the man a chance, Horace," the president said.

"Sorry, sir."

"It's okay, Horace," John said. "The first picture, as I said, was taken at 2300 hours. This shot was taken about thirty minutes ago."

Another picture appeared on the screen, clearly showing six alien vessels. The briefing room immediately broke out in an uncontrollable chatter.

Horace stands up to speak, quieting the room. "Do you have a projected course, or do I even want to know?"

"It appears they are headed straight for our solar system, which would lead me to assume that they are headed here. My team tells me we have three, possibly four days, until they arrive. We are working to get a hard number on that question."

Colonel Law stands and takes the floor. "Have you had any attempts at communication?"

"No, sir. We've had no attempted communication of any kind. To be honest I don't have a clue how to contact them, but we do have another team working on it as we speak."

"We've got to warn the planet about this," Horace said.

"Now, Horace, as science director I know you see the danger of these vessels, but you also know we can't possibly let this get to the public. The panic it would cause would be catastrophic."

"Why does everyone always think of the worst-case scenario when they think of aliens?" Horace stated.

"Horace, if it was one small ship, I would tend to agree with you. But when I see six extremely large vessels, I worry," President Furgison said strongly.

"I have to agree with the president, Horace," Colonel Law stated firmly. "If I want to negotiate or simply say hello, I'll send a single man. But If I want to kick ass, I send a platoon."

The president stood to take control of his people. "All right, gentlemen, calm down."

John breaks into the meeting from the screen. "Ladies and gentlemen, I can assure you that NASA will make every attempt to make contact with the vessels. We are currently approaching SETI to help by using their radio arrays, as well as our own arrays to communicate with them. But it is an extremely long distance, and sound waves only travel so fast. Maybe as they get closer we will be able to make contact. If we do, believe me you will be the first to know."

"Thank you, John, for the heads-up on this."

"You're welcome, sir."

"Now for the time being we will assume they are hostile. We will inform the world leaders of our finding, but we must stress the need for secrecy. The last thing we need is a worldwide panic. And, Colonel, I want our military brought up to its highest readiness."

"Yes, sir."

"I want all essential personnel to be ready to transfer to the bunker complexes at a moment's notice for security reasons. That means every person in this room."

The president paused to gather his thoughts. "That will be all for now. I want to meet again at 0600 hours. Get what rest you can in the meantime because you're going to need it. Thank you all, and thank you, John, for yours and Ben's great work on this situation."

"You're welcome, sir, and I'll pass on the message."

The cabinet members all rose, still astonished at the news they have just heard. They all headed for their homes to get a few hours' rest before the next meeting in the morning.

CHAPTER 8

———•●✳●•———

The Corisole Supreme leader sits quietly in his majestic office, considering the ramifications of his actions regarding the S-3 planet's invasion. As his world's leader, he's worried on two fronts. On one side he has his dying planet and all its inhabitants. On the other is the fear of the repercussions that will surely come to his planet and its people because of his actions. The Galactic Alliance will not take the news of the S-3 invasion lightly, and Corisole will undoubtedly face dire consequences. The leader's only hope is that they will be successful in their plan before Torani can interfere. By succeeding, he knows the punishment will be severe, but at least he will save his people. He is deep in thought, considering these options, when his advisor Nalen enters the room.

"Pardon me, Leader Mirosh, for the intrusion, but we have received a transmission from the planet Torani demanding we contact them regarding our fleet's movements. They are demanding to know why we broke the treaty, and are also demanding the return of our fleet."

"Ignore their transmissions. We cannot afford to break the silence until the invasion is complete. It is imperative, Mr. Nalen, that they know nothing of our plans at this time."

"But what of the Torani fleet?"

"The Torani fleet is of no danger to our planet when they are en route to the Sol Sector."

"Excuse my boldness, Leader Mirosh, but do you think it is wise to invade S-3? The repercussions will be severe."

———

"It's too late to turn back now, Mr. Nalen. The invasion goes on as planned."

"What of our fleet, sir."

"Our fleet has a three-day advantage on the Torani fleet, so they are of no danger to us. Our vessels will arrive in time to set up a defensive position. That will enable us to defend our invasion forces when the Torani fleet arrives at S-3."

"But their vessels are faster than ours."

"Faster yes, but not fast enough to cut three days off their journey. Also, we will have the element of surprise. We have a surprise waiting for them on the Kabult Station should they choose to interfere."

"Sir, surely you understand that the incursion into the Sol Sector is an absolute violation of the treaty. This will most certainly lead us to war with the Alliance."

Leader Mirosh sat quietly for a moment, then reached for the comms. "Science Director Ryndal, would you please report to my office."

"Yes, sir, I will be there immediately."

A short time later, Ryndal entered the chamber of his Supreme Leader. "You called for me, sir."

"Director Ryndal, would you like to explain to my advisor exactly the reason we cannot fail to secure the S-3 planet?"

"Yes, sir," he said as he took a seat with the other two men. "The first reason we cannot fail is quite simple. As you both know our planet is losing its ability to support life on its surface because of a lack of basic resources. We no longer have the ability to grow enough food, and are importing a large supply from various Alliance worlds at this time. Second, our planet is drying up at an accelerated rate and will soon no longer have water to support the population. In one hundred years this planet will be a ball of dust. Even with the extent of our technologies, planet Corisole will be uninhabitable in one hundred years. There's enough food and water on S-3 for thousands of years, and after we cleanse the atmosphere, the planet will be capable of supporting life for eternity if we learn from our mistakes here on Corisole."

"Director, I am fully aware of the state of Corisole," Nalen said irritably. "But you simply cannot expect the Alliance, or the Torani fleet, to stand by as we annihilate the inhabitants of the S-3 planet and claim it for our own. The entire galaxy will come down on us with a vengeance."

"The Torani or any other fleet that enters S-3's space will not be able to withstand the devastating power of our fleet, combined with that of the Kabult Station," Ryndal stated. "Once the Torani fleet, which is the most powerful in the Alliance, is destroyed, all others will bow to our power. We will then be the most powerful force in this galaxy."

"I hope you are correct in your assumption, Mr. Ryndal. The fate of our race depends on it."

"All right, gentlemen," their leader broke in. "We will know more in seventeen hours, and will meet again at that time to assess the outcome of the invasion. That will be all for now, you may leave."

The leader's two advisors stood, then bowed to their leader and left his chambers. The planet's leader sat alone, trusting that he has made the right decision for the fate of his people.

It's four thirty in the morning in Colorado, and another day begins for Bill. After his habitual routine is finished, it's out into another beautiful Colorado morning as his companion spins with excitement. If only he had that much energy this early in the morning. With a cup of coffee in one hand and two bowls in the other—one for the Sassy's breakfast and the other for his head—they head out into that beautiful morning. As he stops to admire the serenity of his valley, his shadow leaves him to make her morning rounds, containing each of her favorite bushes. With the accuracy of a Swiss watch, she hits each one in turn. Then they both head for the studio to begin the day.

The studio is cold and lonely first thing in the morning because Willis always sleeps in, as he did at that age. When he was that age, he was even worse. Out all night partying with his friends chasing girls, then sleeping in all morning. But when you reach the age of fifty-five, you tend to slow down and start enjoying every hour of the day, so the stereo is turned on and a fire is lit to warm the cold studio. Now it is time to start enjoying the day.

With coffee in hand and his favorite station playing on the stereo, he realizes that soon Willis will be gone and the only one he will have to talk to is the dog. She will listen, but she will only lie there and look at him like he's stupid for thinking she can actually understand a single word he says. Bill shakes the thoughts from his head and knows he has work to do. They have to deliver the Dean's statue to Vail today, and since it's going up on the third floor, they'll need Ron and his crane. He grabbed the cell phone off the bench and dialed Ron's number.

"Hello," Ron answered.

"Ron, it's Bill, did I wake you?"

"No. I'm just having a quick cup of coffee and getting ready for the day. What can I do for you?"

"Can you fit me in today?"

"Where?"

"Vail."

"Hold on a minute, I'll check my schedule."

Bill sneaks a puff while he's waiting for Ron to check his schedule.

"I have an opening at two o'clock. Will that work for you?"

"Perfect. The address is 201 Elk Head Lane. You know where that is?"

"I was born in this valley, remember?"

"Right. Sorry."

"No problem. I'll see you at two."

"Thanks a million, Ron."

"No problem, buddy. See you at two."

Bill looks out the studio door and thinks to himself what a beautiful day it's going to be, then grabs the dogs dish so he can feed Sassy her breakfast. "Come on, girl, time to eat." She knew he wouldn't forget. She has her human very well trained.

John spent the night on a plane in order to be in Washington so he could attend the meeting personally. He now sits in the same clothes as the day before, wondering when would be the next time he would be able to shower and shave. He was able to sleep for a short time on the plane, so he felt better, but he also knew deep down that it may be some time before he could enjoy the comfort of his bed. He spent a few minutes getting acquainted with the few members of the president's cabinet that he didn't know, then, like the others, sat waiting for their commander and chief to arrive.

The president enters the room, noticeably as exhausted as the others. After a few minutes of shaking hands and small talk, he took his seat.

"Mary," he beckoned. And his assistant suddenly appeared. "Danishes and a lot of coffee."

"Yes, sir," she replied and headed for the White House kitchen. Mary knows that coffee and sugar is what keeps the cogs of Washington turning.

The president sat eyeing the people sitting around the table and stops at John Alistair.

"John, glad you could make it."

"It is my pleasure, sir."

"All right, so much for the small talk. Let's get on with it. What new information do you have for us, John?"

"Well, Mr. President. My people have been at it since this thing started, and they have determined that the alien fleet is indeed headed for Earth and it will arrive in our orbit in fifty-four hours, give or take an hour."

"Fifty-four hours. I thought they were in the Orion sector?"

"Yes, sir. But at the estimated speed of their vessels, that is the estimated time of arrival."

"They must be traveling at speeds totally unimaginable to us."

"Their technology is hundreds of years ahead of ours, sir."

"Thank you, John. The whole planet appreciates the work you and your people are doing, even though they don't have a clue that it is actually happening."

"You're quite welcome, sir."

"All right. Does anyone have any questions or something else to add?"

"Yes, sir," Elsa replied as she stood. "I have personally contacted all the world leaders and informed them of the coming danger to them and their people. To say the least, I was not taken seriously at first, but we now have every scientist and telescope on the planet at our disposal. I stressed the importance of total secrecy on this subject, and all are in agreement with our assessment. They are all waiting for further news and eager to help."

"Thank you, Elsa," he said as Elsa took her seat. "All right who's next?"

Colonel Law rose to speak next. "Mr. President. Quite frankly, we as a country and as a world have never conceived this kind of threat to be possible. I have had my staff up all night working on this problem and they've come up with a few ideas. We have a few weapons in our arsenal that could be useful. We have our 'Star Wars' system that was designed to stop incoming ICBMs, but we could redirect the satellites toward space and hope they will be affective against the alien vessels. Also, the countries of the world have thousands of ICBMs, which could possibly be used to destroy the alien fleet, but we aren't sure what their orbit will be. We don't know if they will be effective if they stay at an extended orbit. The last option is NASA's classified asteroid deflection platform, which contains eight nuclear projectiles intended for asteroid deflection. They are already at a high orbit and will certainly be effective if we can use them."

"Those are our only options?" President Furgison asked.

"Well, sir, besides loading up the shuttles with nukes and sending them on suicide runs, that's all we could come up with."

"Let's hope it doesn't come to that, Colonel."

Horace is sitting with his hands under his chin, deep in thought about what the colonel has just laid out. After a few seconds, he slowly rises.

"Mr. President. My teams have come up with some ideas, but there are several problems as the colonel has pointed out. Our ICBMs are capable of reaching orbit, but were never intended to be used in space and may not have the distance required to reach the alien vessels. Also, we have no clue what their defensive capabilities are. We have to assume that they have some sort of laser technology, which will make any of our attempts useless. They may simply shoot down anything we throw at them. With that being said, the only available weapon is the Star Wars satellites that have never been used in battle. As far as I know they haven't even been fired in twenty years and will have to be tested. That's all I've got for now, sir, but I'll let you know if we think of anything else."

"Thank you, Horace. Ladies and gentlemen, I expect you to work 24–7 on this problem until we come up with a solution. And, people. If any of you have something hidden deep in your secret bunkers, now is the time to pull it out. We will meet again in twelve hours. I and the people on this planet need some answers, people. Do your best, and thank you all for your input."

The president rose and left the room for the serenity of his office. The remaining occupants looked at each other, wondering what they can do to help the rest of the world protect its people from the alien threat that was currently hurtling at them from space.

John caught a military transport back to Houston, which saved all the trouble of the airport security. Not to mention it's a free ride. He strolled into the control room looking for his colleague and friend Brad Meyer. The two men have been best friend since the Air Force academy, and after the academy they were both stationed in Germany ten long years before they joined NASA to be astronauts. After flying shuttles for a few missions, they both elected to join the team at Johnson, where they excelled and eventually ended up in their current positions. John walked across the room and stood quietly listening to the conversation. He waited for a break to interrupt.

"So what's the news, Brad?"

"Well, we were right about the arrival time. The alien fleet will enter Earth orbit in fifty hours."

"Okay, I don't know if that's good news or not but at least it's accurate. What about the other projects I called about?"

"I have a team working on them as we speak and they should have some answers by noon."

"Thanks, Brad, good work. And tell the guys I appreciate all their hard work."

"Will do, boss. Now are you ready for more bad news? John looked at Brad dejectedly. "What now."

"We have been so caught up in dealing with this alien fleet that we've neglected the six men up in the Space Station."

John's jaw almost hit the floor. "How could we have forgotten them."

"Well, we have been a little sidetracked by six extremely large alien vessels, boss."

"I understand that, but that's no excuse. We have to get those men out of there or they'll be sitting ducks. There's no time for a launch so we'll have to bring them down in the escape pod. How long will it take to evacuate them?"

"We're working on that also. As soon as they made their daily report, we started getting them ready."

"So you told them about the situation?"

"I thought it was only right."

"What would I do without you. I'm heading to my office and then to the shower. Let me know when you can have an evac scheduled."

If John's knees bent both directions, he would be kicking his own ass right now for forgetting those men. If it was him up there, he'd be pissed off. As he entered his office, his phone rang.

"Hello." "John. Colonel Law here."

"What can I do for you, Colonel?"

"John. I want you NASA guys to get in touch with NORAD and touch base. It's been a lot of years since you've had to work together so I'll need you to grease the wheels, so to speak. I've already notified our Star Wars guys and have them working on the problem. I think they should be put in touch with your Hercules team so they are on the same page."

"You got it, Colonel. I'll get back to you in a few hours to let you know what we come up with."

"Thanks, John. And John, please tell them to hurry."

"Good-bye, Colonel."

John hung up the phone and gave Brad a call, giving him even more work to do. Then he leaned back in his chair and put his feet up on his desk and closed his eyes. This has been the longest twenty hours of his life. The shower could wait.

Skoby is on the bridge of the vessel Jayden going over the mission in his mind and trying to determine a plan of action once they apprehend the Corisole fleet. His men are working diligently to make sure that it happens. His thoughts are interrupted by the comms officer.

"Commander, I have an incoming message from the emperor."

"Put it through." Commander Skoby waits as the viewer comes to life.

"Commander Skoby. What is the status on the fleet's progress?"

"Emperor, my engineers have assured me that we are now running at 125 percent. It would be extremely dangerous to risk more."

"Time frame, Commander?" the emperor said irritably.

"We will be in the orbit of S-3 in sixty hours, sir."

"That simply won't do, Commander. The Corisole fleet is ten hours ahead of you, and we cannot let them reach that planet. You must find a way to take ten hours off your time."

"As I said, Emperor, we are already running over the maximum recommended level of our engines."

"Commander, I know I am asking a lot of you and your crew, but we cannot let that fleet reach the planet. The S-3 planet is absolutely defenseless against the power of those battle cruisers."

"Yes, sir. We'll find a way."

"Very well, Commander. Good day."

The screen turns black as Skoby turns to his engineer. "Mock, you heard what the man said. Make it happen."

"Yes, sir. We'll do our best."

Mock turned and left the bridge on his way to engineering. He will have to pull a few more miracles out of thin air.

CHAPTER 9

⸺ •●✸●• ⸺

Parachute, Colorado
October 13, 2020, 18:00

Bill and Willis pull into the driveway and wind their way up to their well-hidden home, after making the delivery in Vail. As they pass the fire pit and stop, Willis jumps out of the truck to open the garage so they can park the truck and trailer. After they finish, the pair headed toward the studio.

"Hey, buddy, you had better go in and get cleaned up. You've got a show to do tonight. And let Sassy out on your way in."

"Yea, you're probably right, that other stuff can wait until tomorrow."

Bill opens the door and turns on the light. He takes one look at the cross, then looks at the fridge. He looks down and notices the dog sitting patiently at his feet. "

What do you think, girl. More work, or beer."

Sassy gave him that tilted head look of hers, then spun in a circle and sat back down.

"Yea, your right. Enough work for today."

He grabs a cold Corona out of the fridge and a smoke out of the pack sitting on top. Then loaded his bowl. He hates the fact that he still smokes cigarettes. Those things will kill ya. He looks down, and his shadow is there as always with her ball in her mouth. He grabs the ball and heads out to the fire pit to relax. "Come on, girl," he said, then shut the door to the studio. Sassy spins in circles excitedly, knowing it's playtime, and she's ready after being cooped up in the house while they were gone. It's time to play with her favorite human. "Go get it," he said as he tossed the ball way down the driveway, eventually landing in the stream. That will keep her busy for a while, he thinks to himself.

After a lot of throws and a few beers, the pair sit at the fire pit enjoying the sunshine. Sassy's ears perk up because she hears someone coming. Bill turns and sees Willis coming up behind them.

"Dad, would you mind if I brought Alice up to stay with us tonight after the show?"

"As long as she doesn't mind sleeping under a mountain, I don't care," he said with a smile.

"She has been dying to come here since I told her about the place, and I guess since it's been almost a year, I'll let her know where I live."

"You learned well," his dad said in between puffs of his pipe.

"We are going into Grand Junction tomorrow to check on new equipment for the band, so it will save me a lot of time."

"Monica is coming up today for the night, so it will give her some female companionship. Nobody likes being cooped up with a crazy old hippy all alone," he said, taking another puff.

"Welcome to my world," Willis said laughing. "Well, I better roll, the show starts at eight and I have to take Alice to dinner. We should be back around twelve thirty."

"Okay, I'll keep the fire burning. Oh, and by the way, you had better stop and see your mother."

"I saw her yesterday. We had lunch."

"Have you told her about Alice?"

"Not yet."

"You better tell her before she finds out on her own, or she'll be pissed."

"Yea, I know. I'll see you tonight, Dad."

"Okay, buddy. See ya later."

Willis jumped into the Jeep and headed down the driveway. Bill cracked another Corona, then tossed the ball back in the stream. "Life is good," Sassy thinks, and Bill agrees.

The sun is setting low over the Washington skyline. The trees are dressed in their best fall colors and clinging desperately to their leaves. The temperature is dropping to its mid-October chill, getting ready for winter to arrive.

Inside the White House, the people gathered in the briefing room have forgotten the beauty of the outside world. The only thing on their minds is the bleak-looking future ahead of them, if there is a future. They are all gathered around the table deeply engrossed in the pages of data that lay on the table in front of them. Numerous pictures and reports have flooded into their possession, so they are sorting through it as best they can with the time allotted. They all place their attention on the door as the president walks in.

"Everyone, please be seated," he said as he walked through the room. "All right, people. John couldn't be with us today, but he will be joining us shortly by video. Do we have any new information to discuss while we wait?"

"Yes, sir. I would like permission to move our fleets out of the harbors," Admiral Hale requested nervously. "I would feel better if they were safely out to sea."

"That's probably a good idea, Admiral. Get the ball rolling. I want them sailing first thing in the morning." "Sir."

"What is it, Horace."

"Sir. Our combined efforts with the other countries have had no success at contacting the alien fleet. We are assuming they are still too distant for communication. In twenty-four hours they should be in range, but they will also be practically on top of us. Then again, if they refuse to communicate with us, all of our attempts will be useless."

"I understand your concern, Horace, but we've got to keep trying."

The main screen lights up with John's image appearing on it. They all direct their attention to it as if he were a god.

"Great. John, glad to see you could make it. You look like shit though."

"Yea, it has been the longest twenty-four hours of my life, and I've flown in two wars, plus flown shuttles."

"Sorry, John. So what news do you have for us this evening."

"Well, Mr. President. The first news is disturbing. Somehow we overlooked the six astronauts on the International Space Station."

Every person gasped. None of them could believe that they forgot about the largest thing that orbits the planet, not to mention the six men on board.

"My god, John. I can't believe we have been so entrenched in our current situation that we forgot about those six men."

"They will be okay. We are undergoing an emergency shutdown and evacuation of the Station. It will take approximately six hours to complete the process. Then they will exit the Station on the escape pod and land at Edwards Air Base."

"Good work, John. Those men are lucky to have you looking after them."

"To be honest, sir, if they hadn't made their daily report, they quite possibly would have remained forgotten. So don't thank me. On another subject. We have reprogrammed the Hercules for multiple targets, but we'll have to wait for the last moment to enter the coordinates since there are six targets and we won't know exactly where they are going to be. How is the army coming with the Star Wars satellites?"

Colonel Law leans forward in his seat to answer. "They have all been activated and are being turned toward space, John. We are going to test fire them in a few hours. Then we will know for sure."

"Well, that's news well received," the president said.

Brad Meyer entered the screen behind John with photos in his hand. He whispers in John's ear, then motions toward the screen with what appears to be a concerned expression on his face.

"What is it, John?" asked the president.

"Just a moment, sir, and I'll put it on the screen." John works the keys on his computer, and suddenly the screen splits, and the image appears in the briefing room. "The Hubble took this shot just minutes ago."

"Is that what I think it is, John?"

"I'm afraid it is, sir. We have detected ten more vessels headed our way."

"Why didn't we see them before now, John?"

"They must be traveling much faster than the others, sir. Our last shot was three hours ago and they weren't there."

The cabinet members stood and moved toward the screen to get a better look. After a lot of pointing and discussion, they returned to their seats looking extremely dejected.

"When are 'these' ships going to arrive, John?"

"Brad estimates twenty-four hours after the first fleet arrives, but we have not determined their exact speed yet. We will get another shot in three hours and we'll have a better estimate."

"So we now have sixteen alien vessels on their way to our planet. Could this possibly get any worse. Well, people, I'm sure you'll agree with me that this is indeed an invasion, and they aren't going to be friendly. My guess is that they tend to annihilate or enslave every human being on this planet."

The room is now out of control with every person in the room trying to speak at once.

"All right, everyone, calm down. I guess this proves the point that we cannot let the public know about this."

"Sir. We have to tell the public about this. They have the right to know," Horace insisted.

"Horace, you saw what just happened and we are all seasoned professionals. Under no circumstances does this leave this room. I don't even want you telling your families."

"But, sir—"

"Horace," the president cut him off, "when the time comes, everyone in this room and all other essential personnel will go into the bunker with their families, but under no circumstances does this leave this room. Am I understood."

"Yes, sir," they all uttered despondently.

"John, that goes for your people too. You have to confine them to the base and kill all outside communications. That includes cell phones."

"Yes, sir. But they're not going to like it."

"How many of your people know about this?"

"Around fifty, Mr. President."

"And how big is your bunker complex?"

"It's rated at three hundred, sir. With all the family members, we'll be pushing the limit."

"Only immediate family, John. It's for their own good. I know it really sucks, John, but it has to be that way. We can't save the whole world if this thing goes south like we think it's going to. Does every person in this room understand what I just said?"

"Yes, sir," they all replied.

"Colonel. I want NORAD locked down also until further notice."

"Yes, sir."

"Now, moving on. Elsa, you will have to tell the world leaders, but stress our point solidly. Is that clearly understood."

"Absolutely, sir," she said.

"Horace, we have ark projects, do we not."

"Yes, sir, they are all around the world."

"Horace, Elsa, get them ready. We'll have to get the world's scientists into them. We can't afford to lose them."

"Yes, sir," they both replied.

"Okay. Let's sum this up now. We have ten more vessels inbound, the ISS to get home, the world leaders to inform, and the ark projects to utilize. Does that just about cover it?"

"Sir," the Secret Service director Allen Whitt declared.

"I insist that we get the cabinet members into the bunker immediately for their sake, as well as the rest of the country. We have to protect the governing body." "I agree with Allen, people. I want everyone here in six hours. Where is the vice president?"

"He's on his way here, sir. He's on Air Force One inbound from China. They are scheduled to arrive in four hours," Whitt said.

"Okay, people. Our next meeting will be at 6:00 a.m. in the bunker briefing room. Thank you all. And, John, no more bad news please."

"I can't promise that, sir, but I'll try."

The president sits with his head in his hands. Never in a million years would he have thought it could come to this. He then rose from his chair and slowly walked out of the room.

On board the Corisole command vessel Rapture, Commander Korg is in his quarters enjoying his evening meal and listening to a classical Corisole ballad when his comms unit chimes. He sets his utensils down and answers it.

"Commander. You are needed on the bridge immediately, sir."

Korg looks at his half-eaten meal, then rises from his table. He turns off his music and then walks through the ship to the bridge. As he enters, he notices Sub-commander Leigh hovering over the scanner.

"Sub-commander, what is it that couldn't wait for me to finish my meal?" he asked angrily. "Commander, the Torani fleet is shrinking our lead on them. Somehow they have cut our lead to twenty-four hours. If they can hold that pace, they will arrive at S-3 only hours after we arrive."

"That is impossible, Sub-commander!" he shouted, as he came over to look at the scanner.

"We had a three-day advantage on the Torani fleet when we departed. How did they make up for three days?" "We have no idea, sir. Their vessels are faster than ours, but the speeds they have been achieving seem impossible."

"Are we running at maximum speed?"

"Yes, sir. Our engineers assured me that we are traveling at maximum power."

"Sub-commander. Inform the Kabult Station that we are going to arrive with the Torani fleet hot on our heels. Then tell engineering that I want more speed."

"Yes, sir."

Korg assesses the data from the scanner. He can see no way the Torani fleet was able to make up so much time. They have to be running their engines at dangerous levels. That fact tells him that they have only one objective. To stop them at any cost. Even the cost of a few vessels.

The Kabult Station, which is in the orbit of the S-3 planet, is now a fully maned battle station. The station was originally created as a small research station, used by many of the Alliance members until four decades ago, when the inhabitants of the planet below began their reach for the stars. Once these beings began exploring the surface of their small moon, it was deemed too hazardous to continue the research on the planet. This decision was made for the benefit of the planet's inhabitants, in order to avoid contamination of the planet's normal evolution. Therefore, the Treaty of 12:7:141 was created to ban further incursions into the system. There are still illegal visits made to the planet on occasion, but these instances are dealt with swiftly by the Alliance Peacekeeping Forces.

The Torani have little interest in the planet since it's almost identical to their own. Torani is also mostly water with landmasses scattered around its surface. They were more interested in the curious evolving beings and their destructive and warring ways. The Torani, having transcended beyond the need for war hundreds of years ago, were merely trying to understand their own past. Their evolution also included thousands of years of war that almost destroyed their world, but after thousands of years they realized the dangers of their ways and turned the planet into the peace-loving Utopia it is now.

The Corisole planet on the other hand has not evolved as the Torani have. Their quest for wealth through the mining of the valuable ores its planet contained has led them to their current predicament. Their planet is now incapable of producing the much-needed provisions to support life on the planet because of extensive mining. The surface of the planet has been virtually destroyed by excessive mining, so they are no longer able to grow enough food for their inhabitants. Water, as well as breathable air on the planet, is also almost nonexistent because of these practices used in this quest for wealth.

The Corisole fleets have searched the galaxy for a new home for decades. With their discoveries being either too distant or too massive an undertaking to convert the environment to their needs, they have set their sights on the S-3 planet. After twenty years of secret preparation, the S-3 moon has been converted into the Kabult Station and was ready for the invasion of the planet, which is now only hours away.

In the control room of the Station, Commander Corisk and Subcommander Misk are going over the final preparations for the invasion of S-3. The mine launch will be the first stage of this process.

"Misk. Are the mines ready for deployment?"

"Yes, sir. All mines are armed and ready."

"Very well, Sub-commander, launch the first stage of the attack."

Misk activates his comms. "Launch control, this is Sub-commander Misk. Launch all mines according to preset configurations."

"Yes, sir," the launch control officer returns.

The two men watch the monitor as wave after wave of mines leave the station, bound for their preprogrammed locations. Commander Corisk directs his attention to his comms officer.

"Ensign Myano. Contact the Supreme Leader and inform him that the invasion has begun."

"Yes, sir," Myano responded.

"Misk."

"Yes, sir."

"I want all defensive batteries made ready for the Torani fleet's arrival. Their fleet has somehow closed the distance on our fleet and will arrive only hours after our own."

"I will coordinate our cannon batteries with those of the fleet upon their arrival."

"Make absolutely sure you do, Mr. Misk, or this will be the shortest invasion in the history of the galaxy.

Corisk continued to watch as the mines left the station for their deadly rendezvous. It is the first hour in the future of the Corisole race.

CHAPTER 10

———•●❋●•———

**Kitt Peak Observatory, Arizona
October 13, 2020, 22:00**

Ben Murphy is perched at the telescope as he normally is at this hour, but tonight for a totally different reason. Tonight he is watching the most unusual target he has ever had. As he watches, he hears Allen enter the building below.

"What's up, Ben?"

"Stars, Allen," he said with a smile, pointing toward the heavens.

"I should know better by now," Allen replied, shaking his head.

"Actually I've been watching those six spots we discovered in the Orion sector."

"Anything new?"

"Well, they appear to be getting brighter, which leads me to believe that they are getting closer."

"Asteroids?"

"Six of them? I don't see how that's possible. I put a call to John at NASA with the coordinates, but he hasn't called back yet to give me an update. Maybe I should give him another call to see what he came up with. By the way, how was your field trip last night?"

"It was really exciting, but tonight it is supposed to be at its peak so I am taking another group up."

"Here you want a look?" Ben said, rising from the chair.

"Sure."

"I'm going to give NASA a call."

Ben strode down the steps toward his office to call NASA. Hopefully John would be in his office at this late hour. To his surprise, he was directed to John's line.

"Hello," John answered.

"John. This is Ben," he said. "You never called me back."

"Sorry, Ben. I can't tell you how busy we've been. Ben, you can't repeat what I'm going to tell you to anyone. It's absolutely top secret, but since you're involved and the president himself told me to thank you, I will tell you."

"What is it, John?" Ben asked curiously.

"You know those spots you found?"

"Yea. What about them?"

"They were six alien ships, Ben."

"Aliens. Holy shit!"

"Yea, but that's not it. They are headed straight for Earth and we just found ten more behind them."

"Invasion?"

"That's our guess. They haven't tried to communicate with us, and any of our attempts to communicate with them has been unsuccessful. Either we can't communicate on their level or they don't want to communicate with us, which would be very bad."

"How much time do we have, John?"

"We estimate the first six ships will enter Earth orbit in about two and a half, maybe three days. The rest of the ships are a day or two behind them. We haven't got a hard number on them yet but we're working on it. Ben, my suggestion to you is to find the safest place you can find and get your family into it. And remember, Ben. Not a soul can find out about this, the results would catastrophic."

"What about, Allen?"

"Can you trust him to keep it secret? Like I said, Ben, this is top secret and if they find out you passed on this information, they'll shoot you and anyone you told in the head."

"He's a professional, John, I think we can trust him. Plus, there's the fact that he was part of the original discovery."

"I'll leave that up to you, Ben."

At that moment, Allen came running into the office.

"Ben, you have to see this," Allen said excitedly. "I turned the small telescope toward the moon and there's hundreds of large meteors coming from the vicinity of the moon."

"John, let me put you on hold for a minute. Don't hang up."

"What is it, Ben?"

"I'm not sure. Give me a few minutes, John, and don't hang up. I'll be right back."

"Okay, Ben, I'll hold on."

Ben ran up the stairs to the smaller telescope and looked through the eyepiece. He rose from the chair and looked at Allen with wide eyes.

"I told you it was strange."

"Allen, don't go anywhere."

Ben hurried back to his office and picked the phone back up, where John was still waiting.

"John. Turn your tracking satellites toward the moon."

"What is it, Ben?"

"Just do it, John. There appears to be large meteors coming from the moon." "From the moon?"

"That's what I said, John. From the moon."

"Okay, let me get Brad on it. Meanwhile I'll also see if the Hubble can spot anything that close. It's your turn to hold."

Ben looked at Allen with a serious expression on his face. "Allen, don't ask any questions, just listen. Number one, those spots were an alien fleet heading straight for Earth. Two, you should cancel the viewing and get your family to the safest place you can find immediately. And, Allen, this is top secret. Understand?"

"I understand, Ben. I'll talk to you later."

"I certainly hope so, Allen," Ben said to his friend as he headed for the stairs.

Back at NASA, John hit the button for Brad's phone on his console. "Brad, I want the Hubble moved right now, as in immediately."

"Okay, boss. What coordinates?"

"The moon, Brad."

"The moon?"

"Brad, please. I'll be right up." John went back to Ben's line. "Ben, I'm going to have to let you go. I'll get back to you. And remember, nobody is to know about any of this."

"Okay, John, but keep me in the loop, buddy."

"I will, Ben. Good-bye."

John left his office and hurried through the corridors to the control room. He went to the Hubble control area, where Allen was working the controls franticly.

"That should do it," Allen said.

"Picture now! Minimum power."

Suddenly the screen on the wall lights up with a live image of the moon—and what appears to be hundreds of objects coming "out" of its surface.

"John, those things are coming out of the moon."

"I better make another call to the president,"

John said as he looked at Brad. John is watching the feed from the Hubble as it comes in. He picks up a phone, and an operator answers. "Get me the president right away." He waits for a moment, and the president comes onto the line.

"Yes, John?"

"Mr. President, I'm afraid I have more bad news."

"You've got to be kidding me, John. What now!"

"Sir, we have detected hundreds of meteors coming from the moon."

"From the moon?"

"Yes, sir. They appear to be coming out of the surface of the moon."

"John, we both know that's not possible."

"Neither is a fleet of sixteen alien vessels, sir."

"I see your point, John. What do you need from me?"

"We need to get NORAD on this right away, sir."

"Okay, John, I'll call Colonel Law and get him right on it, and, John, I'm moving the meeting up to midnight. I'll contact you by video when we're ready."

"Yes, sir, midnight. I'll be waiting."

The line goes dead as the president hangs up. John turns back to his current task.

"Lieutenant Meyer."

"Yes, sir."

"I'm sorry. Brad, I want to know in ten minutes where those 'unknown objects' are bound, and if it's Earth I want to know exactly when they will enter the atmosphere."

"You got it, John."

John stood looking at the feed from the Hubble of the mysterious objects coming from the moon's surface, wondering just exactly what hell could possibly happen next.

President Furgison sat at his desk trying to soak in the disturbing news he just received from John. How could this possibly be happening, and more importantly, is it coincidence that it's happening now. He thinks not. He picks up the phone, and his secretary answers.

"Ruth, get me Colonel Law."

"Right away, sir."

President Furgison waits on the line until Colonel Law answers the phone. "Yes, Mr. President."

"Colonel, we've got another problem."

"Another problem, sir."

"Yes, Colonel. John Alistair just called me. Believe it or not NASA has just discovered objects coming 'out' of the surface of the moon."

"Sir, today I would be able to believe just about anything, especially if it comes from John. What can I do for you?"

"I need you to get NORAD put on red alert. We have way too many things going on right now that just don't make any sense. I want your boys to get busy tracking these objects and see if they can tell us anything. I want to know where they are headed, and if they are headed here I want to know where and when they will make impact."

"Absolutely, Mr. President. We'll get right on it."

"Oh, and, Colonel. Don't take too long."

"Yes, sir."

The president hangs up the phone, thinks for a second, then picks the phone back up. Ruth is on the other end as always.

"Ruth."

"Yes, sir."

"Contact all the Joint Chiefs and the cabinet members, and tell them that I want them as well as their family members in the White House bunker by midnight. That means you too, Ruth," he said firmly.

"Yes, sir," she replied, realizing the severity of the situation. He hangs up the phone, then hangs his head and wonders what could possibly happen next. He now needs to contact Air Force One and let the vice president know of the incoming meteors.

He could very well be flying straight through the onslaught.

NORAD's commander, Colonel Lance Polaski, is in his office reviewing the readouts from the Star Wars satellite tests when his phone suddenly rings.

"This is Colonel Polaski."

"Polaski, this is Jack Law."

"What can I do for you, Colonel?"

The colonel proceeded to inform Colonel Polaski of the new threat discovered by NASA. After a pause, Colonel Polaski speaks.

"Okay, Jack, let me get this straight. Not only do we have sixteen alien vessels headed our way with probably the intent to totally kick our ass, but now the moon is spitting out hundreds of unknown objects at us, and you want to know where they're going to land. Am I on the right page."

"You hit the nail right on the head, Lance. And I needed to know yesterday."

"Okay, Jack, we'll get on it right away. Give me ten minutes and I'll get right back to you."

"Thanks, Lance."

The colonel hurries to the main control room, which is already busy with the Star Wars test results. He spies his second in command, Major Rollins.

"Rollins!" he shouts.

"Yes, Colonel."

"Rollins. I want you to drop whatever you are doing and get every satellite and ground-based system tracking a group of objects coming from the moon. And, Major, let's go to red alert immediately."

"Yes, sir."

Major Rollins starts barking orders. Red lights begin to flash, and bombproof doors start closing automatically. Suddenly on the main view screen the image of Earth and the moon appears with hundreds of lines beginning to appear. Those lines are showing trajectories from the moon and are scattered around the surface of Earth. The major and the colonel look at one another with very concerned expressions captured on their faces.

"Colonel."

"Yes, Major?"

"We have approximately ninety minutes until those objects strike Earth. And from what I'm seeing, sir, it will go on for hours."

"That's impossible, Major, nothing we know of travels from the moon to Earth in ninety minutes," Polaski replied, not believing what he had just been told.

"I understand that, sir. That means we've never encountered anything like this before."

"Thank you, Major. I've got to contact Colonel Law."

Polaski picked up the phone and instructed the operator to connect him with Colonel Law at the Pentagon.

"Lance, what you got for me?"

"Jack, my guys tell me we've got ninety minutes before those things start dropping all over the planet."

"Ninety minutes, can we do anything to stop them?"

"Well, Jack, if we heat up the satellites, as well as use nukes set to detonate in orbit, we may be able to stop 20 percent of the ones we can see. But once those nukes start going off, the EMPs from the blasts could possibly take out every satellite in orbit. That will cut the kill ratio to maybe 10 percent. And we'll also need a presidential order to do any of it."

"We'll have to take the chance with the nukes. Fifteen percent is too much to lose. Heat up those satellites, Lance, and notify the silos as well as the submarines. I'll get you the orders in two minutes. Good luck, Lance."

The colonel hung up the phone and looked at the major, who had heard half of the conversation, and gave him an all-too-serious look.

"Major, heat up the satellites right away. Then notify missile silos and the submarines around the globe to be ready to launch in two minutes. Target as many of the objects as you can. We'll have a firing authorization in two minutes."

"Right away, sir." He then turned to his men and roared, "I want the satellite tracking online and ready to fire now, gentlemen."

His men came alive with purpose, to do the job they have trained a thousand times to do. This time it's different because they have never had this many targets to deal with at one time. The major knows the overall outcome is not going to be good.

Colonel Law reaches for the phone again, knowing the operator will be on the other end. "Get me the president," he orders firmly. Ten seconds later, the president answers the phone.

"Yes, Colonel Law."

"Mr. President, NORAD needs the firing orders for the satellites and ICBMs immediately, sir."

"Nukes, Colonel? I'm not sure I like that idea."

"Sir, Colonel Polaski has estimated that with only the satellites we will only be able to stop 10 percent of the incoming objects, but with the nukes we're looking at a 25 percent kill ratio."

"But, Colonel, nukes in our atmosphere? What about the fallout."

"We will make sure that they detonate out of the atmosphere in space, sir. The only kink is that the EMPs may take out all our satellite systems, but I don't see how we have any other choice. There are enough of these things to destroy most of the planet, sir. I would suggest that you contact the Russians for help."

"This is our only option?"

"It's nukes or total destruction, sir. And, sir, we have less than ninety minutes before they reach the planet's surface."

"Okay, Colonel, I'll send the codes right away. Then I'll call the Kremlin."

"Thank you, Mr. President."

"Colonel. Did you get the memo to be in the bunker by midnight?"

"Yes, sir. I'll see you there. Good-bye, sir."

John paces the floor of the control room at NASA as he watches the screen. The screen is filled with the feed from NORAD showing Earth with hundreds of lines descending toward the surface. One of John's aids comes to him with a cordless phone and informs him that Colonel Polaski is on the line.

"Yes, Colonel."

"John, we have a change of plans. I need you to use the Hercules to help stop these objects. NORAD can only stop 25 percent of the incoming objects with the satellites and our nukes. We need your help."

"Nukes? I heard nothing about nukes. I hope you're at least detonating them out of the atmosphere. And, Colonel, I thought we were saving Hercules for the alien vessels?"

"John, you've only got eight nukes on that platform with sixteen inbound vessels. I think we are better off using them now. I'll send you the launch codes as soon as I hang up."

"Okay, Colonel, we'll do it. Oh, and, Colonel. My guys are estimating that there are thousands, not hundreds, of inbound objects. We are also assuming that they are tied to that fleet somehow."

"So you think it's a preemptive strike?"

"That's our theory."

"John, I'm really starting to dislike you."

"Sorry, Colonel."

"John. How in the hell did they do this without us knowing about it?"

"Colonel. We haven't been interested in the moon for decades. Our sights have been set on Mars and beyond, and with one side of the moon always facing away from us, who would know. Anyone with the correct entry vectors could easily approach the moon without our knowledge. It's a big galaxy and we can't watch it all."

"Okay, John. Send those nukes on their way and dig in deep, it's going to be a rough night."

"Rough night. Colonel, I've got six astronauts trying to get home through a shooting gallery trying to race those objects to the ground. That's what I would call a rough night."

"I'll pray for them, John."

"Thank you, Colonel. We had both better get busy. Good-bye."

"Good luck, John."

John sets the phone down and runs for the Hercules control center. He has to send its payload off to help stop the destruction raining down on the unsuspecting people of Earth.

CHAPTER 11

—•◉❋◉•—

**Torani Command Vessel Jayden
October 13, 2020, 23:00**

On the bridge of the Jayden, the crew is engaged in the pursuit of the renegade fleet that they are slowly gaining time on. It is their obsession to catch it before it reaches the S-3 planet. They must prevent the annihilation of the inhabitants of that planet. Skoby is in his Command chair watching the monitors as Sub-commander Dorin approaches him.

"Commander, our long range sensors have discovered what appears to be thousands of mines being launched from the Kabult Station."

"What makes you think they are mines, Sub-commander?"

"They carry the quantum signature of the Corisole weapons, sir."

"What data do we have on the Kabult Station."

"As you know, sir, the station was created one hundred years ago as a scientific station by the Alliance, for the study of the S-3 planet. It was abandoned forty years ago because of the risk of contamination to the natural evolution of the planet. After sporadic activity for a decade, the Treaty of 12:7:141 was created making the station totally off limits to all Alliance planets."

"Well, it appears that the planet Corisole has not held up their end of the treaty, Mr. Mock. Are you picking up any energy readings from the Station?"

"I am detecting very minimal energy readings, but they could be shielded, sir. It's possible that they have a large base on the station, and are shielding it from Alliance sensors."

"Armament?"

"Unknown, sir," Mock replies.

"I think we should assume that it is heavily armed under the circumstances," Dorin added. "Since they have gone through so much to keep it a secret from the Alliance, not to mention the ability to launch thousands of mines, I'm betting they are heavily armed."

"Engineer Mock. How are our engines holding up?"

"Sir, we cannot get another ounce of energy out of them. We have been running at one hundred and 25 percent for twenty-four hours continuously, and four of our vessels are now lagging six hours behind the rest of the fleet."

"How long before we reach S-3's orbit?"

"Two and one half days, sir. That is if we can continue to run at the current speed."

"Maintain our speed at all costs Mr. Mock. If we lose more vessels they will have to catch up after we reach the S-3 system."

"We will do our best, sir."

"Sub-commander, I want you to try to discover exactly what is inside that station. I don't want any surprises when we arrive."

"Yes, sir," Dorin replied.

The commander began to pace after receiving the new intelligence on the invasion. He has a very uncomfortable feeling about the station. The Corisole have had at least twenty years of uninterrupted time to build it to its current status, and with the ability to build and launch thousands of mines from the station, there's no telling what other surprises it may contain.

Bill and Monica are sitting by the fire pit, on the large lounge chair with a blanket over them (Which the dog has half of) listening to music and watching the stars. The night sky is such a beautiful sight when you are away from the city lights. The stars are bright, and with the added streaking meteors, it's absolutely heavenly. Sassy jumps to attention. She knows someone is coming up the driveway.

"It's okay, girl." Bill tells her, but she doesn't lay back down. "I wonder who that could be? It's too early to be Willis."

As the headlights come up the driveway, he can tell it's not the Jeep, so he gets up and walks toward the oncoming lights.

"Who is it?" Monica asked.

"I don't know."

Sassy starts to bark, so he grabs her by the collar.

"I think it's Alex and Doves car." Devona's father called her Dove, so the name kind of stuck with her.

"This late at night?"

The car pulled up by the fire pit and stopped, then shut off its lights. As the doors swing open Sassy knows who it is, so her tail starts wagging and she turns a few circles before running to greet them.

"Go get 'em, girl." He tells her.

"I hope we're not bothering you. Alex and I went to a dinner party in Grand Junction, and since I knew you would still be up we decided to stop and see how you were doing. I knew you would be out here, it's tradition," she said, looking up at the stars. "Willis isn't home yet?"

"No, but he should be here soon."

"Mind if we join you?" Alex asked.

"Not at all, grab a seat. Want a cold beer?"

"I would absolutely love one," Alex replied.

"I'll go grab another blanket. I'll be right back."

"Thanks," they both reply.

Bill went into the house and returned with a bucket full of Coronas on ice and a blanket. He gives Alex the beer, and Dove the blanket.

"Thank you," they said.

"So have you met Willis's girl friend?" Dove asked.

"No, but he is supposed to bring her home tonight. They are going into Grand Junction tomorrow for some new equipment. Willis really likes this one so I can't wait to meet her."

"Me too," Monica said. "He needs someone besides an old hippy to hang around corrupting him."

"That's the truth," Dove said laughing.

"Speaking of old hippies, would anybody care for some?" Bill asked as he lit his bowl.

"Sure, why not," they all said.

Dove hit the pipe and handed it to Alex, then laid back looking at the stars. "Beautiful night for the showers."

"Yea, it's been quite a show. Better than last year by far," Bill replied.

They all laid back in their chairs enjoying the fire and looking at the stars. It's nice to be able to spend some time with good friends. A few minutes later Sassy's ears perked up. She didn't get up this time because she would know the sound of the Jeep anywhere.

"Here comes Willis," Bill said as he patted the dog on her head.

About that time the Jeep came around the last corner and pulled up in front of the garage. He got out and walked around opening Alice's door, then walked toward the fire pit with Alice in tow.

"Wow, the gang's all here," he said. "Alice, I would like you to meet my mom and her boyfriend Alex." They each gave her a big welcome to the family hug. "My dad's girlfriend Monica." She gives her a hug. "And that old hippy over there is my dad, Bill. Watch his hands," Willis said and laughed. Bill walked toward her with his hands out in front of him, clenching them in butt-grabbing motions, then gave her a big hug. "I told you," Willis said as they all laughed. "How's the show?"

"It's been awesome this year. Quite the light show," his dad answered him.

"We saw a few on the way home, but it's hard to watch them when you're driving."

"Good decision," Dove said. "It's bad enough with all the deer and elk on the road."

"Yea, we drove through a heard of elk coming up the driveway."

"So where's the house?" Alice asked as she looked around curiously.

They all chuckle and point toward the mountain.

"It's in there," Dove said.

"Really?"

"Why don't you take her in and show her the house," Dove said to her son.

"And bring back another bucket of Coronas on your way back out," his dad said, holding out the empty bucket.

"Sure thing, Dad."

They walked toward the hill hand in hand and stopped at what looked like an old root cellar door, which Willis opened.

"Cool," she said as she looked into the kitchen of the house.

The rest of the group remained at the pit enjoying the stars. It was a beautiful Colorado fall evening, and they all enjoyed a cold beer and some good herb, as well as the conversation.

The NORAD control room is now a mad house, but a well-controlled madhouse. They have done this a thousand times in drills. Everyone has a job to do and they all do it well, or they wouldn't be here. The colonel watches his men operate with great pride in their performance.

"Rollins." He barks.

"Yes, sir."

"Do we have the codes?"

"We're entering them now, sir."

"Very good, Major. Let's heat up those lasers and fire them till they melt."

"Captain Rice, you heard the man, commence firing at all available targets, there shouldn't be a shortage."

"Yes, sir, setting on auto lock."

The lasers came to life with bright red beams reaching out for their targets. They are each taking their toll on the incoming mines, but they are no match for the thousands of mines raining down on the planet.

"Are my nukes ready." Polaski asked.

"Yes, sir. All systems are standing by and ready to fire."

"Launch the first salvo of fifty now, and fifty more every five minutes for maximum destruction."

Across the United States as well as around the world, silos dormant since the day they were built suddenly began to rumble as the huge rockets shook the ground as they burst into the sky. The people who have lived among them for most if not all their life's, watched in disbelief as they watched them leave their resting places and rise into the sky. There has been no word of trouble with other nuclear countries in decades, so what could possibly be happening. Whatever it is they know it can't be good, so they run for their fifty-year-old bomb shelters fearing the worst.

"First fifty confirmed launched, sir," Captain Rice reports. The next thirty minutes would determine the fate of the world.

The screen in the control room at NASA is split with two feeds. One image shows the trajectory of the escape capsule from the ISS as it makes its reentry into Earth's atmosphere through the laser fire. The capsule is of Russian design and intended for dry landings. Its final destination is Edwards Air Base in the California desert.

The Astronauts have been extremely lucky to make their way through the shooting gallery that once contained nothing but empty space. Now the six men have to make it to the surface of the planet, and survive the deadly rain of mines. They are out of the pot, but unfortunately jumping into the fire.

The other half of the screen is connected to NORAD's tracking radar. It doesn't look good for the people on Earth's surface as the lasers are slowly being destroyed by the incoming mines. The incoming lines outnumber the outgoing one hundred to one. The ICBMs are taking their toll on the mines, destroying dozens with each blast, but with the massive amount of incoming targets they will be fortunate to destroy a quarter of the deadly objects.

John is standing in front of the screen taking in all the action. He switches one half to the Hubble's live feed, which has now returned to the image of the incoming alien fleets. This image has changed since the last time they viewed the fleets. There are now six vessels in the lead group, and only six in the second group. For some reason four of the vessels are falling back. He wonders what is happening with those four. Are they turning back or simply holding them back for reinforcements. John turns from the screen and watches his people work, then he makes the decision he knew he would have to eventually make.

"Can I have everybody's attention?" he yells above the noise in the busy room. All of his people stop what they are doing, and gather around John to see what their leader has to say. "I want everybody to head for the lower levels immediately. There's nothing more we can do up here. We'll ride out this attack down there, and see what's left when it's over." As the weary crew head for the elevators, John is hit by a strange thought. "Son of a bitch, it's Friday the thirteenth!" Then everything goes black.

All of the Joint Chiefs of Staff, as well as the cabinet members, are waiting deep in the bunker waiting for the arrival of their commander and chief. The bunker briefing room is an exact duplicate of the one in the White House hundreds of feet above their heads. They all have some peace of mind knowing their wives and children are safe in its depths. They pray for the others in their extended families that they were unable to inform about the danger, as well as the rest of the inhabitants of Earth whom they were powerless to help.

The president enters the briefing room and takes his normal position at the head of the long table.

"Ladies and gentlemen, can we have quiet please." As the room quiets he begins to speak. "People, we are at absolutely the most critical point in history since the destruction of the dinosaurs. In the last twenty-four hours we have confirmed the fact that we are not alone in this galaxy. The problem, is that apparently they don't particularly like us very much. We must assume that since we are currently on the verge of being bombarded by whatever these objects are that are coming from the moon, that the two fleets approaching Earth are the invasion force. As far as I can see it's the only scenario that fits, and it all boils down to what happens in the next thirty minutes. Either those objects land peacefully, or they blow the hell out of the surface of the planet. I am currently awaiting a progress report from Colonel Polaski on our situation with the defense systems. As soon as I know, you'll know. That's all I have for now. We can only wait and pray for now. Thank you all for your hard work these last few days.

The president sits patiently in his chair observing the deathly quiet that envelopes the room. He is scheduled in a few minutes to make an emergency broadcast to the nation. It's his horrible duty to be the bearer of the bad news, but it is his responsibility to keep the people informed.

Willis came out of the house with Alice. He is carrying a small bucket of iced beers which he hands to his father, then they both sat down by the fire.

"Thanks, buddy," his father said gratefully. "Who wants one?" They all agree except for Willis and his mother, who don't drink alcohol. He gives one to all the others. "So what do you think of our hole-in-the-wall, Alice?"

"I absolutely love it. It's the coolest house I've ever seen."

"Why thank you," he said with a smile.

"Careful with the compliments, Alice, or we'll never get his head back in through the door," Dove teased.

"It took Willis and I five years to create our masterpiece, but it is worth every minute of it. Our water comes from the stream, our power from the sun. We're totally off the grid. No bill collectors and no reason for anyone to come around.

"Wow, look at that," Alex said, pointing at the sky.

The meteors were streaking across the sky every few seconds, when suddenly there was a series of bright flashes near the horizon as well as a dozen in space that caught everyone's attention.

"What the hell was that?" Willis said, pointing at the distant flashes. "We've been doing this since I was five years old and I've never seen anything like that before."

All of a sudden another series of bright flashes lights up the sky. They all stare with awe at the incredible light show.

"Wow, the last time I saw something like that was back in the seventies, and if I remember correctly, there was LSD involved."

"Bill!" Dove exclaimed. Which was the followed by Her and Monica smacking him on the arm.

They continued to see the flashes lighting up the sky. None of them can believe what they are witnessing.

"That's not normal." Alex warned.

"You got that right." Bill agrees.

"I'm going to see if there's anything on the TV about what's going on," Willis said.

"Why don't we all go inside," Bill said. "I'll put out the fire."

They all grabbed their blankets and headed for the house. Bill used his little bucket to get water out of the stream to put out the fire. He stood watching the sky for a few minutes, then heard a loud explosion toward the west and Grand Junction. Him and Sassy walked halfway down the driveway so they could see in that direction. The sky had a strange glow over the distant mountains. It looked like a forest fire. Strange he thought, then they walked back up the driveway and went into the house.

As the pair entered the house, Bill noticed Willis with the TV remote in his hand clicking through the channels. The screen was blank.

"What's the matter?"

"It's not working. Not a single channel will come in. It's like there are no satellites up there."

"What about a radio?" Alex asked.

"Good idea," Willis answers, then walks over to the stereo and turns it on. He went through all the stations. "Nothing. Am or Fm."

"Wait a minute," Bill said. "I've got one of those old emergency radios." He went into his bedroom and returned a minute later with the transistor radio. After they replaced the batteries and turned it on, they hear the last few words of a message. They all waited for it to start over.

"Ladies and gentlemen, the president of the United States." They all look at each other in disbelief.

"My fellow Americans. As you are most likely aware, there has been an unusually large amount of meteor activity affecting our planet. NASA and NORAD are currently tracking thousands of meteors approaching the planet. We are using every weapon at our disposal to destroy as many of the meteors as we can. They have been able to destroy a large number of them, but unfortunately there are an even larger number still inbound and expected to make impact at any moment. If you are indoors, stay there. If you have access to a shelter, get to it immediately and stay there until further notice. These meteors are quite large and are doing considerable damage upon impact, so please seek shelter at once. We have no other information at this time, so stay tuned to this station for further updates. Thank you, and god bless you and protect you."

"So what the hell do you make of that?" Bill asked.

"I don't know, but I don't like it," Willis replied.

"I'm going back out and check it out. I heard a huge explosion toward Grand Junction before I came in. It looks like a huge fire over the mountain in that direction."

"I'm going too," Willis said as he grabbed his coat.

They went outside and saw hundreds of bright streaks across the sky, combined with a number of bright flashes in space.

"Man, this can't be good," Bill said to his son, shaking his head. "Let's go back inside. We're safe in there with a foot of concrete and four feet of mountain over our heads. I'll make us something to eat while we wait for another broadcast from the president."

Alex came outside to see what is going on. "So what do you think, guys?"

"I think we're in a world of shit," Bill replied.

They all went into the house to wait for another broadcast from the president. They waited early into the morning and eventually gave up and decided to get some rest. Tomorrow they would listen some more and hopefully get some information on the strange occurrence as well as the level of destruction.

CHAPTER 12

---•●✹●•---

Kabult Station
October 14, 2020, 00:30

In the control room of the Kabult Station, all hands can now relax after completing the launch of the mines. These mines were originally intended to be placed throughout the Sol System after the invasion of S-3, to deter any Alliance vessels from entering the system in retaliation. It was later decided that simply clearing the planet of human life would be more efficient than conquering and enslaving them. Once this decision was made they put their time and resources into arming the base for defense, which led to the mines use on the planet surface to clear as many of the humans as possible in one sweep.

The commander is observing the computer image of the planetwide destruction, pleased with the information he is receiving. His concentration is broken by his second in command.

"Commander. All mines have been launched. We will commence with the assault ships in one hour to assure the last of the mines have made it to the surface." Misk informed his superior. "Then we will launch the refueling towers six hours after the last ship leaves the hangar."

"Good, then everything is going according to schedule. What were our losses from their defenses?"

"We lost only 30 percent of the mines, sir. And through the onslaught our mines have managed to take out 90 percent of their satellites."

"With 30 percent fewer mines, what are the damage estimates?"

"Even with the losses, all major cities will be destroyed along with the high priority military targets. We estimate approximately five and a half to six billion out of an estimated seven billion inhabitants killed, sir."

"That still leaves a billion humans, Misk."

"The assault ships will run cleanup missions around the globe. They will destroy any remaining humans they encounter and move on. The two thousand ships should be effective enough to finish the mission in sixty days, sir. We will then send in our ground troops to do a final sweep and destroy mission to get the remaining humans. After ninety days the planet will be ours."

"When is the fleet scheduled to arrive?"

"Forty-six hours, sir."

"As soon as that last ship is launched I want the laser cannons moved into position and maned continuously for use against the Torani fleet. Is that understood, Sub-commander."

"Yes, sir."

"Sub-commander, you are in command. I am going to my quarters to get some rest. Inform me immediately if anything unusual comes up." The commander walked wearily out of the control room to the crew quarters that lie deep within the safety of the base. He is quite pleased with way their plan is unfolding and will now wait for the assault ships to do their job. There are still over a billion inhabitants on the planet's surface to be removed.

Commander Korg is on the bridge of the Rapture monitoring the planetary assault. He can tell by the displays on his monitors that it is going well.

"Commander. The preliminary estimates are coming in from the Kabult Station." Sub-commander Leigh informed him. "They report 70 percent of the mines made it to the planet surface with an estimate of five and a half to six billion of the inhabitants exterminated. The assault ships will be launched in one hour for stage 2 of the assault."

"What's our ETA at the planet?"

"Forty-six hours, sir."

"As soon as we enter orbit I want you to personally coordinate our defenses with the Kabult Station."

"Yes, sir."

The Rapture continues its journey through space to its rendezvous with history for the Corisole people. They have the duty of protecting their investment in the S-3 planet. The Torani fleet will most certainly be in full battle mode when they arrive but they have no idea what awaits them upon their arrival.

The meteors showered the planet with deadly accuracy and the cities of the world were in flames. The meteors created horrendous fire storms that consumed everything in their path as they were intended. New York, Moscow, London, all are now burning piles of rubble like every other major city on the planet. Each mine is capable of leveling a fifty square mile area with their incendiary payloads designed to burn the dead. This combination destroys and cleans the impact area. Real creative, real deadly.

The Pyramids which have stood for thousands of years, now blend into the sand dunes around them and every hub of humanity no matter how young or ancient, are all now destroyed.

The people who were fortunate enough to live in the rural regions of the world were the lucky ones that survived the onslaught. They watched the cities burn from the distant suburbs of America to the hamlets of England. They are now just a glow on the horizon. No matter where you were on the planet the outcome was the same and the remaining inhabitants of the planet saw the total death and destruction. They had not a single clue of the evil that had unleashed it, not to mention the extent of the evil still to come.

Chapter 13

—•●✹●•—

The crew of the Jayden watch helplessly as the Corisole attack the unsuspecting planet, knowing that they are too late to help its inhabitants. It will be another forty-four hours before they can help whatever is remaining of the population. Skoby turns to his second in command for answers.

"Sub-commander, what is the estimated damage to the planet."

"Sir, without being in orbit our estimates are rough at best, but we have estimated that at least thirty-five hundred mines have reached the surface. From our readings, the mines are a combination high yield explosives with incendiary properties added for maximum destruction. Our preliminary surveys show that all of the major cities are now in flames, as well as what appears to be the planet's military installations."

"What about the population?"

"These are only rough estimates, but we've estimated over five billion dead." "That is inexcusable. Such disregard of life is immoral. The Corisole have demonstrated their criminal intent and we will now treat them as the criminals they are. I want our fleet to begin planning for the absolute destruction of that fleet. You will also get our soldiers ready to assault that station. We will end this once and for all. By the time we finish with them, the Corisole planet won't have a military left to harm another living soul. This is by far the evilest act in the history of this galaxy. Ensign Lyle."

"Yes, sir."

"Contact the emperor and send him a full report on the attack. The Alliance Council will want to deal with the leaders of Corisole immediately."

"Yes, sir."

"Mr. Dorin, how many vessels are still with us?"

"We still have six vessels, sir."

"I want all remaining vessels, as well as the Kabult assault forces armed and ready to attack the second we are in range Mr. Dorin. Inform the other four vessels that they are to be ready for battle as soon as they arrive also."

"Understood, sir."

"And, Sub-commander. Keep a close watch on that Station. I doubt we have seen all it contains."

"Yes, sir."

As he paces the deck, Skoby wonders how any species could rain such destruction on another with no remorse for their actions. He knows their reasoning because of the state of their planet, but such disregard for another life form is unforgivable. He returns to his Command chair and grieves for the billions of lives lost on S-3 as he sat and watched helplessly.

Back in Washington the occupants of the briefing room are going over initial reports, and waiting for further information on the situation now occurring on their planet. The president is talking to Colonel Polaski by videophone at his end of the table.

"So how are we holding up Lance." The president has lost all patience with the formality of rank, so he has insisted that everyone drop it.

"To tell you the truth Gene it isn't good. We managed to stop approximately 30 percent of the bombs, but around four thousand still made it to the surface."

"Bombs!"

"Yes, sir. I'm sorry, Gene. Our observers claim that they were high yield explosives with incendiary quality's. Each one had an estimated fifty square mile blast radius. Absolutely a well-planned attack meant to soften us up for the invasion."

"Lance. How could they have launched what appears to be five thousand mines from the moon without us knowing they were even there."

"Well, from what John explained to me earlier, it may not have been that difficult."

"He's right, Gene," Horace said. "We stand on Earth and watch the moon as if it's just a harmless body in space, and we haven't cared about the moon for decades. We've been looking at Mars and beyond. With the right entry vectors it would be possible to land on the dark side and create whatever you wanted. Including a fully armed base evidently.

"Well, Horace, I simply can't believe they pulled it off right under our noses. Elsa, what are the estimates on casualties?" he asked, still shaking his head at the unbelievable nature of what he is hearing.

"We are guessing, and I do stress guessing. The estimate is over five billion."

"Five billion," he said, jumping out of his chair with both hands on the table in front of him.

"Yes, Gene. The bombs were precision guided and very deadly. They had the power of small nukes without the radiation. Literally every major city on the planet was targeted, not to mention the world's military installations. This is a well-planned attack intended for total destruction."

"All right, let's take a step back for a second. Horace, what about our satellites?"

"To know for sure we will have to ask Lance, but our preliminary data shows that we lost over 90 percent of them. The meteor bombs, I guess we could call them, destroyed them on their way into our atmosphere. The only reason you were just talking to NORAD is because they are connected by a hard line buried under Earth, and we both have generator power. "We have lost contact with NASA though. I'm assuming that since Houston was destroyed, NASA was destroyed also. But they do have deep underground facilities that may have protected them from the bombs."

"Lance can you get us that data on the satellites?"

"I'll get it to you as soon as we can. Our systems are currently down and were working on the problem as we speak."

"Thanks Lance."

"Okay, Elsa. I want you and Horace to do whatever it takes to communicate with whoever is left on this planet. We are flying blind here and I want to know what's going on. Our first priority will be to help the survivors of this attack. We need to somehow contact the National guard, Red Cross, and any military that is left and get them busy with helping those in need. Lance. I need you and Jack to somehow get in contact with what remains of our nuclear fleet, as well as whatever nuclear installations that are still armed, for when that fleet arrives. They're all we've got left to protect ourselves. Let's just hope that the rest of the planet's leaders are doing the same thing as us."

"Okay. We've got a lot on our plates so let's get to it. And people, thank you for all your hard work. I couldn't do it without you."

The president sat watching his people go to work. He hopes they can solve these problems for the sake of what's left of his country, and the rest of the world. It's a lot to put on their shoulders, but he knows deep down they can handle it. That's why he chose them for their jobs.

In the darkness of the NASA control room, John wakes in a dimly lit Command center with rubble is strewn across most of the large room. Houston took a direct hit from the attack, but the Space Center is several miles away. With its heavy concrete construction, it was heavily damaged but still standing.

As John started to regain his senses, he began to search for survivors. The emergency lighting which is battery operated cast a dim light across the room. He spotted several of the technicians huddled in the rear corner of the building. They needed to get them to the lower levels where there are medical facilities so they could assess their injuries.

"You men over here," he said to the few he could tell weren't injured. "We need to get this corridor cleared so we can get to that stairwell. Then I want to start getting these people down below to the infirmary."

They all made their way slowly to John and the corridor, but they were all understandably quite shaken up. Suddenly John hears a cry for help underneath the view screen, which is now lying on the floor.

"Over here guys, help me lift this up. There's someone underneath it."

The group ran over to the screen and lifted it up enough for John to see underneath. Under the screen there was a very confused but familiar face. Brad crawled out from under the screen, fortunately not seriously hurt.

"Thanks guys. I thought I was dead."

"Are you all right?" John asked his friend.

"I'll survive," Brad replied wearily.

"Okay. You guys start clearing that corridor, and Brad and I will start looking for more survivors."

The corridor unfortunately led to the elevators, so all of the people who were waiting to use it were crushed by the debris. They cleared the corridor slowly, laying the bodies of their friends out in the control room. After a few hours of moving the debris they had a path cleared to the stairwell. The injured were all accounted for and now ready to move below.

"Okay, everyone, we need to get these people down to the infirmary. Brad and I will go to the generator room and see if it's still operational. We need to get this place back up and running. A lot of people are still counting on us to do our jobs. The president and the rest of this planet are depending on us. Brad, what was the last thing you heard from NORAD?"

"They were only estimating to stop 30 percent of the inbound objects. That was about the last thing I heard, but after seeing this place I'm assuming the rest of the news can't be good."

"Yea, you're probably right. All right, let's get these people down below."

The survivors helped the wounded down the deep stairwell toward help. John and Brad went to the generator room to get the center powered back up. The sublevels are where the communication center is located so at least they can try to reach the president and NORAD.

The emperor's conference room is in an uproar, as the members of the Torani Council try to get a grip on the news that they are just now being made aware of. The emperor rises from his seat and raises both of his large hands to quiet the room. Then he began to speak.

"Gentlemen. Gentlemen. We need order."

"Commander, what is the damage to the planet?"

"Sir, with the inhabitants of the planet still entrenched with wars among themselves, they put absolutely no effort into protecting themselves from other worlds. Their feeble attempt to stop the attack with their primitive weapons was only able to stop approximately 30 percent of the five thousand mines launched against their planet. The remaining 70 percent were able to level every major city on the planet and kill most of what was seven billion inhabitants."

"What do you mean by was?"

"Sir, we estimate that there are over five billion killed." The room burst into an uncontrollable roar.

"This is an outrage." One of the members roared.

"What of our fleet?" another yells over the noise in the room.

"All right, let's have order!" the emperor shouts.

Brydon continues to speak. "Our fleet is running their vessels at top speed. They are still two days from the planet, and losing vessels to engine problems. Believe me gentlemen, we are doing everything in our power to stop this invasion."

The emperor took back control of the room. "Gentlemen, we must contact the Supreme Leader and put a stop to this attack. They will already be considered galactic criminals, and it's up to them to decide to what degree. If the Corisole rulers will not answer our communications, we will send an armed delegation to their planet to try to stop this action. I will notify the Galactic Council personally, and inform you of a meeting date. This session is recessed."

The room breaks out again in uncontrolled anger. The emperor understands their anger; this is an inexcusable crime. The inhabitants of the small planet did not deserve the evil being unleashed on them. No one did.

Inside the Kabult station, the last of the mines are now thirty minutes gone and are wreaking havoc on the planet's surface. The attack ships are sitting in the launch bay ready to be unleashed on the planet below. The second wave of the attack is about to begin and Corisk watches the ballet on the hangar deck with pride. He motions Captain Misk over to where he stands.

"Misk. Proceed with stage 2 immediately. Launch the attack vessels."

"Yes, sir." He walked over to the comms panel on the wall. "Proceed with stage 2. Launch all ships."

The ships came to life and left the bay like bees from a hive. The wellplanned ballet went on until all two thousand ships were launched, and they headed for their predetermined coordinates on the planet below. Stage 2 of the invasion is now under way.

On the planet Corisole, the members of the Supreme Leaders' Council wait for their leader's arrival. As he enters the room, they all rise and he motions for them all to be seated.

"All right, everyone, take your seats. Mr. Nalen, what is the latest word from the Kabult Station?"

Nalen rises to address the members. "Sir, Commander Corisk has informed me that the second stage of the invasion is now under way. The assault ships will enter the atmosphere in exactly ninety minute, and commence with the eradication of the remaining inhabitants."

"And what news do we have from the fleet?"

"The fleet is scheduled to arrive at the planet in forty-three hours, sir. Leader Mirosh, the Torani emperor, is insisting that we contact them immediately. I have forwarded your orders to ignore all communications, sir."

"Good, Mr. Nalen. I will deal with the emperor myself. In the meantime, I want our planetary defenses on standby in case they try to force their way onto the planet."

"Yes, sir."

"That will be all for now and I will inform you of any changes in our plans. Thank you all."

The members all rise as their leader leaves the chambers. They now await the results of the attack which will determine the fate of their world.

CHAPTER 14

———•◦❀◦•———

John and Brad exit the generator room after successfully starting the generators. They make their way into the small makeshift control room. Brad walks over to the console and checks the readings.

"How we looking Brad?"

"We will have full power to all computers and video in a few minutes. The backup dish wasn't damaged and is being raised as we speak. We should be able to send and receive shortly if we have any satellites left."

"Brad, while we are waiting I want you to put some men on clearing the elevator area on the main level so we have access. Have another team go room to room and check for survivors. If they find any bodies, have them lay them in the corridor by the elevator."

"John, we only have twenty survivors out of fifty technicians in this complex, and five of them are in the infirmary. They are scared and tired, so I don't know how much more work I can get out of them."

"For now Brad, we don't have a choice. Once we get the bodies cleared and this place back online. After that is accomplished we will start rotating rest periods."

"Okay, John, I'll get them busy. It might help keep their minds off of other things."

"I'll see if I can get the communications going while you are gone."

John flipped the switch on the console to power it up. An image from the Hubble came on the small screen.

"What the hell," John said. "Brad, wait. Forget the cleanup and get some guys in here now. I want to see if we can get NORAD. What the hell is that?" he said, looking at the screen.

As they looked at the screen they saw a dozen small ships pass from view, then nothing but the moon.

"Those were ships," John said.

"Where's the rest of them?"

"Good question Brad, but I don't think we want to know the answer to it."

"The way things have been going, you're probably right."

"Let's try NORAD."

They switched the satellite frequency and the telemetry from NORAD filled the screen.

"We got 'em," Brad said. "Let me try to get their comms."

After Brad fed the information into the computer, Colonel Polaski's face appeared on the screen.

"John," the colonel said with disbelief. "I was wondering if you made it."

"Just barely, Colonel. I see you guys are okay."

"This place is designed to take a direct nuclear strike. They will have to throw more than that at us."

"Be careful what you wish for, Colonel."

"Yea, I suppose your right."

"Do you have tracking, Colonel?"

"Only low orbit."

"How many were there?" John asked.

"You saw them?"

"Just a dozen or so."

"We've got them at around two thousand."

"Two thousand. These guys don't do anything small do they?"

"Evidently not. What are they? We only have telemetry, not pictures."

"They are small ships. And there are apparently thousands of them."

"You've gotta be shiting me John, do you ever have good news?"

"Sorry, Colonel."

"Oh, I've also been in touch with the president. I'm sure you'll be hearing from him soon. Take care John."

"You too, Colonel."

The screen went back to the NORAD satellite feed. John turned to his guys and gave them a thank you nod.

The colonel cuts his call with John and looks at Major Rollins. "Can you believe this shit?" Polaski asked the major. The major shook his head no. "Major, get me through to the president." "Yes, sir."

Rollins worked his magic, and the video screen soon had the image of Gene Furgison's face. "What can I do for you, Lance?"

"Gene, I just talked to John at NASA."

"Thank god they made it."

"He has more news."

"Bad I bet," Gene joked.

"How'd you guess?"

"You're kidding me. What now."

"Gene, we've been watching more inbound objects and thought they were just more of these bombs, but John got a quick glance of them and they are actually small ships."

"How many Lance?"

"About two thousand."

"Incredible. Lance, let me go to the briefing room. I think everyone else should hear this. Hold on for a few minutes."

"You got it, Gene."

The president paged his cabinet to the briefing room and met them there. Once everyone was seated, he put Lance on the screen.

"Lance, tell everyone what we have just discussed."

"Okay, Gene. Well, people, as I just explained to Gene, I talked to John and we have another problem on our hands. NORAD tracked around two thousand more objects that we thought were more bombs. After talking to John, I discovered that they were actually small ships of some kind."

"What the hell is going to be next, flying monkeys," Colonel Law burst out.

"Let's hope not, Jack," the president said.

"Jack, I need your help. You need to try to get ahold of whatever Air support you can muster. Airplanes, helicopters, ground to air missiles, anything you can find. I can't help on this one, my bullets are too big."

"We haven't been able to reach any of our bases Lance. I Think they have been all destroyed."

"Jack, there has to be something left out there. There's no way they could have gotten everything we've got."

"I'll do whatever I can Lance. But like I said, I haven't been able to get through to anyone."

"Lance, we'll get right on it. Thanks for the heads-up," Gene said.

"Thank John, he spotted them."

"I'm having a hard time doing that lately Lance."

"It's not his fault Gene."

"I know Lance. Stay close to the phone and we'll get back to you."

"Thank you Gene. Good-bye."

The president sat quietly as his staff waited patiently. "Admiral. I'm sorry, Vince. You have to get through to your Navy, and if there are any flattops left out there we need every plane they've got. I want to keep the subs hidden as a last deterrent, so let's leave them where they are at this time."

"Over 60 percent of our fleet was still in port Gene. They were supposed to ship out that morning so I have no idea yet what's left, but I will do my best Gene. I'll see who I can contact and go from there."

"That's all we can ask, Vince. Thanks."

From what the president just heard, things didn't look any better than they have. With 60 percent of the navy in the harbor, they would be lucky to have one battle group and one carrier. The only positive thing is that he knows the men in the armed forces will do whatever it takes to get the job done, whether they are ordered to or not. Gene waves Elsa over to talk. "Elsa, I need to make another address to the people. Set it up."

The guys were all sitting out by the fire pit again so they could talk without the ladies being able to hear the conversation. They didn't want to worry them any more than they already were. It took an hour to talk them into getting some rest. They were all tired and terrified. The guys were all still drinking beer and smoking Bill's pipe, even Willis.

"Ya know, guys, they always claim that the drinking and smoking will kill ya. I think that's the least of our problems now. Those meteors weren't normal, if they were meteors."

"Dad, where's the emergency radio?"

"On top of the refrigerator, why?"

"I'm gonna go and grab it and see if there's any new information on these meteors."

Willis went into the house and came right back out with the radio. He turned it on and they heard the president's voice.

"What was that?" Willis asked.

"I don't know. Just wait a minute," Bill answered.

They listened to the radio static for a few minutes, and then the president's message came on again.

"My fellow Americans. I have been informed by our observers, as well as the science director, that the meteors the struck Earth this morning were in reality, bombs launched by a hostile alien race."

They all looked at each other not believing what they had just heard.

"These meteors, or actually bombs, were precision guided and targeted every major city on the planet. The damage has been catastrophic. I have also been informed that they were launched from a base located in the moon."

"The moon. You gotta be shitting me," Bill said.

"Quiet," Willis said.

"This attack, as I said, targeted every major city and all military installations. The death toll has been estimated at five billion, possibly six billion."

"They're exterminating us," Willis said.

"My friends, this not the end of the story. At four-thirty this morning eastern time, we discovered two thousand small ships breaching our atmosphere headed for the planet's surface. We have no reason to believe that they are friendly and advise you to take whatever shelter you can find. The deeper the better."

"Now, the rest of the information is unfortunately even more dire. NASA has discovered a fleet of sixteen vessels en route to our solar system. We are assuming that they are headed to this planet and are estimated to arrive in Earth orbit in approximately two days."

"Normally at this point I would refer to us as fellow Americans, but I'm going to change that to my fellow earthlings. We can no longer to let our countries be separate entities. We have to stand together as "one planet," and fight for this planet as one. We are under attack by an aggressive alien race, and my advisors and I have determined that they intend to kill every human being on this planet."

"Ladies and gentlemen, I regret having to tell you about our possible Armageddon, but I thought you all deserved the truth. Take this time to gather your loved ones and get away from any cities or towns, and take cover wherever you can find it and stay there."

"I will make another statement in twenty-four hours to update you on our situation. God bless you all, and good luck to each and every one of you. Thank you."

The radio turns to static again, so Willis turns it off.

"You all told me that I was crazy for building this place. Who's crazy now?" Bill said. "We need to get all the vehicles inside. Willis, put the Jeep in the garage and I'll put Alex's car in the studio. As soon as it gets light we need to go lock the gate and camouflage the driveway so nobody knows we're here."

"You don't mind if Dove and I stay here do you?"

"No, I insist on it. And not a word of this to the ladies for now. Understood."

They all agreed.

"What are we gonna do, Dad?"

"I don't know. But I think for now we should lay low and see what happens. We've got enough food to last at least a year if we're careful. We have the greenhouse to grow vegetables. We also have a five-hundredgallon tank of fuel buried for the cars and the generator if we need it. We can hunt and fish, but you will have to wear camouflage suits so you're not seen. If one of us is seen by these aliens, it endangers the rest. Well, that's enough talk about the end of the world for me. We better kill the fire and go inside. We'll come back out in a couple of hours and take care of the driveway."

They were putting out the fire when they saw streaks in the sky.

"Here they come," Willis said, pointing at the sky.

That was all they needed to hear, so into the safety of the house they all went.

CHAPTER 15

Planetwide Summary 2
October 14, 2020, 05:00—October 15, 2020, 16:00

That morning the ships came. The people of Earth were not ready for the new terror the aliens were about to unleash. The shiny V shaped ships moved through the sky like a water bug on the surface of a smooth pond. They darted in any direction of their choosing from target to target, killing every human being that was unlucky enough to be caught in the open.

The skippers, as we began to call them, hunted by movement. Any target that their scanners detected moving was automatically targeted and killed. The skippers would dart to a target and hover only long enough for their green laser tongues to reach down and turn its victim to a small pile of ash. Then it was off to the next victim. The strange thing was that they only targeted humans, and all other life on the planet was spared their wrath. They were fast and they were deadly, but the skippers did have a weakness—they sounded like a huge bumblebee. We finally discovered that if you heard the buzz of a skipper, you got under cover or simply stood still and they would pass you by. The smart ones used this tactic. The scared or inexperienced ones died an instant death.

The governments of the world tried everything they had in their arsenals. They tried surface to air missiles which were very effective, but they lacked the inventory. Like most of the weapons they were destroyed with the military bases. They all tried airplanes to stop the skippers, but they were no threat to the darting abilities of the ships, who simply outmaneuvered them and blew them from the sky with their lasers. It was like shooting fish in a barrel.

The Navy ships were effective for a very short while. They took a small toll on the skippers until the small ships would swarm them and burn holes through their hulls. It seemed that as soon as one was destroyed, the others would come out of nowhere like an angry swarm of bees. There were simply to many of them for them to be effective. The submarines were instructed to remain out of the fight and stay deep and hidden for later use.

It was a terrifying experience to dodge the skippers. You could hear the buzz, but it was hard to tell its direction. So if you couldn't see it, you didn't move a muscle until it had gone on to its next victim.

They targeted the hungry and thirsty. That's how they planned it. They knew that with a surprise attack the people would not be prepared to be out of power, water, and food to survive. The aliens knew that eventually they would rid the planet of what they considered as a disease on this planet's surface, killing it slowly. The human race was dwindling more and more with each hour by the effectiveness of these killing machines. The ones that were still alive knew that all they could do is hide.

On the eve of the third day of the attack, the fleet vessels arrived. From the planet surface the sun made them shine in the sky like a huge star ready to fall to Earth. With the fleet in orbit, the ground troops would soon be dispatched to annihilate any remaining humans. The human race had its days numbered.

The Corisole fleet entered Earth orbit with the Torani fleet hot on their heels and ready to destroy the murderous criminals. The pursuing fleet has turned a three-day deficit into a mere six hours with the miracles created by their engineers.

Sub-commander Dorin turns to his Torani fleet commander Skoby with news of the enemy fleet.

"Commander, the Corisole fleet has entered the S-3 planet's orbit."

"Thank you, Sub-commander. Slow the fleet and hold us at ready, just this side of the systems asteroid belt."

"Yes, sir."

The vessels of the fleet slow to a stop to wait for the remaining four to rendezvous with them. With the fact that they are only six hours behind he is willing to wait and gather his forces for the battle to come.

"Sub-commander, I want all ships officers in the briefing room in five minutes and make sure the other ship commanders are tied in for the pre battle conference."

"Yes, sir."

Five minutes later, they are all in the conference room with the other commanders tied in. "Everyone is ready, sir," Dorin informs his commander.

"Gentlemen. In a few hours we will have the honor of ensuring the continued existence of the surviving beings on the S-3 planet. We also will have the pleasure of destroying the murderous Corisole fleet, as well as their illegal moon base which is responsible for this atrocity."

"As you all know the Corisole leaders, as well as the Corisole fleet, are responsible for the deaths of at least five and a half billion inhabitants on this planet. It was inexcusable that we allowed this atrocity to happen. Unfortunately, we had no idea of the lengths the Corisole leaders would step to replace their planet. I personally can't believe that they were able to hide their activity from the Alliance, and we discovered their plans too late to stop the holocaust."

"Gentlemen, I see how carefully planned out this attack was and that worries me. We have absolutely no intel on that moons defensive capabilities, so we must assume that it is heavily armed and approach it as so. The Corisole fleet on the other hand is vulnerable as it sits in orbit. We will attack this battle field on four fronts. With ten vessels in our fleet, we will hit the Station and the fleet in one balanced attack. I Want the Oran, Braken, Tory, and the Ryden, to set up on in four-point deployment around the station. From these positions I want you to destroy all weapon systems you may encounter. Be cautious, gentlemen, we have no idea what they have for armament, but my guess is that it's laser cannons. We just don't know how many or where they are located. Also, Commanders. This planet relies heavily on its moon so you must be somewhat careful with your attacks. I don't want it destroyed, so use precision when firing your weapons and not force. Do you understand your objectives, Commanders?"

"Yes, sir," the four men affirmed over the comm.

"The rest of the fleet will follow the Jayden to the planet, and at that point we will disperse and take the Corisole vessels one on one. That will fall as it lays, Commanders. I will take the command vessel Rapture, and the rest of you will each select a vessel and destroy it. Use your training as well as your heads, gentlemen, and this should be an easy battle. We have the fleet vessels outgunned, so just use your skills and we will be victorious. That planet is counting on our success. Are we all clear on our jobs as well as our objective?"

"Yes, Commander," they all answered.

"The last four vessels will rendezvous with us in less than six hours. As soon as they arrive we will commence the attack. The commanders of those four vessels will have to prepare en route. All right, gentlemen, let's get ready for battle."

Skoby thinks through the steps of his battle looking for any holes, but can find none. He turns to his second in command.

"Sub-commander, I want you to try to contact the leaders of the planet on all available frequencies. We have been monitoring their transmissions for decades, so you have something to base it on. I want to try to let them know that we are not their enemy, and are here to help."

"Yes, sir," Dorin replies.

The fleet now waits for their comrades to arrive so they can complete their mission. The inhabitants of the S-3 planet will be depending on them to stop the Corisole invasion and save their planet and its people from annihilation.

CHAPTER 16

Parachute, Colorado
October 16, 2020, 08:00

The survivors of the valley were all huddled around the kitchen table having a cup of coffee. The radio sat in the middle of the table playing the same message that it had been playing for the last two days. They have been waiting for more news about the invasion, but have heard nothing.

The ladies have heard the message, and after two days are finally starting to grips with the reality of their predicament. They are still in a state of shock, but the guys have been able to keep them calm. They are all now trying to decide their next course of action. Bill, being the least affected by the strange turn of events, has come out as the leader of the group.

"I think we need to hike down and see what's going on. I just can't sit here and wonder," he said.

"What about the ships, Dad? We can't just go wandering around in the open. Once we leave the cover of the trees in the valley there's not a lot of cover."

"I've got four sets of cammo gear for hunting, so we'll suit up and move as carefully and slowly as possible. I've got to know what's going on. I was out yesterday with my binoculars scouting around, and I noticed something strange about the skippers."

"Skippers?" Willis asked.

"Yea, that's what I call them because of the way they skip around from one place to another. These things are the fastest thing I've ever seen. One minute they'll be hovering over a target and the next thing you know they are miles away looking at something else. I think they hunt by motion."

"I was watching the Interstate and I saw one of them blast a car sky high as it was trying to outrun it. The strange part was that only a couple of miles back another car saw what had happened to the one ahead of it, so it pulled over between two cars on the side of the road and parked. The skipper must have seen it because it went to where it was, but then it just hovered a minute and left. I'm sure they didn't make it too far, but it was strange that it didn't destroy them. The only thing I can figure out is that they hunt by movement. I had six of them fly right over the top of me while I sat under that tree, so I'm almost positive that they do hunt by motion. Something else that I noticed is that you can hear them coming miles away. They sound like a huge bumblebee. That gives us some ability to be able to move around if we know when they are in the area."

They all took in what Bill had just told them as they sat quietly drinking their coffee. Half of them were now more afraid after hearing the horrifying details about the skippers.

"Oh, by the way there's something else too. Some kind of huge tower is standing about two miles to the east. The skippers seem to attach to it for a few minutes then fly off, so I'm assuming that it's some kind of refueling station or something."

"So, anyone want to take a walk?"

The ladies all shook their heads a definite no.

"I'll go," Willis said eagerly.

"Me too," Alex added.

"Let's do it then. We'll suit up and go down and check it out. I'll be right back with the gear." They all ignored the "Are you guys F——ing crazy" looks and got dressed.

The guys walked three miles down the hill where they could get a good look at the town with the binoculars. They had to stop twice because of the skippers, but as Bill thought, with the cammo they just sat still when they heard them coming and they just passed them by.

They laid on the hillside for at least a half an hour watching the town below that was now in flames. Only a few buildings were still standing and completely undamaged by the attack. Willis noticed someone running across a field toward the river with a water jug in his hand.

"Look over there," he said, pointing toward the river.

They heard the buzz as they all watched the man by the river. The man looked up at the skipper in terror and tried to run, but in less than a step, the green laser from the skipper hit him and instantly turned him to ash. They all looked at each other in disbelief. It is the first time they have actually seen the aliens kill a human being in cold blood. A few minutes later they watched helplessly as a family tried to make it out of town to the safety of the forest. The family only made it halfway across the parking lot of the gas station where they were hiding, when suddenly a skipper appeared and turned them all to ash like the first. They all looked at each other wondering who they were and how old those poor children were.

"I've seen enough. How about you guys?" Bill asked sadly.

"Yea, let's go." Alex agreed.

An hour later they were back at the house standing just outside the door.

"Not a word about what we saw," Bill said forcefully. "I don't want to worry the girls any more than they already are," he added. The two others agreed.

"What did you see?" Dove asked as they came into the house.

"Battlement and Parachute are both in flames. There's not much left. With Battlement being mostly trailer houses, they went up like kindling. We'll start in Parachute tomorrow looking for survivors. There's less ground to cover." Bill uttered as he went to the fridge for a beer. "I don't think we will find anyone but we have to check." He stood thinking for a few minutes drinking the whole beer quickly, then looked at the other two men. "You guys want one?" They both nodded yes in agreement. "Let's go out to the studio, I've got some more in there."

Alex and Willis followed Bill outside and into the studio. Once they were inside and the door was closed, Bill gave them both a cold beer and put a CD in the stereo, then he grabbed his bowl.

"Okay, guys, I'm thinking payback."

The others shook their heads in agreement as they drank. Bill walked into the cold cellar and came out a few minutes later with a box full of dynamite and some detonators.

"This is what we used when we made the hole for the house," he explained to Alex as Willis just sat shaking his head in agreement. "How about tonight we get some. And that's just between us guys. If the ladies get word of our plan they will certainly try to stop us." They all agreed, then finished their beers and went back into the house.

Brad and John were sitting in the small control room in the sublevels of the space center. They had crews working on the cleanup of the remaining center, trying to get it back up and running.

The Hubble was fortunate enough to escape destruction from the attack. With the controls reactivated on the Hubble, they had it pointed in the direction of the second fleet, which was still in transit to their planet.

Brad notices something strange and rises, then walks toward the screen as John looks on.

"Those ships have stopped," he said, as he taped the screen with a finger.

"What makes you think that?"

"I've been watching them for the last hour, and they're not getting any larger. It's impossible to be sure without the tracking systems, but I'd be willing to bet their sitting still. They must be waiting for the others to catch up before they join the others. NORAD's radar shows the others already in orbit around the planet."

"So you've been in contact with NORAD?"

"Colonel Polaski sent a message a few hours ago. I didn't wake you since you have to be as exhausted as the rest of us. I'm sorry, it just slipped my mind."

"What was the message?"

"It wasn't good. The colonel was informing us that all the major cities have been destroyed and the attack ships are meticulously targeting the remaining towns. They are going from town to town and killing any remaining people that are unfortunate enough to be seen. It's extinction John. They want us all dead."

"It's ironic Brad, that the governments chose to cut all spending on exploration of the moon because of the Cold War with the Russians and put all their money into defense projects. They totally ignored the moon for decades and look where that got us. Hell we had to fight just to get the funding for our asteroid detection systems. If they would have let us do it the way we wanted, we could watch more than about 10 percent of space and might have seen them coming. It was absolutely stupid."

"No, John, I have to disagree. It wasn't stupidity, it was arrogance. It is totally arrogant to believe that we are the most intelligent and only beings in this galaxy. And to think that no one would ever come to challenge us is ridiculous."

"I absolutely agree with you Brad. I've always felt, and I mean since I was a small child, that we were the little fish in a big pond. That's the only reason I joined the Air force. I knew it was the only way to become an Astronaut."

"John!" Brad yelled with amazement. "We've got a message, and its coming through one of our satellites."

They both stood staring at the written message on the screen.

"It's from 'them,' Brad."

They read the message. "People of the planet Earth, I am Commander Skoby. I command the inbound fleet, which is from the planet Torani, acting on behalf of the Galactic Alliance. The fleet that is now in orbit around your planet, and responsible for the horrendous attack on your planet, is from the planet Corisole."

"This planet has broken a treaty that was created two decades ago to protect your planet from exactly this kind of action. We fully intend to destroy this fleet, along with any other of its entities in its control, in order to return your planet to your control. The people of the planet Torani feel great sorrow for the loss of life as well as the damage done to your societies. We bear the weight of responsibility for not anticipating their actions and assure you that these murders will be dealt with using all our resources. I am also authorized to inform you that we will help in any way we can to rebuild your world."

"We suggest that the remaining population of the planet finds whatever sanctuary they can. This battle will be short but it will be great, and there will be the possibility of debris falling to the planet's surface. The battle will begin in approximately three of your hours."

"We will keep this frequency open in order for you to confirm that you received our message. End of transmission."

"Holy shit, John! Do you believe this?"

"Unbelievable, but at least we now have some friends out there. I need to contact the president. I'll be in my office Brad. I'm going to send this message to the president so he can hear it for himself."

John walked to his office to send the message. Just when he thought things couldn't get any stranger, he gets this dropped in his lap. Will it ever end, he thinks to himself.

After a short rest the guys decided to go back out. Alex is on the east ridge watching the fuel tower, and Willis and Bill have worked their way back into what used to be the town of Parachute.

As they slowly worked their way through the demolished buildings trying to stay out of sight, they came upon the old church and noticed a family hiding in a storage shed behind a burned out house. Bill motioned to them to stay put. As they crept toward the front door of the church, they looked back and could tell that the family was getting ready to follow them into the church. Bill could hear the familiar buzz of a skipper. He told them to stay put, but the father wouldn't listen. The family made it halfway across the empty lot when the skipper stopped above them. They looked up in terror and vanished. They could feel the heat one hundred feet away. Willis stood frozen in place, looking at the four piles of ash where four people had just stood only a second ago. What a terrible sight to see. Bill had to shake him to move after the ship left. They have witnessed the act before, but not so close. It was a totally different and helpless feeling.

They ran through the doors of the church, then heard another skipper hovering just above the building. It had detected them, but since it couldn't find them it went on looking for more victims. A crash behind them startled them both back into the moment and they turned to see at least a dozen people standing at the rear of the building. They recognized a few of the tired and dirty faces of friends from the town.

The Millers and their two children, had run a small coffee shop in town. Standing next to them was Ben and Janet Kerr. There were three children that nobody knew who they belonged to, as well as a woman with a small baby that they didn't recognized. Willis then noticed his friend Bret from high school.

"Tom, I'm glad to see you made it," Bill said as he went over to shake the man's hand.

"It's a pleasure to see you also, Andrea." He gave her a big hug. "It's been hell, Bill. I can't believe we made it this far," Tom said wearily. "You remember Ben and Janet, don't you?"

"Absolutely, I'm glad you two made it also."

"Thanks, Bill," Ben said as he shook Bill's hand.

"Dad, you remember Bret, don't you?"

"Yea. Little league, right?"

Bret shakes his head yes. "This is Maggie and little Lilly. My family."

"Glad to meet you," he replied, shaking her hand and giving Lilly a rub on the head.

"We haven't figured who they belong to yet. We can't get a peep out of them," Tom said, motioning toward the three children huddled in the corner. "I guess they belong to all of us now."

"All right, everyone. Willis and I are going to go over to the hardware store and see if we can scavenge anything useful since we're here. We'll be back in about an hour, then we'll all make our way up to our place. It seems to be safe up there for now."

"Sounds like a good plan, but how are we going to get all these people five miles up the hill to your house?" Tom asked.

"It will be slow going, but you'll have to trust me when I say that we can make it."

Tom shook his head in agreement.

The pair left the church and crept carefully through town toward the hardware store as the others waited impatiently for their return.

The president hurried through the underground corridors of the Bunker complex to the briefing room. He has been informed that there was news from John. He is preparing himself for more bad news. As he enters the briefing room he notices the staff is sitting quietly waiting for him. They all have a relaxed appearance for the first time in days.

"What is it, Elsa?" he asked curiously.

"I think I'll let Horace field this one, Gene," she said, gesturing toward the science director who was sitting there with a very relieved look on his face.

"Mr.—" He stops. "Sorry. Well, Gene, two minutes ago we received a message from John with a separate message attached."

"I'm guessing from the looks on your faces that it's actually good news for once," Gene said, perking up in his seat.

"Very good news, sir, see it for yourself."

Horace started the message and pointed toward the screen where the message appeared. The president carefully listened to the message. As he listened to the message, his friends saw something they haven't seen for days, a smile on Gene's face.

"Well, I'll be dammed. Four days ago we were the kings of our planet. Yesterday we were on the verge of extinction. Today we find out that we actually have had a big brother in the galaxy for decades to beat up the bullies for us. Incredible. Who in their wildest dreams could have expected this. Do we believe them Horace?"

"I think we have to Gene. They contacted us and offered their help. I have the transmitter set to send a reply."

"All right, Horace. You and I will go to my office and send a reply to their message."

The two men left the briefing room to send their message to their new friends.

Commander Korg enters the bridge of the Rapture and addresses his sub-commander as he takes his seat.

"What is it, Sub-commander?"

"We have intercepted a message directed at the planet from the Torani fleet, sir."

Korg rises in amazement and approaches the comms station. "Let's see it."

They both listened to the message that appeared on the screen. When Korg finished he returned to his chair taking in what he has just heard.

"Sub-commander."

"Yes, sir."

"Ready the fleet for battle. Inform the Station of the circumstances and have them be ready to defend themselves. Then I want you to send a copy of this message to the Supreme Leader so he is informed."

"Right away, sir."

"When will the remaining Torani vessels rendezvous with their fleet?"

"We estimate two hours, sir."

'Very well. Inform me of any changes."

"Yes, sir."

Korg rose and returned to his quarters to ready himself for battle. The Torani have confirmed his worries of the battle to come. They will certainly do all that is in their power to put a stop to their plans and save the planet below.

CHAPTER 17

---•●✹●•---

Battle for the Sol System
October 16, 2020, 12:00

The Corisole fleet is repositioned in front of the planet and standing at battle stations awaiting the arrival of the Torani fleet. The Torani fleet has them outnumbered almost two to one but the added firepower of the Kabult Station should make up the difference. They feel confident that they can come out victorious with the awesome power contained within the station. Korg sits watching the screen and waiting for their arrival.

The Torani fleet is also readying their vessels for battle. The stragglers of the fleet arrived over fourteen hours ago but had sustained serious damage to their engines, which required major work before they were ready for battle. With the repairs now completed, the fleet is ready for the attack. Skoby is expecting heavy defenses from the cruisers as well as the station, which is undoubtedly armed with laser cannons. The question is how many and where are they hidden.

The commander has received a message and transmitted it to the emperor. The message was from someone referring to himself as President Furgison, of a place called the United States of America. He now realizes why it was so easy for the Corisole to invade the planet. With the separated countries as well as the separate ruling bodies divided into so many individual groups, it would have been impossible for them to come together to repel the invasion. Now that 90 percent of their population has been annihilated, they will have no choice but to pull together to rebuild their world.

It is now the Galactic Alliance's responsibility to repel the Corisole invaders and bring those responsible to justice for their actions. Second, the Alliance will need to help the planet rebuild to ensure its inhabitants survival. And finally, the Alliance will have to protect the now defeated planet from further actions by other would-be invaders during its weakened state. There are other aggressive races in the galaxy who would take advantage of the planet's weakened state and attempt to take control of the S-3 planet.

Alex has returned from his reconnaissance of the refueling tower. He has spent two hours watching the skippers come and go from the tower and believes he has found a weakness. He believes he can use this weakness to launch an attack on the tower. He leaves the house being careful not to let anybody see him, because they will try to stop him if they do. He went to the studio and gathered what he needed to do the job and put it in his backpack. As he sneaks away from the property, he knows that he has a job to do and he's going to do it. "It's payback time."

Elsewhere on the planet, the people are also getting a little payback. Earthlings are actually a very tough bunch, and after thousands of years of fighting among themselves, they have honed their skills and become quite creative at the art of war. Ragtag militias have been raised to fight the invaders, armed with some of today's best weapons not destroyed by the attackers.

The skippers are very susceptible to ground to air missiles. With thousands of the handheld versions stored deep in bunkers, they were now well armed. The skippers were discovered to be nothing but drones. It was also obvious that they weren't very smart, so they were easily trapped and destroyed by their quest for moving objects. We would simply sucker them in with an unmanned moving target, and blow them out of the sky when they had their attention focused on their targets. With the use of short wave transmissions, the information was fed to the fighters around the world, and now the humans have destroyed most of their fleet of skippers. There are also reports of the refuel towers being destroyed around the globe.

I guess the invaders didn't count on us being so vigilant, or count on the resourcefulness of humans to find ways to destroy their enemies.

The final four vessels have been repaired and are now ready for battle with the rest of their fleet. Commander Skoby entered the bridge of the Jayden ready to take his fleet and his men to war.

"Sub-commander, have all vessels been briefed on their assignments."

"Yes, sir. They all report as ready and awaiting your orders."

"Open a channel to all vessels."

"Yes, sir."

"Attention all vessels. This is Commander Skoby of the Jayden. We are about to engage the Corisole fleet which has unlawfully and without remorse, decimated the inhabitants of the S-3 planet. Because of the extent of their atrocities, we have been authorized to carry out the destruction of their fleet so they can never use it in such a manner as this again. I want these murderers executed for their crimes."

"The Kabult Station is surely heavily armed, so use caution on your approach, and remember, Commanders, that we must not destroy that moon. I expect you to use surgical precision with your fire on this moon Gentleman."

"I want all lead vessels to go in hot and make a strafing run on that moon in order to draw their fire so the second group can set up their attack on the base. The secondary vessels will then be on their own to deal with the base. Once the first group passes the base, we will assume our attack positions and engage their fleet. Good luck, Commanders, and good hunting."

The commander turns to his bridge crew to address his officers. "Men we do this for the sake of the billion people that still remain on that planet, as well as everything the Alliance stands for in this galaxy. Subcommander, signal the fleet that we will commence with the attack in exactly sixty seconds."

Commander Korg readies his fleet for battle with the Alliance fleet. All vessels are standing by and ready, and the Kabult Station has manned all cannons and is also ready for the engagement.

"All vessels stand at ready. As soon as they reach the Kabult Station open fire. We do this for our planet men. Their survival depends on us, so let's not let them down."

Korg watches the view screen as well as his sensors awaiting the inevitable battle to come. He absolutely feels the weight off all his people on his shoulders. His planet needs this planet for its survival and if he fails to destroy the Torani fleet, which is the largest and most powerful fleet in the Alliance, they will not be able to hold the planet and twenty years of preparation will have been wasted.

"Engage all engines," Skoby orders. "Fire as soon as you have target locks and do not stray from the specified attack vectors, but you do have permission to attack any secondary targets you acquire on your approach."

The fleet lurches into action, each vessel knowing exactly where it's heading and exactly what its responsibility is. As the fleet passes the Kabult base unleashing a barrage of fire, they veer off and target the Corisole vessels while their comrades on the remaining four vessels swoop in to target the base.

Korg rises and begins to instruct his fleet. "Watch them they are breaking into two groups." He hits the comms switch. "Kabult Station, they are going to try to surround you. Prepare your gunners for an all-out attack and don't let them through your defenses, Commander."

"Yes, sir." The answer comes over the comms.

Korg hits the switch for the fleet. "All right, gentlemen, we'll break from the spearhead formation as they come in. I will take the lead vessel. The remaining vessels will work their way down through the ranks as they come in. It will be a one on one battle, Commanders, let's show them no mercy."

The skies above the planet Earth looked like the Fourth of July with the flashes of light from the sixteen ever moving spots in the sky, mixed with the lasers reaching from the moon for the nearest target. The remaining inhabitants watched the sky in awe. Having heard the messages from their leaders of their new savior's arrival, they prayed for them to succeed in their mission.

For those who could see it, the moon lit up like a huge disco ball as light flashes emanated from what appeared to be every crater on its surface. The Corisole engineers had done an incredible job creating a spherical firing pattern. It is a truly formidable weapons base, absolutely impenetrable and extremely deadly.

The four Torani cruisers repeatedly attacked the station taking heavy damage with each attempt. The Kabult Station's cannons were extremely effective and taking their toll on the attacking vessels.

"Jayden this is the Ryden. We are taking considerable damage from the station. We need more fire power. The cannons are below the surface and the only way to target them is to get in their direct line of fire. We're sitting ducks, sir."

"Brightstar, Mornstar, break off from the fleet and attack the Kabult base. We will handle the Corisole fleet on our own."

"Yes, Commander," they answered.

The two vessels broke formation and set their sights on the moon base. Their comrades are being pummeled by the station's cannons and desperately need their help.

John and Brad are in the control room working on the NASA systems when Brad suddenly notices something odd in the system.

"John, why do we still have telemetry from Hercules?"

John studies the main board and makes an amazing discovery. "I personally sent the command to launch those missiles, but it must have been interrupted by the strike on our satellite systems."

"So we still have Hercules and eight missiles? We could use them to help. If we were to target the enemy vessels with the Hercules, we may be able to do some serious damage to those vessels.

"It's worth a shot Brad. Let's shove a couple of missiles up their asses and show them that we're still in the fight. We need to get tied in to NORAD, as well as the president's bunker. Get them on the line Brad, we're still in this fight."

Brad worked his magic and soon had the president's bunker on one computer screen, and NORAD on another. The Hubble is still trained on the moon base showing images of the tremendous battle that is taking place.

The Torani vessels aren't faring well against the incredible power of the station's cannons. Now they have something to help their new allies. John hopes their idea will help.

"Gene, Lance."

"What's up John?" the president asked.

"Gentlemen, I have an idea. It seems that the firing order to the Hercules was interrupted during the initial bomb attack which means we still have eight nukes in orbit. We can help the Torani in this battle."

The screens now showed two very excited men.

"Outstanding John. Turn your command of the satellite over to NORAD, and I'll get on the horn to the Torani commander and coordinate our strike with theirs."

Brad typed the commands into the keyboard then gave John a thumbs-up.

"Lance are you receiving the telemetry."

"It's coming in now John. We'll handle the launch and targeting from here."

The president is on the other screen attempting to make contact with the Torani commander. "Commander Skoby, this is President Furgison. Please answer if you are you reading me."

"President Furgison, we are quite busy at the moment. What can I do for you?"

The president informed the commander of the good news and worked out a plan to draw the enemy vessels near the Hercules, in order to cut the weapons flight time and add to the element of surprise.

"Thanks guys. From what I was watching our alien friends were about to get their asses kicked. You may have just saved the day," Gene said, relieved that they could finally do something in this fight.

"Commanders of the Haldeck, Mayden, and Mardeck. If you will take note to the small satellite at location one fifty-seven-point two, you will see one of the planet's orbital nuclear weapons platforms. I want to draw the Corisole vessels near its location so it will be possible for the satellite to target and fire its weapons. You will make passes by the satellite, then get clear, Commanders. These are nuclear weapons and we do not want our own vessels damaged."

"Yes, Commander," they replied.

The Oran and Brightstar have been badly damaged by the station's cannons and have pulled back to a safer position. The Braken has also sustained heavy damage and is reporting fires on four of their ten decks. They are both out of the fight for the time being. Skoby watches as his numerically superior fleet is slowly being dismantled by that station.

The Haldeck is making its first pass by the satellite with the Rapter in pursuit. As the Haldeck passes the satellite it watches the missiles launch, then jumps to top speed and evacuates the area. A pair of fiery projectiles struck the Rapier on its port side blowing a huge hole in the vessels starboard side. The modern warships shields are designed to withstand energy weapons, but are susceptible to projectile weapons and their nuclear blasts. Skoby watches the positive results of the maneuver and sends the other two vessels on their runs.

"Commander Korg, this is the Rapier. We have sustained severe damage. The engine room has taken a direct hit and is on fire. We are." At that moment the Rapier exploded in a tremendous ball of fire and disappeared, leaving only the debris from the vessel floating in space.

"Sub-commander, what just happened?"

"I'm not sure, sir. But the Rapier has been destroyed."

The screens at NASA are bursting out with the cheers of the bunker and at NORAD.

"That's what I'm talking about!" Lance yells. "Now to bag another one."

"Good job, gentlemen," Gene said. "That was some extremely good timing, John. Thank you."

"Glad we could help, Gene. Let's hope we can sucker a few more in before they figure out what we're doing."

The warriors of Earth have scored a kill in the battle to save their planet and now the three separate bases watch the battle a little more hopeful of the outcome.

"Sub-commander, damage reports," Skoby orders.

"The Oran and Brightstar are falling back, sir. The other five vessels are maintaining fire on the station, but are sustaining heavy damage, sir."

"Pull all remaining vessels away from the station. I want them to regroup with us and assault the fleet."

"Yes, sir."

The Mayden is now drawing the Broadstrike into the same trap used on the Rapier. As the Broadstrike passes the Hercules it unleashes another pair of missiles. The Broadstrike detects the missiles, but it is too late for the Corisole cruiser to escape. With a direct hit on the Broadstrike's engines, it suffers the same fate as the Rapier, and the Broadstrike adds to the debris from the Rapier.

"Sir, the Mayden reports another kill. The Broadstrike has been destroyed by the satellites missiles also, sir. The Oran and Brightstar, as well as the Braken are reporting heavy casualties and are still on fire. Their fire crews are fighting the blazes but the damage is considerable and it is doubtful that they can return to the battle."

As the sub-commander finished his report, the Braken succumbed to its damages and exploded, killing all two hundred crewmen.

The Corisole fleet is receiving heavy damage in a fight that they expected to easily win. Korg watches the second of his vessels explode, but is dismayed by the fact that he did not see the laser fire that destroyed it. Then he notices the large satellite on his scanner.

"It's the planet's satellite that is destroying our vessels. Mr. Leigh, target the satellite at location 157.2. That satellite contains weapons and is responsible for two of our lost vessels."

"Yes, sir, targeting now."

"Fire, Mr. Leigh."

The satellite exploded with a blinding flash as the four remaining nukes exploded. The shockwave shook both fleets.

"It has been destroyed, sir. Commander, the Torani have just lost the Braken, and the Oran and Brightstar are adrift, sir."

"Inform the commanders of the Valence and the Skuller to engage the Tory. I want it destroyed. The Harden will fall in with us and attack the Jayden."

"Yes, sir."

The remaining Corisole vessels fell into position and started their attack runs. They have lost two vessels to the Torani's deception and will fall for no more tricks.

"We've lost the Hercules, gentlemen," John said. "But he did his part before they got him."

"Well, gentlemen, it's up to them now," Gene said. "Good work, guys. And, John, we owe you one for this."

"You're welcome, Gene. I'm glad we could actually be a part of the battle."

The three men all watched on their monitors as the battle continued. With John's video from the Hubble and Lance's telemetry from NORAD, they pieced together the happenings above their planet. They have done all they could to help their allies, but now it's up to them to win this battle.

Commander Skoby watches as the Corisole vessels separate into two groups and begin to attack two of their vessels. He has them outnumbered and he isn't going to lose any more lives to these murderous thugs.

"Mr. Dorin. They are trying to cut the Tory off from the fleet. Send the Ryden and the Mornstar to assist. The rest of the fleet is with us. We will destroy the rest of their fleet right now and then finish with that station."

"Your orders have been received, sir."

"Engage squadrons now Mr. Dorin."

The two fleets fought like angry hornets. The vessels of both fleets danced through space attacking the other at any opportunity. The Corisole vessels were outnumbered and unfortunately for them, heavily out gunned by the more powerful Torani cruisers. The Corisole vessel Valence was the first to fall in the melee. She exploded in a magnificent flash as a direct hit on her engines took its toll. The Tory's group made easy work of her and proceeded to pursue the Skuller.

Skoby wanted the Rapture, but the Halden was the next target of opportunity.

"Haldeck, Maydeck, destroy the Halden immediately," Skoby ordered.

The pair veered to meet their foe as the Jayden set course for the Rapture. The Rapture turned toward the unsuspecting Haldeck and delivered a crippling blow to its engines. The Haldeck is now lying stationary in space and at the mercy of the Corisole fleet.

Skoby doubled his efforts and came at the Rapture with every weapon at his disposal. After several exchanges of fire between the two combatants, the Rapture began to slow.

"Mr. Dorin, set course for the Harden and we will join the Mayden. I want that vessel destroyed."

The Harden fought the two superior vessels valiantly, but to no avail. In a short period of time it was adrift in space and also on fire.

"Hold fire. Mayden," Skoby ordered. He realized that he was beginning to think like the Corisole. The vessel was adrift in space and helpless and he would not destroy a defenseless vessel. "Sir, the Skuller is also adrift." With the entire Corisole fleet now disabled, Commander Skoby changes his strategy.

"Tell the fleet to stand down and regroup on us, Sub-commander. This part of the battle is over. Signal the Corisole commander and give him only one chance to surrender. Inform him that if he refuses, we will return and destroy his vessels."

"Yes, sir."

The sub-commander activated his comms to the fleet. "All vessels regroup on the Jayden." He then relayed Skoby's terms to the Corisole commander.

The control rooms of the bunker, NORAD, and NASA were ecstatic. Each screen showed the occupants celebrating the Torani's victory over the Corisole fleet. The president breaks into the celebration.

"Everyone calm down. This isn't over yet. There is still that Station to deal with and we all know how formidable it is."

The celebrations ceased at their commander's words. They knew he was right and possibly the worst part of the battle was still to come.

"Sir, I am receiving a message from the Corisole commander."

"Put it through," Skoby replied.

"This is Commander Korg of the Corisole fleet vessel Rapture. I am now offering my unconditional surrender. I am responsible for this fleet and therefore I am requesting compassion for the lives of my men. We will stand down and await your answer."

"Do you have an answer, sir?"

"Make him wait."

"Sub-commander Dorin, what is the condition of our vessels?"

"Sir, the Brightstar, Haldeck, and Oran are all adrift, but making repairs as we speak. The Braken has been destroyed."

"All right, Mr. Dorin. Put me on to all remaining vessels. This is Commander Skoby. You have all done well against the now defeated Corisole fleet and it is now time to deal with that Station. You know of its weapons effectiveness so therefore we are going to have a different approach this time. We will attempt to avoid direct line of fire and destroy the surface around the cannons. If fate is in our favor, the surrounding structure will cave in on the cannons and incapacitate them. Be careful men, we have seen the awesome firepower of the Station, so treat each run accordingly. Follow me in."

The Jayden set its course for the station, and the final battle has begun.

The Corisole commander sat dejectedly on the bridge of the Rapture scrutinizing the events of the last few hours. He knows that he has not only failed his Supreme Leader, but every living being on his planet. His planet would now be treated like criminals because of the obsessions of its leaders. The leaders of the planet as well as the fleet's members would most certainly be imprisoned or put to death. He grieved for his men and puts the blame of defeat on himself for their loss. He now waits for his conquerors to arrive and decide their fate.

The Torani fleet approached the Station and dispersed around its perimeter, taking heavy fire on their way in. The incredible accuracy of the station took its toll in the first few minutes. The Ryden was immediately caught in heavy fire and destroyed.

"All remaining vessels follow me in to the surface. We can no longer to be surgical with our attacks. If we stay in a tight pattern, we should draw fire from a maximum of four cannons. When you see them open fire I want full spread of weapons fire on that area. Use everything you've got, Commanders, and this just may work."

The four vessels set up with the two center vessels stacked and the two remaining vessels were positioned on each side. With only five hundred yards separating them, it took precision flying of the massive vessels.

After repeated passes, the deadly beams from within the surface began to dwindle. The fleet was taking damage, but as they continued, they were able to create an attack corridor, which enabled them to approach the Station safely and systematically destroy the remaining cannons. After three long hours of battle, they were ready to send their assault teams to the surface.

"Mr. Dorin. Are the shuttles ready to launch?"

"We have shuttles from all four vessels ready with three hundred commandos, ready and waiting for your command, sir."

"You have that Command. Launch the final assault."

The shuttles left their mother ships en route to the surface of the base. They would have to breach the launch bay and detain the unknown number of crewmen inside the Station.

The world looked at a once again quiet space above their planet. The moon had stopped spitting its deadly fire from its surface and the bright flashes that lit up the sky have ceased, leaving only the stationary bright lights hovering over the planet harmlessly.

The leaders of the world rejoice for the stay of execution they have been given by the blood of their Torani saviors. Now they await word from these saviors.

"Well, gentlemen," the president said to the other two men whose facilities have played a huge part in the defense of the planet. "I think it's finally over. John, thank you, and thank your people for me."

"I will, Gene. And you're quite welcome. Good-bye, Gene, I'm going to get some much needed rest before I go topside and assess the damages." John signed off the system.

"Lance, we wouldn't be here without you and your men and women at NORAD. Congratulate them all for me would you."

"I will, Gene. And like John, we all need some rest, so give me a heads-up in about six hours."

"Will do, Lance. Good-bye." The second of the screens faded to black.

Gene gazed around the briefing room at a table full of extremely exhausted, but very relieved people.

"I couldn't have done it without you guys. Elsa, unfortunately you and I each have one more thing we have to do. You need to contact the world leaders and give them a briefing on what has just occurred. Tell them we will be in touch in about six hours. That will be enough time to get some rest and figure out a game plan. I, on the other hand, have to address the nation on our new friends. The rest of you all go get some rest."

The weary people slowly exited the room and headed for their quarters. It has been the most bizarre five days of their lives and they are more than ready to put it behind them.

The sun is starting to set on the Colorado mountains and the father and son, along with their band of survivors, slowly make their way out of what's left of Parachute. As they travel, they watch the sky, stopping occasionally to hide from approaching skippers. It has looked like the Fourth of July, New Year's Eve, and Chinese New Year all rolled into one. They have no idea what is going on, but they are glad it's up there and not down here.

"So what do you think it is?" Willis asked, looking at the sky.

"I'm just guessing, but I think we've got some friends up there, or they are fighting over who gets to finish kicking our ass," his father replied sarcastically.

"Let's hope they are friends."

They continued out of the town slowly, going from gully to gully, tree to tree, hiding from the skippers. As they made their way along the stream they were surprised by a tremendous blast that rocked the mountain. A small mushroom cloud rose in the direction of the fuel tower. The father and son looked at each other curiously.

"Payback?" Willis asked.

"Payback," his father replied with a smile. Then they continued on their journey to the safety of the canyon with their small group of survivors.

The Kabult Station was taken without a shot being fired. The massive attack had done considerable damage to the Station. Rubble was strewn throughout the station and the crew was absolutely shell shocked. They rounded up all the crewmembers and shuttled them to the Torani vessels to detain them. The fleet then sailed back to where the Corisole vessels have been detained. Then the prisoners were transferred to their own vessels under guard for detention. The Torani didn't want them on their vessels.

"Sub-commander, put together a team of commandos. We are going over to the Rapture and personally accept Commander Korg's surrender, then I'm going to put him and his officers in our brig."

"Yes, Commander."

The commander, along with his team, loaded into one of the Jayden's shuttles to put the finishing touches on this battle. His men have fought valiantly, but unfortunately he has lost hundreds of valuable lives at the hands of the Corisole fleet.

Chapter 18

——— • ● ✿ ● • ———

White House Bunker
October 16, 2020, 19:00

The leaders of the world have been filled in on the existence of their new friends from a distant world. The president has recorded the message to his country and the cabinet members were able to take a short nap before being called back to the briefing room. The Torani commander is waiting on an open video line to speak with the only leader he is familiar with on the planet below. They are all waiting patiently when the president's secretary comes in and whispers in his ear.

"Ladies and gentlemen, we're ready."

The screen activates with the president's command and the Torani commander appears on the video screen. He is a large humanoid with skin colored the brightest gold. His eyes are a brilliant blue color, and his hair and the spikey whiskers on his chin are pure white. They all stared as he started to speak, surprisingly in their own language.

"People of the planet you call Earth. I have been directed by the emperor of the planet Torani to deliver this message to you. As you are well aware, three days ago your planet was attacked by a fleet sent from the planet Corisole. These beings violated a galactic treaty that was originated to protect your planet's natural evolution."

"These criminals will be prosecuted by the Galactic Council to the fullest extent of galactic law and we now have their fleet under our control, and their fleet commanders imprisoned onboard our vessel until they can be transported to Torani to stand trial for their crimes. I can assure you that their punishments will be severe and swift."

"We are deeply saddened by the loss of life on your planet, and hold our Alliance of planets responsible for allowing the Corisole planet the opportunity to carry out their evil plan. We have sensor networks to protect the planet Earth, but somehow they were able to bypass these networks in an attempt to claim your planet for their own. We are sorry we did not learn of this evil plan sooner."

"For the next few days we will be removing the Corisole machinery from the planet's surface as well as the remaining automated eradication vessels that are still operating on the planet. I must stress the dangers they still present, as they are still operating on prearranged mission objectives. So please avoid any contact with all Corisole machinery as it extremely deadly."

"Our emperor Ardesnal, and our ambassadors are leaving the Torani planet as we speak to come to your planet Earth. They will arrive in five days, and upon their arrival they will meet at a place of your choosing with all the leaders of our worlds, to decide how to proceed with the relief efforts."

"In closing I would like to again give our condolences for your great loss of life and strongly stress the importance of avoiding the Corisole technology. We will contact you again in five days to receive the coordinates for the meeting. Thank you."

The screen went blank as everyone in the room still continues to stare at it in disbelief of what they have just seen and heard. Gene Furgison immediately takes control of the situation and his advisors.

"Elsa, you have five days to contact all the world's leaders that survived the destruction. I'm sure that John and Lance can help you make contact with them."

"Horace, get on the horn with John and find out all you can about these aliens and their ships."

"Jack I want you to find out exactly what forces we have left in this country, as well as the seas. Get with Lance and Vince, they will help."

"Allen I need you to rally any police, National Guard, Red Cross, and your security forces. Then you are to start conducting search and rescue operations. There are a lot of hurt and needy people out there."

"People, the human race just received a stay of execution, so let's take advantage of it. Now let's get busy. And people. Thank you for everything." They all immediately started their appointed tasks. Gene was right. The planet has been given a chance, so they needed to take advantage of it.

The exhausted group finally reached the bottom of the driveway and they are headed for the house when Willis hears a noise and motions for them to stop and be quiet. He is pointing to the east ridge when suddenly they hear someone approaching. All of a sudden Alex bursts through the thick bushes with the biggest grin you ever saw. Bill and Willis look at each other and smile, then look back at Alex.

"So, I don't suppose you know what all that commotion was just before dark?" Bill asked, already knowing the answer to his question.

"Payback," Alex said, still grinning ear to ear.

They continued up the valley and quickly came to the house. When they arrived the ladies automatically began helping to make the new arrivals comfortable by bringing them into the house and immediately began hydrating and feeding them. They were all half-starved, especially the children.

They pulled the cars and the trailer out of the garage and created a rather large living area for the refugees. They created beds for everyone, and with an old fashioned wood stove it would remain quite comfortable. It wasn't much, but it was more than these people had seen in days.

After they were all fed, the children were sitting in the living room watching TV. Thank god for DVD's. They all slowly dosed off and rested for the first time in days. The adults were all gathered in the kitchen talking about the last three horrible days, when Willis came in with the radio.

"Hey, everyone, listen to this."

He sat the radio on the table. The prerecorded message was already playing. It was the president's voice on the message.

"This is the message as we received it from the commander of the Torani emperor."

The message was played in its entirety, and the president decided to omit nothing. When the message was finished, the president addressed his country.

"You have all heard the message from Emperor Ardesnal. We assume it was given in good faith and urge you to heed its warnings. I hope it gives you some peace of mind during these hard times. This recording will be repeated for the next five days until we have new information to give you and if any new information comes to our attention, we will of course broadcast it on this frequency. Thank you, and god bless."

"Can you believe this shit," Bill said. "Four days ago I'm working in my studio enjoying life. Four days later our planet has been destroyed and the human race is facing extinction. Now we're standing here with one aliens foot up our ass, and another one pulling it out claiming to be our friend. What next?"

"I don't know about you guys but after the last three days I'm ready for a whole bunch of beers, and a few bowls. If anyone wants to join me, I'll be in the studio."

Bill went out the door and to his studio where he knew everything he needed was waiting for him. A few minutes later others wandered in to join him.

Commander Korg is in his quarters on board the Rapture awaiting the arrival of the Torani commander. The Torani have already stationed commandos on the remaining Corisole vessels to ensure the vessels security, and Torani engineers are currently making the vessels ready to be escorted back to Torani, where the crews of the vessels will stand trial for their crimes. As the commander waits, he is going over the last five days in his head trying to discover where they went wrong. The plan was perfect. If they had not been spotted leaving the Orion sector, he would now be standing on the planet's surface below. He is shaken from his thoughts when the door chimes and Commander Skoby enters with a group of six commandos.

"Commander Korg. I have no time for pleasantries, so we'll make this quick. First, I want your unconditional surrender." Commander Skoby towers over the Corisole commander by at least three feet and is using it to intimidate his foe.

"Very well, Commander. I, Commander Korg of the Corisole fleet, do hereby surrender my men, as well as my fleet vessels to the Galactic Alliance." The commander then ceremoniously surrendered his weapon to the Torani commander.

"Now I want you to recall all the weapons of war that you have stationed on the planet."

Commander Korg activated his comms and contacted his bridge crew who were currently under close guard. "Sub-commander, this is Korg. I want you to initiate a recall of all weapon systems on the planet's surface immediately, is that understood."

"Yes, sir, I will do it immediately," Leigh replied as he looked at the armed guards on his bridge knowing that he had no other choice.

"Now, Commander, you will surrender yourself and your officers to my men."

The Corisole commander left his quarters surrounded by the commandos. He was now bound to rendezvous with his other ship commanders and their officers in the Jayden's brig.

Willis came running into the house, panting as if he were running. "Dad, you've got to see this, they're leaving."

They all went into the yard by the fire pit, just in time to see the last of the skippers heading up into the sky. They knew that they had to be leaving because they've never seen them actually go up.

"Would you look at that," Bill said.

"I told you, they're leaving."

They sat at the pit watching the rest of the skippers rise into the sky. Good riddance, Bill thought to himself.

"We'll wait until the end of the week before we use the vehicles again," Bill said.

"What about gas?" Bret asked.

"We've got five hundred gallons in the tank. Come Saturday we'll start combing the countryside looking for survivors. We should be able to get more food and supplies from the deserted ranches. They seem to have been left standing."

After they stopped seeing the skippers rising into the sky, they went back into the house to finish their lunch. Just maybe, "life would be good again."

John and Brad are on the elevator heading for the surface where they haven't set foot since the night of the attack. As the doors open, the stench of the dead is over powering and fills the control room. They both cover their noses and hurry to the front door of the building.

"We need to burry these people Brad. They were all our friends and deserve a proper burial."

"Well, seeing as we are standing on a sea of asphalt John, that could be difficult. I think burial is out of the question. We'll have to burn the bodies."

"Yea you're right." He agrees. "Let's look around and see if we can find anything useful."

"Like what, a time machine."

As John and Brad searched the Space Center's outer buildings, they came to a hardened concrete hangar. Inside the hangar, they found two F-18 fighters and a deuce and a half truck. The next building was the rocket assembly building, which was partially collapsed by the attack. The two men entered the assembly building and found that the door to the lower levels was blocked by a pile of rubble. After thirty minutes of hard work they were finally able to open the doors. As the door opened, John and Brad stood amazed as a dozen workers stumbled out.

"Are you guys okay?" John asked, noticing that they were severely dehydrated. "Brad, go and get the truck."

Brad ran to the hangar and brought the truck back a few minutes later.

"Everyone in, we have food and water in the control center. Is there anyone else in there?" John asked.

"Not alive," one of the men said wearily.

"What's your name?"

"Buchman, sir. We ran for the stairwell as when we saw Houston go up in a ball of fire. The shockwave collapsed the building as soon as we hit the stairwell."

"You were lucky to make it. Let's get these men back to control, Brad," he said as they were helping the last of the men up into the rear of the deuce and a half.

They drove to the control center with the twelve men, who were all tired, hungry, and dirty, but glad to be alive after three long days trapped in the dark stairwell.

Gene is sitting at his desk going over reports given to him by his staff on the estimated losses of life, and damage to his country. Ruth enter the office and sets another file on his desk.

"What's this one?" he asked as he picked it up.

"It's from the secretary of state, sir," she replied as she turned back at the door.

"Lose the sir, and tell Elsa I want to see her."

"Yes, Gene," she said nervously, calling her boss by his first name.

A few minutes later, Elsa knocks and enters his office.

"Elsa to be honest with you I'm not in much of a mood to read any more reports so why don't you take a seat and just fill me in," he said as he put the file on a stack with fifty others.

"Sure thing," she said with a smile as she sat down.

"I wasn't able to do very well at contacting the other world leaders. Apparently the other countries weren't as prepared as we were. I have been able to get through to the Russian, Chinese, Japanese, British, Australian, Indian, Saudi, and Canadian leaders. But with the communications down we've had to rely on short wave communication, which is slow because we have to depend on curriers to relay the messages for now. We're still working on contacting the others."

"So what are the latest estimates? These are guesswork to say the least," he said, holding up the file on the desk in front of him.

"They aren't good Gene. The latest estimates put the death toll at nearly 80 percent and that's a low estimate. Most countries are optimistic, counting on the rural areas to drop that number. Thankfully the Corisole planned on their attack ships and their invasion forces to mop up the rest of humanity. It's going to take months to get a final number. The good news is that they didn't destroy our livestock or agriculture, we assume they were saving it for themselves."

"Okay, Elsa, we give the Torani three days. Then we go all out. Allen is already engaged in the search and rescue, so we will need to get on rebuilding. It's going to be a massive undertaking, but we've got to start somewhere. Let me know when you contact the remaining leaders."

"Sure thing Gene." She stood and left the office knowing the meeting was over. The president locked fingers behind his head and thought about the incredible job ahead of them. They now had the incredible task of rebuilding an entire world.

Skoby is surveying the reports on the Corisole retreat from the planet when his door buzzes. He calls for whomever it is to enter, and Subcommander Dorin entered the office.

"Mr. Dorin, what can I do for you?"

"The Corisole withdrawal from the planet is going well, sir. We have accounted for all but one of the assault ships. We are assuming it was totally destroyed."

"You must be certain, Sub-commander," he stated firmly. "We cannot risk any Technological contamination of the planet."

"Yes, sir. Also, sir, the fuel towers are all accounted for and ready to return to their vessels, but with the destruction of the three Corisole vessels, we have twenty-five towers that we can't put aboard for transport back to Torani."

"Then we will store them on the Kabult Station until we can arrange transport," Skoby replied.

"We have another problem, sir. The Kabult Station was badly damaged and it will take two days to clear the debris from the landing bay. There are also fifty assault ships and around a hundred mines to remove from the station."

"Okay, Mr. Dorin. As soon as the work is completed, move the towers to the Station and make sure that the towers are not left unguarded until that time."

"Yes, sir," Dorin replied as he turned to leave.

"And Mr. Dorin, make sure that the commander of the Mornstar ejects and destroys all Corisole armament as soon as they reach open space. I want absolutely nothing left of the Corisole war machine but its crews and vessels when they reach Torani space. Also inform the commander to personally supervise the transfer of all Corisole prisoners into the Alliance Detention Center upon arrival to stand trial for their acts."

"Yes, sir. Consider it done."

The commander, as well as the Alliance, are determined to see all involved in this act punished. The commanders and crews of the Corisole fleet, as well as the Supreme Leader and his council members will all pay for this near extinction of the earthlings with their lives. Billions of lives were ended, but they will be made example of to ensure it never happens again.

CHAPTER 19

Parachute, Colorado
October 19, 2020, 08:00

The adults are gathered in the kitchen discussing their plans for the immediate future, while the children are in the Livingroom watching cartoons on the DVD player to keep the occupied. There are things that need to be taken care of outside of the valley. The invasion has left death and destruction around the globe and someone has to pick up the pieces. That task has been left to the survivors.

"I think we need to start going out daily to look for survivors," Bill said. "Today Alex and I will search Parachute, and, Willis, I want you and Bret to check out the ranches along the river. There aren't too many between here and Rulison, so you should be able to check all of them today."

Bill knew the next part would be terrible to carry out. "Now for the most horrible, but unfortunately the most important part of these trips. All of the unfortunate people who didn't survive will have to be dealt with. We need to burn all the bodies we come across, it will take too long to bury them all. Find some gas cans and fill them with diesel at one of the ranches. There's bound to be a diesel tank on one of the ranches, and any bodies you come across, you need to pile up and burn them."

The two very young men had a sickened expression on their faces.

"I'm sorry, but it has to be done. If we don't burn or bury the dead, it will allow disease to run rampant across the country side and it will eventually end up here. I for one, don't want that to happen." As he explained, the people in the kitchen looked at him horrified with the thought of having to burn the bodies of their friends.

"We will need some help then. It will take too long for just the two of us," Willis said.

"You're right. Tom, why don't you go with them. Hook up one of the trailers to the Jeep for any survivors you come across."

"Okay, Bill," Tom replied.

"Ben I want you to come with Alex and I if you would."

"No problem, Bill."

"All right then its settled. Let's hook up the Trailers and get started."

"What about weapons, Dad? We have no idea what we'll run into out there."

"I guess you're right. Willis I want you to be extra careful when you approach the ranches. People might be getting pretty desperate by now and they may shoot first and ask questions later. I've got guns locked in the cabinet. I also want everyone to carry a white cloth with them just in case," he said as he was getting the key off the nail by the door. "If you come across any guns or ammo, make sure you bring it back with you. We may need all we can get if things go bad."

"Okay, Dad."

The guys gave their ladies a hug and a kiss and made ready to leave. They then went to the garage and hooked up the trailers, then they loaded into the vehicles to leave. As they drove out of the property they gave each other a wave and went on their way to do the job nobody was looking forward to, but they all knew had to be done. They hoped that they would find survivors because it would make the horror that faced them more bearable.

The truck and its three occupants pulled slowly into the town that used to be Parachute, Colorado. Almost the only buildings left standing were one gas station, and the church where they witnessed the horrible death of the family, but thankfully found their friends.

They parked in front of the church because as their friends had done, its where people gather in times of trouble for hope. Bill looked at the four black spots on the ground and shuddered as he remembered the awful event. It is something he will never forget.

Five days ago, the population of the two connected towns of Parachute and Battlement Mesa was around six thousand people. Today it stands at eighteen. They hope to add to that number today.

"We'll comb the north side of the freeway today and move to the other side tomorrow," Bill said.

"We should drive over to Harry's Haulers. There will be diesel there for sure," Ben said.

"Good idea, Ben," Bill said as he started the truck.

They crossed the freeway and made their way to the commercial park used by the drilling companies. They pulled up in front of Harry's shop, got out of the truck and headed toward the Partially destroyed shop. The smell or decomposing human flesh was overpowering.

At the rear of the shop they found the bodies of four men, that fortunately none of them knew. They carried the bodies out in the lot and piled them up. There was a storage tank for diesel, so they filled some five gallon cans for the truck, then used a bucket to get gas to burn the bodies. They piled some dead tree limbs on top of the bodies, then poured the diesel over the pile and lit it with a match. Before leaving they checked through the rubble of the other buildings. Finding no other unfortunate victims, they drove back across the bridge to the church.

By noon they had they had covered every street on the north side of town and fortunately for them, only found twelve more bodies which were taken care of in the same manner as the first. The inhabitants either evacuated or were among the many hundreds of black spots that dotted the landscape.

Since they had finished so soon, they decided to start on the south side of the freeway. They started at the High School because it is all the way at the west end of town. They thought that they would start there and work their way back toward home.

Surprisingly the school was still standing because of its concrete construction, so they went in to check for survivors.

"Alex you check the gymnasium and we'll check all the classrooms," Bill ordered. As usual he has the need to be in charge.

"On my way."

They headed in opposite directions, searching as they went. After checking a half dozen classrooms, the two men heard Alex yell for them. They quickly left the room and ran for the gymnasium.

"Alex, what is it?" Bill asked as they entered.

"People!" he yelled.

At the rear of the gymnasium, lying on a stack of rubber mats, were twenty people who were all still deeply terrified, but glad to see other living human beings. They rose and most of them ran to their rescuers. The three men checked the rest of the school for more survivors but none were found. Thankfully they found no more bodies either.

With twenty-eight new survivors, eight of which they picked up on the way out of town, they decided to head toward the valley. They honked the horn of the truck on the way out of town to try to attract any other survivors, or at least let them know that they weren't the only ones left alive. Their main objective had changed, it was now to get the survivors to the valley for food and water. They would have to check the rest of the town for survivor's tomorrow.

As they were ready to leave town, Alex thought of something.

"How are we going to take care of all these people?" Bill thought for a second then it came to him. He looked at Alex and said, "Storage." Then pulled into the parking lot of the shattered hardware store. After a few minutes of rummaging through the debris he held up his arm in victory. In His hand was a pair of bolt cutters. He waded his way out of the debris and back to the truck.

"We'll go through the storage sheds for camping gear," he said, quite proud of himself for thinking of it.

There were three storage facilities in town and they were all still standing. They went from unit to unit gathering anything they thought would be useful, then headed for the safety of the valley.

The other group spent the day going from ranch to ranch checking for survivors, but they found none. They must have all left when they saw the shit hit the fan. Luckily for them they found no dead either and were spared the gruesome task of burning the bodies. All the livestock was wandering around carelessly as if nothing had happened at all. They looked at each other, shot three cows and gutted them, then loaded them on the trailer. They would definitely need the meat in the weeks to come. They found a freezer on the porch of the next ranch and loaded it up too. After they were finished they headed for home with their booty.

When Bill came up to the house he noticed the Jeep was already sitting in front of the studio. Bret and Willis were busy hanging the first of the cattle in the tree they use to dress game. In this country most people are hunters and know how dress an animal.

The ladies came out of the house to greet the new arrivals. They rounded them up and led them to the fire pit to stay warm and began the task checking them all for injuries.

"I need some volunteers to set up all these tents," Bill said as he was unloading the trailer separating the supplies. "It's going to be dark soon."

Monica went over to him and gave him a hug and a kiss, knowing that he hadn't had the most enjoyable day.

"Thank you. You have no idea how much I needed that."

"You're welcome. What can I do to help?"

"Get these people some water. they are all very dehydrated. I'll start a fire in the barbeque so we can feed them all."

"You got it baby," she replied and grabbed Alice on her way to the house to help.

"Hey!" Bill hollers to her before she got inside. "Beer and a bowl," he added.

She nodded at him and went inside. Don and Tom, being avid hunters, went over to help the two boys dress the animals so they could be hung in the cold cellar. Bill has had absolutely enough for one day, so he sat down in his chair by the fire pit looking at the dirty, confused, and scared faces all around him. They were all sitting quietly in a state of shock, not knowing what to do next. He was sure that they haven't heard the broadcasts, and have no clue what has happened, or what's going to happen next.

"Willis!" he hollered to his son, who came running over at his father's call.

"Start a fire in the big barbeque, will you please, I'm exhausted."

"Sure, Dad."

"Thanks, buddy," he replied as he leaned back in his chair.

Bill looked behind him as Monica and Alice came out of the house with Dove and Alice in tow. They all had gallon jugs of water and some plastic glasses. Monica had a six-pack of beer in each hand and Bill's bowl in her pocket ready to be fired up. She's a great woman he reminds himself. Alex walks over and Bill hands him a cold beer.

"Thanks, I can use this. Where should we set up the tents?"

"I would say over there in the trees by the hill," Bill said, pointing at the mountainside. "It should be out of the wind."

"How many?"

"Well, let's get some volunteers and keep going until we have enough. I have no idea who belongs to who, so we'll just keep going until we have enough."

"Yea, you're probably right. Thanks for the beer."

Alex rounded up eight men and began setting up the tents. They decided that there were thirteen families, so that was the number to achieve. Bill grabbed four beers and walked over to where the guys were working on the beef. They were all quite grateful for the frosty treat.

Bill brought out a portable CD player and set a case of beer next to it. The ladies confiscated both, and took them over to the barbeque, where they began to cook for the crowd. The people on the mountain enjoyed a peaceful night for the first time in six days. The town of Parachute, or should we say Bill's valley, just grew to thirty-eight.

After a good meal, the families all chose a tent and put their children to bed. They sat talking quietly among themselves about what had actually happened over the past week. Most of them were unaware of the president's messages. Bill brought out the small radio and let them listen to it for themselves. An hour had gone by filled with questions about the last week. Once all their curiosities were satisfied, they thanked their host and settled in for the night. There was plenty of gear, so everyone was quite comfortable.

Ben and Janet have decided to adopt the orphans since they had no children of their own, and they had taken quite a liking to Janet. With everyone safely in bed, Bill put out the fire and went into the house with the others. Tomorrow would another day of searching and burning. He wasn't looking forward to it, but hopefully they would find more survivors.

Chapter 20

--·•✦•·--

The briefing room is humming with the people taking in groups around the table. The satellite systems are starting to come back online, and the other countries are also getting auxiliary power back online to power their computers and communication systems. The president is wandering from group to group, trying to stay on top of the situation. He eventually made it back to his seat and brought the group to order.

"Elsa do we have any new information on worldwide damage estimates?"

"We have only been able to contact twenty countries because the rest of them haven't been able to restore power yet. We do know that out of these countries, their power supplies have been cut to almost zero. The aliens destroyed anything that they considered to be a hazard to the planet. The coal and nuclear power plants have all been destroyed leaving nuclear wastelands around the nuclear plants. We still have solar and wind farms, but the infrastructure has been destroyed so we can't utilize it. The same goes for the hydroelectric dams. Operational but no way to get to the power."

"Then that should one of our main objectives Elsa."

"We don't have the manpower or equipment yet to do it Gene."

"I suppose your right. Okay, let's forget about the power. What about the people?"

"That number has improved. We now estimate the world population at two billion. Gene if I can speak freely here, it's like they were trying to wipe out everything that was harmful to the planet. I heard it said once that humans were like a virus. A virus feeds off its host and multiplies until the host can no longer contain it, then goes on to another host. We

---

117

all know that humans are the biggest threat to this planet." She shook her head sadly. "Maybe we can't blame them for trying to take it from us before we destroyed it."

"One thing for sure Elsa, is that we will remember that when we do rebuild. I want you to set up a meeting with the other leaders at six o'clock tomorrow evening. Maybe we will hear more from our new friends by then. We will also want to make another broadcast afterward, to inform the people of what's happening."

"I'll do my best Gene."

"Thanks Elsa, that's all I can ask for. That will be all for now People."

The president makes his way through the safety of the corridors thinking about the people who weren't as fortunate. He still has his family safely locked in the bunker and feels great guilt that so many others have lost all. They were not spared the horrors of the last six days as he and his family were, because they had no bunkers to hide in.

The surviving population of Parachute woke to a beautiful Colorado morning. Having slept in after a late evening getting the new arrivals settled, they had a late breakfast under the golden aspen trees. October in Colorado is the Most beautiful place on the planet. The bright golds and reds, mixed in with the dark green of the pine trees, are breathtaking. With the perfect stream running through it, there's no place on the planet Bill would rather be. Unfortunately, the beauty will be torn apart with the coming images of tragedy they will face.

The men have all been fed and are as ready as they will be for the day. They gather at the garage to decide what they will do today. There are more men today that will make the job at hand a little easier.

"All right, guys, listen up," Bill said. "Now since we only have two vehicles, one of today's jobs will be to find a couple of more. Willis, when you were at the ranches yesterday did you see any trucks?"

"There were a couple of old trucks at a couple of them."

"Good. Old ones are the best because if the keys aren't in them they are easy to hotwire, and the steering columns don't lock. Take Tom, Bret, and Ben. What's your name?" he asked one of the newcomers.

"Chad Hall."

"Okay, Chad, you go with them too. Now one of you does know how to hotwire a car I hope."

"I do," Tom replied as he raised his hand.

"Now you need to get two trucks, and you should be able to find two trailers. In one truck I want Bret and Tom to continue searching the ranches along the river. Ben you bring the second truck back to town to help us. Okay."

"I'll be there as soon as I can."

"Willis, I want you and Chad to go into Morrisana and check it out."

"Okay, Dad."

"Remember to be careful on the ranches, and if I were you I would just tie the white flag on the antenna so it's always there. You can take all the guns today we won't need them in town. If everybody's ready, let's get to it."

"Okay, Dad. I guess we're out of here then."

"One more thing guys. Try to keep track of the empty ranches. Tie a rag on the gates or something to mark them. We'll go back in a week and see if they are still empty. We have some people here who can use the houses and the livestock will have to be taken care of also. If you find anyone alive, tell them that we are thinking about turning the High School into a new Town Hall. In a few days we will get someone to be there during the day, all right."

"Okay," Willis said. Then he gave Alice a kiss and jumped in the Jeep.

The others said good-bye to their wives and joined Willis. They headed down the driveway for another day of searching, and if they were lucky they would only find live ones.

"I need two volunteers to go with me."

Two men stepped forward with their hands raised.

"What are your names?"

"Jesus Chaves."

"Barney Byrd."

"All right, Jesus and Barney, let's head into town."

The two men also hugged their wives and got into the truck.

"Ready, Alex?"

"Ready as I'll ever be," he answered with a smile. The last few days had hardened him to the reality of the job.

"Can you ladies do whatever you can to make this place a little more comfortable for these people. Hand out whatever camping equipment we have, then have a couple of the guys drag out those generators in the garage. There are extra lights in the studio that can be strung up for extra light at night. Also show them where all the supplies are. Let's make them feel like they belong here. Thanks for your help.

"It will give us something to keep us busy," Dove said. Monica and Alice shook their heads in agreement.

"All right then. We should be back around dark. We'll see you then."

The men said good-bye to their wives and were off to Parachute. The new guys had no idea what they were in for, and Bill didn't tell them.

Meanwhile on the Jayden, Commander Skoby is in his quarters talking to Commander Bryden of Fleet Command vessel Empress. The emperor is on the Empress and currently en route to Earth.

"We will be in Earth orbit in thirty-six hours, Commander. The emperor is quite pleased with your performance in this matter. We have informed the Corisole leadership of their fleet's surrender, but they haven't acknowledged our communications so we're assuming that they aren't pleased with the outcome of their invasion."

"I wouldn't think they'd be pleased. They gambled their futures on the invasion and the power of the Kabult Station and lost. Do you think they will retaliate by attacking Torani?"

"They would be fools to do so. They only have two cruisers in their orbit to rely on, and if those cruisers so much as move an inch, the Alliance will destroy them."

"Yes, I suppose you are right. Has the Supreme Leader stepped down?"

"Our sources on the planet claim he is being defiant, but the people on the planet would be foolish to follow him. The Corisole planet relies heavily on imported goods from Torani to survive, so they would be cutting their own throats to let him remain in office. The people will revolt and eventually he will be handed over to the Alliance for judgement."

"Let's hope the people don't wait too long. If they do it could mean armed commandos being sent to their planet. We will expect you in thirtysix hours and we will continue this conversation then, my friend."

Skoby kills the comms, and leaves for his bridge to check on his men and the status of his damaged vessels.

Bill and his men made a quick job out of the rest of Parachute since there was really not much left on the south side of the freeway. They then went up the hill three miles to Battlement Mesa. On the way up the road they spotted Ben and motioned to him to follow them.

It's the first time they have actually been to the town since the attack and Bill doesn't expect to find anything pleasant. The town of Battlement Mesa was thrown together in the seventies for one of the oil companies to house their oil shale workers. The buildings were hundreds of wood framed apartments below, and a huge trailer park with hundreds of seventies trailers all side by side. It is now cheap housing for the thousands of people who can't afford the ski valley rates. It was a fire trap and it burned like one. The whole town was now nothing but burned out homes.

As they drove very carefully to avoid the bodies that were everywhere you looked, they realized the unbelievable loss of life. The residents that weren't burned in their homes were lying in the yards and streets. It appeared that they died from either the extreme heat, or the smoke. The dead as well as their pets were everywhere. The stench of the dead was unbearable.

"It's terrible," Ben said. "I knew a lot of these people."

"We all did," Barney replied.

"Guys, it's horrible but it has to be done. We'll have to go street to street and there's a lot of streets to cover," Bill said sadly. "Since there's so many dead, why don't we use the big pit the kids used to ride their motorcycles in to burn the bodies."

"Yea, we're going to need a lot of room from the looks of it," Barney agreed.

Bill sat for a minute looking at the carnage. "We might as well start here and load the trailers, then haul them to the pit to be burned."

They started loading the dead. There were men, women, children, and even their pets. It would haunt all of them for the rest of their lives.

After the two vehicles split that morning, Willis's crew stopped at the ranch where they had seen the first truck and they were lucky because the keys were in it. They hooked a trailer up to it that was parked on the other side of the barn and sent Ben on his way. A few miles down the road they found another pair for Bret and Tom to use.

Willis and Chad headed for Morrisana, and Bret and Tom checked the ranches they couldn't get to the day before. Both groups covered a great deal of ground. It was a good day. They found all but four ranches in Morrisana empty. They told the ranchers about the High School and went about their task.

Bret and Tom were able to cover all seven miles between Parachute and Rulison. They found two ranches still occupied, and the people were safe and healthy. They told them about the school also and continued on their way. After they reached Rulison they decided to turn around and head back to the valley. They were driving back when Bret spotted it—a big pull behind the diesel generator. What a lucky day. They found no dead bodies, and now this prize. They dropped the trailer and hooked up their prize and headed for home.

After four hours of hauling the dead and piling them in the pit the men poured sixty gallons of diesel over the corpses and burned them. They had cleared all the streets in one day, and wouldn't have to witness any more of the horror of picking up the dead bodies of their friends. Since they weren't worried about the fire spreading in the pit they lit the fire and drove away.

A few blocks down the street Bill pulled over to the side and waved Ben up alongside. "Ben I think we should check those two subdivisions on the way home. You take the one over by the Middle School and we'll take the other one. Let's not search for any more of the dead today, but as you're driving through, honk your horn and look for survivors. We'll come back tomorrow and check that area for dead. Thankfully it will be the last time we have to do it."

"I'll see you at your house in a little while," Ben said, then drove off.

A little over an hour later, Bill pulled into his yard with ten more people who have survived the massacre. Only ten more. There are now around ninety people in the area which used to have a population of around six thousand a week before. Where did they all go? There's no way they burned that many bodies, so they either fled, or the skippers were very effective.

Bill walked over to the fire pit where the others were gathered. "So Tom, I see you brought home a new toy."

"We couldn't resist. We'll go back for the trailer in the morning."

"So how did everyone's day go?"

"Really good," Willis said. "We covered the entire valley all the way to Rulison. I found four families in Morrisana and they found two over by Rulison."

"Any dead?"

"None. You?" Willis asked.

Bill told the story of Battlement Mesa as the rest of the people listened in horror. By the looks you could not only see the horror, but also see that they were glad they weren't there to see it.

"Well, it's getting late, we better feed all these people," Bill said as he looked around.

"We're on it," Monica replied as she walked up behind him and handed him a cold beer. "We've already got a bed of coals in the barbeque, and as it turns out, Mr. Wright used to be a butcher, so we have a lot of meat ready to roll."

"Wow, I didn't eat this good before the shit hit the fan. There's veggies in the greenhouse. The tall smelly ones are mine. I don't know about the other guys, but I know I want a shower."

"You need one. You smell like death," Monica said sadly.

"Hopefully for the last time in my life," Bill replied.

After they showered and ate dinner, they sent the kids to play with the dog which made her very happy. Bill came out of the cold cellar with a case of beer and set it on a picnic table that the guys had drug out of the studio. He excused himself and went into the house and returned with his own bucket full of frosty coronas. Monica gave him a strange look.

"It's my valley," he said, not caring if he was being rude.

"That isn't what I was going to say," Monica responded. I was wondering where you keep getting all this beer."

"I told you, I've got enough supplies for a year. I can drink a lot of beer in a year." He smiled and gave her a kiss.

"Okay, gentlemen, tomorrow we hit the subdivisions. With four vehicles it should take no time at all. I don't know about you, but I want to finish this shitty job. I've smelled enough dead bodies for a lifetime."

They all agreed, then sat back and enjoyed the evening. After a few beers Bill started to relax. Monica is sitting on Bill's lap and Alex and Dove are sharing a blanket. Willis and Alice, along with Bret and Maggie, have gone into the house to relax. Everyone else who wishes to, is sitting by the fire watching the kids play with Sassy, who by the way is doing her job and wearing them out.

Tomorrow will hopefully be the last day of searching. Then they can start getting the people into homes and off Bill's mountain.

They all wake hoping this will be the last day of the terrible job they have inherited. Winter is right around the corner and they have to get these people settled into homes somehow. After days of dealing with the dead they were getting used to the task. It's strange what you can get used to. After four hours they were ready to take a break.

"Smoke 'em if you got 'em," Bill said as he sat down and lit his bowl.

Willis came over and sat down beside him. "Think we'll finish today?"

"We should. We only have two more blocks to search."

"I can't believe we haven't found any more survivors today."

"Maybe some will show up at the school today. I had the ladies put some signs up by the freeway just in case some stragglers come into town, and we should start seeing more people now that the aliens are gone. We need to start thinking about sending out scouts to the other towns to see what's going on. Chad, how would you like to take Roberto with you to Rifle tomorrow since he speaks Spanish?"

"I can do that."

"One town per day will be enough, unless someone wants to go in the other direction. And Chad, take some diesel with you just in case. Also make sure they are on the same page. Search, burn, rebuild."

"You got it. But I'm sure we're not the only ones on the right page."

They all went back to the awful job of stacking and burning the bodies they were pulling out of the rubble.

CHAPTER 21

---•●❀●•---

The emperor is standing on the bridge of the Empress as they enter the Sol System. He wants to see the planet that has been the center of attention for the past nine days. Nine days he thinks to himself. Is that all it takes to change the history of a world. "Commander Brydon, place us in the orbit of the planet."

"Yes, Emperor, I will put us in stationary orbit over the continent we have been in contact with."

"That will be fine, Commander. Contact the Jayden."

The commander motions to his comms officer.

"Torani vessel Jayden, this is the Empress."

"This is the Jayden," came an answer.

"This is Emperor Ardesnal on board the Empress. I require the transponder settings to contact the planet below."

"I will send them over directly. When you contact the planet you will be received by a human who calls himself the president of a country called the United States," Commander Skoby replied.

"It's apparent why this planet was so easily defeated. Individual countries are not the way to administrate a planet. The Torani discovered this hundreds of years ago, after thousands of years of war," the emperor commented.

"Perhaps they will learn from this terrible lesson. Since the Earth leader is accustomed to communicating with me, I will make contact, then transfer to the Empress. They should be more contented by such an arrangement."

"Very well, Commander. We will stand by for the transmission."

"I will contact you as soon as we raise them. Skoby out."

"Commander Brydon, contact me in my quarters as soon as we make contact."

"Yes, Emperor."

The emperor retires to his quarters to await his first contact with the human leader. He has a lot to discuss with the leader, and wants to make sure he is prepared.

Commander Skoby is now engaged with his comms officer with the task of making contact with the president.

"Ensign, we need to make this connection immediately. The emperor is an impatient man and will not settle for less."

"Yes, Commander. I have the message already on its way and we are simply waiting for a response."

The president is awakened by a call from his secretary Ruth. He wipes the sleep from his face and goes into the other room to finish the conversation.

"Sir, the Torani are trying to contact you." Ruth still has a hard time calling the president by his first name.

"Have everyone meet me in the briefing room."

"Yes, sir."

Gene runs a quick comb through his hair and heads through the halls to the briefing room. As he enters the briefing room, his staff is already assembled and waiting. He doesn't know how they do it. Horace is already at the communication console answering the call.

"This is Horace Hunt speaking. I am the president's science advisor. The president is just entering the room, so please stand by." Horace lets his boss take over.

"Commander, what can I do for you?"

"President Furgison, it is Commander Skoby. I have the emperor waiting to speak to you. I will now transfer you to the Empress, where the emperor is standing by to receive your communication."

A few seconds later, the emperor comes onto the screen. On that screen is another of the golden aliens wearing his royal attire.

"President Furgison, I am pleased to make your acquaintance."

"The pleasure is mine, Emperor. I have awaited this conversation with you and would like to thank you and your people for stepping in and saving our Butts."

The emperor looked slightly puzzled by the response. "President Furgison, I am Emperor Ardesnal, the leader of the planet Torani. I would first like to put forth my deepest regrets for the loss of life to the planet Earth, and I can assure you that the Corisole leadership, as well as all involved in this tragedy will be severely dealt with. An act such as this has never occurred in the history of the galaxy, so we at the Galactic Alliance will act swiftly. We currently have all the Corisole fleet's personnel in custody, and will be sending troops to the Corisole planet if the Supreme Leader does not surrender himself and his staff."

"Emperor, what will be done about this situation?"

"These criminals will most certainly be put to death. The Galactic Alliance has stiff penalties for such unheard of acts."

"If I may speak freely, Emperor, they deserve no less. They have murdered over five billion people on this planet, and knocked us back to the stone age."

"Stone age? Oh yes, you are referring to your ancient past. President Furgison, the Galactic Alliance has decided that we will help you rebuild your seriously damaged planet as we feel somewhat responsible for that damage. The Alliance should have predicted the Corisole planet's actions."

"Their planet's ecosystem is failing swiftly, and they have been searching for a replacement planet for decades. With the time on their planet running short, they decided to take the simplest route, which is why they covertly invaded your planet. The Alliance had no idea what they were intending. It was fortunate for all that we observed their fleet en route to your planet or we would not be speaking this day."

"Emperor, how did they create a base large enough on our moon to launch this attack. And please Emperor, call me Gene."

"Very well, Gene. Your moon was used by the Galactic Alliance as a research facility for almost ten decades."

"You have been on our moon studying us for a hundred years. How did we not see this base during our Apollo missions?"

"The facility was well disguised. The Alliance manned the post continuously until you were able to leave your planet's orbit and start exploring your moon. At that time, it was considered too large a risk to continue, so all research of your planet was banned by the Alliance. We couldn't risk damage to your planet's natural evolution. Enough damage had already been done by other species encroachment into your atmosphere. Two decades ago a treaty was established that made it a crime to do so."

"You are talking about the 1947 Roswell incident, correct."

"I'm not familiar with the name but the date is correct. Gene." He called the human uncomfortably. "After that incident, the Alliance put strict standards on their research."

"In my opinion, they weren't strict enough, Emperor," he said angrily.

"I understand your anger, Gene, and again I cannot stress enough the sympathy we feel for the people of Earth."

"I'm sorry, Emperor. The people of this planet will be in your debt forever. If it wasn't for your fleet, we wouldn't be talking today. You must convey our appreciation to the Alliance, as well as your people, for saving this planet."

"Gene, I want to arrange a meeting with the leaders of your world in order to discuss the rebuilding of your planet. Can this be arranged."

"Emperor, many of the planet's leaders are either dead, or we simply cannot contact them yet. We aren't sure which is the case, but we are currently trying to remedy this problem. If we had another twelve hours it would be helpful."

"Then we will contact you at this frequency in twelve hours to continue our talks. I will warn you Gene, that there will be conditions instituted in order to continue this process, and you should be ready to consider them. I will await your next communication. Thank you, President Furgison."

Gene looked at his staff as the screen went blank. He is awed by the conversation he has just had and wonders just exactly what the emperor meant by "conditions."

"Horace, I want you to get in touch with John at NASA and get the communications set up. His people seem to be the best at pulling off the impossible. We'll do this at Johnson. They already have the power and the satellite to do the job. Elsa you have twelve hours to get all the other leaders connected to this line for the meeting. John and Horace will assist you with the tie in of the communications. All right, people, let's fire up Air Force One and head for Houston. It's wheels up in six hours. And someone call John and tell him we're coming."

They all jump to attention and gather their things. They have a job to do and a deadline to meet.

The emperor has having just finished his conversation with the Earth leader, and activates the comms to talk to Brydon.

"Commander, I want this frequency kept open until further notice. I have scheduled another meeting in twelve hours. They may contact you for help with the link. If they do, I want your men to do everything in their power to help."

"I will do everything I can, sir."

Brydon looks to his comms officer who has heard the conversation.

"You heard the emperor's orders, people."

John is awakened by a knock on his door. Brad sticks his head in to wake him.

"Rise and shine, boss. You better tie on your boots and tighten your belt, we've got a job to do."

"What's going on now?"

"The president and his staff will be here in about nine hours. We have to set up a multilink communications network for a meeting between all the world leaders and the Torani emperor."

"At least they aren't asking for much. How in the hell are we gonna do that?"

"I'm not sure yet, but we'll figure it out. We're going to need the big screen as well as the main control rooms equipment to do it."

"Well, then we had better get all the guys we've got up there getting the place cleaned up. How many men do we have?"

"We have thirty-two counting the assembly guys."

"That'll have to do. How much time do we have?"

"Twelve hours is what the man said."

"All right, let's get the place cleaned up, then get main power established and we'll go from there." John and his men will do their best to make this happen. The world is depending on them and they certainly aren't going to let them down.

Chapter 22

———•◎•———

Parachute, Colorado
October 22, 2020, 06:00

The alarm rings. It's four-thirty in the morning, so it's off to make the coffee, light up a smoke, then off to the can. Amazing he thinks to himself, not even an alien invasion can interrupt the morning routine. Now that the cleanup work is done there's some time to relax.

Monica comes out of the bedroom and gives him a big hug, and a good morning kiss which he always enjoys. The two haven't had much time together in the last nine days. Wow, nine days is all it takes to totally change every life on a planet. "Life isn't really good right now." It makes Bill wonder what the next nine days will have in store. Actually, he probably doesn't even want to guess. Monica is pouring a cup of coffee as he sneaks up behind her and gives her a squeeze. She looks back and purr's like a kitten.

Sassy the dog wakes up and does a big stretch. Bill knows exactly what it means since he's such a well-trained human. Coffee in hand they go out so she can make her rounds. You would think she was a male the way she hits exactly the same bush every morning.

Monica comes out and snuggles up under his arm. It's getting colder every week with winter coming.

"So how ya holding up baby?" he asked.

"Well, for a person who has probably lost every person in her family, and every other person she knows except the people inside this house. Has absolutely no idea which way her life will lead her, and has the entire population of a town living in the front yard, not too bad."

"That's the spirit. You're a strong woman, you'll survive."

"I'm not that strong. It just hasn't caught up with me yet, and right now I can't afford to let it."

"I know exactly how you feel. I've had to burn most of my friends, and a whole bunch of people I didn't know. I've somehow became the leader of two towns, which is a job I have no desire to have. Imagine, me, a leader. I liked things just the way they were. No headaches, no responsibility, no worries. I built this place so I could live my life in peace, and to enjoy my art."

"You should be happy. You still have your life, and me and Sassy and I to enjoy it with. You still have most of your family with you so far, which is more than most can say. As far as your art, you can still enjoy it, there's just nobody to sell it to. But when you think about it, who needs money now."

"Yea, I suppose your right."

"I'm always right," she said with a big smile.

Roberto came walking up with Sassy in tow.

"Coffee?" Monica asked.

"If it's not too much trouble."

"No trouble at all. Black I hope?" she said as she left for the house.

"That will be fine, thank you. What will we do now Bill?" Roberto asked.

"I'm not sure yet Roberto, but we'll think of something."

Actually he did know what they had to do, but wasn't looking forward to it. They had to rebuild a town. Monica returned with the coffee, and they all sat quietly looking at the Fall colors that were already starting to fall off the tree's. Winter will be early this year so they had better hurry.

The men at Johnson are working as fast as they can to get ready for the president's arrival. The men have cleared the runway of debris, And the control room is now powered up. They are busy checking the communication in order to see what needs to be repaired. With two hours remaining, it would be close.

"How we looking on your end Brad?" John asked as he crossed the control room.

"Not bad John. The men are rebooting the equipment right now so we can see what needs to be fixed."

"Great job Brad. We've got to pull this off, Gene is counting on us. Too much depends on this meeting. Air Force One will be landing any minute, and times running short."

John was a little bit concerned about the time, but also knew his men would pull it off.

The men made their final check of the two towns, driving from street to street honking their horns and hoping to find more survivors. They found none. After they had finished their final checks they all met at the High School. Bill called them all over to his truck.

It's only my opinion, but I think this is as good a place as any to start the new town. There's plenty of room in the parking lot to pull in a bunch of trailers. We have a water source because this side of town is gravity fed from the tank on the hill, and all we will have to do is get a generator up there to pump water from the well. We already have the one that Tom and Bret found, and we can get more generators from the drilling yards for the school and the houses. The only problem I see is getting the sewer up and running. We can hook into the school's sewer line but the plant is down. Jesus, the sewer just became your problem. Get someone to help you find one of those generators and see what you can do. There's no shortage of diesel fuel in this valley, so that won't be a problem for a while."

"You got it," he replied.

"The school will be perfect for the town office, and we can even open the school back up to give the kids a little bit of normality in their lives. We will have to find us a doctor since we don't know if the hospital in Rifle is still standing."

"Roberto and Chad went to Rifle today, so we'll find out about the hospital when they get back," Alex said.

"Well, if it's still there we will have to see if they have any extra medical supplies. If they don't we'll have to check Glenwood Springs or Grand Junction, so let's hope Rifle is still standing."

"The next thing on the list is homes. I saw quite a few travel trailers as well as motor homes in the storage lot. We can use them temporarily, but they won't be very comfortable when January arrives, so we need to scour the country side for trailer homes that weren't destroyed. Well, move them here and set them up for now. Maybe next year we can start rebuilding some of the homes. So for the rest of today, let's forget everything else and go house hunting. Let's start with the small stuff."

The men climbed into the four trucks and began their hunt. Four hours later the parking lot was lined with travel trailers and motor homes. Bill wished he had guys like these when he owned his construction business, they would have made him rich.

"Barney." Bill called.

"Yea."

"Take Jesus and go over to the drilling lot and see if you can find some cable to wire all these up to the generator."

"We'll be back in an hour."

"Oh, and if you can grab another generator. We'll need at least three to power everything."

After Barney and Jesus left, Tim Vance came over to Bill.

"Bill, I've got an idea for gas for heat."

"What is it?"

"There are several big propane tanks in the lot where I used to work across the freeway. I worked for them for five years, and there's nothing I can't do with gas. We can haul some of the tanks over here and hook the whole shebang up to 'em. As far as gas, we live in the largest gas field in the country, and there is a tanker loading facility about ten miles down the road. We would have a lifetime supply," Tim explained, quite proud of himself.

"Good thinking Tim. Why don't you get on it first thing tomorrow?"

"Will do."

There is only one other thing that Bill is worried about, security. There was no need for it on the mountain, but being this close to the freeway they could get some unsavory characters coming through. They need a security force, and the trick would be picking the right man to do it.

Air Force One has already landed as scheduled. The president and his immediate staff are waiting in NASA's control room, for John's men to put the finishing touches on the connection.

John and the Torani communication officer have set the system up to bounce the multiple video feeds from the Torani vessel to NASA. They hope the setup works correctly.

"John are you ready to test the feed?" Horace asked.

"Let's give it a shot," John said, holding up his crossed fingers.

"Brad, tie us in to the Torani vessel."

"Patching us in now, John."

All of a sudden the large screen, which is now just leaned against the wall comes to life with the images of eleven of the world leaders. They are all waiting silently for the Torani emperor.

"Were hot, John," Brad said, looking quite pleased.

Gene was called over to a seat in front of a small computer monitor, which he would use for the meeting.

"It's all yours, Gene," John said.

"Thanks, John," he said to his friend, then began the conference.

"Ladies and gentlemen, I'm glad to finally see your faces. It's a pleasure to have you with us today. We are all fortunate to be alive and joining together on this historic day. This will undoubtedly be the most important conference call in history. In a moment the Torani emperor will join us from his vessel. After his statement, I'm sure we will all be allowed to ask questions, so please hold your questions for after he finishes," the president explained as the leaders all started to all speak at once.

"Ladies and gentlemen, we have to have order," Gene stated over the roar. "We must be respectful, and take turns with our questions. Since I have already spoken with the emperor, I will be the one to moderate the conference. I have asked you all to get a six by six card to hold up when you have a question. I will be as fair as possible, and everyone will be able to ask their questions, but let's not repeat ourselves."

President Narkoff of Russia raises his card.

"Thank you, Mr. President. What is your question?"

"How do we know these aliens are actually here to help?"

"Mr. President, they did save our asses, so to speak, from the Corisole invaders. I would take that as a sign of friendship."

Prime Minister Harker of England raised her card.

"Yes, Prime Minister Harker?"

"Mr. President. You have already communicated with them. What do you think their intentions?"

"I truly believe they are here to help us rebuild our planet. The emperor has expressed his condolences for our losses, and expressed his great rage at the Corisole's actions. He seems absolutely sincere to me, but you all can make that decision for yourself."

"One more thing everyone. They are an alien species, so please refrain from any facial expressions when you see him. All right, everyone, I am getting the signal that we are ready to start. Please be courteous and patient. Thank you all."

The twelfth section of the screen came to life with the emperor's image. The members are noticeable surprised by his regal appearance. His gold skin and bright blue eyes, accented by his white hair and perfectly manicured spiked beard, are all awe inspiring.

"Emperor Ardesnal, it is truly a pleasure to see you again. I would like to take a minute to introduce you to some of the leaders of our planet."

The president introduced each leader in turn. He can tell that they are quite amazed by the unique alien being.

"Emperor Ardesnal would like start by making a statement. He will then take your questions. Thank you for being patient.

"Leaders of the planet Earth. I would like to start by voicing the Torani peoples, as well as the Galactic Alliance's, deepest sympathy for your horrendous loss of life. This loss of life is the largest ever recorded in galactic history. We regret that we were not able to arrive to your assistance sooner. We dispatched our fleet as soon as we discovered the Corisole fleet in transit to your planet, but unfortunately we had no idea of their plans to use the moon base against your planet."

"We were unaware of the illegal base they had created in your planet's moon. This moon base was originally created as a very small research station used for the study of developing races. The galaxy was intrigued by the only planet in our galaxy that was not capable of interstellar travel and still evolving. Once your race had the ability to leave your atmosphere, it was determined to be harmful to your evolution to continue our research. After the facilities closure, it was deemed illegal by the Alliance to return to your moon. The Corisole planet ignored the treaty that was created by secretly building the Station that is now inside your moon, along with the weapons system it contains."

"Now, to move on. With the Corisole planet's ecosystem almost depleted they searched for a new planet. After many years of searching, and no other planets that would fit their timetable, they set their sights on Earth, which has brought us to the situation we are all in today."

"I understand their motives, but don't condone their actions. All involved in this invasion will most certainly meet their deaths upon their return to Alliance space. They will of course be tried for their crimes first, but I assure you that will be the final outcome."

"Now we will move on to the rebuilding of your planet. The Torani people are committed to helping you rebuild your necessary life sustaining utilities within reason. We must put forth certain terms to be adhered to."

A nervous murmur rose from the leaders.

"First, the people of each of your countries will surrender all weapons of mass destruction. All nuclear, biological, and chemical weapons will be handed over to us for disposal."

"Second, each country will refit all military vessels for peaceful purposes, as there will be no need for such destructive weapons in your future."

"Third, this planet will come together and elect one world leader, and one world government, to lead this planet's people into a peaceful way of life. You're separated governments are the blight that infects your planet's peaceful existence and must be disbanded."

"As long as the Torani have watched your planet, and monitored your transmissions, we have seen only war and the pursuit of power over another. These wars have all been fought over politics, Boarders, religion, or the quest for more wealth through resources. These practices cannot continue if you wish to achieve a peaceful world that cares for its inhabitants. You notice I say inhabitants. Inhabitants are of one world. People are separate entities of separate countries."

"Our fourth and last demand, is that your world no longer relies on what you refer to as fossil fuels. If this planet continues on its destructive path with the use of these fuels, you will find yourself in the same predicament as the Corisole planet within a few hundred years. Your planet is on the verge of destruction, and if we are to help you, we will not stand by and let you destroy it."

"If you do not agree to these four conditions, we will not help you, which will leave your planet in a state of total destruction and destined for extinction. We have no desire to rule your planet or its inhabitants, but we will not help you if you don't agree to these four conditions."

"This is all I have to say at this time. Now I am sure you all have questions, and I will answer them all honestly."

The eleven other screens burst into a display of anger at what they have just heard, and all of the leaders were trying to talk at once.

"Ladies and gentlemen. Ladies and gentlemen." Gene raised his voice the second time to get their attention.

"We cannot talk at once as was established at the beginning of this conference. So let continue in a respectful manner." "We will begin with President Narkoff."

"Thank you, Mr. President. Emperor Ardesnal, the Russian people are grateful to the Torani warriors for their efforts, as well as loss of life during the battle with the Corisole invaders. We are truly in their debt, but you cannot expect us to simply discard our defensive forces."

"President Narkoff. With the removal of all offensive weapons on this planet, and the introduction of a world government, what need will you have for defensive forces? The planet may require a worldwide police force to enforce the new laws you will create, but you will have no need for armies. The Torani's very distance past was dotted with instances of bitter war among ourselves, as well as with other planets. After several millennia we grew to realize the error of those practices, and became the peace loving society we are now. We are speaking from experience here when we make these demands of you. It is for the good of all the people on your planet."

"We will consider your recommendation, Emperor," Narkoff replied, yielding to the next question.

"Next will be the German Chancellor Merkel."

"Emperor, I would first like to welcome you to our planet, and thank your people as well as the Alliance for your help. Now to move on, Emperor. The many people of the planet Earth have a strong sense of pride in their heritage, as well as their countries. You are asking us to give up all that our people have fought and died for to ensure our future generations happiness," the Chancellor stated respectfully.

"Chancellor, with all due respect, your planet's people have fought and died for ten thousand years for such beliefs. After thousands of generations, it is all too clear what has been passed on to the future generations. You still wage war over borders and beliefs. Your past leader Hitler destroyed millions of innocent lives because he believed that your beliefs and heritage were the only one that should be worthy of existing on this planet. Are you putting forth that you still believe in this archaic philosophy."

"Of course not, Emperor. The German people today are greatly disturbed and ashamed of these actions, and would never condone such behavior in the future."

"Then you have learned the error of your ways, and should do so again."

"Thank you, Emperor Ardesnal." The Chancellor sat melting into her seat like a child, after being scolded by its parent.

"Prince Azeere of Saudi Arabia, you will be next."

"Thank you, Mr. President. Emperor, the people of my country, as well as the people of the Middle Eastern countries, have concerns of what you demand. Correct me if I'm mistaken, but are you suggesting that we simply turn over the natural resources of our countries, which are the life lines of our countries. We of the deserts are not as fortunate as other countries to have the fertile lands to grow crops or to raise livestock, which makes us rely on the other countries of the world for much of our food. We absolutely rely on the income from our oil to survive."

"Second, Emperor, the Middle Eastern people are extremely devout to their god. We would rather die than renounce our beliefs. You have no idea what you ask of us," the prince returned the conversation to the emperor.

"Prince Azeere. I am by no means asking your people to give up their religions. Even the Torani have religious beliefs, but they are here," he said, putting his hand on his huge chest. "We do not build huge temples, or wage wars in the name of our gods. Your religions refer to your countries as the birthplace of mankind, as well as religion. Well, your countries are the birthplace of war. You have waged war for millennia in the name of you gods, and still do today."

"Now for the second part of your question. I am not saying you have to give up your countries resources. I am simply saying that this world cannot continue to use these resources for fuels. There are many other uses for your oils, and you are well aware of that. If this planet converts to other sources of energy, it would free other countries of this burden and let them concentrate on what their lands are best suited for. This would in turn, leave you with the responsibility of producing the world's petroleum for the remaining uses. Your people would benefit from this responsibility. Your people, as well as this world, must adapt to a new way of thinking to survive. I hope I have clearly answered your question."

"Yes, Emperor. I believe you have," Azeere replied.

"If there are no more questions, I will turn this conference over to the emperor for any further comments. Are there any other questions at this time?" President Furgison asked. The leaders all sat quietly, so President Furgison turns the floor back to the emperor. "We have no more questions at this time, Emperor."

"Very well, Mr. President. Leaders of the planet Earth. The other inhabitants of this galaxy have watched your young planet for thousands of years. You have grown to be a very resourceful species. We have also watched you develop extremely dangerous habits that affect this very planet's well-being. You poison its atmosphere, as well as its lands and oceans. Your frivolous behavior has quite frankly put you on the verge of extinction."

"If this planet adopts one Earth governing body you will lose the desire to rule others, and eventually learn to work together for the common good of the planet. With this desire to rule others removed, you will have no need for armies, as well as weapons that are capable of destroying this planet many times over. And finally, by realizing that every individual has the right to believe in his own afterlife, you remove the religious wars that have plagued this planet since the beginning of civilization."

"People of Earth. You have a decision to make. Continue on your path of selfishness and destruction, as well as the abuse of the planet you all live on, and I will assure we will not help your planet and you will end up in the same position as the Corisole planet is in now."

"Your other choice is to take the wise path which leads to a healthy planet and population, all working together to make their world a better place for all that live on it. As I have said, we have no desire to forcibly change the natural evolution of your planet or its inhabitants, so the choice is yours. We will await your decision. Take your time, consult among yourselves, and I will suggest, make the best decision based on the desires of the entire planet. Thank you all for attending."

The emperor's screen went blank, leaving them all thinking of what they had just heard. The board then erupted in uncontrolled, and incomprehensible mayhem. "Ladies and gentlemen, quiet please," Gene repeated himself numerous times until the mayhem ceased.

"Ladies and gentlemen, we have a decision to make. We either come together as a planet, or we continue on our current path and slowly destroy each other, and our planet." Gene declared, then hung his head dejectedly.

"I have imagined since I was very young what it would be like to live in a world where a person could travel the entire planet, without worrying about the persecution of nationality or beliefs. Not Russians or Americans. Not South American or Asian. Not European or Middle Eastern. What wonderful place that would be to live in," he added, pausing to take a drink of water. "I for one, am ready to take this planet into a new future. We will meet again in ten days from today. That should give you all enough time to decide exactly what kind of a planet you would like your future generations to inherit. Thank you all."

The screens all went blank, and the control room is completely quiet. They all realize the importance of the last thirty minutes to their futures. John leans over and whispers to Brad, "So what do you think?"

"I think it's about dammed time."

John looked at his friend and shook his head in agreement.

"John, thank you and your people for all their hard work," the president said. "We're going to head back to Washington. Can you send a couple of your guys with us to help us get our communications back up to par?"

"You can have as many as you need. We've got things here pretty much under control."

"Thanks again, John, and you too, Brad. From what I hear we couldn't have done this without you."

"You're welcome, Mr. President," Brad said proudly.

Gene and his cabinet filed out of the control room and boarded Air Force One, then flew off for Washington. They all had a meeting to get ready for in ten days.

CHAPTER 23

—•●✹●•—

Parachute, Colorado
October 29, 2020, 06:00

Bill stands in what is now his empty front yard, waiting for Sassy to make her rounds. A cup of coffee in his hand and a Camel hanging in his mouth. He was thinking about quitting smoking cigarettes, but what the hell. If there's one thing he has learned from all of this, is to enjoy today because there might not be a tomorrow. Aliens may come down and take a big crap on your world.

Monica wandered out to where he was standing, and they enjoyed the first quiet morning in what seemed like forever. The turning leaves are blowing across the valley. The woman you love is standing next to you. Aliens aren't trying to kill you. "Life is good."

"So what's on the calendar for today?" she asked.

"I'm not sure yet. We've got the settlement set up and running, but more people come every day so it keeps us on our toes to keep up. Actually Alex keeps up with it. We all elected him as the new mayor of Parachute."

"Alex is the mayor?" she asked interestedly.

"Yea. Alex is the mayor. Tim, Barney, and Jesus have been put in charge of the utilities, and Allen Wright used to be a Sheriff's deputy, so he got the Sheriff's job. Roberto and Chad have volunteered to be his Deputy's. Ruth was a teacher, so she was elected to run the school, with Dove and Hellen Byrd to help with the teaching."

"Sounds like things are starting to get back to normal."

"Well, as close to normal as can be expected I suppose. Now I can get back to normal."

"You don't know the meaning of the word," she joked.

"That's true, normal really isn't in my vocabulary."

"You want to come with me to Rifle today? I want to see for myself how things are going."

"Sure, I haven't been out of this yard in weeks."

Bill knows she's looking forward to a trip, but she hasn't been off the mountain since the invasion. She has heard the stories of the carnage, but hasn't actually seen it for herself. This trip won't be pleasant for her. Bill called the dog, and they all went into the house to get ready.

"Mornin', guys," Willis said as they came in.

"Mornin'," they replied.

"What are you up to today?" his father asked.

"Pretty much the same as yesterday. Bret and some of the guys are helping me go through the destroyed houses, and salvaging anything that can be used later. We've collected a lot of good stuff, and it could be a long time before we get this kind of stuff again."

"Great idea. Come springtime we can start rebuilding some of the houses. The foundations are all still in good shape.

"That's what I figured."

"Where are you storing it all?"

"Outside town at that commercial storage yard. There's a lot of room, plus the buildings are all steel or concrete and still standing.

"Well, keep up the good work," Bill said, giving him a slap on the back. "It will give the people something to look forward to in the spring. If I were you, I would use that to your advantage. Spread the word about the storage yard and you'll get a lot of extra help."

"What are the two of you up to?"

"We're going into Rifle."

"Be careful." Willis warned. "It's not normal out there yet."

"I always am."

Willis left the house with Alice at his side. He's trying to keep her busy. She has been worried about her family like everyone else. It's still too dangerous to travel to go looking for her family because there have been reports of gangs running the roads, robbing people for food and whatever else they can get.

Gene and his staff are back in Washington, and in the briefing room talking among themselves, when John and Brad Suddenly walked into the room unannounced. Gene is surprised at their appearance.

"John, how the hell are you. We didn't expect to see you," he said. "Good to see you too, Brad," he added.

John and his crew gassed up one of the F-Eighteens so John and Brad could make the trip to Washington. It's been a while since either one of them have actually flown one of the fighters but it's like riding a bike to an Air force pilot.

"Actually, I'm a little bit tired. It's been quite a few years since either one of us has sat in the seat of a fighter."

"How did he do Lieutenant Meyer?" Gene asked, pointing a thumb at John.

"Not bad for an old timer," Brad joked.

"You should have let me know you were coming. I would have sent a car for you."

"Couldn't get a cell signal," John joked.

"You wouldn't happen to have a cup of coffee around here, would you, Mr. President?" Brad asked.

"You drop that Mr. President crap, Brad, and I'll even find you a couple of Danish. We're going to have one leader from here on out, remember."

"You got a deal, Gene," Brad replied.

John and Brad went over to a small table where the coffee and Danishes were kept and helped themselves. Gene proceeded to where Elsa was working.

"Elsa, what's the news on survivors. It's been weeks, we should be able to put some hard numbers together."

"We have Gene, but you have been so busy with the other leaders, I haven't wanted to bother you."

"I'm not busy now."

"All of the major cities were totally decimated, and as far as we can tell there were only a handful of survivors. The Corisole hit them with enough fire power to make sure there were no survivors. The state capitols are setting up refugee camps across the nation, so we will be able to at least start getting families in contact with their loved ones. By the end of next month, we should have exact numbers."

"Next month! Elsa by the end of next month winter will have set in."

"I understand that Gene, but at least the interstates are open, so we hope the survivors will head south. There's no shortage of vehicles lying around right now.

"What about the storage depots. Red Cross, National Guard, those types of organizations?"

"The news is sporadic. We simply can't get in contact with them right now."

"We can talk to aliens in space, but not to people in our own country. There's something seriously wrong with that picture Elsa."

"I understand your anger Gene, but the individual states haven't stepped up to the plate on their end on this one."

"Elsa, if by the end of the week we don't have every National Guard station and military base in this country talking to us, I'm gonna be pissed. You personally make sure that Jack, Vince, and Allen understand that within the next five minutes, understood," he said, on the verge of anger.

"Absolutely, Gene." She instantly rose from her seat and went to pass on Gene's message.

Gene stormed down the hall to his office to cool down. He sat at his desk thinking about the ridiculous state of his communications, when there was a knock at the door and John stuck his head in.

"Sorry to bother you, Gene."

"No problem, John, have a seat," he said, pointing to the chair.

"Actually Gene I just want to talk."

"Want a drink?"

"Hell yes."

Gene went over to the bar and pulled out a bottle of Bourbon, then poured them both three fingers of the whiskey.

"So what do you think of the emperor, Gene?" he asked, then took a drink from the glass. "Thanks I needed that a week ago."

"You're welcome. I like him and agree with everything he said. Every problem comes down to three things. Oil, Borders, and religion. Deep down I've always known that it would take this kind of thing to happen for the rest of the world to realize it and come to their senses."

"I agree 100 percent, Gene, but as we both saw in that room the other day. That stupid mentality is still there."

"Yea, I was shocked by what I heard too."

They sat silently enjoying their Bourbon for a few minutes, when John finally broke the silence. "You know Gene, at NASA we all know deep down that we are not alone in this galaxy. So what do we do? We send deep space probes out into the galaxy, and have powerful radio telescopes pointed at all parts of space saying, "Hey, here we are and we don't know shit about you, but why don't you come and visit, or maybe come kick our asses and get it over with." John shook his head and finished his drink.

"I Know what you mean John. It's like standing in a dark alley with a stack of hundred dollar bills in your hand, and expecting to buy a pack of smokes when you walked out. It's just not smart." Gene was staring at his empty glass. "Another drink?"

"Absolutely," he said gratefully, holding out his glass. "We've got to nail them down Gene. We have no idea what they intend to do to help us. Currently we have no power source that can replace fossil fuels. Our battery technology isn't far enough along to remove the combustion engines from our cars and trucks. Our solar and wind power might work for providing electrical power now since there's only 10 percent of Earth's population left, but the infrastructure is shot. It would take years to reestablish a working system."

"What we need to do John, is make them give us some of their technology which they are totally against. John tomorrow you and I are making a very long distance phone call. Get a list together of what you think we need from the Torani, and we'll see what happens," Gene said with a smile. "How's noon sound?"

"Sounds good to me. I'll be ready."

"This is just between you and I John."

The two men clicked their glasses together and drank their Bourbon. Then John rose, shook Gene's hand and left the room. He has a lot of thinking to do to get ready for their meeting tomorrow.

Bill and Monica drove along the frontage road toward what used to be the town of Rifle. They have no idea what to expect when they get there. Chad and Roberto tried to explore the town a week ago, but the streets were cluttered with debris and impassable, so they returned empty handed.

This is the first time either of them has been out Parachute since the attack, and are both quite curious as to the extent of the damage to the other towns. As they neared Rifle they began to see the remnants of the attack. Destroyed homes dotted the landscape, and burned out cars were pushed off to the side of the road. The last ditch effort to escape the death and destruction was evident. With the roads cleared, it meant that they were trying to reach the same goal as Parachute, a feeling of well-being.

As they drove through the streets of Rifle, they couldn't help but notice that they were still clearing the bodies after two weeks has passed. Rifle was a much bigger town, but after two weeks, he couldn't believe it. Monica was sitting so close now that she was practically sitting on his lap. She had witnessed none of the cleanup of their town, and this was her first glimpse of the brutality of the invasion. He could tell how terrified she was because he could feel her shaking.

"This is what you've been doing for the last two weeks. How did you even want to get up every morning knowing this is what was in store?" she asked with a horrified expression.

"I did it for the same reason they do it. Because we had to, so disease wouldn't run rampant throughout this valley. It would have killed us all if we didn't."

Bill pulled up next to a few masked men standing by a truck and trailer. One of them walked over to see what they wanted.

"Hello," Bill said as he stuck his arm out the window to shake the man's hand.

"Hello. Are you lost?"

No. We came in from Parachute to see just how hard you were hit. My names Bill by the way, and this is Monica."

"Nice to meet you Bill, and Monica, always nice to see a pretty face. My names Jim. How many survivors?"

"Nice to meet you Jim. We started with thirty-eight but we're up to about one hundred, and they come straggling in every day."

"One hundred, that's all. I think we're up to about three-hundred now."

"Wow, from the looks of things, how did so many survive?"

"Most of the houses are old and have cellars. Plus, there were a lot of people in the gas fields when they attacked. They all came home to this."

"Sorry to hear it, Jim," he said, shaking his head sadly. "Do you have a city hall set up yet?"

"Yea it's in the basement of the hospital. The new concrete building held up really well. The hospital is even still operating."

"That's good because we don't even have a Doctor yet. Well, it was nice to meet you Jim, but we've got to go to the city hall to touch base with your mayor and let him know what's going on."

"All right. Glad you two made it."

"Thanks Jim. Take care."

They both gave Jim a wave and steered the truck toward the hospital. A couple miles down the road, they pulled the truck up in front of the hospital and got out. There were people going in and out of the door as they walked in. It was a very busy place. They went into the building and went to the reception desk. "Excuse me," he said to the receptionist. "I'm looking for the mayor's office."

"Down the stairs to the end of the hall on the right," she answered without even looking up.

"Thank you," he replied and walked away, not wanting to bother any further.

So down the stairs they went, then to the end of the hall, and to the office on the right side. Inside was a small woman who looked very busy.

"Can I help you?" she asked, holding out her hand. "I'm Betty, Betty Simpson."

Bill and Monica both shook her tiny hand.

"Yes, I'm Bill and this is Monica," Bill replied.

"Nice to meet you, but I'm quite busy. What can I do for you?"

"We came in from Parachute to see how you were making out."

"You're the first people we've seen from Parachute. How many people made it?"

"We started with thirty-eight from both towns, but we're up to around one hundred now with the newcomers."

"Thirty-eight, sorry to hear that."

"Thank you."

"So what is it I can do for you?"

"Not much really. We just wanted to touch base with you and let you know that were there, and wanted to see how you made out. Have you heard about up valley?"

"From what I've heard, Silt and New Castle ended up much as you did. Glenwood was hit hard with it being such a narrow valley, and they're still digging through the rubble. As far as anywhere east of there, I have no clue."

"Thank you Betty. If you need anything our office is at the High School."

"Well, I have to get busy, you two take care," Betty said as she picked up the mic of a CB radio and continued with her work.

As the two walked down the hall away from Betty's office, Bill smacked himself on the side of the head.

"Stupid, stupid, stupid," he said.

"What's wrong?"

"CB radios. I can't believe I didn't think of that. It goes to show what technology does to you. It makes you stupid," he said, disgusted with himself.

The two of them made their way out of town and began their journey back to his valley. Now he had more work to do. Tomorrow he would have to collect some radios and get them dispersed throughout the town and the surrounding areas. It will be another step toward their rebuilding.

Chapter 24

——•●✳●•——

White House Bunker
October 30, 2020, 12:00

Gene and John are tucked behind a small computer terminal in Gene's office, trying to contact the Torani vessel Empress. After A few minutes the screen comes to life, and the image of the Torani Commander Brydon appears.

"President Furgison, what can we do for you?" Commander Brydon asked.

"Commander, I know this is unexpected, but I would like to speak with Emperor Ardesnal."

"This is an unannounced transmission, Mr. President, I'm not sure there is anything I can do for you."

"Please, Commander, it's important."

"Very well. I will see if the emperor is available to speak with you."

The screen changes to the image of what must be the Torani flag. There is a blue planet with what must be islands dispersed like the spots on the back of a ladybug. After a few more minutes, the emperor appears on the screen. He is dressed casually, instead of wearing his royal attire that he wore for the last meeting.

"President Furgison, this is a highly unexpected communication. What can I do for you?"

"Emperor, I know this is not a scheduled meeting, but we really need a few minutes of your time before the next meeting. I would like to clear a few things up if I can."

"Yes, go on," the emperor replied curiously.

"Emperor, this is John Alistair. He is the leader of our space program. We both have a few questions we would like to ask if we may," Gene said respectfully.

"It is highly irregular, and may even be considered unfair by the other leaders, but I will allow it."

"Emperor, I am John Alistair. I would like to ask you a question about our energy problem."

"Proceed."

"Sir, our technologies in solar and wind power production may be able to sustain the population now that it's numbers are depleted, but the problem is that without fossil fuels, we cannot rebuild and operate the factories to continue the changeover to these technologies. We have Hydroelectric dams that are still operational, but the infrastructure was destroyed along with our cities. It will take many years to repair the damage to the system. My question is, what can Torani do to help?"

"Mr. Alistair, as you know from the meeting, it is against all we believe in to give technology to any civilization that can interfere with its natural evolution, so I'm not sure I understand your question."

John looked at Gene with a small smile and continued. "Emperor, I guess I'm curious about those fuel towers that the Corisole used to refuel their ships. The people around the planet have already seen them in operation, so they are not new to this planet, and the people know they produce energy."

Gene smiles as he thinks he knows where John is going with this.

"The people of this planet have known of the dangers fossil fuels pose to their planet, and they also know that nuclear reactors don't pollute the atmosphere, but the fuels from these reactors are one of the most destructive and poisonous by products that exist on this planet. With no other way to turn I fear they will choose to take the same path. What I am asking is if the towers can be somehow utilized to power our planet in order to bypass the use of other fuels."

John waits patiently for the emperor's answer, with his fingers secretly crossed.

"Mr. President, your scientist is a very wise man in more than one way. I will have my research people look into this possibility. I must agree that this technology would not be a shock to your society, but the problem is, it is quite powerful and dangerous. In short I don't know if we can trust you with the technology. I will consider this problem along with your request."

"Emperor, what if we allow your people to live on our planet to help us adapt our systems to except this new power. It would be a unique opportunity for both of our planets," Gene asked hopefully.

"This is an interesting proposition, President Furgison. Your scientist, as well as yourself, are very wise men. Your planet is almost identical to Torani which is undoubtedly why the Corisole desired it. Your atmosphere would have to be cleaned, but with our technologies it could be accomplished in a few years, but this we will talk about that at a later date." The emperor pauses to consider what has been asked of him. Then continues. "I will consider your proposition and have my researchers examine the possibility of your plan. We will meet again, but with all of your leaders in two days. Please inform your leaders of this meeting and I will give you my decision in two days."

"Thank you, Emperor, for your time and patience," Gene said respectfully.

"Thank you, Mr. President, for piquing my interest in his interesting proposition of a union of our two planets. Good day, gentlemen."

The screen went blank, and the two men look at each other, smile, and give each other a big high five.

"That was brilliant John."

"Same to you, my friend. Imagine the power those towers can produce."

"You just want inside of one of them," Gene said. "I think that deserves a Bourbon?"

The two men enjoyed a glass of the Bourbon as they considered the magnitude of the conversation they just had with the emperor. Not only may they get the use of the fuel towers, but they have also possibly created a partnership with the Torani planet.

It's a frosty Colorado morning as Bill waits for his shadow to return from her travels. He's standing there in his PJ's, slippers, and his old cowboy hat that he always wears. As the black dog runs up the driveway he hears a noise behind him. He doesn't turn because he would know that beautiful smell anywhere.

"How's my baby this morning?" he asked.

"A little cold."

He turns to see Monica wearing nothing but a long tee shirt. Or should he say that it was wearing her. She is an absolutely stunning woman, at fifty years old, she didn't look a day over thirty-five. With her very youthful body, and her long blond hair hanging down over her now cold nipples almost to her waist, and those beautiful blue eyes, she is absolutely stunning he thought to himself.

"More coffee?" she asked.

"What did I ever do to deserve you."

"I'm still trying to figure that one out," she said, smiling as she said it. "Give me your cup."

He sat down by the pit petting the dog, and looked at the now almost bear trees. Everything looks so lonely in winter. There's no snow yet but it's coming any day now, you can feel it in the air.

"Here you go," she said, startling him back to the moment. "So what ya up to today?"

He tapped the side of his head.

"Oh yea, stupid," she said and laughed, then headed back toward the house with Sassy at her side. "You really need a new hat," was the comment as she walked away.

"This one is just getting broke in. Besides, where you gonna find one?"

"Watch me."

He followed her into the house, where Willis was in the kitchen getting some breakfast.

"We're gonna have to get a cow, I hate not having milk," he said, holding a bowl of dry cereal.

"I'll work on it."

"So what are you up today?" his son asked.

"I'm going to steal some radios."

"What the hell do we need with more radios? We've got a houseful of them."

Bill explained what he had seen at the hospital the day before.

"CB's like the truckers use?"

"Yea, we will be able to communicate all up and down the valley. I can't believe I didn't think of it. I gotta go get dressed."

"Mind if I tag along?" Monica asked.

"It would my pleasure baby. You better go get dressed, I'll join you in a second."

After getting dressed he filled a thermos with coffee, and was ready to head out the door when Monica came out wearing a flannel shirt and her blue jeans. How he loved those jeans.

As they drove down the driveway toward town, they had to stop for a few minutes and wait for the Elk to cross the road, which isn't unusual. He looked over at Monica.

"I love it up here," he said, then drove off down the road.

An hour has passed since the president arrived at Johnson Space Center in Air Force One, with John and Brad on their tail in their commandeered F-18. The meeting with the emperor, and the world leaders, is scheduled to start any minute, and Brad's making some last-minute preparations for the meeting. They are all in the control room, which most of them now consider their home.

"We should be ready to go in a few minutes, Gene."

"Great, Brad. Are the other leaders waiting?"

"All standing by, sir," John replied, as the leaders all started to appear on the screen.

"Two minutes, John," Brad said.

"Mr. President. Your seat," John said, pointing to a computer station. "Thank you, John," he replied, then turned to the communication station. "Ladies and gentlemen, we will be starting in a minute. I need to know how we stand on the emperor's terms. Let's start with President Narkoff." "Mr. President, the Russian people have been a strong people throughout history, but throughout this history we have seen little peace. After much thought and a great deal of turmoil between myself and my advisors, we have decided to agree with these terms. This decision is not only the best decision for my people, but for the entire world. We will immediately begin dismantling our nuclear weapons, and gathering our biological and chemical weapons for disposal. It will be a pleasure to live in a world where we will not have to fear the future. Thank you."

"You wished to speak, Prince Azeere?" Gene asked the Arabian leader.

"Yes, thank you. I have been authorized to speak for all the Middle Eastern countries. The people of these nations control a very small amount of these weapons, and are happy to see them rid of this planet. We are on the other hand concerned with what will become of us. Our nation's wealth is under the sands of our lands. For over fifty years this wealth has maintained the health and welfare of our people. We do not have fertile lands on which to grow the foods to feed our people as most of you enjoy. With few large cities in our countries, and a largely nomadic people, we estimate approximately ten million people still live in our countries. How will we feed them? Our people are also extremely devout to their faith, and to ask them to deny it is something they will not do, even if their survival depends on it." The prince sat back expecting an answer.

"Prince Azeere, I can assure you that nobody will be asked to give up their faith. None of us are expected to do this. The problem is not with faith, it's with the fanatics who believe that if others are of a different faith they are unholy, and do not deserve to live. You have been dealing with these fanatics the same as we have. You cannot deny that it's the way they think, and it cannot be allowed to continue. It will be your responsibility to deal with them. Faith is a good thing. Persecution because of faith is not."

"Now as far as the feeding your people, Prince, we are all now one people so to speak, and this world will take care of all its people. With so many of all our people murdered by the Corisole, the population of this planet will never have to worry about food for a very long time. There will be a surplus of food in almost all countries, and you will also have to learn to utilize what fertile lands you do possess."

"The Chinese president will now speak," Gene said, considering the prince's question answered.

"Thank you, President Furgison. China will gladly forfeit all our weapons of destruction. The Chinese people yearn for peace on this planet, and whatever is required to achieve it." "China is a very large country with vast rural areas for growing food. We estimate that there are still one hundred million people in our country, and with this meager amount of people and so much land to grow food, we should easily be able to feed a good portion of the planet. Our concern is fuel. If we are not allowed to use fossil fuels, how do we ship this food to the rest of the world. We have the largest commercial fleet on the planet, and no way to utilize it."

The Chinese president waited for an answer to his very valid question. President Furgison tried to calm his doubts.

"President Ho. I am going to ask the Torani to allow us to continue to use fossil fuels until we can refit our transportation. They will not allow fossil fuels for power because we do have other technologies, but they must temporarily give a little on transportation purposes. Does that answer your question?"

"Yes, Mr. President."

"I believe the Swiss president would now like to speak."

"Thank you, President Furgison. Switzerland has suffered greatly. With most of our population in the cities, the death toll was severe. We estimate that only one hundred thousand of our citizens survived in the villages that were not targeted by the Corisole attack ships."

"We do grow a small amount of food for our people, but not enough to support our needs, so we will need help. Our greatest loss is financial. As you all know we were the financial capital of the world. We do have huge gold reserves, but what good is gold now. To say the least, my friend, we are concerned for our welfare. Thank you."

"Ladies and gentlemen, we will no longer have to worry about wealth as the Swiss president has noted, but gold does have other uses which were never considered before because it wasn't considered cost effective. I have a feeling that with new technologies being developed it will play a very important part. We may find that other worlds are in need of it also, and may be able to trade technology for gold. This is unknown at this time."

"We must all assume a different role in the future. Not as leaders, warriors, and bankers, but as keepers. We must keep our world and its many people's safe from harm. We must make sure that we take care of each other to survive this catastrophe, and build a future for our children's children for millennia."

"Now, my friends, for the reason this meeting was called. Now that we have all agreed to the Torani's Terms, I will personally ask them to postpone the ban on fossil fuels for five years to refit our transportation, and ask them to provide any technology they can to help with our power problems. If anyone is not in agreement, please speak now because the emperor is waiting as we speak for us to contact him."

There was silence among the leaders, so Gene took that as a sign that they all agreed.

"All right then, I will now contact the emperor."

Gene gave Brad a nod, indicating that he was ready. The screen started with the Torani flag. Then the emperor appeared.

"Emperor Ardesnal, it is a pleasure to talk with you again."

"It is also my pleasure, President Furgison, as well as the rest of your leaders. I assume that you have discussed our terms and come to a decision."

"Yes, Emperor, the people of the planet Earth have agreed to your terms," Gene informed him.

"Very good, you will not regret your decision. Soon your world will become a strong society, without petty differences to keep your world from greatness. The Torani planet was once as your planet, but evolved into a peace loving society. The Corisole planet has made us break this tranquility for the first time in almost one thousand years. For this they will be punished. They will also be punished severely for the damage they have done to your planet."

"Now back to the points of this meeting. First, you will provide the locations for removal of all nuclear fuels, as well as biological, and chemical weapons, for their removal and destruction. Our sensors can detect them but it will be more efficient if you collect them in central locations. We will remove your ballistic missiles from their locations, as they are difficult for you to move."

"Now on a matter that was brought to my attention by President Furgison. A power source for your planet. It has been suggested by John

Alistair, to adopt the power source used by the Corisole towers to refuel their attack ships, to power your planet. By adapting this source, it will give your planet a clean power source for the next hundred years. After much discussion with my science advisors, we have decided to implement the use of these towers, and my advisors assure me that it will be a safe and reliable source of power once we adapt it for your use. Starting one week from today, we will start positioning these towers in precise positions around your planet. Once the towers are distributed, we will station personnel on your planet to adapt these power sources to for your use."

"We will then land vessels to build small bases to house our technicians on your planet, while they construct the infrastructure that will allow these towers to supply the power you require. Many of your people will be needed to assist them with this task, and we hope a healthy relationship can be established between our two people. It will take many of your years to fully implement the use of these towers worldwide, and will require hundreds of your scientists, as well as laborers to accomplish the task."

"Now to our next point. The Torani see your separation of countries as an obstacle to the unity of your planet as well as its recovery. First, we would like you to choose a central location from which to govern your world. Next, a single leader will be selected from the current world leaders, as they are the most qualified to govern the planet, and you will need regional governors to help with the people's needs. Since there are seven continents on your planet, I suggest seven governors to maintain peace until your people adapt."

"You will then adopt a set of laws for all the people of the planet, which are acceptable to all. This will most certainly be the most difficult task in this process. Unfortunately, every society needs a force to enforce the laws created. Without the threat of retribution for breaking the laws, they will not be effective, so you will build a world police force based on the fair enforcement of these laws. I know this will be difficult, but your people are accustomed to living with laws, just not on such a grand and singular notion."

"I believe this completes our requirements of your planet. If anyone has any questions, now is the time."

"Thank you, Emperor. I know of one question we would all like to ask."

"Continue."

"The leaders would like to ask that you delay the ban on fossil fuels for five years on our transportation only. With the removal of the power plants, factories, and millions of other transport vehicles in the equation, the effect on the planet will be extremely minimal. You must understand, Emperor, that with so few people spread throughout the planet, it will be impossible to provide food and other necessities without proper transportation. We need at least five years to refit our transportation to alternative powers."

The emperor contemplated the question for a minute, then made his decision.

"Under the current circumstances we will agree to your request, but I think you will need more time to accomplish this task. I will grant a ten-year time period to convert your transportation. We have calculated the fuel remaining on the planet and it is more than sufficient for a ten-year period, so there will be no further refinement of fuels allowed."

"I think we will agree that offer is quite fair, and we will work diligently to meet the deadline. Are there any other questions from the leaders?" Gene asked.

"Mr. President, I have a question," John said. "Emperor, I am John Alistair. I am in charge of space exploration on our planet," he stated confidently.

"I am familiar with you Mr. Alistair. What is your question?"

President Furgison has a smile on his face knowing that John has something up his sleeve.

"Emperor, since you are going to station people on our planet, I would like to request that you allow a group of our scientists to travel to your planet, along with an ambassador to join the Alliance Council. Since our two planets will be entwined for at least a decade, I think it would be beneficial to both our planets." John then took his seat, knowing the emperor's answer would change his view on the galaxy forever.

"John Alistair you are a creative and curious man. It would be my pleasure to have you on the planet Torani," he said, with what could be considered a smile.

"It would be my honor, sir," John replied.

"Then it is settled. The Empress will be leaving Earth space in two weeks' time. You will select two assistants, and your leaders will choose one ambassador to accompany us to Torani. That will be all for now. This meeting is adjourned."

"Thank you, Emperor," President Furgison said. Then the Torani screen went blank. "Are there any other questions?" He was actually afraid to ask at this point.

"Yes, Mr. President," the British prime minister replied. "What if they put these bases as well as technicians on our planet, and they decide not to leave?"

"Well, Prime Minister, would that be such a bad thing. We have a big planet that has a lot of extra room right now. Also, we had better get used to dealing with other species if we are going to join their Alliance. An Alliance that will eventually want to station their own ambassadors here on Earth."

"All right, everyone, I will have my staff contact you with the timetable for the weapons removal as soon as I get that information. I think we should set up a face-to-face meeting with the emperor, preferably at our new World Headquarters before he leaves for Torani in two weeks. We will have to select this site before then. Thank you for your participation in this historic event."

The screens all went blank one by one until Gene was standing alone with John.

"John," he said quizzically.

John stands beside him grinning ear to ear.

"You never cease to amaze me. Remind me never to play poker with you, you've always got a hole card," Gene said with a smile.

"Mary!" he shouts. "Ten glasses, and a bottle of Bourbon. And grab that box of cigars on my desk. Major, could you take Mary to Air Force One and give her a hand?" Mary and the major left to fill the president's order. The rest of the cabinet came over to shake both the men's hands. It was a good day for humanity, and they all had a good feeling about the new Torani alliance.

CHAPTER 25

———•◦✵◦•———

Parachute, Colorado
November 3, 2020, 06:00

Bill entered the kitchen after him and Sassy took care of their morning ritual. Today he was wearing only his long underwear and his hat. He loved living on the mountain.

"Hey, babe," Monica said laughing.

"Good morning," he returned, adding a kiss.

"Radio day?"

"You guessed it."

Bill and Willis Had spent the last three days building radio sets for the new town, so it will be able to communicate again. They plan to give a few of them to the ranchers, one for the school and one for the Sheriff's office. The others would be spread out through the town, and the people will be happy to have any communications again.

"Breakfast?" she asked with a smile. "I've got eggs and milk."

Harvey and Myrtle moved on to one of the ranches outside of town. It had chickens, a few pigs, and a small herd of cattle roaming free on the property, so Bill helped fix the coop and a few fences and It's now a perfect little ranch. The best part is that they get to reap some of the benefits.

"Steak and eggs?" Bill asked.

"Steak and eggs it is. Why don't you get dressed and wake the others up?"

They still had four other people on the mountain, but it would be back to normal in a few days. Alex and dove have found a good sized trailer on one of the ranches and moved it into town. They would be moving in a few days. Bill came out of the bed room in his ratty old sweats and sweatshirt.

The others are right behind after being awakened by the smell coming from the kitchen.

"You will never change will you?" Monica said, shaking her head at him.

"Never," Dove replied. "I tried to buy him new clothes for twenty years, but he always looked just like that."

They all laughed, but Bill doesn't care. He is comfortable, and "life is good." That's all that matters to him.

They ate a great breakfast for the first time in three weeks, then went across the lower valley passing out the radios. It was a huge step in getting life back to normal for the people of Parachute.

With the city destroyed, and the White House in ruins, the leaders of the United States see no end to their stay in the bunker. They are looking for another sight, but with the most needed infrastructure, Camp David is the only other option at this time, but they are determined to stay in Washington.

Gene habitually travels the halls, in search of anything to keep him ahead of the new world game of survival. He steps into what is now serving as Elsa's office.

"How are you today, Elsa?" he asked.

"Exhausted Gene. I've got the first reports on the refugee camps. We had to load communication gear on helicopters to contact them, but the data is now rolling in."

"How many are we tied into?"

"We've connected thirty-five states so far, and the rest will be online within the week. The numbers are improving, and we can now confirm one million survivors in the thirty-five camps."

"That's a lot of people in each camp Elsa."

"Yes, it is, but it seems that they are only staying short term. The people have taken it upon themselves to rebuild their towns. The major cities will most likely remain abandoned, because they are so heavily damaged that we don't think anything is salvageable. Plus, the fact that nobody has even attempted to remove the dead making them biological hazards."

"It's great that the people are pulling together for the common good, it's the first stepping stone in a unified world. Great work Elsa, keep it up."

Elsa's phone rings as they talk. "Yes. Okay, I'll let him know." She hangs up the phone and returns to Gene. "Gene, Jack is looking for you. He's in his office."

"Thanks Elsa. Get some rest, you look tired."

"I will Gene."

The president navigates his way to the colonel's office, and as he enters, Jack doesn't even notice his visitor because he is mesmerized by what he is watching on his computer.

"Jack, you wanted to see me?"

"You have to see this. It's amazing."

Gene stands behind the colonel and watches the video of the collection of their nuclear missiles. "How the hell are they doing that?"

"I have no idea, Gene. Antigravity beam, magnetic, we're not sure, but it is amazing, isn't it."

The two men watched the video as their missiles simply, and slowly, rose from their resting places, into the bellies of large hovering ships from the fleet vessels. There was feed from around the world showing the same practice worldwide. The nuclear waste dumps, Chemical and biological facilities were also cleared in the same manner, after their contents were relocated to the exterior of the facilities. There were even pictures of nuclear tipped missiles being taken directly out of the submarines launch tubes as they sat in the ports.

"How long is it supposed to take for them to finish, Jack?"

"It won't take long. They've got a fleet of sixteen smaller ships from their fleet working diligently on the removal. Three days, maybe four tops to finish. It depends more on how quickly we can make the stuff available."

"So that means that all nuclear vessels are now useless."

"That's right, but what do we need them for now. We no longer need warships. There are several conventional vessels remaining from the invasion that can be used to police the seas, but just barely enough. Lucky for us they left most of the shipping vessels alone. We'll be needing those more than ever now."

They continued watching the unearthly sight with awe. After several minutes Elsa stuck her head into the office.

"I figured you'd still be in here. Amazing isn't it. Gene, can I have another minute?"

"Sure Elsa, what is it?"

"Have the leaders decided on a location for the World Headquarters?"

"Actually we have. We've decided on the manmade Arabian island. You know, the one shaped like a big Palm tree. After a lot of searching worldwide, it seemed to be the best location. It was only slightly damaged in the attack, and it's easily accessible, so the Saudi's volunteered it for our use. I guess it's their way of having an impact on our future."

Earth 2020

159

"Well, sir, we have exactly thirty-six hours to ready it for the emperor's arrival. We also have to have all the world leaders in that location to vote on the new world leader."

"It's being taken care of Elsa. Don't worry. Now get out of here and get some rest."

"Okay, Gene."

"Jack I've got to talk to John. I'll talk to you later. And Jack."

"Yea Gene?"

"You'll ruin your eyes if you watch too much TV," he said, as he waged a finger at him.

"Yes, Mother," he replied.

Gene returned to his office to give John a call. He caught John in his office, working on his list of scientists for the team.

"Gene, how are ya?"

"Good John. Have you selected your Torani team yet?"

"Not yet Gene. I'm going over the applicants now. There is quite a long list of interested scientists."

"You've got eight hours John. We're meeting in Saudi Arabia at the new World Headquarters at 1800 hours tomorrow. You can travel with me if you would like."

"Buy me a ticket and I'll be there."

"Consider it done John. See you in eight hours. We are going the day before to prepare."

"Oh, Gene, you had better make sure the people are notified of the return of the towers or we will have some really freaked-out people around the planet. And, Gene, I'll be the one on the tarmac with a suitcase so you can find me," he said comically. "See ya then, Gene."

Gene laughed to himself, imagining the sight of John standing alone on the tarmac with his suitcase. It's good to know that people can still have a sense of humor after such a traumatic turn of events.

Bill and Willis have just returned from a very long day. With the first snows starting to fall the people of the valley are pulling together to get ready for winter. The crews of men went from ranch to ranch helping to repair the barns for the livestock, and the hay that was still stacked in the fields needed to be dealt with so it wouldn't mold. They spent the day cutting and splitting wood for their winter heat, since almost none of the ranches had power yet. It is like they have all been thrown back to the distant past and they all have to depend on each other to survive.

"Oh, I ran into Bret today," Willis said as they sat in the kitchen. "He went to Grand Junction the other day to check out the damage. He stopped in Dubuque on the way, and from what I gather it's a ghost town, totally destroyed and deserted."

"What about Junction?"

"He said that the streets weren't cleared yet so he really couldn't tell too much, but he did say that the people were still wandering around in a daze like zombies. They are scavenging through the rubble for supplies. I can't understand why, because Bret said that there was a refugee camp at the airport. They stopped to see if any of their families were there, but they didn't find any of either one of their families sadly."

"If there's a refugee camp, that means that the government is involved which is a good sign. The people simply can't do it all by themselves. We've been fortunate to have very committed people to help with Parachute, as well as a small population to deal with."

"You want a sandwich?" his dad asked.

"Sure."

They were getting the fixings for their sandwiches when they heard a new message on the small radio."

"Hey, listen," Willis said as he turned up the radio that they always now keep turned on. "There's a new message."

Monica and Alice heard the radio and joined them in the kitchen.

"What's going on now?" Monica asked.

"We're not sure yet, it's just starting over," Willis replied.

"People of Earth, I'm coming you tonight, not as your president but simply as another inhabitant of this planet. I am here tonight to update you on our situation, and since many of you have missed the earlier messages, I will start at the beginning and give a very brief update of these events."

"Twenty-three days ago, this planet was ruthlessly attacked by an alien race of beings from the planet Corisole. These beings used our moon as a base, to launch a covert attack using our planet's meteor showers to disguise the attack, which destroyed every major city on the planet. After this attack they sent automatically piloted ships, in an attempt to destroy the rest of humanity."

"Another alien race of beings from the planet Torani, discovered the motives of the Corisole and came to our rescue. By destroying most of the Corisole fleet, and imprisoning their soldiers, they have saved this planet and its inhabitants from extinction. The death toll from this attack has been estimated at over five billion lives. The Torani leader has assured me that these invaders will be dealt with swiftly and mercilessly. The fleet soldiers as well as the rulers of Corisole will pay for their crime with their lives."

"Now, in order to receive assistance from the Torani, they have put forth conditions. These conditions are that first we hand over to them for disposal, all weapons of destruction on this planet, which we will do happily.

"Second. They insist that we dissolve all individual world governments, and create one governing body to rule the entire planet. There will no longer be borders to fight over, or separate governments to start these wars."

"Third. We will cease the use of fossil fuels, as well as nuclear fuels for the production of power. We are all well aware of the damage these fuels do to this planet, but we have refused to adopt new technologies to stop it. We have been given a ten-year grace period, in which we may use fossil fuels to power our transportation needs until we can adapt them to a new source of power."

"For the last and final point. Within the next few days you will begin to see the Corisole fuel towers return to the planet. Do not fear these towers, because they will be refit to provide a reliable energy source for this planet for at least a hundred years. With the implementation of these towers, the Torani will need to send a minimum of two hundred technicians to our planet to live and help us convert to the power. We ask that you treat them like the friends they have become to our planet. The Torani will also need an army of laborers, as well as hundreds of our own scientists to complete this task, so we will inform the populations of these jobs when they begin."

"Ladies and gentlemen, this is truly the first day of this planet's future. By all working together, we will make this one planet, with one people to enjoy the paradise it can become. We can also look forward to a future which will span the galaxy. I hope you will join me in the anticipation, of lives containing only peace and harmony, as one people, on one planet."

"Thank you all, and good night."

The radio began the message again and Willis turned it way down and set it back on the fridge. The inhabitants of this small piece of the world looked at each other with absolute amazement. Each one of them is silent and deep in thought. Bill is the to break the silence.

"I have always said that it would take an alien invasion to bring this world together as one. I just never believed that I would see it in my lifetime."

"If you didn't think you would see it in your lifetime, why did you build this house, Dad," Willis stated. "If they put one of those towers around here, I'm going to try to get a job. I think it would be cool to work with the aliens, as long as they aren't all slimy or something gross," he added with a chuckle.

"You want to know what I would like?"

"A beer and a bowl," the three of them said in unison, then walked away shaking their heads.

Gene is sitting in his office deep within the bunker, listening to the message as it plays over the radio. Ruth sticks her head in and informs him that John is on the phone.

"John, what's up?"

"Nothing at all. Heard the speech and wanted to say, great job."

"I hope so. I feel so guilty about not keeping the people better informed. I can't imagine how it felt to not know that their leaders were there to help," he said sadly.

"Don't beat yourself up Gene, we've been a little busy trying to keep the world in one piece."

"You got a bottle of Bourbon handy?" Gene asked.

"Just so happens I do. One of yours," he replied.

"Well, have one with me and I'll see you in seven and a half hours, John," Gene said, pouring a shot for himself.

"I'll be waiting with suitcase in hand. See ya tomorrow." He hung up the phone and grabbed the Bourbon.

They both sat back in their chairs and drank to a new world.

CHAPTER 26

—•◉•—

Dubai, Persian Gulf
November 7, 2020, 18:00

The leaders of the world now stand in the grand courtyard of one of the magnificent Palm Island luxury hotels. This location has been chosen for the new world government to house its headquarters. The United Arab Emirates have donated the structure as a gesture of good will to the planet. They are all awaiting the arrival of the Torani emperor, to proceed with the business at hand. The election of a world leader and the posting of a Torani ambassador. Gene spots Elsa chatting with a group of his colleagues, and walked over and joined the group.

"Elsa, you pulled it off. I knew you were the right person for the job," he said, shaking her hand.

"It wasn't easy getting them all here, Gene. I had to call in a lot of favors to make all the connections to get them all here, I didn't think I was going to pull it off."

"How many did you get?"

"Forty-four is all. I wish it was more. There are almost two hundred members of the UN so we only got a quarter of the leaders.

"Forty-four will have to do Elsa. You should be proud that you got that many after all that has happened."

The prince approached them from across the Courtyard, and shook the hands of his American friends.

"Prince Azeere. It is a pleasure to be here on this beautiful island." Gene remarked as he shook the prince's hand.

"I thought it a fitting location from which to rule a planet. As this island rose from the sea by the sweat of numerous countries, our planet will rise to greatness from the same island, in the same manner."

"It is absolutely beautiful, Your Highness," Elsa commented.

"You shall both tour the island once this bit of business is concluded," he promised. "We have quite a task ahead of us today, and for many days to come also. I must leave you now to greet the rest of the leaders." The prince bowed politely and went on his way.

"Where is your pal, John?" she asked.

"If I know him he is looking for the perfect people to take to Torani with him."

"What about the appointment to ambassador?"

"That will also be decided today, by a vote of the members."

A small ship approached from the western skies, and came to a hover above the courtyard. The leaders all cleared the courtyard allowing the ship to land. They all waited to get a glimpse of the Torani emperor. The door to the ship opened, and after a moment the emperor exited the craft.

The emperor was very large. His seven-foot-tall golden frame crowned with a pure white mane running to the bottom of his shoulders was impressive, if not awe inspiring. As he approached the crowd, his bright blue eyes took in the surroundings. At his heels were four guards clad in bright red uniforms. Two of the guards remained to guard the ship, while the others followed him at a distance to allow him to greet the crowd.

President Furgison approached him first.

"Emperor Ardesnal, it is indeed a pleasure to finally meet you in person," he said as he shook a very large hand.

"This is our host, Prince Azeere." The prince gives him a polite bow, then offers his hand in friendship. "Emperor Ardesnal, it is my honor to welcome to our planet. If you would please follow me, we will proceed to the main chamber."

"This is a beautiful island, Prince Azeere. I am inspired by the creativity of your people." He remarked as he walked with the others toward the building, admiring the scenery as they went. "This island was constructed with the help of many of our countries. We spent many years constructing this island and are all very proud of it."

"As you should be. Torani is a world of hundreds of islands, but nothing quite as unique as this."

The leaders all made their way into the main hall, where there was a table at least sixty feet long, with chairs surrounding its perimeter. There were two large chairs at each end. The emperor was led to one, and the prince chose the other. The prince then gestured for all to take a seat.

As the emperor sat, his guards took their stations at each side of their leader. The prince motioned for the servants to bring wine and water for the guests. After all of their glasses were filled, the prince rose and offered a toast.

"A toast to our new friends, who have most certainly saved us from certain death, and will now help us save our world." They all drank to a new future.

The emperor watched curiously then does the same. He looked at his glass curiously. "This is exquisite, what is it called?"

"It is called wine. It is made from crushed and fermented grapes," Azeere explained.

"Exquisite."

"We will have to send a few cases with you to Torani. It will please me to arrange it."

"That would be very nice. Now could we please get to the business at hand." The emperor stood to address the members of the Earth government. "Ladies and gentlemen, we have collected the weapons and poisons from your planet, which will be destroyed as soon as we reach open space. You have chosen this symbolic place for your World Headquarters, so the next step is for you to elect a world leader to guide your people into the future. How will you make this decision?"

"We will have a vote. This is how we decide important matters on our planet," Gene explained.

"Very well, then should we proceed?" the emperor asked, not knowing exactly what to expect.

Amazed at the emperor's haste, Gene rises to speak. "We have already narrowed it down to seven candidates by an earlier vote today. These candidates are." He reads the names from a card. "Prime Minister Mankle of South Africa, Chancellor Rowland of Switzerland, Chancellor Ono of Japan, President Perez of Peru, Prime Minister Melner of Canada, President Narkoff of Russia, and Prime Minister Aston of Australia. Now if all the members would please cast two votes. One for the new leader of Earth that will be put in the white box, and one for the Torani ambassador to be put in the blue box," Gene said, standing between the two boxes, with one hand on each of them. "Let's begin the process of a new world, gentlemen."

Gene returned to his seat to cast his votes. For several minutes, the members wrote down their selections and placed them in each of the boxes.

When they were finished two of the prince's guards, each taking one, carried them to a table at the side of the room. Two of the Earth members were chosen to count the votes. The final count was completed, and a card with the results was handed to the prince to announce the results. The prince looked at the cards, and then rose from his seat.

"Ladies and gentlemen. It is my pleasure to announce the first leader of the planet Earth.

Chancellor Martha Rowland of Switzerland. Congratulations Chancellor."

The surprised Chancellor rose to speak. "I would like to thank you all for the trust you have bestowed in me to hold this historic, and honored position. I assure you I will not let your trust be dishonored." She sat as the members applauded.

"Now for ambassador to the planet Torani." He reads the card and nods with approval." I think a better choice could not have been made. The ambassador to the planet Torani, is President Gene Furgison." The prince applauds, as the rest of the group give him a standing ovation. The Torani emperor stands and gives him a respectful bow. "Thank you all for this great honor. Of course I'm not sure how excited my wife and children will be," he joked.

"Thank you all," he finished and took his seat.

The Torani emperor rises, and the room gets very quiet. "Leaders of the planet Earth. Today you have taken the first step into the future of your planet. You are also one step closer to joining the ranks of the galaxy as an equal. By putting aside your differences and coming together as one planet, you have breached the first barrier to equality in this galaxy. I must also admit that your choice for ambassador was indeed a wise one." He gestures to Gene and applauds. "Now I must return to my vessel to prepare for the journey to my home planet. We also have many details to complete before we leave your planet. Thank you all for your hospitality." He rises and gives the members a respectful bow, then makes his way toward his ship with his guards at his heels. The members followed him to his ship and watched the ship fly off into the sky.

John walks over to Gene and whispers, "I guess we're gonna be shipmates."

"Very funny. My wife is going to divorce me," Gene said with a smile.

They both stood looking at the beautiful view in silence, thinking about their futures. They would be among the first group of humans to travel to another planet.

CHAPTER 27

—•●✹●•—

Planetwide Summary 3
November 8, 2020, 12:00

The fuel towers have started to reappear around the globe, each placed strategically for maximum effectiveness. Some of the planet is still without radio communications, so the reappearance of the towers to the planet created a panic in those locations. The only relief to the panicked populations was that no attack ships joined them.

The towers have all been set at their established locations. The largest of the continents requiring a greater number of towers to support them. The North American continent had a need for a total of four towers, one of which was placed on the mesa above the town of Parachute, Colorado.

The towers, all now setting on their assigned locations, are due to go online in one year's time. The work is just beginning and it will be a challenge to make the deadline. Even when the towers are powered up, there is no delivery system to distribute or receive the power. The scientists of the two planets are working feverishly to resolve this problem.

Most of the citizens of Parachute are at what is the new downtown. Today for the first day the church will hold services for the townspeople. They are still without a minister, but the people want their children to attend Sunday school, hoping to bring a sense of security back into the children's shattered lives.

After church, the residents gathered at the city park which lies on the bank of the Colorado River. With the huge Cottonwood trees, it was beautiful during the summer and fall, but with winter now having arrived, they are all bare but the people didn't let that cast a shadow on their day.

They were among friends and enjoying the sunshine, regardless of the dropping temperatures. They are all gathered today for the last barbeque of the year. A bandstand has been erected containing the equipment from Willis's collection. There is recorded music playing now, but the band made of a few volunteers will play soon. The barbecues are all hot, at least a hundred pounds of meat ready to be cooked, and fresh baked breads and pies lay on the tables, all brought by the ladies for the people to enjoy. This will most certainly be the last nice weather of the year, and they all intend to enjoy it.

The music is playing over the speakers set up alongside the stage. People are dancing, and the children are playing, it almost feels like nothing happened almost four weeks ago. The band climbed up on stage. Willis will play guitar, Alice, who has a beautiful voice will sing, and Bret has volunteered to play the drums.

"I need one more guitar player. Anyone want to volunteer?" Willis asked.

"I'll do it," Tim Vance said as he neared the stage. "I used to play in a band years ago."

The band warmed up for a short time then started to play. They played a variety of classic rock as well as Country music. This wasn't the normal group of Metal monsters they usually play for, so they kept it easy. All of a sudden three large ships flew over the park and flew toward the mesa where the tower has been placed. Bill walked up to the stage and asked Willis for the microphone.

"Well, folks," he started. "With people coming from the surrounding area as well as the galaxy, I guess we'll see the town grow a bit since they put the tower on the mountain," he said, pointing at the ships as they landed. "Actually I can't wait to meet one of them. But for now, let's just have some fun, eat some good food, and listen to some good music. He handed the microphone back to Willis, then he whispered something to him, Willis then turned to the band and said something to them. They all smiled and began to play David Bowie's "Space Oddity." Bill looked at Monica, who was wearing a big smile. There's no sense in letting a few aliens ruin a perfectly good day.

For the next few days, tractor trailers full of supplies began to roll into town. These trucks carried bulldozers, loaders, dump trucks, everything you would need to build a new town.

After clearing the burned homes from the land, they brought construction trailers and mobile laboratories. They then brought in a hundred mobile homes to house the workers, and fenced off a large section for the Torani to live in. I guess they thought the huge aliens needed to be protected from the puny humans. The tower has created new Boom Town on Battlement Mesa. It's ironic that the town started the same in the quest for energy from shale oil over thirty years ago.

Bill and Willis have drove down the mountain to see what was going on, and were now standing by the truck watching the people run around like a bunch of ants on an anthill. They all have a job to do and they were very busy doing it. On the side of the office was a sign. Help Wanted, Laborers Needed. Willis looked at his dad. "What do you think?" Willis asked as he read the sign.

"Well, I'm not interested, but your young, and with this going to become the new energy source, it would be a great idea for someone your age. Plus, if you start now, you'll learn it from the ground up and you'll be way ahead of the curve in the future."

"Yea, plus I get to meet some aliens," he said, smiling as he did.

"Just be thankful they're the friendly ones."

"Yea that first bunch sucked." They both laughed.

"Go in and check it out. See what they've got to offer. It sure can't hurt to try. I'm going over to the mayor's office, I'll be back in half an hour."

"Okay, I'll see you when you get back."

Willis went into the office to check on a job, while his dad jumped into the truck and drove off. He wasn't as interested in the job as he was in the aliens. He really wanted to see them.

The new Earth ambassador is sitting in his office deep within the White House bunker, when there is a knock at his door. Then a familiar head stuck inside.

"John to what do I owe the pleasure, and believe me it's usually not a pleasure when you come through my door," he said smiling.

"Gene, I'm hurt," he said, smiling back at him. "I've been thinking about our little journey."

"Little," Gene replied sarcastically.

"Yea, right. Anyway, Horace is going to be busy heading up the research on the collectors needed to receive the power from the towers, so he won't be going to Torani for some time. Brad is going to be the new head of NASA, so I would like to ask Ben Murphy to come along. That is if he's still alive, I haven't talked to him since the attack."

"That sounds great, but why are you asking me, it's your show?"

"I need a favor. I need a helicopter and a pilot, to fly to Kitt Peak and see if I can find him."

"That's all." He was relieved that it was all he wanted. "You got it, I'll set it up. When do you want to leave?"

"Today."

"Not to change the subject John, but who is going to be your third choice?"

"She's a Russian Astrophysicist. Olga Krishkoff. She's at the top of her field."

"I know her, she's top of the line in more ways than one," Gene said, winking at his friend.

"That doesn't hurt either, but she is the best on the planet at her job. Besides, it will give Marsha someone to talk to."

"Marsha isn't coming," Gene said sadly.

"She really doesn't want to go?"

"She wants absolutely no part of it. The kids would love to go live with the aliens, but she'll have no part of it. I can travel between planets when I get a chance. My parents have a ranch in Texas, so she can stay with them," Gene explained sadly. "Oh and by the way John, come Monday Elsa will have my job. By unanimous decision she has been elected as the new leader of the American District, as we've decided to call it."

"American District. I like it, and you couldn't have made a better choice for the best person to take care of it in my opinion. Now, about that chopper."

"I'll get right on it."

Gene picked up the phone and pointed at it humorously, as he began to talk to the captain at the airbase he gave John a salute, and John walked out the door headed to the base. It was time to find Ben Murphy.

Horace Hunt is the new district science director and has decided to use the Area 51 base in Nevada as the site to do the research on the power amplifiers and collectors. The base is absolutely undamaged because of its remote location, as well as being well hidden. It is also one of the best research labs on the planet.

Horace and his researchers are standing the tarmac of the base waiting for the Torani scientists to arrive. The transport shuttle came in low over the mountain that disguises the lab, and lands fifty yards away on the tarmac in front of them. The engines shut down, the door opens, and four very large Torani scientists exit the craft. As they approach Horace and his men, one of them steps to the front of the group and speaks.

"I am Engineer Mock of the Torani vessel, Jayden. These are my assistants."

Horace greets them with a short bow, which he discovered in Dubai was the correct greeting. "It's good to meet you, Engineer Mock. I am Horace Hunt and these are my colleagues. If you would all follow me, I will show you our laboratory and living quarters."

"What of our equipment?" Mock asked.

"I will have transportation brought here to transport it. If you would like you can leave your men here to help load it onto the truck."

"Very well. I will leave two of my men, the other will come with us."

Horace left two of the scientists to help load the Torani equipment. The others then loaded into the truck and drove to the underground lab. For Horace it was the first day, of what will soon be his very interesting future.

Bill is in Battlement Mesa at the construction site, and has been watching the unstoppable action going on around, as well as above him for over an hour. The Torani are using small shuttles to ferry the workers to the top of the mesa. He turns when he hears Willis come up behind him.

"So what's the verdict?" he asked his excited son.

"They want people to help erect the towers' emitters, which will send the power out of the station to some kind of collectors. The Torani scientists will be in charge of adapting the towers. This guy knows absolutely nothing about the technology, and we aren't expected to either. All they want now is laborers to help build the town, then eventually help build the infrastructure for the towers to relay the power. Then I guess we are going to help build the collector stations also. From what I'm guessing, this guy knows about as much as I do right now. The good thing is that they are providing housing, food, and some kind of credits that will be used in the future for money. Money has gone right out the window from here on out."

"Yea, right now money is about as useful as tits on a boar hog," Bill replied. "So do you have a job?"

"Yea, we start in a week. The aliens have to get the towers anchored before we can start. Get this. They are going to shuttle us up to the job on one of their shuttles. Cool huh," he said with a huge smile.

"Let's head for home," his dad said. "I told Monica we would be home for lunch. She's going to barbeque some steaks for us."

"Okay, but can we stop by Bret's, I want to get him over here quick. They are only taking so many guys from this area. They have to spread the work throughout the valley. Plus, I want to be able to at least work with someone I know."

"No problem."

They stopped by Bret's trailer to let him know about the job, then went home to their valley for a steak and a cold beer for lunch. "Life is good."

John is driving up the twisting road to the observatory in a National Guard Jeep. When you arrive in the presidential helicopter, they give you anything you want, and he always loved driving these old Jeeps. He eventually pulled up at the bottom of the huge Telescope and went inside.

"Ben, are you here?" He hollered when he was inside. "Ben, Its John. John Alistair."

He heard footsteps, then suddenly Ben came out of a small office. He grabbed John and gave him a big hug.

"Hi, Ben," John said, surprised. "A handshake would have worked."

"How the hell are ya John. You're the last person on the planet I expected to see. Good to see ya man, and I'm real glad you survived."

"You too Ben. I guess they didn't consider your telescope a threat huh."

"I guess not, thank god. I sat here and watched the most incredible show you could imagine. There were things coming out of the moon like a disco ball. Spaceships were blasting other spaceships. Absolutely mindblowing. So what brings you to my mountain, John?" he asked with a very curious look. "I know you didn't come all the way up here just to say hi."

"A proposition, or should I say a job offer," he said, raising his eyebrows.

"I'm afraid to ask," Ben said with his head cocked back.

"I want you to come with me to another planet."

Ben looked at him and sat down in a chair, absolutely confounded by what he has just heard. "Exactly what have you been up to for the last few weeks John?"

"The Torani, which is the alien race that saved our asses."

"Yea, I heard on the broadcasts." Ben interrupted.

"Anyway, as I was saying. I conned the Torani into taking three of our scientists to their planet, to study their solar system, as well as their space craft's. I am allowed to take two scientists with me."

"Let me guess. You conned the aliens into a poker game, and this was in the pot," he joked.

"Close enough," John answered with a smile.

"Who's the other one?"

"Olga Krishkoff. You know her?"

"Yea, she's like Miss Russia, with an astrophysics degree," he answered while making the curves of a woman with his hands.

"So I've been told."

"I'm in buddy. I wouldn't miss this for anything."

"Get your stuff, were out of here in ten minutes."

"I'll be ready in five."

"I've got the president's ride waiting for us at the guard station."

"Ah, pimpin', I like it," Ben said, adjusting the brim on his imaginary hat. He was ready in four minutes. "Ready to fly?"

"Let's roll."

As the two men got into the Jeep, Ben stopped and took one more look at the observatory, then they left on their way to fly off to another planet and a new life, filled with the unknown.

Chapter 28

---•◦❀◦•---

Johnson Space Center, Houston
November 12, 2020, 12:00

Air Force One is now sitting on the tarmac at Johnson. Next to the large airplane is the Torani shuttle that will take the Earth men to the Empress for their trip to Torani. At the bottom of the ramp leading into the shuttle stands the group that is going to join the emperor on his vessel. The travelers are saying their good-byes to their friends, and Gene's ex–cabinet members are all lined up to shake the hand of the new ambassador as he leaves for the most important job of his life. He started with the new American governor, Elsa Ault.

"Elsa, I don't know what I'll do without you to do all my work for me," he said as he shook her hand, then gave her a big hug.

"I'm sure you'll manage. You can find a tiny Torani woman to be your new slave," she jokingly replied.

"I'm not sure there's such a thing as a tiny Torani, but I'll look for one," he said with a big smile. "You, gentlemen, take care of this little lady, and tell Horace good-bye for me."

"They have set up transmitters for communication between the two planets so we can stay in touch, and if you have any problems, just contact Brad Meyer here at NASA. He's running the show here now, so he's your man to pull of the miracles from here on out. All right everyone. I really hate long good-byes so I'm going to say so long for now, and I'll be in touch." Gene stood up straight and saluted his faithful advisors, then walked up the ramp into the shuttle.

John and Brad are standing with the other group containing the other two scientists. Ben is busy beginning the flirting with Olga, who is politely ignoring his advances. "I will contact you as soon as we get settled Brad.

I'll send you a message at least once a month. I wouldn't want you to get lonely," he joked as he shook his old friend's hand. "It's all yours now, so take care of her," he added, pointing toward the Center.

"You know I will. I've been waiting for you to retire for some time now so I could get my hands on her," he said smiling. "I was beginning to think you'd have to die before it would happen."

"It's time for us to go Brad, take care." After saying good-bye to his friend, John walked over to Ben and Olga. "So are you two ready for this?"

"I've been waiting for this my entire life," Olga replied. "I just never thought it would happen."

"How about you Ben?"

"Beam me up, Scotty," he said with a smile.

"Then let's do this, people."

The three scientists climbed the ramp behind the new ambassador, with the Torani guards bringing up the rear. The group all stopped momentarily to take one last look at their planet before they began the greatest adventure of their lives, then boarded the shuttle to fly into their futures. John recognizes the importance of leaving Earth from this location, as he headed for the stars.

The heavy equipment is still busy clearing what is left of the destroyed town of Battlement Mesa, in order to make way for its new residents. They make quick work of it as they push it into piles for it to be loaded into trucks, then hauled to the pit burying the ashes of the dead.

Willis and Brad pull up in front of the superintendent's office ready for their first day of work. He is busy talking to one of the truck drivers, so they wait for him to finish.

"What can I do for you, gentlemen?" their new boss asked curiously.

"We were told to report here to start work today," Willis said, extending his hand. "I'm Willis, and this is Brad."

"Bob's the name. Bob Schrader," he replied, shaking their hands.

"You two grab a couple of shovels and help those loaders get this mess cleaned up. That will be your job for the next couple of days." "You got it, Bob. Thanks," Willis said.

"Well, this is pretty much the same thing we've been doing for the last month, only now we have heavy equipment to help," Bret said.

Overhead the shuttles were busy ferrying materials to the top of the mesa for the tower. Willis looked at Brad and smiled. "I can't wait to get onto one of those things," he said. They both watched the shuttle fly to the top of the mesa, then went about their task of helping to clear the rubble for the new town.

Except for a brief tour of the Empress, the group of travelers spent most of their time in their quarters. Beyond the meals they ate with the emperor, they were kept away the rest of the crew. In a way it has been a strange trip.

Today they are entering Torani space. The Torani planet is in view from the windows of the observation deck, and they stood admiring the beauty of the large blue planet. In many ways it is much like Earth, only with hundreds of small islands instead of large continents. The emperor entered the large room and noticed the wonder of his guests.

"Well, my friends, what do you think of our planet. It's much like yours is it not."

"It is much like ours," John replied. "Are the oceans salt water like ours?"

"Yes. The same as your planet we have salt water seas, surrounding what we call territories."

"I noticed your two moons," Ben said. "Doesn't that create a drastic effect on the seas?"

"Yes, it does. We have quite large tidal surges compared to your planet, which is why all territories have very large sea walls on their shores."

"Is this the only habitable planet in your system?" Olga asked.

"It is the only habitable planet, but we have a settlement on another for the mining of the materials needed to build ships and power our planet."

"Emperor, what is the possibility of touring one of your shipyards or orbital stations?" John asked.

"Mister Alistair, you are truly a curious man. All in good time, my friends. First, we will get you settled at our university, where you will be closer to your labs. I will allow a short tour of our fleet station when we arrive, but the shipyards are very dangerous places, so I will have to plan that at a later date," the emperor said, patting him on the back with his huge hand.

"Return to your quarters and gather your things, we will be docking soon. A member of the crew will come and get you when it is time to leave the vessel. After a short tour of the Station, you will be shuttled to the surface, where I will meet you at a later time. Enjoy your tour, my friends."

The emperor left them on the observation deck, where the earthlings all looked at each other excitedly. It will be their first day on another planet, which is something every one of them has waited their entire lives for.

"Well, here we go, kids," Ben said. "Were going to Disneyland," he added comically.

"All right, let's get this show on the road. I'll see you when they come and get us," John said.

They all exited the observation deck together, en route to their quarters to get ready for their first day on a new planet, all of them excited about the months to come.

Horace is standing at one of the computer terminals with the Torani scientists. They are showing him a diagram of the collector they will be building.

"So what you're telling me is that the collectors are to be a titanium shell with a polymer insulator, covered by solid gold to collect the energy," Horace asked curiously.

"Yes, and once it is collected, it is fed through a series of complicated microprocessors to convert it into useable currents. Then the currents will then be transferred to your power stations for use in designated areas. Once we have built the facilities to manufacture miniaturized collectors, there will be no need for these power stations. The current will simply be pulled from the atmosphere," Talor explained.

"Why can't we simply produce the miniature collectors in the first place?" Horace asked.

"Your planet hasn't the ability to produce them at this time. We must build facilities to produce the components to create the collectors. There is no other way we can accomplish the task at this time," Talor added.

"Then we need to build hundreds of these collector stations to tie into the planet's infrastructure to start with. It seems to me that this will take years to accomplish," Horace states.

"Yes, it will be a very timely process Mr. Hunt, but once the stations are constructed it will go much faster."

"Once we complete these stages, what is there to insure these towers will continue to produce power. It can't be an infinite source. What exactly is their power source?"

"That is not for your people to know at this point. When we feel you are responsible enough to use it wisely, we will answer that question," Talor explained in a superior tone.

Horace nods in approval, understanding that he is totally at the mercy of the Torani to release whatever information they wanted. For the time being he would have to accept the circumstances and work as best he can to make the system work.

CHAPTER 29

---·•❀•·---

Planet Torani, Capital City, Carista
November 20, 2020

It has been three days since the earthlings landed on Torani, and the ambassador is in his quarters and has begun to meet the other members of the emperor's staff. It's not much different from being president, but somehow he feels like a fish out of water. Gene is comforted by the easygoing demeanor of the Torani diplomats and easily falls into his new position as ambassador.

After his meetings Gene decided to go out and tour the city. The Architecture of the planet is quite unique. The structures are all either round or elongated, with smaller ones stacked on top the others. Not a single sharp edge or corner is seen except the sharp spires on the top of each structure. These spires, which are the power collectors for all the individual structures, pull energy from the atmosphere by some unknown technology.

These structures are also built without a single seam being apparent anywhere, not even where they meet the ground. It's as if they grew from the surface of the planet, not built by the hands of the inhabitants. Strange. All of the structures are a spotless white, giving the city an aura of cleanliness and peacefulness.

The waterfront is protected by a huge sea wall to protect the cities from the planet's large tides created by the two moons that orbit it. At fifty feet high, and the same as everything else, not a single seam in its entire length of hundreds of miles. Every island on the planet is surrounded by one of these walls to protect them from thirty foot tides, and the severe storms that the endless sea can produce. With two moons, you can have a severe gravitational pull on the planet's seas, creating these unbelievable tides.

179

Grass, trees, and shrubs, are growing in every available spot of open ground that bring bright colors to the spotless white city. The grasses which are the brightest turquoise color you've ever seen, and actually the same color as the Torani's eyes, are all neatly mowed and trimmed, bordered in also seamless curbs. The curious trees, some of which are hundreds of feet tall, are similar to mushrooms in shape with no leaves at all. They vary in color from deep reds, golds, to vibrant blues like something out of a fairy tale. The shrubs all match their tall cousins in color and appearance.

Riding the Torani seas, are huge white ships with gold sails to catch the winds. The ships like the structures appear to be one solid piece with the masts seeming to be growing out of their decks. The sails are a shimmering gold that almost seems to change color in the Torani sun. They are absolutely amazing, and beautiful to watch.

Occasionally you may see what are similar to Earth's dolphins swimming alongside the ships. These Torani Dolphins are spectacular with their twenty-foot-long bodies, and a single fin down their back that runs the length of its body. They are also quite ominous, because of a threefoot snout lined with razor sharp teeth.

Torani is a strange but beautiful planet, and so far Gene Furgison has only seen a small part of one city. He plans to venture out into the countryside to witness its wonder when he can get a free day to travel the inner part of the island.

John, and his team of scientists, have been given quarters on the edge of the university, which is located on the outskirts of the city. Their group has also toured the islands spectacular sights, but have a greater interest in their magnificent lab which is filled with the finest equipment they have ever encountered. The team has spent the last few days familiarizing themselves with this equipment that they will be using in their studies. The Torani may speak English, but all the systems are in the Torani language so they have been trying to learn the language, but after several days of stumbling through the task, their teachers decided that it would be easier to change their computers to English instead.

The junior scientist assigned to help them adapt to their surroundings, as well as their assimilation into the science center, is called Cloric. He has been their savior on this new planet. Cloric entered the lab, where the three newcomers were still studying the Torani technology.

"Ah, Mr. Cloric," Ben said as he rose to greet him. "We were wondering if we could take another little tour of your city?" he asked, putting his arm around the shoulder of the young but still very large Torani.

"I see no reason that would be a problem, but I had better check with my superiors first," he said, pulling away from the earthling's grasp. Apparently they were uncomfortable with Ben's type of friendliness.

Cloric leaves the room and returns a few minutes later. "My superiors have approved your request. You are free to travel the capitol at your leisure."

They left the center and walked through the streets of Carista watching the strange new people, and enjoying the magnificent Architecture as well as the scenery.

"Mr. Cloric, how is it that your people speak our language so well?" Ben asked curiously.

"We have been monitoring the broadcasts from your planet for almost seventy years. I guess it started as a curiosity, then our children started to pick it up quite quickly. It started as what you would call fad, and after many years it seemed that the children could speak it quite well. Then eventually the children grew up. It has become our main language, as well as most of the galaxy's language because of its ease to learn."

"What do you mean by, across the galaxy?" Ben asked. "Exactly how many inhabited planets are there in this galaxy?"

"There are ten planet systems with secondary outposts on their nearby moons."

"Are they friendly," John asked.

"Not all are friendly. There are two species out of eight that are sometimes troublesome. The Boral, which are a humanoid, cyborg hybrid. And the Antarian are an insectoid species. These two species have been known to attack vessels traveling through their systems, so we have learned to avoid them," he said as he noticed the very confused expression on Ben's face. "Do you not believe me, Ben Murphy?"

"Oh, I believe you, Cloric. It's just that I'm finally getting used to huge gold aliens, and now I'm trying to visualize the cyborgs, and huge ant people," he said, shaking his head.

John laughed loudly, while Olga shook her head shamefully.

"Actually they are more like your Earth roaches."

"You asked," John said, looking at Ben and laughing.

They walked through the streets of the city which were a light gold almost yellow color. As they passed a female Torani she stopped and watched the humans walk by curiously. She had the same golden skin and blue eyes, but had large firm breasts and her white mane went all the way to the top of her hips, accentuating her beauty. Ben elbowed John and gave him the Groucho eyebrows. John Laughed, and Olga rolled her eyes and walked away down the street in disgust.

"Cloric I've noticed almost no differences in your people. The skin color and eye color, along with the hair are all the same," Olga said cautiously.

"Yes, we are a very pure race genetically. You are among one of the select few races that have even been allowed on the surface of our planet. The galaxy's delegates rarely get any closer than the Torani Space Center, which is used for the meetings and trade negotiations. We would never consider crossbreeding with another race as you humans do. We strive to remain a pure race."

"I'm not sure how to take that," Ben said.

"I mean no disrespect Ben Murphy, but humans have been breeding with other species since the Neanderthal," Cloric clarified.

"Only ones like Ben," Olga said.

"Ouch," Ben said, feigning hurt.

"That's correct Cloric, but had the Neanderthals not done so, we wouldn't be here today," John said.

"Yea, we'd all still be like Ben," Olga added sarcastically.

They all laughed. Even Cloric got that joke and laughed with them.

"Oh, you can laugh?" Ben asked, looking at Cloric.

"Yes, we do like a good joke, as you call them. I will try not to be so serious in the future Ben Murphy. Would you all like some food and drink?" he asked, motioning to a café.

"Sure," they all answered together.

They walked across the crowded street to the quaint little café and Cloric led them to an outdoor table. "Please sit and I will order some Torani dishes and refreshments." Cloric motioned to a table.

They sat and talked while the Torani patrons stared curiously at them and whispered.

"I don't think they are used to seeing humans," John said.

"Not yet," Ben replied.

"Why are all of your building built so smooth and round," Olga asked.

"As you may have noticed even the trees on this planet are smooth and round. This planet suffers from very severe storms quite often, so like nature we create smooth surfaces for less wind resistance. When you go into the interior of the island you see the structures begin to be more random in their shapes," he explained.

"Interesting," Olga replied. "I would like to tour the interior one day."

"What is the chance of us touring one of the shipyards, Cloric? We are all very interested in the Torani vessels and their propulsion systems. We are all space scientists and are intrigued in your advanced capabilities." John asked the question knowing his request would be refused, but he wanted to start the process somewhere.

"That, my friends, will be an entirely different matter. We cannot let your planet be corrupted by our advanced technologies. They are capable of terrible destruction if not used correctly, and there are also galactic laws forbidding any transfer of technology to developing societies." Cloric warned.

"The day the Corisole came to our planet it permanently changed the natural evolution of our species," John said forcefully.

"I agree," Olga said. "We have had your technologies thrust upon us in the most ferocious way possible. I believe we should be able to evolve, so to speak, in order to better protect ourselves in the future. Our planet is weakened severely, and I'm sure that every planet in the galaxy now knows that."

"Cloric we are not asking you to give us the technology, we would simply like to explore the physics, so we can peruse our assimilation into the galactic family," John stated as respectfully as possible.

"I do understand your request as well as your desire. I will discuss it with my superiors and try to schedule a tour."

"That's all we ask," John said.

With the business out of the way, they all sat enjoying the Café's cuisine of very unique dishes and refreshments. Ben is still trying to get Cloric to laugh more, but it's hard to do when Cloric just doesn't get the jokes.

After touring the city, Ambassador Furgison spent the day in numerous meetings with the emperor, as well as his advisors. The next meeting has caught the Earth ambassador's interest. This meeting is with the Corisole ambassador. The ambassador has been held in custody since the invasion of Earth, and the emperor is also eager for this meeting.

"Guards, bring the Corisole ambassador Kaloren to these chambers," the emperor orders.

The guards left the chambers to collect the Corisole ambassador from his cell.

"Emperor, where do you stand with the planet Corisole?" Gene asked.

"The leaders of Corisole will all be treated as criminals. Every member of the leadership had to have knowledge of the plan to take your planet, and they have all broken one law that can never be broken in this galaxy. Not only have they broken this law, but they have done it in the vilest fashion imaginable. For hundreds of years there were systems that wished to enter the Sol System and claim it for their own, but the Torani, along with a majority of the other planets in this galaxy, created the Galactic Alliance to protect planets like yours. This Alliance passed many laws protecting, not only your planet, but every planet in this galaxy. The most recent of these laws is the Treaty of 12:7:141, which was created by the Alliance to protect your planet from future contact with any Alliance planets until your planet was able to at least travel freely within your own system. For the past two hundred years, many systems in the galaxy have visited your planet at will, which endangered your natural evolution, so the treaty was enacted to put a halt to these practices."

The guards brought the Corisole ambassador into the chamber in irons and sat him down at the center of the room. Gene was absolutely speechless. Sitting in front of him was the living image what of every alien sighting or abduction victims have claimed to have seen. The ambassador was a tiny gray-green alien with large black eyes and no nose or ears to speak of, along with thin fingers dangling from his hands. "I'll be dammed, Roswell was real." He thought to himself.

"Ambassador Kaloren, I would like you to meet one of the humans your planet tried to exterminate. This is Ambassador Furgison from the planet Earth," the emperor stated loudly.

The Corisole ambassador squirmed as if he was trying to disappear into his chair.

"We have the remaining three commanders of the Corisole fleet, as well as all of their crewmen in our prison as we speak, and you will soon join them. Your Supreme Leader as well as all of his staff are all fugitives and will soon also be apprehended. We are waiting at this time, for a new leader to be appointed to your planet so we can continue the legal process. "If your planet doesn't abide by galactic law and turn these criminals over to the Alliance, it will have sanctions placed against it that haven't been seen since the Antarian invasion of Velnor one hundred years ago. I will give you ten days to have your new leaders turn over the fugitives, or these sanctions will be put in to play. Ambassador, you know your planet cannot survive with these sanctions, so you will persuade them to comply with the Alliances demands if you truly care for the wellbeing of your people."

"Now, Ambassador, I will also say that you know very well the punishment for these crimes, and there is no way for you to escape your punishment. But for the sake of your planet only, I am giving you these next ten days to make them understand what unsteady ground they all stand on. That will be all. Guards, take him back to his cell and give him access to communications for two hours each day."

The guards escorted the ambassador from the chamber. Gene can't believe what he has just seen. How could his government have withheld information from him that could have saved five-billion lives? Unbelievable.

"Emperor, my people have been claiming all sorts of things, including brutal abductions at the hands of beings whose descriptions match the Corisole exactly. And up until five minutes ago, I didn't believe the abduction stories were true. Evidently they haven't obeyed the treaty since it was established," Gene said, shocked by the truth. "I hate to admit it, but the governments of the planet hold a part of the responsibility for this attack. They withheld the truth about the Corisole incursions to our planet because it would create fear within the population. Well, Emperor, sometimes it's good to be afraid." The emperor agreed with a nod. Then the two men rose and left the chamber for their offices.

CHAPTER 30

---•◦❈◦•---

Battlement Mesa, Colorado
November 25, 2020, 07:00

Willis has been working on the Battlement project for almost a two weeks now, and is up early getting some breakfast before work, when his dad comes into the house with the dog.

"How you doing this morning?" Willis asked, as he reached down to pet Sassy.

"Good, but it's getting dam cold in the mornings. Snow's gonna start falling any day."

"I hope not. We're supposed to start working on top of the mesa today. They finally have the towers anchored."

"You better dress warm. It's even colder up there."

"I'm on top of it, Dad. Today I get to ride in one of those shuttles. I've been waiting for a week for this day." The smile on Willis's face was huge.

"They are all living in Battlement now, aren't they?"

"Not yet. We finished fencing off their area yesterday, then the craziest thing happened. They rolled out what looked like a huge round mat on the ground, pushed a button, and poof, instant igloo, weirdest thing I've ever seen. Actually, so are the aliens. I mean Torani—we're not supposed to call them aliens. Plus, I don't think I would want to piss one of them off."

"Why not?" Bill asked, now very interested.

"Because they're huge and mean looking. The Torani are over sevenfoot-tall, with gold skin and these blue eyes that make you feel like they're looking right through you. They do have the coolest beard I've ever seen though, it's pure white like their long hair that runs down the back of their necks, and spiked like a Punk Rocker. They actually look really cool when you think about it. Take me to work and I'll show you one."

"Punk Rocker aliens huh, I gotta see this."

After their breakfast they grabbed their coats and headed for Battlement. When they arrived at the new town, Bill thought it was incredible how much the town has changed in two weeks. All evidence of the destruction has been cleared, and a hundred new trailers now stand where the old ones were burned to the ground.

"Where did they get all those trailers?" Bill asked.

"You know the government, if they need something they'll find it," Willis replied. "Pull over there," he said, pointing at a group of people standing by one of the shuttles.

"Holy shit. They are big aren't they," Bill said as he spotted one of the aliens.

"I told ya so."

Every hair on Sassy's body stood straight up, and she started growling at a creature she has never seen before. They both looked at her and laughed.

"All right, Dad, I gotta go to work," he said, pointing at the ship.

"Tell them you'll pass on the probing," Bill said, smiling.

"You can count on it."

"Be careful up there," he cautioned as his son walked away.

Willis turned and waved, then walked over to the shuttle, where Bret was already waiting for him. Then they both climbed into the shuttle with big grins on their faces. Bill started up the truck, and headed down toward Parachute with the dog who looked like she had just been electrocuted.

Once on board Willis sat down next to Bret. "So you got any idea what we're going to be doing today?" he asked.

"I talked to Bob and he said we would be doing pretty much the same thing. They moved all the equipment up to the top to clear the land for the facility."

"All right, guys!" Bob hollered to quiet the crew. "This is Dorahk. Dorahk is in charge of everything on the top of the mountain. If he tells you to do something you do it. Understand?" They all nodded in agreement. Then Bob continued. "We are going to clear the top of the mountain to get ready for the foundations. Does anyone know how to read blueprints?"

Willis raised his hand. "I do," he said.

"Willis, right?"

"Yea, that's right."

"You can read blueprints?"

"Been doing it most of my life."

"Okay. I want you in the trailer studying those prints. We start setting footings tomorrow, and Dorahk will need someone to help run the show up there."

"Question?" Willis said with his hand raised. "What are we planning to use for concrete?"

"We spent the last week repairing the plant in Rifle," Bob answered.

"Can I chose an assistant to help me?"

"Yea sure," Bob said.

"Want the job?" he asked Bret.

"You bet. It beats the hell out of running a shovel."

"Get on those prints as soon as we land Willis, it's going to get crazy up here in the next few days."

After they landed on the mesa, the first day of the tower project began. Dorahk explained to the men what he wanted the men to do, and they did it without question. They were all happy to have a purpose again, and repowering the planet was a very important job.

Bill pulled the truck up in front of Alex and Doves house, where Alex was standing outside. Bill and Sassy got out of the truck and walked over to where Alex was standing.

"Morning Alex."

"Good morning to you two," he replied as he petted the dog, who is still a little puffed up. "What's her problem?"

"She saw an alien," Bill answered, laughing as he said it. "She didn't know what to make of it."

"I heard they were quite a sight. Come on in and have a cup of coffee."

They all went into the house where Dove was cleaning up after breakfast. "Want some coffee?" she asked as she turned around. "What's the matter with her?" she asked curiously.

"Saw an alien," Alex answered for Bill.

"Okay," she said, slightly confused.

"You guys should see them. I saw them when I dropped Willis off at work." Bill explained in detail what they looked like to the very interested pair.

"They're working on Thanksgiving?" Dove asked.

"I don't think the aliens know what a pilgrim is," he joked.

"So Willis is working with the aliens?" she asked uncomfortably.

"Yea. The work is finished at Battlement, so they moved up on the mountain to start the work on the tower today. He got his first ride in one of their spaceships. He was grinning ear to ear when he got in it."

"Most people would be afraid," she said with a worried-mom expression.

"Yea most, but he's like me. You know, beam me up. Well, thanks for the coffee, and I've got to run. I just wanted to stop really quick and see what was going on. I promised I would take Monica into Rifle today. They scavenged everything they could out of the stores in town and put it in a hangar at the airport, so we're going to go check it out."

"It's all free?" she asked.

"It's free if you really need stuff, but if you have things you don't need to trade for it, they really appreciate it. It helps to keep it stocked, and they can help more people that way. All right, me and the Chia Pet are out of here. You two take care."

The two wanderers headed for the truck to begin the rest of the day's travels. They had a lot to do today and had to keep moving.

Chapter 31

---•●✷●•---

Planet Torani Emperor's Chambers
December 4, 2020

The leaders of the planet Corisole have been turned over to the Alliance and are now in the Torani Detention Center. The people of the planet greatly feared retribution that would fall upon the people of the planet if they did not agree with the Alliance demands, so they captured the leaders and turned them over to Alliance security. The emperor and the entire Torani Council are all in the council chambers to file charges against the criminals. Ambassador Furgison is also in attendance as a witness if needed.

The Supreme Leader as well as his council are led into the chambers to face the consequences of their act. The Supreme Leader has been left with the dignity of wearing his royal robes throughout the proceedings, which are expected to last at least a month.

The Earth ambassador watches with anger, as the beings that are responsible for the death and destruction on his planet are led to the guarded section below and seated. Gene would like to do a little anal probing of his own right now, he thinks to himself with a hidden smile. It would be sweet revenge. Gene shakes the disturbed thought from his mind and returns to the moment.

"Leaders of the planet Torani." The emperor starts to bring the room to order. "We are here today to bring charges against all those involved in the S-3 invasion. The question of guilt has already been answered, but since we live in a civilized galaxy charges will be formally filed against all those involved, followed by a trial."

"There have been two crimes committed in this case. The first being the blatant disregard for the Treaty of 12:7:141, which if found guilty carries a sentence of twenty-five years' hard labor in the Triomicium mines on our sixth planet Harken. The second crime of genocide against a peaceful planet carries a sentence of death. These charges will be weighed against all involved, including the crewmembers of all vessels involved. I ask you now to plead to these crimes."

The chamber remained silent as none chose to plead to the crimes. Already aware of their fate, they know that this hearing is only a formality, and the end result is already known to all.

"I will take your silence to be a not guilty plea, so we will continue this matter in thirty days from today at the Galactic Alliance Station. Before we adjourn today I would like you to meet Ambassador Furgison of the planet Earth. You should be informed that he will personally testifying at the trial if needed, to verify the extent of your brutality. This hearing is now adjourned. Guards, remove the prisoners and return them to their cells."

The leaders of the Corisole all rise and leave the room surrounded by the guards. Then the Torani Council also rose and silently left the chamber. The ambassador remained in the chamber to talk with the emperor.

"So those are the men responsible for five-billion deaths on my planet," Gene said angrily. "I know it sounds rash, but I can't wait to see them all executed. How many defendants are there in all?"

"There are almost seven hundred in all. There are one hundred leaders and Command officers, and almost six-hundred crewmen," the emperor stated.

"It's not a very even trade is it?" Gene replied.

"No, it is not, my friend," he said sympathetically.

The two men then rose and left the chambers.

CHAPTER 32

— • ❀ • —

Area 51, Nevada Desert
December 25, 2020

Horace and his crew of four scientists are in the lab along with now five Torani researchers. They have all worked very hard over the last month to create the prototypes for the power emitters and collectors, as it has been decided to call them. The power emitters are of a very strange configuration to the Earth scientists, as are the collectors. The emitters resemble a large ribbed clamshell, eight feet in diameter, with golden fingers extending twelve inches from the end of each rib. The collectors are similar, but much smaller at only four feet in diameter.

Engineer Mock and Mr. Modar have spent the last month building a miniature fuel tower for the test that is about to occur. After a very busy month, they are finally ready to test the fruit of their labors. If this test is successful, they will be ready to start the production of larger versions of the two.

They have also assembled a transformer system that is identical to the ones used at the power stations scattered around the world. They have hooked up an array of large spotlights to test the power, which should be quite sufficient for the test.

"Are we ready to test the system?" Horace asked, as he admired the golden shells.

Mr. Talor confers with Mock and his assistants, and returns to where Horace is standing. "Yes, Mr. Hunt. It appears that we are ready."

The collector is one thousand yards away, resting on the tarmac in its cradle next to the transformer. The lights are spread across the wide runway connected by heavy cables. The emitter is in its cradle next to the small tower also connected by a heavy cable to handle the current. The extraordinary thing is that they are both pointed at the sky.

"Shouldn't they be facing each other?" Horace asked.

Mock hears the question and comes over to answer it. "Let me explain Mr. Hunt. The emitter array directs the energy directly into the atmosphere, eliminating the need for millions of miles of wires to carry it. It is then collected directly from the atmosphere and transferred to the transformer. Once it is perfected, the collectors will be as small as a Pit bug."

"Pit bug?" Dan asked curiously.

"Never mind," Horace said.

Mock walked over and activated the tower, which made only the faintest humming sound. "Are you ready, gentlemen?" Mock asked his technicians.

"We are ready, sir."

Mock tripped the circuit breaker on the emitter, and a second later the lights across the runway lit up brilliantly. Horace walked over to the emitter, absolutely amazed at what he is seeing.

"Is it safe?" he asked.

"Absolutely," Talor said as he waved his large hand over the top of it. "It simply saturates the atmosphere with an energy force that is absolutely harmless. The collectors then draw in the energy and change it to useable power.

"Amazing," Horace said as he rested his hand on the emitter. "Congratulations, gentlemen, we've done it. Merry Christmas, gentlemen."

Horace shook his team's hands gratefully, then turned to the Torani crew to do the same but stops himself, and bows respectfully. Now they can construct the large versions of the emitters for use on the towers, as well as the collectors for the stations around the world.

The family is at Dove and Alex's house for the Holiday. The small town is decorated with any Christmas lights they could find, to help the children deal with their new lives. The church also has a hay ride going around the town for anyone that wants to enjoy it, hoping to add to the Christmas spirit.

Willis is sitting on the couch with Alice, trying to help her with her holiday blues. Alice is having a hard time dealing with Christmas without her family. Like most people, she just doesn't know if they are still alive.

Dove and Bill found out two weeks ago, that their two daughters and the grandkids were still okay and hoped that they could make it to the dinner. Bill on the other hand has heard nothing about his two sons in Oregon and hopes that they are okay, along with the two grandchildren.

The guys went hunting the day before and bagged a wild turkey for the meal. They also have a small ham which was a gift from one of the ranchers for all their help. Most people treat them like heroes because of the way they jumped in and helped everyone that survived the attack.

Dove and Monica were in the kitchen working on dinner, and the rest of them were in the Livingroom watching a DVD on the TV, when there was a knock at the door. Willis got up from the couch and went to the door to open it. In the door came six people that no one has seen since the attack. Doves two daughters Fawn and Tiffany along with their husbands, came through the door with Tiffany's children Karizma and Gabe in tow.

Dove was so happy that she dropped what she was doing and ran in the room and hugged her grandbabies until their eyes almost popped out. Then she hugged her daughters with big tears rolling down her cheeks.

As Willis started to shut the door Fawn stopped him. There was one more guest. She opened the door and Alice's Mother walked into the house. Both in tears, they ran to each other and hugged each other for several minutes, crying in each other's arms. There wasn't a dry eye in the place now. It was now a very "Merry Christmas."

The families ate their Christmas dinner and spent the rest of the evening recounting the events of the last few months. They were luckier than most to still have most of their families under one roof for the holiday, and were already making plans for a future they never imagined they would have.

CHAPTER 33

----•◉●•----

Torani Space Galactic Alliance Station 1
January 5, 2021

The Galactic Alliance Station is one of two in the galaxy. The Torani station is known as Station 2, of the Galactic Alliance. The leaders of the galaxy have all been called to the Station to hear the charges against the Corisole criminals. Attendance of all galactic leaders as well as their ambassadors is required for galactic trials such as this one, to assure the insurance of galactic law. No system should ever consider themselves above it as the Corisole have done. Galactic law is final, and is always carried out swiftly to maintain those laws. This finality assures compliance by all.

The leaders are all now filing into the main chamber of the Station. They are expected to come to a verdict on the charges against the one hundred leaders and officers, as well as their crews. The Torani emperor, who is now six years into his ten-year term as leader of the Galactic Alliance, is sitting at the center of a large crescent table with the Earth ambassador at his side. The others are filling the seats next to them. After the leaders were all seated, the accused were brought into the chamber. They are led to a central seating area where the Corisole leader is sat in the front with his commanders, and their officers behind them. He is the main target of these charges, but none will escape justice.

The emperor calls the trial to order. "Members of the Galactic Alliance, and inhabitants of the M-420 Galaxy. We are all called here today to hear testimony on the charges filed against the Corisole leadership, as well as its military leaders and the crewmembers involved. The charges are as follows."

"Count on, the defendants did knowingly violate the terms of the 12:7:141 Treaty by entering the S-3 system, and did interfere with the evolution of the S-3 planet. This charge, if found guilty, is punishable by a sentence of twenty-five years' hard labor in the Triomicium mines on planet Harken."

"Count 2, the defendants did knowingly, as well as ruthlessly, commit the act of genocide against the S-3 planet. This charge, if found guilty, is punishable by death. We will now hear the prosecutor's opening statements."

The prosecutor rises from his seat wearing the traditional red robes of the court. "Thank you, Emperor Ardesnal," he said with a bow. "Members of the Galactic Alliance. We are gathered here today to decide the guilt of these beings who are all accused of horrible crimes against the helpless planet Earth, as it is called by its inhabitants."

"Gentlemen, the Corisole criminals did knowingly, and covertly, use the Kabult Station for the sole purpose of the total annihilation of the inhabitants of Earth. This act is a direct violation of the 12:7:141 Treaty, which was specifically enacted to protect the inhabitants of Earth. There is no defense against these charges, as they have spent the last twenty years refitting the Kabult Station for this invasion."

"The next charge states that they did commit genocide on the planet's inhabitants. Gentlemen, the defendants are not only guilty of genocide, but premeditated genocide. They have planned this act for the last twenty years, and the evidence against them is airtight. There are over five billion corpses on the Earth planet as we speak, and this trial is merely a formality of this judicial system."

"Members of the Alliance. With the evidence at hand I recommend a guilty verdict on both counts, although I do feel that the crewmembers who were following orders only be charged on Count One in these proceedings and be sentenced to the mines on the planet Harken for a period of twentyfive years. Thank you, gentlemen." The prosecutor took his seat knowing that his job was done. The evidence was solid as a rock, and the defense had no chance at disputing it.

The representative for the defense rose wearing the blue robe of his position. He approached the center of the elevated semicircular table, then began to speak. "Distinguished members of the Alliance Council. My Clients Have volunteered to enter a plea of guilty for all charges against them. The Supreme Leader of Corisole has asked me to plead leniency for his military commanders, as well as their crews. These men were only following his orders and should not be held responsible for the crimes of their leadership. With no other evidence to present, the defense rests its case. Thank you, gentlemen."

The representative for the defense returned to his seat and waited, knowing that there is nothing he can do for his clients.

"Gentlemen," the emperor began, "the prisoners, as well as the council, will remain in the main chamber while the council adjourns to my chambers to deliberate the evidence."

The council members all rose and followed the emperor into his private chamber. The only ambassador to join them was Ambassador Furgison because he is the only representative from the planet Earth present.

Once inside the chamber, the members are all seating themselves around a round table to decide the Corisole prisoners' fate. The emperor rose to speak to the assembled members.

"My friends, we are not here to decide guilt as we already have a guilty plea from the accused. Our task is to determine the extent of the blame. There is no question that the Supreme Leader and his cabinet members should face the death penalty. As to the fates of the remaining defendants, I will now hear from the members of this council."

The Supreme Leader of Velnor, which is a sister planet of the Corisole race rose to speak. "Members of this council. The leadership of Corisole has committed an inexcusable act and should be punished severely for this atrocity. The commanders of the fleet vessels should also face the same fate, but the vessels' crews in my opinion should be shown leniency in their punishment as the defense has stated. Now as far as the crew of the Kabult Station, I feel that they should bear the same punishment as their leaders because of their twenty-year period of involvement. Thank You." The small gray leader of Velnor took his seat.

The planet Antaria's leader Xystrl then rose wearing a suit that enabled him to survive outside their hydrogen atmosphere. The six-foottall insectoid being, which looked similar to what the earthlings call cockroaches, had to speak by means of a translator integrated into his suit. The Antarian language is incomprehensible to most races, so the translator is necessary.

"Alliance members. The Antarian people agree with all recommended punishments, but also demand the destruction of the Corisole fleet. Their leaders must never be able to attempt this Kind of action again." The Antarian leader sat, not saying more.

"Thank you, Leader Xystrl," the emperor said after he was seated. "Leader Crowath, you are next."

The Klosk leader stood to address the members. The Klosk are a warrior race that are quite intimidating. With the size of the Torani and their bodies totally covered in brown hair they are quite a ferocious sight. Luckily for the inhabitants of the galaxy, they have become less aggressive over the last few hundred years, and evolved into a race of defensive warriors who volunteer their services to the Alliance.

"The Klosk feel that all involved in this ruthless attack should put to death. Take it from me, gentlemen, there is no innocent warrior in battle. Had the Klosk attacked that planet, we would expect death before we stepped on the vessel to leave our planet, and hope that our people were strong enough to hold the planet after we were dead."

The Klosk leader returned to his seat, and Ambassador Furgison rose without being asked.

"Gentlemen, I am Ambassador Furgison from the planet Earth. I have been invited in this chamber because I am the only representative to my planet. I do not consider myself a vindictive person, but I am going to speak for the five-billion inhabitants of Earth who were murdered in cold blood. I want every individual that was involved in this invasion to be put to death for their evil act. Like the Antarians, I also feel their fleet should be destroyed to deter future actions of this kind. Thank you."

The ambassador takes his seat and a very large hairy hand gives him a slap on the back in approval, that almost knocks the wind out of him. The other council members react in a number of ways to the ambassador's statement. Then the emperor rises to demand order in the chamber.

"Gentlemen, please." They all quieted to listen to their leader. "We are all here today to pass judgement on those responsible for the tragedy on Earth. If there is nothing more to add You will now enter your verdicts into your stations."

The members all entered their verdicts according to their beliefs, which are within the members' rights. After many tense minutes, they have all finished and returned to the main chamber where the defendants are still being held. The emperor has received the verdict and stands to read it.

"I will now read the verdict handed down by the members of the Galactic Council. The council has accepted the guilty plea of the leaders of Corisole. We also find all other defendants guilty as charged. The punishment for these crimes will be carried out as follows."

"All Corisole leaders, as well as all military personnel will be loaded onto the three remaining Corisole cruisers. They shall then be escorted to open space where these vessels will be destroyed with all aboard. This is the verdict handed down to you."

The council chamber came to life in a stunned commotion. Most of the members are pleased with the verdict. However, the Velnor leader and ambassador are upset with the severity of the verdict toward the crews. But they also know that they are bound to abide by it for the good of the galaxy."

"Gentlemen, we are bound to do our duty," Ardesnal stated. "The prisoners will now be escorted to the Corisole vessels and will then be escorted by the Torani fleet to the assigned location for execution. Guards, remove the prisoners, and inform the detention center to move the remaining prisoners to the vessels. This session of the Galactic Alliance Council is now recessed."

The members rose and slowly exited the chamber. This is the first time in galactic history that such a massive execution of prisoners has occurred. The prisoners were then led from the chambers to meet their doom. They would pay for their terrible crimes with their lives.

CHAPTER 34

---•◦❀◦•---

Torani Shipyard Orbital Station
February 15, 2021

The three Earth scientists have finally been granted permission to tour the Torani shipyards. Cloric fought long and hard for his new friends to be able to visit the Station, by finally winning over his superiors, and assuring them that the Earth scientists would not enter any forbidden areas. The group is now disembarking the shuttle on the lower level of the station.

"My god this thing is huge," Ben said, as he looked at a ship that was even larger than the Torani fleet vessels.

"Actually, Ben, this is one of our interplanetary shuttles used to ferry ore from the Harken mine," Cloric explained as they made their way to the elevators. "We can board and inspect the bridge and the crew quarters. That is all that has been allowed."

"How long does it take to construct a shuttle this size?" Olga asked.

"Depending on the availability of materials, it can be finished in a year."

The elevator rose to the bridge level, and they walked into the hallway leading to the shuttle's bridge. John has been silent, amazed by the awesome scale of a project of this size. He could park hundreds of space shuttles in the cargo bay alone.

"How?" John asked. "How do you refine enough metal for one of these ships?"

"It's a long and arduous process, but as you say, 'To make a long story short.'" Ben gives him a thumbs-up for his use of the English language. "We mine the ores for the engine parts and fuel on Harken, and the ore for the hull is mined on Corisole. The engine metals and parts are manufactured in space because they are ten times as dense, making them ten times as heavy. There are large enough sections of the station designed to produce the engine parts, but the hull plates are much too large and are manufactured at a separate orbital facility."

"Could we tour that facility?" Olga asked.

"No, it is fully automated and much too dangerous to tour."

They toured the bridge and crew quarterdecks. The workers were moving around with a sense of purpose, all very accustomed to what they were doing.

"Didn't the executions of the Corisole prisoners have an effect on the Corisole planet's production of your ores?"

"The Corisole rely too heavily on imports from our planet to survive without them," Cloric replied as he led them back to the elevator. "They supply our metals. We supply them with life."

"Can we look at the engine room, Mr. Cloric?" Olga asked as she pointed at the rear of the huge ship.

"I'm afraid it is still in the vacuum of space at the present time. As soon as the rear plating and the cargo doors are finished, they will start on the engines. It will be another two months before they start on the engines."

They then returned to the shuttle and flew back to the university. John still can't Get accustomed to how easy it is for them to travel in space, it took months to plan a spaceflight on Earth.

After they arrived back at the university, John left his three friends and strolled through the city to the magnificent capitol building. After getting directions from one of its occupants, he walked the seamless corridors until he found his way to the ambassador's quarters, which were located high in the interior of the building.

Gene is going over reports sent to him from Elsa. She has been steadfast about keeping him informed of the happenings on Earth, and contacts him weekly with updates, as well as many questions the new governor has for her old boss. There is a knock at the door that interrupts his thoughts. He rose from the desk in his office and answered the door.

"John, where have you been for the last couple weeks? I've missed our talks. These guys don't exactly know what a sense of humor is," he said as he shook his friend's hand vigorously.

"Sorry, Gene, I didn't mean to deprive you of my incredible wit."

"Sit, John, please."

They walked through the exquisite décor of the ambassador's quarters to Gene's work area and sat. Gene removed one of the bottles of Bourbon that he brought from Earth out of a drawer.

"Bourbon?" he asked with a smile.

"Absolutely," John answered. "I'm getting accustomed to the Torani brews, but nothing beats a shot or two of good Tennessee whiskey."

"Hear, hear," Gene replied as he poured them both three fingers of the smooth intoxicant. "To what do I owe the honor John?"

"I talked to Brad Meyer at NASA yesterday."

"And what's the major up to these days?"

"Actually Gene he claims to be quite bored, and wants us to get him clearance to visit that Moon Base. I know the Torani don't want us anywhere that technology, but it is our moon."

"Wow, the moon huh," he replied as he sipped the whiskey. "I can understand his interest. And as you said, it is our moon."

"All he needs is a shuttle, and the permission to go. They can assign him a couple of Torani scientists to assist him if they're worried about the technology. I see no reason we shouldn't be able to use our own moon as a research station. Everyone else has been doing it for decades."

"I'll have to run that one by the emperor, John. I know you understand that as well as you understand their position on us getting anywhere near their technology."

"Gene," he said, leaning forward. "We have an alien power source on our planet. We have joined our planet with theirs and have their people living on our planet, as well as our people living on Torani. We are now at a point in our space program where all we need is the engines to achieve flight beyond our solar system, Gene. We need to beg, borrow, and steal if we have to, to acquire our own ships to do so. They can teach us anything we need to know. That's what friends are supposed to do." He then sat back and sipped his whiskey.

"Okay, John. I'll bring it up the next time I meet with the emperor, but I can't guarantee anything. The emperor likes and trusts you so that might help with our argument."

"That's all I ask, Gene. Here's to flying through the galaxy someday." John declared as he held up his glass.

The two men sat and talked for a long while, both having a lot to disclose to the other. John told the story of his visit to the shipyard. He also revealed what he discovered about the Corisole planet's life line depending on Torani imports. All paid for with the much needed ores from the Corisole mines, which in turn is the reason for the planet's degeneration. Gene was unaware of the Torani's control over the smaller planet, which started the wheels turning in his brain.

They finished a few drinks, then wished each other luck in their new quests and said good-bye. Their new jobs keep them both very busy, not leaving much for extra time to pursue trivial matters.

As the sun rises over the snowcapped Colorado mountains, we find Bill standing in the snow completing his and the dogs morning ritual. Willis and Alice have moved into one of the government homes at Battlement, and him and Monica are all alone now. "Life is good."

Willis gained the foreman position on the tower complex project, and was able to put his brother in laws to work, helping their families and his sisters, by giving them housing and income for other items.

Alice and her mother have spent the last month and a half enjoying their strange new lives as well as each other's company. It's fulfilling to the both of them that they still have a special tie to the world.

Dove could not be happier now that she has her daughters and grandchildren to hover over like a mother hen. The joy of finding them both safe, as well as the relief, has made hers and Bill's lives much happier. They were both extremely worried about their children, and Bill still waits hopefully for word on his other two sons.

Sassy hears the Jeep coming up the driveway and does her happy dance, which demands that she spins in circles barking. Strange creature, just like her master. Bill calms her down as they both walk over to the Jeep.

"No work today?" he asks his son.

"Nope, we're finally starting to get some time off. I brought you guys some milk and eggs. They have a supply depot in the camp to keep the workers happy," he explains as they unload the groceries.

"Thanks, buddy, Monica will appreciate this."

They made their way into the house, where Monica was busy making breakfast.

"Oh goodie," she said. Willis handed her the bags. "I've been out for a few days. Thank you," she added, giving him a hug. "So how's work going?" she asked.

"It's going good. We finished mounting the new emitter yesterday, and as soon as we get the collector mounted at the transformer station we'll be ready to hook them into the power wires."

"Emitters, collectors. What's that?" Bill asked curiously.

"The towers use the emitters to shoot the energy directly into the atmosphere so it can be pulled back in at the collector arrays at the old transformer stations, then transferred into the old power grid. It's totally safe, you could lay right on top of one of these things and it wouldn't hurt you. The hard part is going to be getting all the wires fixed that run from the stations. It will be another six months before we get all the towns wired, and with all the people they've got working on it, they figure the world will be powered up in a little over a year."

"The whole world huh."

"Dad, we've got hundreds of people, and probably a million worldwide working on this. Then once they get the factories built they are going to build mini collectors for houses, cars, boats, you name it. Problem solved."

"All right, you two, I've got to run. I just wanted to bring this stuff to you. I promised Alice and her mother that I would take them to Grand Junction today. They're supposed to have a few stores for the workers can use their credits to buy stuff. The aliens couldn't destroy all the ports and warehouses, so supplies are finally starting to roll in."

"Okay. Be careful, and tell everyone we said hello," his dad said as they headed out the door. "Bye." Then he closed the door and looked at the two girls looking at him.

"You two want to go for a ride? I'm getting curious how the rest of the state is making out."

"Sure," Monica replied, patting Sassy on the head. "We'd love to go for a ride."

They gathered a few things for the trip and went on a postapocalyptic journey.

Chapter 35

Johnson Space Center, Houston
March 1, 2021

Brad crosses the tarmac to the awaiting shuttle. John and Gene have pulled off the impossible. Brad and his team have been granted access to the Station. With the power generators still operational and the weaponry ready to be removed, they intend to create a fully manned research station.

As he nears the shuttle he spies Horace Hunt and some of his assistants. With him are four Torani researchers who are admiring Johnson for the first time. They have watched this facility remotely for decades, as the people of Earth made their reach for the stars. Now that the tower problem is solved and they are waiting for the production facilities to be constructed, the emperor has ordered Mr. Talor and Mr. Mock to accompany the Earth scientists to the Kabult Station.

"Brad, it's good to see you again," Horace said, holding out his hand. "I would like you to meet the Torani's head researchers here on Earth. This is Mr. Talor, and his team which you will be acquainted with later. And this is Chief Engineer Mock."

"A pleasure to meet you, gentlemen," Brad said as he shook all their hands.

"The Torani prefer it if you bow to them," Horace said to him quietly in his ear.

"I have a hard time bowing to anyone, Horace," he replied forcefully.

They all entered the shuttle. Brad a little slower than the others, as this was his first time aboard one of the ships. Once they were all aboard and seated the shuttle gently rose into the sky and began its journey to the Kabult Station.

"How long will it take to reach the Station?" he asked.

"About two hours," Horace replied. "Just sit back and enjoy the scenery."

Brad watched out the window of the shuttle as the Station slowly got larger, and Earth shrunk behind them. It used to take them months of preparation and two days' flight time to make the journey to the moon.

As the Station grew steadily larger, his heart began to beat faster. He has always dreamed of walking on the moon, which is why he joined NASA in the first place. After what seemed like no time at all, they entered the landing bay of the Station into the hangar section. The air lock closed behind them and the atmosphere was restored, and they were now ready to depart the shuttle.

The passengers of the shuttle stepped onto the steel deck of the hangar, that was used to launch the brutal attack on Earth and kill five billion of its inhabitants. The Earth men stood silently taking the immense size of the structure.

"This is where they launched the attempted annihilation of our planet." Horace remarked, saddened by the memory of the event.

"Shall we proceed into the Station?" Mock asked, motioning to a huge pair of doors in the hangar.

The group walked down an extremely large corridor that led to another set of doors. The doors opened, and when they walked through them they entered the main bay and crew quarters. The sight was not unusual to the Torani, but to the Earth men, it took their breath away.

The room was big enough to fit at least two football fields inside. The ceiling was so far above the floor you could have put the Empire State Building inside of it. One hundred and fifty levels ringed the immense room that were used for the storage of the mines and attack ships. Two large elevators, one on each side, reached fifteen hundred feet to the top level, that were used to move the deadly cargo. There had to be some kind of artificial gravity in the Station because it felt just like walking on the planet below. On one side of the huge structure was an enclosed section that was one hundred feet wide and reached the entire height of the wall. These compartments were used to house the crewmen, and also contained the many labs. How was this place created without the knowledge of Earth below?

"Can you believe that we didn't have a clue what was going on right over our heads," Brad said to Horace.

"This isn't all of it." Mock declared. "There are a hundred miles of tunnels that lead from the central reactor chamber to the one hundred defense batteries that encompass the surface of the moon. All but twenty of the cannons were disabled during the battle."

"Can we see the power core?" Horace inquired, assuming the answer would be no, knowing their technology was such a touchy subject.

"Yes, you can," Mock replied. "The technology is similar to the fuel towers' cores. It will give you the knowledge you will require to maintain the towers in the future." He knew that he was most likely going against the emperor's wishes, but in his opinion, it would be criminal not to teach the human scientists the engineering of their power source, as well as its extreme dangers.

As they all made their way toward the power core, the Torani were walking a familiar path, but the Earth men were walking into the future.

After a long conversation with the Earth ambassador, it has been decided by the emperor that the Earth scientists will be able to study their technology related to space travel. Gene's argument was based on the fact that there were only one billion Earth inhabitants, and if they were to survive in the galaxy, they needed to be trained to exist in that galaxy. He also argued that since Earth was only about fifty years from achieving reliable intersystem travel, that the matter of interference with their natural evolution should be dismissed. The fact that his entire planet has witnessed these types of technologies also made it wrong to deny them the ability to defend themselves militarily, as well as diplomatically, by creating friendships with other systems.

After many days of meetings, it was decided that the Kabult Station should be turned over to its rightful owners, because the Torani had no legal claim to it. There will now be a permanent Earth presence on the Station to develop a defensive system to protect their planet from both natural and unnatural threats to Earth. The human race has just jumped two hundred years into its future.

John and his team have been in their lab studying miniature versions of the engines used on fleet vessels. After days of work they decide to take a break and enjoy a nice lunch in the city. They end up at what is now their favorite café in the city.

"Garson," Ben said, snapping his fingers. "Usual please."

The waitress returned a minute later with what would be considered wine on Earth.

"Thank you," Ben said with a wink. The waitress smiled in return as she walked away.

Ben Murphy has spent a great deal of time in the seaside café. As an Astronomer, he is of absolutely no use when it comes to the physics of space travel. In his off hours he has created a friendly relationship with the waitress at the café. She finds his sense of humor amusing.

"Ben, if I were you I would be careful with the way you flirt with the women on this planet." John warned.

"Oh she just thinks I'm funny, and you know how much I like a good audience. Besides, I come in here all the time and she knows me."

"I'm just saying, Ben, that you need to remember what Cloric about the purity of their race."

"I'm truly hurt, John," Ben said, grabbing his chest.

"You are awfully quiet tonight," John said to Olga.

"Yea, I haven't even seen her roll her eyes once," Ben added.

"I am trying to get my mind wrapped around the physics of their engines. It's amazing how they get such enormous power out of a mineral."

The waitress returned a few minutes later with their meals. They have come to love the Torani cuisine, and always try something different.

"Thank you Tashike," Ben said with a smile.

Tashike blushed, as much as a seven-foot golden alien can blush that is, and walked away smiling. Olga rolled her eyes and shook her head.

"There she is," Ben said, pointing at Olga's eyes. "And I'm just trying to be polite."

"Be careful Ben." She warned him.

They enjoyed their meals along with the beautiful Torani weather, then paid their tab with the Torani credits they had been given. They have to get back to the lab and continue their work on the engine designs. They were here to do a very important job for their planet and didn't plan on letting them down. They are responsible for Earth's future in galactic space travel.

A roaring fire is blazing in the fire pit. The days are starting to lose their bitter chill so Bill is sitting by the fire drinking a beer and throwing the stick for the dog. As she runs back toward him with her stick she stopped and looked down the driveway. The Jeep came around the last corner with two people in it. Sassy spun twice then ran to greet them.

Willis pulled up to the house and parked, and Sassy mugged him as he got out of the Jeep. She then ran around the other side to see who was with him. The Jeep creaked and rose as his passenger exited the vehicle, and the dog came running back around the front looking like a pissed off porcupine. Bill watched as a very golden man walk around the Jeep.

"Sassy come." He called to her, then grabbed her collar and made her lay down next to him.

"Dad, I would like you to meet my friend Mortisk," Willis said as they walked toward the fire.

Bill stood and looked up at a very large alien. "How are you," he said, holding out his hand.

Mortisk looked at him curiously, holding out his hand, but not grabbing Bill's. Bill grabs the large hand and shakes it vigorously as Willis rolled his eyes and shakes his head no.

"I am well," Mortisk answered, confused by the greeting.

"Please sit," Bill said, pointing at a large rock.

"Got a cold beer?" Willis asked.

Bill went to the house and returned with his bucket and Monica in tow. He handed Willis a beer then turns to Mortisk.

"Cold one?" he asked. Then opened one and handed it to Mortisk anyway.

"Thank you," Mortisk answered politely. He took a drink from the small bottle in his huge hand and gave Bill an agreeable nod.

Monica elbowed Bill in the ribs.

"Oh, Mortisk this is Monica."

Mortisk stood and bowed politely. "It is my pleasure to meet another of your beautiful human mates," he said respectfully.

"Thank you," Monica replied, blushing from the compliment.

"So what brings you two up here Willis?" his father asked.

"Mortisk wanted to see more of the planet, so I brought him up to see the house."

"Then take him in and show him around," he said as Monica sat down next to him and petted the puffed up dog.

"What's her problem?" she asked.

Bill pointed at Mortisk.

"Oh." She laughed.

Willis gave Mortisk a tour of the house and studio to show off their creation. They returned minutes later and sat down by the fire.

"Your home is quite unique," he stated politely as he looked around the valley. "And this part of your planet is quite beautiful. We have places like this on Torani, but our trees and grasses are quite different," he explained and then finished his beer.

"Would you like another, Mortisk?"

"Yes. It is much like our Chimork, quite pleasant."

Monica opened another beer and handed it to Mortisk. He rises and bows as she hands it to him. They were sitting by the fire enjoying the sound of the stream and the heat from the blaze, when Bill reached into his shirt pocket and pulled out his bowl. Willis gave him the "What the hell are you doing" look. Bill lights the pipe and takes a few deep draws. Mortisk smells the air and looks at Bill.

"That smells much like our Nitrob. May I try it?" he asked curiously.

Willis rolled his eyes at his father. He can't believe his father is getting the alien stoned.

"Be my guest," he said as he handed him the pipe.

Mortisk lights the pipe then smokes it until it's gone, then hands it back to Bill.

"Very flavorful, but not near as strong as our Nitrob. I will bring you some the next time I come."

The humans broke out in laughter. Mortisk looked at them wondering what was humorous about what he had just said.

"Mortisk, you and I will get along just fine," Bill said, still laughing.

The earthlings, and the Torani, sat at the fire for hours drinking and smoking, enjoying the rest of the Colorado day. As it started to get dark, Willis decided that it was time to leave, so Bill slapped the big alien on the back, shook his hand, then bowed. He figured he might as well cover all the bases.

"Mortisk, you are welcome here anytime," Monica said politely.

"Thank you, Monica," he replied, then made his way to the Jeep that Willis has already started to warm it up. Today would be a day that neither of them would forget. Meeting their first alien, and then finding out that he wasn't really that alien at all.

Today is the day that Willis and his workers get to see the results of all their hard work. The collector station was constructed at the old transformer station to distribute the power, and after two weeks of fixing the existing lines and hooking the new homes into the grid, it is time for the test.

On the mesa, Mortisk and his leader Dorahk energized the tower. With a low hum, the high voltage is ready to be fed into the emitter. Dorahk remained at the tower as Willis and Mortisk flew the shuttle to the collector station. After they arrived, Mortisk called Dorahk on the comms and told him that it was time to engage the emitter. Within thirty seconds, the collector assembly began to hum. Willis could tell by the look on Mortisk's face that it was working. They contacted Dorahk and gave him the good news.

"We did it?" Willis asked, knowing the answer was yes.

"We did it," Mortisk said smiling.

Within minutes the town began to light up. The new town could now shut down the noisy generators after six months of the constant roar and begin to return to what would be considered a new normal.

Chapter 36

---·•❋•·---

Galaxy Wide Summary 1
April 15, 2021

The people of Earth are returning from the darkness. City streets are lit at night again, and the factories are running again to produce the much needed and missed goods. The nations ports are once again operating their huge cranes making the work easier for the longshoremen to unload the most needed goods to be loaded on the trucks, then shipped to the remaining populace of the planet. Life is returning to as close to normal as it can get under the circumstances.

The planet took a simple thing as electricity for granted thinking that it would always just be there. With what seemed like just the flick of a switch, the whole planet was thrown into darkness. It's like anything in life; you don't know the value of things until you lose them.

On the other side of the coin was the problems that would arise after the power was turned back on. The gas and water leaks had to be dealt with. No matter how meticulous the power grid workers were, once the grid was energized the fallen power lines were a hazard around the globe. Also, every single piece of equipment that was turned on before the attack, now had to be shut down. This became a worldwide task.

The men of the Space Center have no homes to go back to. Their new homes have been brought to the Space Center by truck and set up a mile away on the shores of Clear Lake, just off Trinity Bay.

Johnson is now also the home to a massive refugee camp, set up on the Centers large tarmac. The people from the north had migrated to the southern states to escape the cold and starvation of winter. Now that spring is here and electricity is coming back online, the masses are beginning to leave for the comfort of their home states. The Space Center will soon be back to normal, if there ever will be such a thing again.

Brad is sitting at John's old desk in what is now his office. The Space Center is once again fully operational with the return of electricity, and totally cleared of debris. With the communication buoys that have been deployed between Earth and Torani, communication between the two planets is almost normal with only a ten-minute lag time. Because of this lag time Brad and John have gotten into the habit of sending complete messages between the planets, and waiting for the return message. Brad has just received an answer to his last correspondence with John.

"Brad. I was more than happy to help you reopen the Lunar Station." (They renamed the Station to try to remove the memory of what it was used for.) "If you and Horace have the same problem that we are having, you aren't allowed to learn much about their power sources. I have managed to change the mind of the Torani emperor with Gene Furgison's help. He made them understand the importance of our understanding these systems, and I explained how we need to master these systems for the continued prosperity of our planet, as well as the safety of the planet and its people. Their scientists will be teaching Horace and his men, as well as our three personnel on Torani, the entire engineering and physics of these power systems.

"Your message yesterday informed me of the existence of twenty remaining laser cannons on the Lunar Station. I have convinced the Torani to leave them intact for the defense of the planet. The Velnor planet, which is the sister planet to Corisole, has shown a sense of resentment toward the deaths of the Corisole prisoners, as well as the disarming of the Corisole planet as demanded by the Galactic Council's decision. I am personally concerned about the Velnor. They now have the third largest fleet in the galaxy. This is because of two hostile races that occupy their portion of the galaxy, and are accused of raiding vessels that travel through their system. I don't trust them Brad."

"I want you to assemble a ten-man team and accompany Horace and his men to the Lunar Station. I want your team to live and work on the Station on a permanent basis. After Horace learns all he can on the Station he will return to Nevada to begin building our own version of the power units from the knowledge he gains. Engineer Mock and a small crew of his men will also stay on the station to help bring the cannons back online. Good luck, Brad, and welcome to the future of the human race."

The planet Corisole has elected a new Supreme Leader, as well as a new cabinet. They are currently in session regarding the results of the trial, and the sanctions imposed by the Torani since the attack on Earth. The Supreme Leader now wants to determine their next course of action.

"Members of this council, we are here today to discuss the events of the last six months, as well as the future of the Corisole planet. Our previous leadership has brought the planet to the brink of destruction."

"The attack on the Earth planet was an ill-advised course of action to save our planet. The past leaders have dreamt of the colonization of Earth for the last thousand years. As a species we were once the most powerful species in this galaxy and our planet was once a paradise much like Torani, but through the quest for wealth and power by the mining of this planet for its precious metals, we have brought it to the absolute brink of destruction. We have turned the paradise into a barren dust ball that can no longer support its own inhabitants. We must now make a decision on the future of this planet, and without our fleet, we must now rely on Velnor for protection. The problem is that Velnor no longer wants to waste its resources on a planet that is as barren and near death as Corisole, so the Supreme Leader Irkan has offered our population sanctuary on their planet. They feel that by removing the three billion inhabitants from this planet, they can save it."

"The Velnor have estimated that with the use of atmospheric processors the planet can be regenerated in one hundred years, and the Corisole people can then return to their home. We must stop looking to the stars for a replacement planet and heal the one we already have. It will take centuries of work and sacrifice to reach this goal, but at least we will have a goal to achieve." "Are there any questions at this time."

The ambassador rises to address the council. "My friends we have lived in harmony with inhabitants of this galaxy for a thousand years. Against my recommendations, the previous leader has cost us all respect in the galaxy and we must now work to earn that respect back. Since we are one of two known planets that are able to mine fuels for the fleets, we have contracts with many systems in the galaxy. I say that we convince these systems to aid us with the rebuilding of our planet. It is their need that has destroyed this planet, so therefore they should help us restore it. The other option is for them to supply us with a replacement planet, and we continue to mine this one. Our previous leaders went about this in the wrong manner, which has cost us everything. Thank you."

The ambassador returned to his seat and the Supreme Leader once again rises to speak.

"Members of this council. The ambassador has presented a very interesting idea that I think we should consider seriously. I want you to contact the leaders of these systems and present our plan to them. We will convene this council again in two weeks to discuss our findings. At that time, we will make a decision on our future path. Thank you, council members."

The chamber slowly cleared of its members with the Supreme Leader remaining behind to weigh his options carefully. He has been put in charge of a dying planet and must decide the best course of action for his people.

The Earth scientists have been awarded the total freedom to study the science of the Torani propulsion systems. Olga has spent the last week aboard the Torani shipyard assisting with the building of shuttles for the other galactic systems. John has convinced the science leaders of Torani that it would be the most productive way for them to study the new propulsion systems. Olga is absolutely thrilled and has been having the time of her life.

Meanwhile on the planet's surface, John has been in numerous meetings with the Science Council regarding the engines, as well as the conversion of the Lunar Station. Gene has been at his side for support the whole time and John's next pursuit is to be granted a vessel to shuttle them to Earth and back. Gene is also going to make the trip to see his family. He misses his wife and children, and needs a break from galactic politics.

Ben has been studying galaxies that haven't even been viewed by the Hubble. The Torani technology can see ten times farther and fifty times clearer than anything on Earth. He loves his new toy and has spent every available hour studying these galaxies.

Ben has also been working very hard on another project. He now has a second love which comes in the form of a seven foot Torani woman named Tashike. Tashike has become enamored with the humorous, but also very loving earthling. John is not fond of this relationship, and has warned Ben repeatedly of the dangers not only to himself, but to the union between the two planets. He hopes Ben listens.

With the power on throughout Colorado's cities, the people have returned to somewhat normal lives. Ranchers and farmers are trading their goods across the district, so the people are now able to get all the meats, produce, and even fresh milk that they need.

The factories are working again which is providing other necessary goods. For the first time in over a hundred years there is no unemployment in the American District, if not the entire world.

The family is all gathered in the valley for the spring barbeque, along with several friends from town and their children. Also in attendance is a pair of Torani. Mortisk and his wife have been invited to join in the ritual. The Torani workers were allowed to transfer their families to the planet Earth. The people of Earth welcomed them quite affectionately, as they are all very pleasant beings. Mortisk's wife Hyal has been easily adopted into the mountain clan. For all involved. "Life is good."

Bill sits at his usual spot at the fire. It is the most comfortable place on the planet to him, and it is "his" mountain kingdom.

The rest of the men are seated around the fire enjoying the refreshments. Bill is very thankful that they reopened the breweries, because his supply of Corona was getting dangerously low. The children are busy playing with a very wet, but very happy Sassy in the stream. The ladies are happily working and gabbing together in the house, working on the food for the barbeque. Bill of course, has cases of beer on ice in small horse trough sitting close to the pit, as well as his usual stash of smoking supplies for all to enjoy at their leisure.

"So how's work going?" he asked Willis.

"Not bad. We're almost finished with the entire state. We've managed to get all the cities powered up, and are moving out into the mountain areas," he explained while he played with the fire with a stick.

"How's the city business going, Alex. You tired of being in charge yet?"

"Actually its finally gotten to where I can breathe. All of the utilities are up and running with the help of Tim and the guys. We haven't had to worry about fuel shipments since the power came on, and we even have garbage service now. Life's getting easy again," he said as he tipped his beer.

"Mortisk!" Bill yelled as the alien walked over to where they were all sitting.

"Yes, Mr. Bill."

"I told you, Mr. Bill was my father," he said, joking with the large alien. He loved joking with Mortisk because he just hasn't quite got the hang of when someone is teasing him.

"Sorry, Bill," he said, dead seriously.

"How's the wife like Earth?"

"Hyal loves these mountains. She was raised at the edge of the sea, but loved the mountains of Torani. She thinks your mountains are even more beautiful than the ones on Torani."

The ladies are starting to wander out of the house, and seek out their other half's. Monica came over and sat in her usual seat, Bill's lap. He offers them all a beer.

"I love your home," Hyal said sweetly.

"Thank you, Hyal. It is a pleasure to share it with you."

Mortisk taps her on the leg and she reached into her bag and pulled out a large pipe. Bill's eyes got very big.

"Nitrob?" Bill asked, rubbing his hands together.

"Nitrob," Mortisk said with a grin and handed Bill the pipe.

Bill took the pipe and grabbed his lighter to light it. Mortisk reached out and stopped him.

"There's no need for that," he said, pointing at the lighter. "Be careful now."

Bill took a big hit off Mortisk's pipe and about coughed his lungs out. Hyal takes the pipe from him shaking her head, then hits it herself and hands it to Mortisk.

"Nitrob," Bill said with a thumbs-up as they all laughed at him.

The adults all enjoyed a little Torani herb and soaked in the Colorado sun, while enjoying the good company of their friends. It was amazing how two species separated by so much space can be so similar.

The men are then informed that they get to cook, so they grab a few huge trays of meat and teach Mortisk the fine art of drinking beer and barbequing.

I've never seen such a happy alien Bill thinks to himself, then laughs out loud.

"What's so funny?" they all asked.

Bill called them over to where he was standing behind Mortisk, and they all laughed too. Standing in front of them was a seven-foot-tall alien with a beer in one hand, a set of tongs in the other, wearing a kiss the cook apron. It was an absolutely hilarious sight.

"Willis. Go get the camera. I have got to get a picture of this or nobody will believe me."

After a lot of good food, and even more beers and bowls, it was officially declared a "good day" by all.

PART 2

CHAPTER 37

---•●✹●•---

Earth Lunar Station
July 1, 2021

The Lunar Station has been a very busy place over the past few months. The scientists, as well as fifty technicians, have spent every waking hour converting the station's systems to the earthlings' needs. The Station is now the planet Earth's first Space Command post.

The Torani have been permanent residents of the Station, helping the Earth men reactivate the defensive systems, along with the badly damaged cannons. After months of hard laborious work, they have cleared all the debris from the cannon bays and restored power to the magnificent weapons. The cannons are not only meant for military needs, but they also have the ability to destroy very large asteroids and will be the planet's protector from the system's wandering demons. The sensor arrays on the moon will guarantee that the planet that has been annihilated countless times by these heavenly killers, will never again suffer the fate of the dinosaurs.

The science department of NASA now inhabits a large number of the labs on the Station, with a Hubble control center being one of them. NASA has been informed of the Torani's incredible telescopes, and is waiting patiently for the privilege of the incredible viewing technology. Being that it is not a dangerous or military technology, Earth has been granted the use of it.

Brad and a small crew are now in the process of learning to maintain and pilot the Torani shuttles since the Torani will eventually return to their home planet, and the men of the station will be on their own when it comes to transportation. Brad is currently in his office studying the schematics of the shuttles when he receives a recorded video message from John.

"Brad, my friend. I am happy to hear of the progress you are making on the Lunar Station, and happy to see that all our hard work is finally paying off. I envy your job. You are doing what we have dreamed of for decades, and are now seeing those dreams come true. I have a request in now to return to Earth for a short time to tour the Station."

"Dr. Krishkoff and I have made tremendous leaps forward in the field of engine construction as well as their dynamics, but for some reason they won't let us learn about the fuel technology. We now know how to build and maintain these engines, but have no knowledge of the composition of the fuel. It's a closely guarded secret for some reason."

"The Torani have allowed us to assist in the construction of one of their vessels which has enabled us to learn a great deal. We will pass on this technology when we return. It will help considerably with the proper construction of the first Earth shipyard."

"I can't wait to see you again, my friend. I'm not sure on the exact date yet, but I will see you soon. I haven't had time to learn to pilot the shuttles yet, so you'll have to take me for a spin and give me a crash course. Without the crash that is. I will see you soon, my friend. Good-bye."

Brad turns off the view screen and sits reviewing what he has heard. He's glad he has John and Gene on his side on Torani or they wouldn't be where they are now. The ship building technology is a big bonus to his plans with the Station, but he has to wonder as John has, why they won't give up the secrets to the fuel. They will teach them how to build and fly the things, but not make the fuel for them. Maybe they just want a hole card for themselves.

John and Ben are relaxing in the meeting room after a hard day's work. After his time in the shuttle program with NASA, John worked for a short time as an Aeronautic Designer for a military contractor and has been playing with his own design for a new ship for Earth, and Olga has been working on the engine designs. Ben is sitting with what could be called a laptop in front of him, gazing at the incredible images from the Torani telescope.

"Back already?" John asked Olga as she entered the room.

"I was asked to leave while they fueled the engine core. Why will they teach everything else and not even give us a glimpse of the fuel," she commented, frustrated by their actions.

"For some strange reason Olga, they don't want us to have all the pieces of the puzzle," John replied.

"That's the frustrating part of this whole process. They show us how to build the engine, and how to operate and maintain it, but they won't let us learn how the fuel is produced to power it," she explained angrily.

"I've been talking to Brad on the Lunar Station and he makes the same point. He's as frustrated as we are."

"All right, enough of work for today," Ben said. "Let's go get something to eat."

"You just want to go flirt with your girlfriend." Olga teased. "I really like her. She is actually very funny, and she enjoys my company. Plus, she never gets tired of my jokes. That's a rare combination for me," he said seriously.

"Just remember what I said, Ben," John warned.

"Don't worry, buddy. I'm not going to create a galactic scandal. Come on, I'm hungry."

They all followed Ben out of the room to stroll the streets of Carista, and having a few drinks and some food did sound good about now.

Gene is in his office watching a message that he just received from his wife and children.

He had a system set up at his father's ranch in order to help with the loneliness they have all experienced with him so far away.

He recorded his own message today, informing them all of his return visit to Earth the following month. He has promised his children a tour of the Lunar Station, which they are very excited about. Unlike their mother, they love space as much as their father. He is getting ready to send the message when his comms system buzzes. He activates the monitor and a strange face that he thinks he has seen before appears on the screen. It is a reptilian being from the planet Zaxin. The ambassador, he thinks.

"Ambassador Furgison, I am Ambassador Tronext of the planet Zaxin. I know we have not personally met, and it is unusual to call unannounced, but I have a very upsetting and personal matter that I must speak to you about. I would prefer that you did not mention this to anyone until after we have met."

"I will be in my office on the Galactic Station in two weeks from today for other business. It would be to your advantage to meet with me at that time. I cannot explain at this time, but I assure you that it is important to your planet. Thank you, Ambassador Furgison."

As the screen went blank Gene sat perplexed by the mysterious message. That was quite curious, he thought to himself. Why the intrigue.

But the Zaxin ambassador did say that it was important to his planet, so he would defiantly make the meeting.

Mortisk is at his home in the Torani settlement. The temporary housing has now been replaced by permanent dwellings resembling the ones on Torani, with their oval stacked construction much like the ones on the Torani coastline. They even have the spires at the top to draw the energy from the atmosphere. One day all homes on Earth will have these spires also.

The large alien is in his front yard playing with his new toy. It seems that the Torani have a fascination with our Automobiles, and they all have found a variety of these vehicles. Mortisk has managed to acquire a two thousand fourteen, Chevy Camaro ragtop. The convertible top is a necessity because of the Torani's seven-foot frame. He has also discovered the joy of cruising the Convertible through the breathtaking canyons and mountains of Colorado.

The Torani workers all now have their wives and children on the planet. Their children play at the playground with the Earth children, as if it were a normal everyday occurrence. It's amazing how easily children can adapt to their environments.

The residents of the Torani settlement have all been invited to the town picnic, at the park by the river. As always there will plenty of good food and music for everyone to enjoy, as well as a Fourth of July fireworks show at night. The town received the fireworks as a gift from the government contractors, to show their appreciation for all the hard work the townspeople put into the project. It will be a fun, as well as relaxing day that they all need. Bill and Monica are outside playing with Sassy when Willis drove around the final corner of the driveway. As usual the dog does her circles and runs to greet him, then follows him to the garage.

Bill and Monica follow them.

"What's up, son?" his father asked

"I need to hook up the trailer and load up the equipment for the show today. Want to give me a hand?"

"You bet. I'll get the doors."

Bill opened the huge wood doors and helped back the Jeep up to the trailer. "When are you two coming down town?"

"Probably around ten. We're going to help get everything set up. I'm bringing the firewood for the barbeques, so I need to get their kind of early to get things started."

"It's gonna be a blast. Everyone, even the Torani workers are gonna be there," he said. "Let's load up the amps first."

The equipment was stored in the rear of very large garage by Bill's indoor greenhouse. Among the variety of vegetables is his dad's "personal garden." Willis walked by the garden, then stopped and backed up a few steps. "What the hell is that?" he asked.

"Mortisk gave me some of his 'special' seeds," he replied, making the quotation marks with his fingers.

"They are glowing!" His eyes were big as he looked at them.

"I know. Weird huh," Bill said as he began collecting the equipment.

"Am I gonna have to keep an eye on you two?"

"Won't do any good."

Willis shakes his head in disbelief, then joined in the loading. "You're teaching the aliens bad habits."

"He brought that habit across the galaxy with him. Don't blame me."

After they finished loading all of the equipment on the trailer, Willis thanked him for his help then headed for the park, where Alice and her mother would be waiting. It's a beautiful Colorado summer morning, and as he drives down the driveway he thinks to himself. "Life is good."

The park is starting to fill with the residents of the two towns. The bandstand and dancing area are being completed for the day's entertainment, and the barbeques are being lit for the day's feast. Everyone has shown up to help in any way they can to make the day a success.

The ranchers supplied the meats and vegetables for the feast. There were tables loaded with every kind of dessert you could imagine provided by the ladies of the area, and barrels full of ice and refreshments for both children and adults lined the gazebo. It is like any Fourth of July picnic ever held before.

Bill and Monica are sitting on the tailgate of the truck with Sassy lying on a rug behind them, watching the crowds begin to fill the park. Willis turned on the sound system and makes it official; the party has started. All of Bill's children walked up to the truck to say hi and get hugs. Sassy rose from her nap and got out of the truck to go play with the grandkids. Well, actually, all the kids. There's no such thing as to many kids, or to many sticks to play with, so off she went. Willis came over handed his dad a cold beer.

"Thanks, buddy," he said to his son, who knew that in his dad's opinion, it was long past Miller Time.

"You're welcome," he replied. "Here they come," he said, pointing out the red convertible followed by several other cars from the Torani settlement.

"You really are a bad influence on him," Monica said as the big gold alien pulled up wearing a cowboy hat.

"I have no control," he answered, throwing his hands in the air.

They all laughed and then just stood back and watched. The music is playing, friends and family are plentiful, and the beautiful Colorado weather, it just doesn't get any better than this, Bill thinks to himself. He walked over to the very large cowboy and shakes his hand, then gives his beautiful golden wife a hug.

The day went off without a hitch. The people danced and ate to their hearts content, and the children danced and played with their friends as if nothing at all had happened to their planet. It was a perfect day for all.

After the sun went down they shot fireworks into the sky as the music played for all to enjoy. They ate, drank, and danced till midnight. It was a Fourth of July that nobody would ever forget, and a relaxing day that everyone desperately needed.

Chapter 38

—•●✹●•—

Torani Space Galactic Alliance Station
July 15, 2021

The Earth ambassador is entering the Alliance Station after a short shuttle ride from the surface. Gene did not come alone. He has confided in his friend John, about the strange request made by the Zaxin ambassador, who also thought the request to be very unusual. He decided to accompany Gene to the meeting.

The two Earth men walked through the Station admiring the view of the star system through the surrounding portals on their way to the Zaxin ambassador's office. Unlike Gene, he hasn't met any other of the members of the Alliance but the Torani. A small gray alien walks by them on their way, which stops John in his tracks. He looked at Gene in disbelief.

"The stories were all true." John declared, not believing what he has just witnessed.

"It appears so John. That is the Corisole ambassador."

"The grays are the ones that attacked us?"

"Not that one, but yes."

They continued their way through the station, stopping occasionally to watch shuttles fly by the busy Station, and to look at the odd beings walking by paying absolutely no attention to the earthlings.

Eventually they came to the ambassador's section and entered the Zaxin Consulate. In the outer office was a reptilian being that looked at the humans curiously.

"Is Ambassador Tronext available?" Gene asked.

The ambassador's assistant spoke into a comm system in a totally unintelligible language, then motioned toward a door behind him. They followed the creature into the office where they were greeted by the Zaxin ambassador.

"Good to meet you, gentlemen," he said, looking at Gene curiously as he shook both their hands. "I assumed that this would be a private meeting."

"Ambassador Tronext, there is no person in the galaxy that I trust more than this man. This is my chief of operations of our Space Exploration Center on Earth. John Alistair, I would like to introduce you to Ambassador Tronext."

"It is my pleasure, Ambassador," John said respectfully to the reptilian ambassador.

"I hope you don't mind my bringing him to this meeting, but I value his input on unknown dangers, and from your message I am expecting an unknown danger. And, Ambassador, please call me Gene."

"Very well Gene. You both may call me Tronext."

The two men wait as the ambassador gives his assistant some instructions.

"Gene," Tronext said uncomfortably. "I am a citizen of the planet Zaxin. As a member of the Alliance I feel I should share some information with you that I am not sure that you are unaware of." He stopped to consider his next words carefully.

"Gentlemen, I feel that you should be made aware of the way this galaxy actually operates. Most all races in this galaxy are dependent on the Torani planet. The Torani have absolute control of the one thing we all need if we choose to travel in this galaxy. Most of the systems have the ability to build their own vessels and travel to all reaches of the galaxy, but the Torani have absolute control of the minerals used in the production of fuel for these vessels. The Torani have one small planet that uses our galactic prisoners as slaves to mine these ores."

"Five-hundred years ago the Corisole planet was much like your planet Earth. It was a fruitful planet with numerous areas for growing food, and had an ample water supply to sustain both the agriculture and the people. During this time the Torani were the only race in the galaxy capable of galactic travel, and slowly they dished out whatever technology they wanted to the highest bidder. They made a deal with the Corisole after the discovery of the rare metal on their planet, to give them the technology as long as they fed their needs for the precious metal. This deal has led the Corisole people to their current predicament."

"As the technologies were spread throughout the galaxy by the Torani, trade between the systems began to sprout new technologies. New life such as the clone planet Zakorin and the Boral, which are a clone cyborg hybrid, were the result of this sharing of technologies. But as the fuel began to become rare, and with the Torani being the only race to know the closely guarded formula, enticed the other systems with wealth to search the galaxy for the rare mineral. After a century of searching the Corisole discovered the mineral on their own planet."

"The Corisole were a very curious scientific race, who gladly traded their mined ores for a fleet of vessels to explore the galaxy. But with all things of value, greed and corruption soon follow. The Torani and the Corisole entered into a partnership which enabled the Torani to build their shipyards, and control the production of space vessels, which brought the planet great wealth, which you have witnessed."

"The Corisole planet also flourished with the partnership because of the fact that other than the small Torani moon, the Corisole are the only supplier of the rare Triomicium ore. Unfortunately, all good things must come to an end and two hundred years ago a cruel Torani ruler decided to take the Corisole planet for their own. A horrible attack was launched against the planet having the same result as the attack on your planet. All of the Corisole inhabitants were annihilated except enough to work the mines as slave labor. At this time there was no Galactic Alliance or systems powerful enough to stand against the Torani."

"After one hundred years of slavery, a new ruler was elected on the Torani planet, which offered the Corisole people their freedom, and helped many of them relocate to the planet Velnor in the Krobata System. A greedy few stayed on Corisole to continue to mine the ore with the help of the Torani ruler. They mined the ore in trade for space vessels and supplies to maintain the remaining population of their dying planet."

"This period in history was a peaceful and industrious period in the history of the galaxy. The Alliance was created, and two stations were built in the galaxy in the name of peace and justice. These stations are still maintained in the pursuit of that goal."

"Now, as before, with time things change. The previous emperor of Torani was killed in a mysterious shuttle accident three decades ago leading to the rise of once again oppressive rulers, which has led to the present Emperor Ardesnal. Ambassador, let me assure you that your planet was not saved for mercy, but because of greed. The 12:7:141 Treaty was not created to protect your planet. It was created by the Torani and Corisole planets to keep your planet's inhabitants from reaching galactic status, as well as protect its secrets."

"Gentlemen, with this long story being told it comes down to one fact. With the Corisole planet almost depleted of the Triomicium ore, your planet is the only planet in this galaxy known to exist that contains this rare ore. I believe you call this ore "Gold."

The Earth men looked at each other in shock, as well as worry for the fate of their world. Everything they have been told by the Torani has been a lie.

"My friends your planet is in great danger. The Torani did not kill the Corisole to save your planet. They killed them because they were double crossed by the Corisole, when they attempted to gain galactic power by annexing your planet and its wealth for themselves."

The ambassador then sat back and filled his glass with water to let the humans assimilate all the information he has given them. Gene was the first to break the silence.

"Why did the Alliance allow the Torani to destroy the Corisole planet, as well as enslave their people."

"As I've said. They have lied to you. The Galactic Alliance is a very young entity that was created less than a century ago. Also, at that time the Torani fleet was the most powerful force in the galaxy, and none dared challenge them. Plus, the fact that they controlled and still control all Triomicium in the galaxy. They make the rules, gentlemen."

"Why have you waited so long to tell us of this deception?"

Gene asked angrily. "Gene," he said kindly. "You must believe me when I tell you that we only discovered the presence of Triomicium on your planet the day I contacted you. One of the Corisole leader's assistants had survived the cleansing and came forward," he replied.

"What do you mean by cleansing?"

"The trial of the Corisole invaders was a ruse, created to hide the truth. I wondered myself why no one was allowed to speak at the trial, as well as thought it was peculiar that the council voted to have all involved executed. The vote was tampered with to cleanse all knowledge of the Corisole's true goal in invading your planet. I covertly asked the other council members about their votes and discovered the horrible truth."

"So what do we do now to stop them from doing to Earth, what they did to the Corisole planet two hundred years ago?" Gene asked, thinking that without being able to protect themselves his planet was basically screwed.

"I would estimate that the Corisole planet has approximately fifty years of production before their planet is out of Triomicium ore. The Torani will most likely let you rebuild your planet for them. The population has already been purged, so there should be no further extermination of your race. They will need the remaining inhabitants to mine the ore. My best guess is that you may have twenty or thirty years before they invade."

John burst in. "That's why they haven't let us see any data on the fuel for the engines. They have showed every single thing about building a ship except that. Then add in the fact that it will take at least ten years to build the facilities to build ships, they just don't care if we know how to build them. It will only add to their facilities if we do," John added.

"So what are we going to do now? Just wait for them to come and wipe us out in thirty years like the Corisole did!" Gene shouted angrily.

"Gentlemen, I suggest that we proceed very carefully," Tronext replied. "If the Torani discover that you know of their plan, your world will be instantly invaded. I will find out whom we can trust of the council members to help us. In the meantime, you should make your planet ready for the imminent invasion. I understand that you still have cannons on the orbital station. You need to build on that technology to start." Tronext raised his water glass to drink then stopped. "I think we need something stronger than this." He emptied the glass back into the pitcher and reached behind him and took a bottle off the shelf containing a blue liquid, along with two more glasses, then poured them all a glass of the contents. They all sat silently drinking the liquid.

"Thank you, Tronext. You are truly a friend of the people of Earth," Gene said, holding up the glass, and took another sip of the very strong liquor.

"Be careful, my friends, that is what you thought last time," Tronext returned with a sly expression.

"We owe you one, Ambassador," John said as he stood and extended his hand.

"We owe you more than one," Gene added as he shook the reptilian hand.

The two men left the ambassador's office and spent an hour walking the decks of the Station, knowing that they may never get another chance. Once they were back on the shuttle and had a chance to speak, they had a very short and very quiet conversation.

"We need to get back to Earth right now," John said quietly. "We've got a lot of work to do."

"I've got a ship scheduled in two weeks. Get your team ready to leave. And John. Squirrel away all the data you possibly can."

John gives him a nod and the two men rode in silence all the way to the planet's surface.

After a long quiet ride back from the Alliance Station, and a quiet walk across the city, John entered the crews living quarters at the Learning

Center. His friends are busy with their work from the day, so he went to the bar and grabbed a bottle of Bourbon, then sat on the large couch with a glass in his hand, but drinks from the bottle. Ben and Olga looked at each other and shrugged. Then Ben broke the silence.

"It can't be that bad," he said.

"Wanna bet," John replied and took another drink from the bottle.

Ben and Olga grabbed a glass and shared a drink with their friend as he explained the conversation he and Gene had with the Zaxin ambassador. After ten minutes he finished the story and took another drink of the bottle as he waited for his friend's comments.

"Do you believe him?" Olga asked.

"I'm not sure what to believe anymore, but it does explain why they won't let us anywhere near their engine cores, or the fuel."

Olga nodded in agreement. "What are we going to do now?"

"I'm not sure yet, but I do know that I'm not going to let them get away with it. We've got maybe twenty years to get ready, unless they discover that we have uncovered their plan. If they do, we're screwed. We have to keep this absolutely secret for now."

"Blueprints," Ben said.

"What do you mean?" Olga asked.

"We need to steal the blueprints on those ships and engines without them knowing, and build our own. Two can play this game," he said with a smile.

"Good idea, but I bet we can con them into giving them to us," John replied.

"They do seem to trust us with everything but the fuel data," Olga agreed.

"Okay then. We leave this planet in two weeks and nobody needs to know that for now, not even Cloric. We'll get all the data we can get our hands on loaded into our computers and take it with us. Agreed."

"Absolutely," Ben replied.

John filled their glasses again and they toasted to their plan. They have two weeks to try to get enough data to save their planet.

Gene has been communicating with Horace in order to see what the Torani are up to on Earth. The production of the emitters and collectors are in their final stages, so the Torani scientists are eager to go home. They weren't allowed to bring their families because of the secrecy of the Nevada base.

Gene has informed him of his return in ten days, which will allow the scientists to ride along on its return trip to Torani. Gene didn't tell Horace about the meeting with the Zaxin ambassador because he was pretty sure that their communications were monitored. Absolutely no chance can be taken with the secret. If the Torani find out that they know, it's game over for Earth. The most important thing Gene learned as president is the value of secrecy. It will be nice to see his family again he thinks, trying to get his mind off his discovery. His comm unit activated, and the emperor was on the screen.

"Ambassador Furgison, could you join me in my office please," was all that was said. Then the screen went dead.

Gene has a really bad feeling because of everything that has happened. He left his office and went to see the emperor.

Gene entered the emperor's office after making his way through the halls of the building. "You wanted to see me, Emperor?"

"Yes, my friend. Please sit."

John takes his seat nervously, not knowing why he was called to the ruler's presence.

"So, my friend, I understand that you are going back to Earth."

"Yes, I am," he answered. "I haven't seen my family in months, and I think we both know how wives can be when they don't get their way. Don't we, sir?"

"This is true," the emperor replied, then changed the subject. "My security chief informed me that you took a trip to the Alliance Station recently."

"Yes, I was explaining the incredible engineering to John Alistair, and he simply had to see it," Gene replied, trying to stem the ruler's curiosity. "I didn't think it would create a problem giving him a tour. He was also very eager to meet other alien species, so I introduced him to some of the ambassadors," he stated to try to throw the ruler off the trail.

"Well, I hope John enjoyed himself. I know what a curious man he is," the emperor replied, seeming to be satisfied with Gene's explanation. "I understand your science team is going to join you on the trip."

"Yes, they are all quite homesick right now and I thought it would be a good break for them."

"When are you scheduled to return, my friend."

"We will return on the next available vessel. There's no reason to schedule a special trip for our return," he replied, wanting to climb over the large desk and grab him by his golden throat for calling him his friend. "Well, Emperor Ardesnal. I have four days to get ready for my trip, and I've got a lot of work to take care of before I leave. If there's nothing else, I will get back to it," he said and stood to leave.

"Have a good trip, my friend. I will see you upon your return. You can fill me in on the efforts on your planet when you return. Good-bye, Ambassador."

John left the leader's office and walked through the halls wondering just how much the emperor actually knew about the meeting with the Zaxin ambassador. He is fairly sure he covered his tracks, but he still has to be careful. They are all obviously being watched very closely.

Ben has escaped the others to visit his very special friend, knowing that he will be leaving for Earth in four days. The hour is late and Tashike is just finishing her workday.

"Would you like to go for a walk?" Ben asked.

"I would like that very much," she replied with a smile.

Ben helped her on with her jacket, and they headed for the street. They walked quietly along the magnificent sea wall enjoying the ocean view. The two were an unusual sight as the seven foot Torani woman walked next to the five foot nine human, both uncaring of what anyone else thought.

They stopped at one of the viewing areas that were built into the seawall. Ben turned Tashike gently toward him. "I will be leaving in four days for Earth, and I don't know if I will be coming back. I have very important work to do on my planet," he explained, as he looked up into her big blue eyes that were now starting to weep.

"Could I come with you to your planet?" she asked, almost pleading.

"Will they allow it?" he asked, his tone now hopeful.

"We are not prisoners on Torani. We often travel to other worlds. I will have to file the proper requests, but it should not be a problem," she replied, not wanting to be separated from her funny little Earth man and willing to leave her home planet to remain with him. "

I would give my right arm to have you on Earth with me."

"That will not be necessary," she said seriously.

Ben laughed at her innocence. "It's just a figure of speech," he explained. "There is nothing in the galaxy I would like more, and you can stay as long as you want," he said, taking her rather large but delicate hand. "Our vessel is leaving for Earth in four days, so you better file those requests tomorrow."

"I will make sure that I am on that vessel," she promised him.

They walked back to her house, and he waited for her to open her door. "You will be there, won't you?" he asked.

Tashike grabbed her funny little man and kissed him hard and long.

"I'll take that as a yes," he said happily.

Tashike smiled at him lovingly as she closed the door. Ben turned from her house and walked through the Torani streets, thinking about the wonderful life he would be beginning with Tashike. Thirty minutes later he walked into the groups quarters at the Learning Center. His friends were both very busy at the computer stations. "Busy?" he asked.

"Trying to get this information downloaded before we leave. There's thousands of pages to copy," John replied.

"I understand Cloric has asked to go with us." Ben really liked Cloric and would like to have him on Earth.

"Actually they denied his request. I feel sorry for him, he really had his hopes up. But on the other hand, we can't afford to let our secret out so it might be for the best."

They all agreed with John but felt bad for the young Torani. He has really become one of the team and they'll all miss him. John and Olga resumed their work as Ben poured himself a couple fingers of Bourbon and relaxed on the sofa, retracing the events of the evening. Tashike's decision to accompany him to Earth has made him the happiest person in the entire galaxy.

CHAPTER 39

Area 51, Nevada Desert
July 22, 2021

Horace is in his office going over the designs for the fuel towers. The engineering is pretty straight forward but he can't seem to wrap his head around the power signatures, because he wasn't allowed to participate in the building of the miniature fuel tower. The Torani claimed that it was too dangerous, but he thought there was more to it than that. He is suddenly disturbed by his assistant.

"There's a Brad Meyer here to see you, sir."

"Show him in." Horace knows Brad as John's replacement at NASA. "Brad, how are you."

"Been real busy on the Lunar Station," Brad replied.

"That's what you get when you try to fill John's shoes. Please, sit."

The two men have a seat at Horace's cluttered desk. Horace then pours himself a glass of water.

"Care for some?" he asked. "You have to stay hydrated out here."

"Yes, please. Have you talked to John?"

"No, but I got a strange message from Gene telling me to convince the Torani to go home on leave."

"I received somewhat the same message from John. He told me to have all but my labor force, take a vacation and go see their families. It actually wasn't that hard to convince them. Any clue why he wants them to leave."

"None, but I know Gene well enough to read between the lines, and I don't like the feeling I'm getting."

"John asked me to touch base with you and give you these." Brad handed Horace a C D.

"What's this?"

"The blueprints to the Torani laser cannons. They're identical to the Corisole cannons on the Lunar Station. Don't ask me why, because he didn't say."

"Now I'm really starting to get a bad feeling Brad."

"I know what you mean Horace. Well, I've made my delivery so it's time to get back to the Lunar Station."

"You got your own shuttle, didn't you?"

"Sure did. They even taught me to fly it," Brad said with a big grin. "Gotta go, Horace. I'll see you on the sixth at Johnson to welcome them home."

The two men gave each other a salute and went about their business. They both knew that the future held something important in store, but neither one had any idea of the importance to the future of the planet.

The guys are all now enjoying the weekend ritual of cold beers and a fire in the pit. It didn't take much convincing to make them all believe that it was the best place on the planet to be. The radio is playing a CD real low so they can talk, and the ladies are lying back enjoying the warm Colorado night with the ones they love. Mortisk suddenly rises to address his friends.

"My dear earthling friends. I would like to thank all of you for your friendship, as well as your kindness. You all have made my beloved Hyal and I feel like a part of your family, and for that we are both very grateful. I would now like to take this opportunity to tell you that our family will soon be growing by one. My dear Hyal will be giving us another life to add to this family." Mortisk took his wife and pulled her to her feet and kissed her lovingly.

The ladies all mobbed her with hugs as soon as he was finished, like she was one of their sisters. Mortisk is assaulted by the manlier handshakes and slaps on the back, then Bill rises to speak.

"Friends and family, I would like to make a toast," he said, holding his bottle in the air. Everyone quiets to listen to him. "I have been lucky enough. No, let me rephrase that. We have all been lucky to call Mortisk our friend from the first day we him. With the addition of his beautiful Hyal, our family grew by two wonderful lives, and will soon become three. A toast to Mortisk and Hyal, and our universal family." They all clinked their bottles together and drank to the expecting couple.

"Thank you all," Hyal said in tears. "Even on Torani, I do not have friends as you. You have blessed me with your friendship, and have made me feel like I belonged since the day we first met. Thank you all," she repeated as she was hugged by her friends.

Bill excuses himself and returns a few minutes later with a box of cigars.

"Gentlemen, to the new addition to our family," he said, passing out the cigars. "I know you don't smoke these things, so I have a special one just for you." He pulled a cigar-sized joint out of the box and handed it to Mortisk. They all laughed and applauded as he lit it, enjoying a smoke with his friends.

Mortisk leaned over to Bill. "Thank you, my friend."

"You are welcome, my friend," he replied with a pat on the back.

The ladies are already planning for a new baby, months ahead of time as usual. The men are celebrating, as men like to do on pretty much any occasion when Bill stands once more.

"All right, everyone, quiet please. I have had an idea in my head for the last few months."

"That must have hurt," Monica joked.

Everyone laughed at her humorous remark.

"Funny, but true. That's why I'm glad to finally say this. I want to put an idea on the table. We have this beautiful valley all around us and I am proposing that we build our own town here in this valley. I built this house to get away from society, but lately I feel lonely when you are not all here. All of the people who are here and considered a part of our family and are welcome to add to this valley. Mortisk that goes for you and your family too." He sat back down and waited for all that were present to take in what he had just put forth.

"I, my friend, would be honored to live on your mountain," Mortisk said in agreement and handed Bill his very large smoke.

"I'll be happy to have you," he replied, holding it up and laughing.

This special group of friends and family all sat together and talked late into the night. It will be a new day tomorrow, and things will begin to change on the mountain.

CHAPTER 40

---•●❈●•---

Johnson Space Center, Houston
August 5, 2021

The space center is alive with hundreds of people from the center and the surrounding area, all there to welcome the first people to venture to another world. Brad waits patiently for word of the shuttles approach, which should be momentarily. Horace, Elsa, and the rest of the ex-president's advisors wait for the arrival of their good friend. Gene's family is also waiting for their very missed father and husband.

The Air Force band is playing on the tarmac to add to the atmosphere, and add to one of the greatest days in the history of the human race. Brad is informed that the shuttle is inbound and passes the word. The shuttle lands gently on the tarmac and the ramp extends to meet it. The first one out of the vehicle is the new ambassador who is immediately surrounded by his family. Gene's friends then all welcome him back to Earth from his new post.

John, and his friends Olga and Ben, who had surprised the others with his news of Tashike joining their group, all made their way to where the NASA crew was waiting to greet their friends. The group has a very important job to begin, but that can wait for tomorrow. They all have a very big "welcome home" party to attend today.

Bill has spent the last few days gathering earth-moving equipment to begin work on the new homes. They have decided to build six of the new homes before winter sets in, so he has spent the last few days marking out the spots for the homes.

He is standing outside with the dog drinking his morning coffee, wearing nothing but his boxer's, slippers, and his hat, waiting for his help to arrive. With Willis, Mortisk, and Bret, working on the power grid and only off on weekends, he and the other guys will have to carry the weight. Winter is only three months away so they need to hurry. He suddenly realizes that he will have to start getting dressed in the morning before he does his morning ritual. Well, he'll just have to make that one big sacrifice for his friends he figures.

The American District is still operating from the depths of the White House while the new headquarters is being constructed above. The rubble has been cleared, and the construction has begun on the modern building that will soon house the leader of the American District.

Elsa has called a meeting of her staff at the request of her old boss, Ambassador Furgison. The staff are all now in the briefing room of the bunker awaiting the arrival of their trusted leaders, both new and old. As Elsa enters the room with her guest, she calls the meeting to order.

"Gentlemen, we are called here today at the request of our former commander and chief, and new ambassador, Gene Furgison."

Gene rises and greets his old friends. "Good day everyone. First off, let's drop the ambassador crap. I'm still just your old friend Gene, and one of a billion other people on this planet that this new information pertains to. My friends what I am going to tell you must not leave this room. At this point I'm not even sure if we should tell the other world leaders yet."

The room is suddenly deathly quiet as Gene recounts his story of the conversation he had with the Zaxin ambassador. As he told the story, the mood in the room went from one of interest, to one of extreme anger and disbelief. For the Torani to make them believe that they were actually helping us for the good of the planet was one thing, but to convince the world to willingly give up every weapon they had to defend themselves against a future attack was a brilliant ruse. When Gene finished the barrage of questions began.

"So do you think we can believe the Zaxin ambassador, Gene?" Elsa asked from Gene's old chair.

"Elsa I have a hard time believing anything at this point, but with what he has told me about the execution of every single Corisole member that had knowledge of the plan, as well as them keeping us totally in the dark on the fuel composition. I have to lean toward yes. I do believe him. The nail in the coffin was when I was called to the emperor's office less than twenty-four hours later. He questioned me with the skill of a seasoned C I A investigator when he learned of our visit to the Zaxin ambassador's office. They obviously have had us under close guard."

"Do you think that you convinced him that it was just a curious visit on John's behalf?" Elsa's new security chief Whitt asked.

"I simply told him that I was giving John a Tour to satisfy his curiosity, and believe me when I say, that he does know how very curious John is, so I think he bought it."

"So where do we go from here Gene?" the Defense secretary asked.

"Actually Jack, that's where you and Horace come into the equation. Horace now has a complete schematic of the laser cannons that are based on the Lunar Station. You both need to get to Area 51 and get to work producing and strategically placing these things as quickly as possible. With a worldwide battery system, we should be able to repel any attack that is launched at us. We all saw the destruction they unleashed on the Torani fleet during the battle."

"What about building our own vessels from the blueprints John's team brought back from Torani," the admiral asked curiously.

"Vince, I have Horace, John, and Olga Krishkoff working on that as we speak. With enough time and manpower, I'm sure we can pull it off, but our Achilles heel will be the time."

"How are we going to hide the fact that we are building starships, Gene?" Elsa asked.

"We're not. We use the freighter designs and convince the Torani that we are going to go into the freight business. Even if they don't buy it, they might let us build them anyway, expecting to add them to their own fleet after they take control of Earth."

Elsa sat quietly for a moment contemplating their next move. "We can't do this alone Gene, we need the Russian and Japanese research facilities to help with the cannons. We have no choice but to call a meeting of the world leaders, so we will schedule a meeting in Dubai in one week. They both have as good of labs as Area 51, and we need them. And, Gene, you can't let any of the other leaders know that you gave me this information. I want them all to feel as we are doing this as a planet."

"You got it Elsa."

"All right, everyone. Like Gene said, this has to be kept top secret. Nobody but the people in this room know about any of this yet, so let's keep it that way. The Torani scientists have all gone back to their planet for a little R and R and we intend to take full advantage of it. Horace and the others can start work on the cannons immediately, and after the meeting in one week we will get the other districts involved."

"That will be all for today. Let's get busy."

As the others were leaving, Elsa cornered her old boss. "So do you think we can pull it off?"

"With enough time, yes I do. The kicker is that we have to keep the Torani from discovering our plan," he answered.

"I'll see you in one week, Gene. Go spend some time with your family."

They shook hands and Gene left the bunker en route to Texas where his family was waiting for him. He has spent months on Torani and is ready to relax.

John and his team have been invited to the Station to tour the massive structure. They hope to get a close look at the reactor room, but the Torani have left a skeleton crew of technicians to watch over the reactor, which throws a monkey wrench into their plan. They are now in Brad's office waiting for an opportunity to get into the reactor room.

"Have you made any headway at all with the fuel analysis Olga?"

"They haven't let us get within a mile of the fuel. If we had even a microscopic sample of it, we could break it down and determine its composition and discover how it works."

John rose and activated the video of the reactor core, watching the Torani technicians as they guarded it. Then he opened his laptop, turned it on, and went to where Brad was seated.

"Brad we have complete diagrams of the engines." He showed Brad the images. "We just can't discover how they work without the fuel."

"Then we need that fuel," Brad replied. "That has to be our first priority."

"They have a storage vault for the fuel, don't they?" John inquired.

"Yes, but there's no way into that vault. The electronic lock is unsurpassable."

"Then we need a world-class thief," John replied slyly.

Everyone's attention was now piqued.

"Where the hell do we find a safecracker?" Ben asked.

"I don't know, but you can bet one of Gene's, or should I say Elsa's FBI guys do," he stated with a sly smile. "I'll get them to find us one."

They all agreed that it was a good plan, but how do they get rid of the Torani long enough to make it happen was the question. Brad rose and grabbed his jacket.

"Shall we go look at the reactor core. They can't stop us from doing that."

The group would play it cool for now. They have no other projects started at the present, so they might as well enjoy a tour of the Station.

Chapter 41

---•●✦●•---

The Valley
August 10, 2021, 10:00

Things are going well on the mountain. The men have been able to complete preparing the first two holes for the houses. They will pour the footings as soon as they get the rebar to put in them. The government has guaranteed them all the concrete they need for the new town. The administration has approved full compensation for any company that helps with the rebuilding of the district. The people of the American District provide all the labor, and the government supplies all the material. It's a win, win situation for all involved.

Bill called Willis and Mortisk over to where he is working. "Willis, did you ask Tim Vance if his uncle still had those concrete forms?"

"He does and they are even still on the trailer, so all we have to do is go hook up and haul them here."

"What about the rebar? You said you had about around fifty tons left on the mesa right."

"Yea, at least that much. If you want, Mortisk and I will go now and fire up one of the shuttles and get it."

"That would be great. You two do that and I'll have Tim take the truck and chase down the forms. You said that you had plenty of lumber over at your storage yard right?"

"Yea, and there's also a forklift and a truck with a forty-foot flatbed sitting there to haul it with. I bet there's at least enough for the first three or four houses. I think we have enough of everything we need for the first four, but we'll have to find the rest someplace."

"We'll get a couple of guys started on that tomorrow. Okay, guys, I'll finish this and you two make a steel run. We've got to pour concrete tomorrow. What do you think Mortisk, about two hours?"

"About that," Mortisk said. He's finally learning to loosen up with his language.

"I'll have lunch and a cold beer waiting when you guys get back."

"Deal," Mortisk replied.

The two men headed for the Jeep. and Bill stood looking over the excavations. Five days and they were already to pour concrete. Good job guys, he thinks to himself.

Ben has borrowed a truck from the Motor Pool at Johnson. He has earned a vacation and he is taking it. The NASA crew doesn't have a big need for Astronomers right now, so he figured he would take advantage of the free time. Ben promised Tashike that he would show her the most beautiful mountains on the planet, and he wasn't going to break that promise. With the ability to get anything they need free at the district bases they can travel almost anywhere they want without having to deal with the locals in the cities. He mounted a fifty-five-gallon drum in the rear for gas so all they needed to worry about was food and water on their trip.

His plan is to go over the Colorado mountains through the Vail and Aspen area, then loop down to his observatory at Kitt Peak in Arizona and drive back across the deserts to Johnson. Tashike has never seen a desert and is excited to see something that Ben called a cactus.

He looked over at the beautiful golden woman sitting next to him. Tashike hasn't said even ten words in the last hour. As they are leaving the destruction that was once Denver and heading up into the mountains, he reached over and touched her hand. She looked over at him sadly.

"The destruction is horrible," she said as they left the city behind. "It must have been a beautiful city."

"The entire country was beautiful before the Corisole invasion," he answered angrily.

"I am sorry," she replied.

"It's not your fault, it's ours."

"Yours, what do you mean. The Corisole did this to your planet."

"We ignored all the signs. There were constant sightings of objects in the sky, which nobody took seriously, and the governments of the world also kept the truth from the people so they wouldn't be afraid. We were also arrogant enough to think we were the smartest beings in the galaxy, which is totally ridiculous. The worst part is, we found out the hard way that we're the stupidest and most gullible beings in the galaxy."

He squeezed her hand again, and looked west toward the pine-covered mountains leaving Denver in the rearview mirror. They drove in silence into the mountains of Colorado, both thankful for their time together.

Gene has come to Johnson at the request of his friend John, from his family's ranch outside Dallas where he has enjoyed the last few days riding horses on the large ranch his father owns. He walked through the Center to John's new office and knocked on the door, then stuck his head inside the office.

"Gene come in, I'm glad you could come."

John grabbed a pair of glasses off the small table next to his desk and filled them half full of Bourbon. Gene looked at the glass, then at his friend curiously.

"What can I do for you John?" Afraid of the answer he was about to get.

"Gene I need a favor. Do you still have connections in the FBI.?"

"Sure, why do you ask?"

"Well, Gene, I need the best thief the planet has to offer."

"What are we going to steal now John?"

"We need someone who can crack one of the most secure electronic locks ever made. We're going to break into the fuel vault on the Lunar Station and get us a sample of that fuel. If we can get a sample."

"We can reverse engineer it," Gene finished for him.

"Exactly," John replied.

"All right, John, I'll see what I can do. Give me a couple of days."

"So how's the family?" he asked, changing the subject.

The two men enjoyed their drinks while Gene explained to the bachelor, the pleasures of being a husband and a father. John listened contentedly to his tales.

Mortisk and Hyal are at Evans station fueling up the Camaro, when an Air Force–issue pickup truck pulls into the parking lot and up to the gas pump next to them. Hyal climbs out of the car and approaches the truck slowly at first, then runs to the side of the truck and started banging on the window. Inside the truck a startled Torani woman looks out the window absolutely speechless. Ben watches curiously as the door of the truck flies open and the two women hug each other madly and begin to cry.

Ben watched a Torani man walk over wearing of all things, a cowboy hat and Earth clothes. They both stood there watching silently as the two women hug and cry in each other's arms.

"I take it they know each other," Mortisk said dryly.

Ben looked at Mortisk and laughed loudly. "Finally, a Torani with a sense of humor," he said, holding out his hand. "Ben Murphy," he said, still laughing.

"Mortisk," he replied as he shook Ben's hand.

Hyal drags Tashike over to where the two men were standing watching them. "Mortisk, this is my best friend Tashike from Carista. Remember the café by the seaside," she said very excitedly.

"Yes, the Ocean Mist."

"Oh Tashike, you both must stay with us tonight. We have a small house, but we will make room. We are actually building a new one in the mountain. We are going there right now, please join us," Hyal asked, as giddy as a schoolgirl.

"Yes. You must join us for a barbeque," Mortisk added as he put the nozzle back in the pump.

"I never pass up a barbeque. Actually I thought I'd never get to go to another one," Ben said.

"Follow us," Hyal said as she stepped back into the convertible.

Mortisk joined his wife in the car, straightened his hat in the mirror, and started the cars roaring engine. As he pulled onto the street, he can't resist the temptation to smoke the tires and smile at his wife as she slapped him on the arm playfully.

Ben looked at Tashike with a very large smile. "I'm going to like this guy," he said, then followed them down the street of the small Colorado town.

Bill is walking toward the house after putting more wood in the barbeque. Alex, Willis, and the rest of the family's men are sitting by the stream in the shade of the aspen trees. As Bill takes his seat Sassy's ears perk up, someone's coming up the driveway, and they can tell by the rumble that it is Mortisk's Camaro. As he came around the last turn toward the house, they notice a green Air Force–issue truck following him.

Bill stood and walked toward the two vehicles with the dog at his side. The vehicles park and he sees two people he doesn't know, and one of them is a very beautiful Torani woman. Mortisk and Hyal lead the two newcomers over to where Bill and the curious dog were standing.

"Ben, this is my friend Bill."

"I can see where he gets his fashion sense from," Ben said laughing, noticing the beat-up old hat Bill was wearing. "Glad to meet you."

"He's hopelessly vulnerable," Bill replied, also laughing. "Pleasure to meet you."

Hyal introduces her dear friend to the rest of the men then, then lead her into the house for her to meet the rest of ladies.

"Beer?" Bill asked.

"Thought you'd never ask," Ben replied gratefully.

"Have a seat, Ben."

Bill introduced Ben to all the guys sitting under the trees, and after the introductions were finished, Ben looked around at all the construction that was going on. "Looks like you've got quite a project going on here," Ben said.

"We're building six more houses."

"More?" Ben asked, looking around, then noticing that Hyal and Tashike had disappeared.

Bill pointed at the ancient looking door. "Care for a tour?"

"In a few minutes." Mortisk interrupted, then handed Ben a very large pipe. Ben smelled the pipe and looked at Bill. Bill threw up his hands.

"I had nothing to do with this one. Oh and you won't need a light."

Ben shrugged his shoulders and smokes the large pipe. "Wow," Ben said. "Yours?" he asked Bill.

"No, his." Bill laughed.

The men sat talking among themselves for a while, then Bill took Ben in and showed him the mountain home and introduced him to the ladies who were all busy talking with their new friend. After a great meal they all sat around the fire pit enjoying the beautiful summer night.

Bill leaned over to Ben. "So what do you think of our new town?" he asked, motioning to the mountain.

"Got room for two more citizens?"

"Absolutely," Bill replied, handing Ben another beer. "Absolutely."

CHAPTER 42

—•●✿●•—

Johnson Space Center, Houston
August 12, 2021, 12:00

John is in his office at the Space Center, sending a message to Cloric at the Learning Center, trying to get the plans for a shipyard from the Torani to build freighters for the planet. The Torani shouldn't deny them the chance for the challenge of building their own vessels. He leaned back after sending the message and his phone rang.

"Hello."

"John, Gene here. I found the guy you asked me to find for you. He's a British man named Laurence Mann. I'll contact him at our meeting in Dubai tomorrow."

"Dubai huh?" John replied.

"We thought it was best to get all the leaders involved in this. I'll be back at Johnson day after tomorrow, hopefully with your new man."

"Be careful Gene. You know how important this is."

"John, as president I was the most careful person on this planet. You should know that."

"Sorry, I forget sometimes."

"No problem, buddy. I'll see you in two days and well set this plan into motion. Gotta go John, take care."

"Good-bye, Gene."

John hung up the phone and thought for a while about the days to come, then headed for the Communication Center to contact Brad on the Lunar Station. He had to schedule a ride to the moon.

The world leaders have all been summoned to World Headquarters to attend an emergency meeting. The leaders are all quite curious about not only the suddenness of the meeting, but the secrecy of the topic to be discussed.

The district leaders are all slowly filing into the main chamber. The number has grown by half and all the new members have been filled in on what is to be expected of them as a member of the council.

After they are all seated, Leader Rowland calls the meeting to order. "Ladies and gentlemen, we are assembled here today at the request of the man who is directly responsible for this great organization. I welcome the ambassador to Torani, Gene Furgison.

The room applauds as Gene takes the podium to speak. "Members of the council, it is indeed a pleasure to once again be among my friends from around the world. My friends, I have called you all here today in regards to information that has been brought to my attention about the Corisole invasion of our planet, and our Torani saviors."

The ambassador tells the story in its entirety of the Torani deception, as well as their desire to eventually conquer Earth in the future. He explained the need to build the shipyard and construct the warships disguised as freighters as quickly as possible, as well as the conversion of the Lunar Station for their defense. After all of these topics were made clear to them, he made it absolutely clear of the importance of secrecy regarding everything that he has just told them.

"Ladies and gentlemen, you have no idea of the level of my regret for getting us into this predicament. I like everyone else was quick to trust our mystery saviors, and feel deeply responsible for falling for their deception."

The members then began voicing their outrage at what they had just heard. Leader Rowland called for order in the chamber several times before the members quieted to let her speak.

"Ambassador Furgison, I for one am glad you made these decisions. Had we not fell for the Torani ruse we would still be a world in turmoil, and most likely still living in the ashes of our Countries. This terrible disaster has brought this planet to an all-time high. We all now work together as one for the greater good of the planet Earth. Had we not made the pact with the Torani, they would have certainly finished the job that the Corisole started. We also, would never have discovered the truth behind their intentions from our many true friends in the galaxy that you have gained throughout the process. So in my opinion, Ambassador, we all still owe you a great deal of thanks."

The leader once again sat to let Gene speak. Gene rose and slowly walked up to the podium. "What I need from all of you now is the use of your best scientists, as well as the use of your labs to work on our defenses. Next, my friends, we must have the utmost cooperation between the districts to complete this task."

"Last and most importantly. As I have already said, we have to maintain secrecy. If the Torani discover the fact that we know of their plan, or if they discover our manufacturing of the laser cannons, we will not even have to worry about building the freighters because we will already be dead. I will await news from your districts on whatever help you can provide. Thank you all for your participation."

Leader Rowland again takes the podium. "It is perfectly clear which path we should take on this matter. We will meet again in thirty days. At that time, we should have all we need to proceed with our plan, but until then we must have absolute secrecy. Not even your families are to know of this. Thank you all. This meeting is adjourned."

The members all filed out of the main chamber talking among themselves. As he walked, the British prime minister came to Gene and began to talk quietly.

"Ambassador, I have what you have asked me for," she whispered to Gene.

"Thank you, Edna."

"We were lucky to find him since all the state's prisoners were pardoned, but he has agreed to help us," she said, motioning to a door.

Once they were inside the room she introduced him to the most talented thief that ever lived. "Gene, I would like to introduce you to Mister Laurence Mann."

Gene shook the hand of the man standing in front of him. Laurence was no spring chicken at almost sixty years old, but Gene knew that with age comes experience.

"It's a pleasure, Mr. President," Laurence said respectfully.

"That's ambassador now. You have been told of our need I assume."

"Yes, I have, and let me tell you that it would be my pleasure, as well as an interesting challenge, Ambassador."

"Edna you have no idea how much help you have been, thank you," Gene said as he shook her hand.

"Are you ready to go, Laurence?"

"Do we get to fly in one of those shuttles?"

"My position does have its advantages."

"Then let's fly."

They bid the prime minister farewell and made their way to Gene's personal shuttle. Laurence Mann is not only going to the moon, but he is going to pull off the most important heist of his life.

With the day's unusual events to soon unfold, Brad and John are sitting in his office watching the monitor for the reactor room. Brad has been doing this for days, to try to establish the Torani's routine. Gene and his passenger should be coming into his office any time since they arrived at the Station ten minutes ago, and they want to be ready for any questions their guest may ask.

As Gene enters the office with the man they have been waiting for, they get up to greet their coconspirators in crime.

"Glad you made it Gene."

"Gentlemen, I would like you to meet Laurence Mann."

"I never in my life expected to be in the moon," Laurence said, shaking their hands and looking around the office.

"Would you like to see what you're up against, Laurence?" John asked.

"Let's have a look," he replied.

They all went to the monitor for the reactor room, and John pulled over a stool for Laurence to sit on as they watched the video screen.

"I'm not sure how you want to proceed, but I have days of footage for you to study if you would like to see it," Brad said.

"That would be the best way to begin."

They all sat at the monitor watching the video that has been recorded, answering all of the thief's questions as they did. Laurence jotted down notes as he watched, noting the times that the Torani took their breaks and slept.

"They don't seem to be very concerned with security do they?" Laurence commented. "There are times when there is nobody in there for hours."

"The Reactor cannot be opened while it's operating, which makes it secure. Their only concern is the vault," John said, pointing at the vault on the screen.

"Brad, you need to find our new friend a job to do so he can blend in," John said.

"I'll make him my new assistant. I can go anywhere I want on this Station unnoticed. Besides they pretty much all ignore me now, so I really doubt they will even pay any attention to Laurence."

"Gentlemen, I am going to hit the road, or space I guess. Whatever. Laurence, you're in the best hands in the galaxy, and anything you need these guys will get it for you. And remember that the entire world is depending on you to pull this off."

"My blind grandmother could do this job, and she's bedridden. Don't worry about a thing."

"Thank you Laurence. And thank you two also." He shook all of their hands and then made his way to his shuttle where the Torani pilot was waiting to return him to Earth.

Brad and John watched the thief as he watched more of the video. Suddenly Laurence turned to them.

"Let's see it up close."

The two men looked at each other and shrugged their shoulders.

"Let's Go."

They walked the corridors through the Station that led to the reactor room. The fate of the world rested on the shoulders, or should we say, the fingers of the thief.

Bill and Sassy are returning from a short morning walk as the guys start to show up for work. Willis, Mortisk, and Bret have managed to get two months off to work on the homes, so they hope to get the six homes under dirt. Once this part is finished, the cold of winter and the snow won't stop the progress. They already have three of the houses covered, and some of the guys have started the interior work. With so many homes to supply, the only problem is the solar power. Mortisk is sure they can get a collector for the town which will solve the problem and not damage the appearance of the valley. Bill insists that they keep it as it was, with nothing visible when they are finished.

When Mortisk was on Torani his main study was engine dynamics and power conversion, which is why he ended up working as a technician on the tower project.

Bill greets Alex and Dove as they pulled into the lot. They are going to make the trip to Gypsum today, which is one of two remaining sheetrock plants in the American District, and has also created many jobs for the area. The importance of rebuilding the planet has actually created a shortage of workers worldwide, for all the factories needed to manufacture the needed materials. Alex is going to take the big trailer and go to the factory, to get the drywall they need for the homes as the push is on to get them finished on the inside before winter hits.

"Good morning, Bill," Alex said, climbing out of the truck.

"How's everything coming?" Dove asked.

"Great. Willis and Bret Brought up all of their booty from after the attack, so we have all the plumbing and electrical supplies we need for at least the first three houses. We'll be ready for the sheetrock in a few days on the first one," Bill answered, opening the door for her.

"Happy birthday," she said, handing him a small box.

"Thank you. What is it?" he asked foolishly. "Never mind I know, just open it." He opened up the box, and inside was something he hasn't seen in many years. "Thank you so much," he said, pulling a big gold chain bracelet out of the box. The bracelet was a gift to him when they were on vacation in Florida, while he and Dove were still married. He had forgotten all about it until now.

"Where did you find it?"

"Alex and I thought that since the storage units weren't destroyed here, that we would go to Aspen and see if ours was still there. Luckily the building was still lying in a pile, so we dug through it to our unit and it was still there. We loaded it all in the truck and brought it home. That was in the bottom of one of my old jewelry boxes."

"Here, this is from me." Alex handed him a very expensive cigar. "It's not much but I knew you would appreciate it."

"Thank you both so much. To be honest, I forgot my own birthday." He put the bracelet on his wrist, and the cigar in his pocket. "For later," he added, patting his shirt pocket.

Alex headed back toward the truck. "Let's hook up that trailer and we'll be on our way."

They hooked up the trailer and the trip was under way for their first load of drywall. Things were starting to come together. To Bill it was like old times when he had his construction company. It's always fulfilling to see progress.

The rest of the family as well as the other workers arrived soon, and picked right where they left off the day before. They wanted as much work as they could be done by noon because they all knew it was Bill's birthday, and that always meant a party. Actually, Groundhog day was a good enough reason for Bill to have a party. Since the mountain was in such disarray, they planned on using the park for the party, and the whole town would undoubtedly be there to celebrate.

Gene left the Lunar Station and informed his pilot to take him to Washington, where they had just landed. He had to talk to Elsa. He walked freely into the White House, which was strange not having a hundred guards and security people guarding it. Elsa's office was in his old office in the bunker, so he had no trouble finding her. Gene knocked, then let himself in.

"Come in, Gene," Elsa said, getting up to greet him.

"It fits you well," he commented, pointing at the desk.

"It seems a little big to me."

"That doesn't last long."

They both sat at the desk and got comfortable.

"So what does your thief think?" she asked.

"I left our new friend with John and Brad so he could snoop around for as long as he needed. They'll set it up so he can move freely throughout the Station until he decides the best way to proceed."

"You think he can do it?"

"To the best of our knowledge there's nobody better for the job. Edna Harker said that he was a thorn in their ass for twenty years before they finally caught him."

"How is the prime minister taking the news?"

"The same as the rest of the leaders. Not well."

"They sure pulled one over on us didn't they?"

"Look at it this way Elsa. If they hadn't of, we would have ended up like Corisole. At least we have the advantage of knowing they are coming."

"Care for a drink Gene?"

"Just one. This job makes you like that stuff, doesn't it?"

"Yea, I'm going to start smoking again too," she said laughing. "I understand that you're heading back to Torani soon."

"I have to play the part. They can't think anything is different, and I also need to stay in contact with the other ambassadors. I'm going to con the emperor into sending me and my new staff on a galactic cruise too."

"That's smart. Who's your new staff?"

"John for sure, and I think I'll ask Allen Whitt if you can spare him. He used to work for the CIA, so he knows his stuff."

"He's all yours if he wants the job."

"Oh, and there's one more thing I need to borrow."

"What's that?" she asked curiously.

"I need a ride back to Johnson after I'm through here. I had to send the shuttle back to the station. Can I borrow your ride?"

"It's yours as much as it is mine. Help yourself."

The two leaders sat and talked throughout the afternoon. Not about business, but about everyday life. It was nice to forget the world's problems, even if it was only for a few hours.

The guys quit working at noon and loaded everything they needed for what they knew would be the best barbeque of the year.

Bill now sits on the tailgate of his truck with his old hat on his head and one of his best girls by his side; unfortunately, it's the hairy one. They watch the people he has come to call his family and dear friends, enjoying the warm August afternoon.

The music is playing, people are dancing and singing, and the children roam safe and free throughout the park without a care in the world. Mortisk is at the river enjoying his new hobby. Bill has taught him to fish and he's hopelessly addicted to it now. The large alien is becoming more human every day. Ben comes up with two cold beers and hands one to Bill, then sits down on the tailgate next to him.

"Where's the girls?" he asked.

Bill pointed out into the crowd of inebriated women who are dancing and having the time of their lives.

"It's nice to finally see happy people," Ben said, looking around the park.

"How's that for happy." Bill was pointing toward the river at a totally contented alien.

Ben smiled at the sight. "I trust that one, I think." "What's that supposed to mean?" Bill asked, almost angry at the comment.

"I'll have to explain it another day. You'll just have to trust me for now."

"Trust is earned, Ben, and I've known him a lot longer than I have you."

"I'm sorry, Bill, I didn't mean anything by it. It's just that I learned a few things on their planet that I am sworn not to repeat, that make me not totally trust them. Let's drop the subject, okay."

"Agreed," Bill replied.

The two men were sitting quietly enjoying the sun and the music, when Mortisk came up the bank with a beautiful trout on his line.

"What do you think?" he said, holding it up for them to see.

"Nice one," Ben said, now wishing that he was fishing.

"Take it over to the barbeque and they'll gladly cook it for you. They taste best right out of the water," Bill said as Mortisk was walking away.

He looked back as he was walking away. "I'm one step ahead of you," he said smiling.

He gave the fish to the men that were manning the barbeque, who took it gladly to cook for him. He stopped and grabbed three beers, then came back to the truck handing each of them another.

"To good friends," he said, holding up his bottle.

"Here, here," they both replied.

As they clinked their bottles together, the large alien's big blue eyes got even bigger as he spotted the bracelet on Bill's wrist. He set his bottle down and grabbed Bill's hand to examine the bracelet more closely.

"What is this?" he asked.

"Just something I thought I lost a long time ago, and was given back to me today as a birthday gift."

"May I see it?" he asked, holding out his hand.

Bill removed the bracelet and handed it to Mortisk to examine. He examined it quite closely as the two men watched.

"What's wrong."

"Do you know what this is, my friend."

"Yes, it's solid gold."

"My friends, this is Triomicium. This is what powers our space vessels, as well as our planet," he explained, still not believing what he was holding.

Ben could not believe what he has just heard. Bill might not think much of Mortisk's statement, but Ben certainly does.

"What do you know about Triomicium?" Ben asked.

"On my planet I am what you would call a fuel engineer." Ben's eyes got real wide with interest. "I was brought to this planet to adjust and maintain the fuel flow in the Corisole towers, in order to create the power for this planet." As he explained, he handed the bracelet back to Bill. "Gold is common on your planet?" he then asked curiously.

"It's quite valuable, but also quite plentiful. Why do you ask?"

"I am not certain. I need to think about this."

Mortisk sat quietly on the trucks tailgate, thinking and drinking his beer. Hyal and Tashike, along with Monica, came over to see what the guys were up to. The cook came over with a plate covered with potatoes, vegetables, and a perfectly cooked trout that he handed to Mortisk.

"Go eat your fish, we'll join you in a minute," Bill said, pointing at the picnic table. Bill and Ben then both locked their respective lady's arm in theirs and wandered toward the party.

Willis and his friends were having the time of their lives playing music for all the people to dance to. He is happy to see how much they all appreciate how much his father has done for them to get their lives back. They are all here to celebrate his birthday with him and show their appreciation for all he has done for them.

The party went on late into the night, with everyone enjoying another classic park barbeque. Ben and Mortisk were unusually quiet, but tried very hard not to let anyone else notice it. Ben would wait a day or two to talk to Mortisk about the Gold. He's sure he can trust him, but he has his orders and must be careful with the information that he possesses.

CHAPTER 43

Planetwide Summary 3
August 27–September 1, 2021

The Valley
August 27, 2021

The next few days went on as the ones before. The hillside was excavated, and Bill was supervising the concrete work which is now half finished. Bret and Willis are busy running the utilities into the houses, and Mortisk has been working on the collector for the town. All in all, the project is coming along quite well and they should have the first three houses finished by October. They have actually thought about starting the other three this year.

Ben has decided that he had better get back to Johnson to inform John about his discovery. John would be greatly interested in the Torani fuel technician. Tashike is Going to stay with Hyal to save her the long journey, and he has promised to be back by the first of the month.

The men on the Station have been very busy. They have spent the last month studying the laser cannons in great detail since they have been given access to them. Horace returned to Area 51 two days ago to begin the process of recreating the cannons. The Russian district as well as the Japanese have sent teams of physicists, as well as metallurgical scientists, to assist with the research on the project. Horace and Olga are heading up the project.

On the Station, Brad and John are helping Laurence to succeed with his own project. The schedule is set, and in two days their thief is going to make his attempt to breach the vault. They must acquire the fuel sample to continue with their plan. John will be returning to Johnson in a few hours. He has received a massage from the Space Center claiming that there is an emergency at the base. It's curious that there was no explanation with the message.

Ben has spent the last twenty-four hours on the road to get back to Johnson. He met with John as soon as he arrived and they both agreed that Gene needed to hear what he had to say. It is now six o'clock in the evening and they are all in John's office for the meeting.

Ben pulled the bottle of Bourbon from the shelf and poured them all a drink. Gene is quite curious about what the two men are about to tell him.

"Guys, I've got a Torani fuel technician," Ben said. "You can drink those now."

"What the hell are you talking about," Gene said as he sat down his glass on the desk.

Ben began the story of his trip, and the one-hundred-billion-to-one odds of Tashike meeting Hyal at a gas station in a tiny little burned-out town in Colorado. He told them about the seven-foot alien wearing a cowboy hat and driving a red Camaro convertible. He then told them about his friend who is building his own town in a mountain, and how that friend came to his birthday party wearing a gold bracelet.

"Ben," John said, stopping him, "would you please get to the point."

"I'm getting there, don't interrupt," Ben replied, then took a drink from his glass.

Ben then told them how the seven-foot beer drinking alien fisherman, almost had a heart attack when he saw the gold bracelet on his friend's wrist, and proceeded to tell them that gold was the ore used to make the fuel to power his whole planet, as well as their space vessels.

"Brad, we already know about the gold," Gene said impatiently.

"Would you two please let me finish."

Ben then told them how the seven-foot cowboy-hat-wearing, beerdrinking alien was a Torani fuel technician.

With all this being said, John grabbed the bottle and filled their glasses again and sat back in his seat and looked at Ben.

"You've gotta be shitting me!"

"Not even a little bit," Ben replied, grinning.

"Did you say anything to him about what we know?" Gene asked.

"Absolutely not, but I notice a sense of worry in his mood afterward."

The three men sat and thought and drank for a few minutes, then Gene sat forward and you could tell he had a plan.

"Gentlemen, load up we're going to Colorado," Gene said.

"You driving, I'm beat," Ben said.

"I'll borrow some wheels. How about Air Force One," he said as he grabbed John's phone.

Three hours later, they were on board Air Force One and on their way to the airport in Rifle, Colorado, of all places.

Bill is standing outside with his coffee in his hand, and a joint hanging out of his mouth. Sassy has changed her routine somewhat since most of her bushes are now no longer there, but she doesn't care, she found new ones. Monica comes out and laughs at him standing in nothing but his hat, boxers and an old pair of sneakers.

"Going for a fashion statement this morning I see," she said, looking at the sneakers.

"You know me. I'm a trendsetter," he replied with a smile.

"Please don't let Mortisk see you like this or Hyal will kill me. And I don't need a seven-foot alien woman pissed at me."

Sassy's ears perked as a car was coming around the corner of the driveway.

"You should get some clothes on," Monica said.

"This is my valley, and there's a No Trespassing sign on the gate," he said, walking toward the strange car.

The car rolls to a stop and Ben gets out of the driver's side.

"I didn't know it was a formal affair," Ben said laughing.

"Ben, how the hell are ya. I didn't expect you back so soon," he said, shaking his hand.

Bill looked at the house when he heard the door shut, and Monica was already coming out with his robe. As he's putting it on two more doors open on the car.

"Looks like you need a pair of fuzzy slippers," one of the men said.

"The dog ate them," Bill replied.

About that time Bill noticed who the man with the jokes was. It was Gene Furgison, the president of the United States.

"I'll be dammed, Mr. President. Pleasure to meet you. You didn't tell me you hung out in this kind of circles, Ben."

Bill puts the joint back in his mouth to free his hand and shakes the president's hand.

"Old friends," Ben said. "And this is my old friend John Alistair."

"From NASA, right? I'm a bit of a space buff," he added as he shook John's hand. "Gentlemen, let's get a cup of coffee."

"In your mountain?" Gene asked, pointing at the door.

"Don't ask," Ben said, laughing.

The four men, and the now really happy dog, disappeared into the mountain. Monica had already disappeared to make herself look perfect, being a woman.

"So to what do I owe this special visit, Ben?" he asked as he put his now-extinguished doobie in the ashtray.

Gene told the story from the beginning. From the Zaxin ambassador, to the thief on the moon. Bill listened in disbelief as he rolled another joint. About that time Willis and Mortisk walked in the door. Gene watched as the seven-foot alien in a cowboy hat, takes the freshly rolled smoke from Bill and lights it.

"Willis, Mortisk, the president of the United States."

"Actually I'm not the president anymore. I'm the ambassador to Torani now."

"So they demoted you because of all this, huh," Willis said with a smile.

They all laughed, which lightened the mood in the room at least a ton.

"Guys, the ambassador here has a story to tell," he said as he poured everyone some more coffee. Monica came in looking her best and began making some more.

"Before we get started, Gene and John, this is Monica."

They all shook her hand and introduced themselves. Gene and John then retold the story. When they had finished, Willis and Monica stood absolutely speechless because of what they had just heard. Mortisk sat silently. After smoking most of Bill's joint, he handed it back to him, then spoke.

"My friends I am shocked at what I have heard. I cannot believe that the Torani emperor would fall to such evil levels. This galaxy once went through a very dangerous and deadly period of time. Like your planet, the quest for power was the most important thing. As children we were told the stories of the wars, and the evil of such greed and destruction. I have a hard time believing that a Torani would stoop to such evil, but the Zaxin race is known for their honesty. Their race bases its society on the basis of truth and the pursuit of justice in this galaxy."

He paused to drink his coffee and gather his thoughts. "After seeing this," he said, grabbing Bill's wrist, "I believe what you are telling me. I am sorry, my friends, for the evil my planet has brought upon Earth. I am not worthy of your friendship." He stood and handed Bill the hat that he had given him. "I am ashamed to be Torani."

Bill handed him back his hat, then looked at the three men. "You've got a plan, don't you."

They all listened as Gene and John explained the plan to arm the planet and the Lunar Station over the next ten to twenty years. When they had finished, they looked at Mortisk and asked the question they came to ask.

"Will you help us?" Gene asked him.

Mortisk thought about the great task they were taking upon themselves. Then spoke. "My friends, I will help you but you must take my advice. First, call off your thief. If he is caught, or if they discover the missing fuel, all will be lost. You cannot have the risk of this knowledge reaching the emperor. If it does, all will be lost."

"The cannons are the best defense against the Torani vessels. The power can be pulled directly from the towers, but we will need to create force fields to protect them from bombardment from space. I know very little about this technology, but perhaps we can enlist a designer to help us. Most Torani will feel as I do about the emperor's plan." He paused to think and John jumped in.

"We are going back to Torani soon. I will be at the Learning Center and maybe I can convince them to let me learn about the technology. To them it will just be another of my many curiosities," John said with a smile, looking at Gene.

"You may be right. Especially if you base it on the maintenance of the Station's force fields," Mortisk said. "I would also point out that trying to build vessels at this time would be a waste of valuable time and resources. The answer is in building hundreds of smaller fighter craft armed with smaller laser cannons. These craft can be built secretly on your planet, and will have the ability to exit and reenter the atmosphere like the Corisole attack ships."

"That is a great idea," Ben remarked as he was getting another cup of coffee.

"You should have everything you need on this planet, to succeed with your plan. The most important part will be secrecy. If they find out, you will be destroyed." Mortisk sat and thought for a minute. "The Torani have given you shuttles, correct?"

"Yes, we have five," John said.

"Get your people together. You will need your most secret bases to hide this from them, and I will help you any way I can."

Gene offers his hand to his new friend. "Thank you Mortisk." Then he looked at Bill and at the ashtray. "You got another one of those. I haven't smoked that stuff since college, but I could use it right now."

"That's what they all say," Bill said.

They all laughed, then Mortisk pulled his pipe from inside his jacket. Bill looked at Gene and pointed to Mortisk. "He's got the good shit."

The men talked for many more hours trying to sharpen their plan. With John being a pilot, Mortisk was sure he could teach him to fly the shuttles. Since they had five of them, they could use them to fly between the labs. The Torani cannot trace the shuttles movements unless they are in orbit and they will have no ships in orbit for some time.

After they had finished they went outside and noticed the guys were all busy at their jobs. The ones that that noticed them stop and point. They couldn't believe that the president was in their valley.

"Ready to go, Ben?" John asked.

"I'm staying for now, but I'll give you a ride to the Airport if I get to keep the car. I'm sure you can find your way back when you need us. We'll be waiting."

"You guys take care now. We can't afford to screw this up," Bill said, giving them an awkward salute.

"We'll be in touch," Gene said as he returned the salute, then got into the car.

The three men left the valley and drove back to the Airport. They have a world to save, and now they have a plan to do it with the help of a Torani specialist named Mortisk.

The men arrived at Houston six hours later and hurried to John's office to put a stop to the heist. They hurried to the comms center to raise the Lunar Station.

On board the Station Brad is at the monitor watching the feed from the reactor room. The Torani always take their break at 1400 hours and are always gone for exactly thirty minutes. They are all ready to put their plan into effect.

Laurence has spent days studying the locking mechanism and is confident that he can easily open the vault. The Torani are obviously not concerned with theft. It appears to Laurence that the lock is more of a safety feature, which makes his job rather simple as an experienced thief.

Brad watches as the thief easily opens the vault door and acquires his treasure. The treasure is a Gold ball about four inches in diameter, and very heavy as Laurence picks it up with both hands and admires what would be worth around a Million dollars to him. They now have to quickly analyze the orb and return it before it is discovered that it is missing.

Five short minutes later the thief enters Brad's office with their booty. Brad locks his office door and takes the orb from Laurence's pack, then sets it on his desk to examine. He is amazed by not the weight of the object, but its beauty.

He has the tools ready to take a sample of the orb and is ready to begin, when his comm activates with a communication from John's office at Johnson. He sets down his tools as Laurence watches him and looks at his watch. They have less than twenty minutes to return their prize to its original resting place before the Torani return. Brad answers the comms knowing that only John could be on the other end.

"Brad. We have to stop Laurence," is the first thing John said. "We've found another answer to our problem."

The two men looked at each other amazed at what they have just heard.

"John we've got it sitting right in front of us," Brad replied.

"Shit. We've got to get that thing back in the vault."

"What about our plan John?"

"Brad the plan has just changed. We've got a Torani fuel technician."

Brad stood there speechless and looked at Laurence. Laurence realized the value of John's statement.

"How the hell did that happen in just a few hours John?"

"A billion to one odds, and a very long story Brad. You've got to get that thing back in the vault now. Get a very small sample and get that thing back in that vault now."

"You got it John."

The comms went blank and the two moon men looked at each other.

"You better hurry," Laurence stated as he handed him a very small drill, then looked at his watch to express the lack of time.

Back at Johnson, John looked at the very concerned Gene. "I can't believe they pulled it off."

"Laurence is the best John. I didn't have a doubt that he could do it."

"I've got to talk to Elsa," Gene said.

"I'll go with you. I haven't been to Washington in a while."

They both sat back and waited for Brad to call them back. They were hopeful that the reply would be that they were successful.

Back on the Station the thief was already en route to the vault to return the orb. He had fifteen minutes to get there and replace the treasure in the vault. This was a peculiar situation for him. He has never been in a rush to return something to a vault before.

After getting the good news of the successful return of the fuel to the vault, the three friends flew to Washington and are now sitting in the new Oval Office of a very new, and different White House. The construction is still under way, but Elsa's office is finished, and she couldn't spend another day in that tomb which has been her home for almost a year. She sat listening to Gene's incredible story about the cowboy hat wearing Torani that just happened to be a fuel technician.

She laughed at the thought of the seven-foot cowboy, and cringed at the thought of the risk they had taken on the Station. When Gene was finished, Elsa was quiet for a moment, then spoke.

"Well, at least your alien has good taste. He drives a Camaro." Then she laughed, relieved that all had ended up for the best. "So where do we go from here?" she asked the two men sitting in front of her.

"John and I are returning to Torani. We can't afford to let them get suspicious. Is Allen Whitt on board to act as my assistant?"

"I talked to him two days ago and he's up for a little action. He hasn't played the spook role for five years, so he's almost giddy at the chance. Who are you taking with you John?"

John stood and started to pace as he thought. "I'm really not sure. We've been so busy I haven't even thought about it. Ben has no desire to return, and Olga will be busy with the cannon project. I'm going back to study the force field designs. We've studied them for years at NASA but haven't gotten anywhere."

John continued to pace, then he turned to the others and you could that he had his man. "We have to nail down the engineering of the force emitters and there's nobody better than Jack Lee. He's the best dammed computer engineer on the planet. As far as I know he's still in Japan."

John looked at Elsa, and then at the phone. "Chancellor Ono," was all he said.

"I'll get on the horn and contact him," Elsa said.

Gene turned and helped himself to a glass of Bourbon. "Old habit," he said. "Elsa, we need you to get ahold of the Chinese, Russians, and Japanese. Anyone who has secret bases, because we're gonna need them.

We've got a hell of a lot of work to do, and it has to be done in absolute secrecy. Can you do that for us?"

"Absolutely Gene. The best part of being secretary of state was that I got all the juicy information. I not only know who, but where." She smiled and poured two more Bourbon's. "Sounds like we've got a plan, gentlemen. I will make sure all the others are informed when I'm in Dubai on the thirteenth. I guess I won't see you two until you get back in six months. Oh, and John. I'll have Lee at Johnson in two days if he's still alive."

"Thanks Elsa."

"We'll see you in six months, Elsa, be careful," Gene said, setting down his glass.

The two men rose and shook Elsa's hand, then left the office bound for the presidential taxi. If you had to travel, Air Force One was the only way to do it.

September mornings are the best there are in Colorado with their absolutely perfect temperatures. Ben and Bill are both standing in the morning air drinking coffee and completing the morning ritual.

When John left Colorado he left Ben a Small satellite dish used by the SEALS so they could communicate. Today is the day they have scheduled for him and his new alien friend to go to Houston and start teaching John to fly the shuttles. Mortisk has managed to get the Torani to give him a shuttle permanently. He convinced them he needed it to check locations of the grid around the district, which will give them the freedom of movement they need in the months to come. Ben and Bill are waiting for him to arrive.

"So what's on the agenda for today?" Ben asked as they waited.

"Willis and I are going to start the restoration of the hillside today. I want the valley to look exactly like this," he said as he pointed at his home.

"I love the idea. Total stealth, not to mention the protection from the elements."

"It's great protection from aliens too. That's already been proven."

Ben agreed with a nod. A few seconds later the dog's ears perked up when she heard something coming.

"Here they come," Bill said, pointing at the dog.

The shuttle came up the valley just over the treetops and landed in the driveway. Mortisk exited the shuttle and walked over to them with Hyal on his arm and an empty coffee cup in her hand.

"Got an extra cup," she asked.

"Monica's in the house, she'll hook you up."

"Thank you," she replied.

They went into the house for another cup of coffee before the day begins.

"So what's your game plan for today?" Bill asked Ben.

"We're going to Houston and pick up John so Mortisk can give him his first flying lesson on the way to Area 51. Horace wants to meet Mortisk. We'll be back by dark."

"Those things are that fast huh."

"Faster," Mortisk answered, smiling. "We'll take it easy today since it's John's first lesson."

After another cup of coffee, Mortisk and Ben kissed their ladies and climbed aboard the shuttle. It rose gracefully into the sky, then disappeared over the mountain.

"Wow. My day is going to be boring compared to theirs," he said to Monica.

"You'll get over it. Besides, you've got a lot of work to do, so you better get dressed."

Bill bowed politely and obeyed his better half. He did have a lot of work to do and needed to get busy.

Ben and Mortisk are standing on the tarmac at Johnson after their quick journey from Colorado. Mortisk stands looking around the base with the curiosity of a teenager. He has studied the early days of space travel, but has never seen it. It was an amazing experience for him. There was a shuttle parked on the runway that escaped the destruction and Mortisk couldn't help but to walk around it and imagine flying the ancient spacecraft.

"I have studied your early space history from the rocket flights to the space shuttle missions. It is amazing to stand this close to history."

"This is where we watched our first man walk on the moon," Ben replied. "It doesn't seem like much now."

"We all learn to walk before we run," he said to his new friend.

A Jeep is coming across the massive tarmac toward the shuttle. It stopped and John climbed out, then walked over to the two men.

"Ready, Captain?" Ben joked.

"That's colonel," John reminds him.

"Yes, sir." Ben saluted comically.

"Mortisk. How are you today?"

"I am fine."

"Shall we get started?" John asked. "You have the coordinates to the Nevada base, right?"

"They are programmed into the flight computer," Mortisk replied.

"Then let's fly," John said as he cracked his knuckles.

The three travelers entered the Torani shuttle on day 1 of John's training, and they will take care of business while they are at it. Horace is expecting them at the Nevada base in one hour.

Horace is waiting in his Jeep as the shuttle comes over the mountain that hides the base within. It circles the base then comes in for a rougher than usual landing Horace noticed. The door opens and the three men exit the ship. Horace knows two of the men but does not recognize the Torani. He thinks he would remember one wearing a cowboy hat.

"Landing was a little rough," Horace commented.

"My first landing," John replied.

Horace looked at him with a surprised expression. "That was you flying that thing?"

"Gotta learn some time."

"Scared the hell out of me," Ben said.

John looked at his friend and laughed. "Shall we go inside."

They all climbed into the Jeep and went into Horace's new playground. Once they were inside Horace led them over to something covered by a large tarp. Horace ripped the tarp off the object and the men all looked with wonder at what Horace had hidden.

"A Corisole attack vessel," Mortisk said, as he went in for a closer look and rubbed his hand over the surface. "This is good, my friends. We now have the model for our laser fighters."

Horace looked at them curiously. "Who is this?" he said, pointing at the Torani.

"Horace, I would like you to meet Mortisk. He is our Torani fuel technician."

"You're shitting me."

"Not at all, my friend. He is literally a gift from the heavens," John replied, looking up.

"Horace, Mortisk is our friend and he stands against everything the Torani are trying to accomplish on this planet. He's actually one of the planet's newest citizens." Horace takes a minute then decides his next course of action. "Then show me how it works," he asked, putting his hand on the ship.

Mortisk spent the next three hours giving the scientist a crash course in the engineering of the ship. He removed the ships shields and showed them how the power was produced, then transferred and stored for engines and weapons. After three hours Horace was one large step closer to his goal of totally understanding the power source.

"Incredible," Horace said. "I just jumped fifty years into the future. Thank you Mortisk." He then bowed which made Mortisk look at him oddly. Mortisk grabbed his hand with his own big hand and shook it firmly.

"You are welcome, Horace."

John climbed down from the ship that he was inspecting closely. "We need every person we can possibly fit in this lab working on this Horace.

Get ahold of the Russians, Japanese, British, whoever you can get to get this rolling. Elsa is lining up the rest of the world's research facilities for our use. You need to teach them all you have just learned, and Mortisk will be back in one week to answer any questions you may have for him."

"I'll get my engineers working on doubling the size of the ship so we can fit the laser into the fuselage," Horace said, thinking out loud. "Mortisk, can you come to the base once a week to answer questions?"

"Yes, Horace, I can do that."

"All right then," John said. "Time for more flight lessons. Let's hit the road."

"The road?" Mortisk asked, puzzled by the comment.

"Just a figure of speech," Ben said to the puzzled alien.

Horace escorted them back to the shuttle where they all then shook hands and parted ways. After Dropping their new addition and his old friend off at the mountain, and five hours at the helm of the shuttle, John was beginning to feel at home in the new craft. As he walked across the tarmac at Johnson he had a thought. Now they would have to build simulators for the laser fighters.

CHAPTER 44

—•●❀●•—

Planetwide Summary 4
September 13–December 25, 2021

Dubai, United Arab Emirates
World Headquarters
September 13, 2021

Elsa appeared before the leaders with Gene and Horace at her side. They explained the need for the world's supreme scientists to travel to the Nevada base for a period of time, to train in the physics of the Torani fuel systems and reactors. Horace has requested engineers, as well as scientists, for the production of the alloys they will need for the reactor cores and fighters.

Gene assured the council that he will do all he possibly can on his Tour of duty on Torani, to meet with the other leaders of the galaxy in order to discover their true Allies. With Allen Whitt acting as his assistant, they intend to discover everything they can about the other systems, and return in six months with an idea of who they can trust.

The council adjourned with a better sense of the fate of their planet's future than they have had for the past year. They have a renewed sense of hope as well as purpose for Earth.

John has spent the last month with Mortisk, learning to master the new craft as well as maintain and service it. After a month Mortisk is confident with his abilities. John has now become the teacher, as he teaches Brad everything he has learned. The training time has allowed them to make regular trips to the Nevada base to stay in the loop on the goings on at the labs.

Laurence Mann, after completing his task for the fate of the world, has earned a new respect from the world. He is no longer treated as a threat, and with a great deal of gratitude from the world leaders, tours the planet unmolested as a guest of any district he visits.

Brad's next task is to create the new simulators for the fighters with Mortisk's help. Mortisk is the only one on the planet that has piloted such a craft, therefore he is invaluable in the project. They will then begin the task of training the qualified recruits for the program.

John and Gene, along with Allen Whitt and Jack Lee, will be leaving for Torani in eighteen days. They all have very important jobs ahead of them for the sake of their world. John and Jack will be extremely busy studying the science behind the much needed force field technology, while Gene and Allen will be deeply involved in the task of creating a secret alliance of planets, that will only include those that they believe they can totally trust with the newfound evidence they have uncovered about the Torani's future plans for galactic domination.

Olga has returned to a secret base in Siberia, where she will lead with the creation of the engine cores for the new fighters. Olga is the only person on the planet that has spent time on the assembly of the cores during her time on Torani, which makes her the only expert on the subject other than Mortisk.

All aspects involved in the task of saving their world are now in high gear and they all need to grab the wheel and drive hard to the finish, with hope that they can beat the Torani to the finish line.

Horace has very busy greeting his new teams. One hundred and fifty scientists have now assembled at the Nevada base, so he has had his work cut out for him.

The weekly question-and-answer sessions that Mortisk has attended has brought the world's scientists up to speed on the basics of Torani fuel technology, and in the weeks to come, Mortisk will lead them as they disassemble the Corisole attack ship. The ship is to be enlarged to accommodate the laser cannon assembly and a pilot.

All is going well and soon Earth's scientists will be able to return to their own labs and double the efforts from the knowledge they learned at the Nevada facility.

Gene is busy enjoying the last three days on Earth with his family. He has spent the last two weeks on the ranch undisturbed by the galaxy's problems. Riding the unmolested ranch with his father, as well as his wife and children has been the most peaceful experience he has had in the last year, and he has enjoyed it immensely. It's a wonderful place and he wouldn't want his family anywhere else on the planet at this time.

The last of the hay has been bailed for the winter, and the cattle have been culled for the sale and shipment to the people of Earth. All of the district ranches, as well as the farms, now use regional co-op's to distribute the food, as well as the seed and feed they need to operate. There are no more worries of whether a farmer can afford to grow his crops, making farming now a very respected occupation in the world's eyes.

It's Christmas in the valley and the first four homes are finally finished, and the last two homes are 90 percent finished but livable. The garage has been converted to the new meeting area because it is too cold outside for most of the residents to sit at the fire pit. This spring there are plans to build a large recreation center for the residents of the town to enjoy.

Today the valley is filled with the happiness of its residents. The children are playing in the snow with the dog, as well as the new sleds that Santa brought them. We told them that the aliens couldn't find his secret workshop on the North Pole. Bill is by his fire as always, keeping it going for the happy but cold children to warm themselves.

Monica and the rest of the ladies are sitting with Willis and Alice. The pair have informed the others that Alice is now three months pregnant, so as women do, they are already planning for a new member to the growing family and enjoying themselves doing it. So many loved ones were lost during the attack, and Bill still has nightmares about the disappearing family at the church, as well as the hundreds of bodies they had to burn during the cleanup.

A very happy alien came into the garage with a big Cuban cigar in his mouth. He plans on smoking this one since Hyal gave birth to the town's newest resident at four o'clock this morning. Mortisk is the proud new father of a bouncing fifteen-pound baby girl. Hyal has been mobbed by the ladies all day and is finally getting some well-deserved rest.

Out by the fire pit, Monica wanders over and sits in Bill's lap and gives him a Christmas kiss, which is much appreciated by the old hippy. Mortisk walks up and hands them both a beer and sits down.

"How are you, my friends?" He was exhausted from the last twelve hours—and his first eight hours of fatherhood.

"We are perfect," Monica answered. "How's Hyal and the baby doing?"

"Sleeping," he replied.

"Do you have a name yet?" Bill asked.

"Earian," the proud father replied. "In honor of the first Torani born on Earth."

"Well, congratulations, old man," Bill said.

"I am not old," the very tired alien replied.

"You soon will be." Bill laughed as the large gold man thought about what his friend had just said.

It was a perfect day for all in the valley town, Bill thought, as he watched the kids playing. "Life is good," he thinks to himself. Then he handed the very tired alien a cold Corona and a lit joint, knowing very well the man's current state after a new child is born.

"Thank you, my friend," Mortisk said as he took a seat at the fire with his best friends on this planet—and maybe in the galaxy. He sat with the others, quietly watching the children playing in the new snow, on a wonderful Christmas day.

PART 3

CHAPTER 45

⸱●❀●⸱

Torani Vessel Tarkon M-420 Galaxy
January 1, 2022

It is New Year's Day on Earth as the four Earth men returned to the Torani capitol, and Gene has put Allen into play, disguised as his assistant. As an ex-CIA man, he will come into play on their six-month trip. John returned to the Learning Center with his new partner Jack Lee, and put him directly working on the Torani force field systems. Cloric is still working with the earthlings, but deeply saddened by the fact that Ben didn't return with John. Cloric and Ben had become good friends, and Cloric will miss the funny little man dearly.

Gene has requested a vessel to travel to the other systems to "extend relations." His quest for allies is just beginning, and with Allen by his side he hopes not to make the same mistake as he made with the Torani. The Earth ambassador has requested to visit the planet Zaxin first on their trip, where Ambassador Tronext is patiently awaiting their arrival.

The emperor has given them use of the royal vessel Tarkon to use in their journeys. The Tarkon is a high velocity vessel, and will cut half the time off that of the large Torani vessels. The two men should arrive at Zaxin in seven days, and during that time Gene and Allen will be enjoying a view of the galaxy that no humans have yet witnessed.

"Unbelievable, isn't it," Gene said to Allen as he entered the observation area.

"The last three months of this have been unbelievable to me," Allen replied as he walked nearer to the large view port.

"After getting to know the emperor, what do you think of him?" Gene asked curiously.

"I think he's a coldhearted son of a bitch who would sell his own mother for power, if he hasn't already. I've been around some of the coldest, most bloodthirsty bastards on the planet Earth, but none of them are as cool and collected as that man."

"I know what you mean. Since I found out the truth about him, it makes my skin crawl to be in the same room with him. When you bow to greet him, you expect to rise with a dagger in your back," Gene said this all quietly because you didn't know who was listening, and you could be sure that the emperor has someone watching them very closely. "We'll spend a few days with the Zaxin ambassador and see what new information he has for us. The Zaxin people are willing to help in any way they can, so we need to use that to our advantage in gaining allies to our cause."

The two men then stood quietly as they watched the stars fly by, what a view. They are all still the same stars around them, but they look at them from a totally new prospective today.

John and Dr. Lee have spent the last week on the orbital shipyard, admiring the vessel that John has been studying since its infancy. Fortunately for John the time he was away didn't interfere with his studies, as he had Cloric record the construction while he was absent. He is studying the structural designs when Jack Lee enters the lab with his face still in his laptop as he walks.

"What do you make of these systems? They are like nothing I've ever seen."

"Jack, everything on this planet is something you will never see anywhere on Earth."

"Yea, right. The whole vessel seems to be operated by a high-tech fiber optics system. But not normal optics, they are really unusual."

"I'll get Cloric to get you research material that you can study, so you can understand the science behind it."

"That would be great, because right now all I'm doing is guessing."

"Jack there's one thing you need to learn about the Torani. As long as it doesn't have anything to do with the fuel or the engine cores, you just have to ask and you can get it. We've got three months to get as much data as we can on those force fields, so we need to stay focused on that target."

"Six months isn't enough time to study this stuff. It's like me trying to teach you Chinese, and I'm Japanese John."

"Just do the best you can Jack, and remember that Cloric is a junior scientist, and he really likes to show the earthlings just how much smarter he is than them."

"The Ocean Mist is open, you hungry?" John asked, changing the subject.

"Yea, they serve a great Torani Sushi," Jack replied with a smile.

The scientists needed a break and the food at Ben's favorite hangout is wonderful, so they took a break from their work and went for some food and drinks.

The ambassador, along with his new assistant, are now en route to the Zaxin planet aboard the Tarkon's landing shuttle. The two Earth men look in awe as they approach the Capital city of the borderline desert planet. The almost Mars like terrain is bright red with sparse vegetation, purple in color.

The cities which are housed in massive domes, have the appearance of terrariums and are spread across the planet's surface. The Zaxin planet has an Earthlike atmosphere but very dry, and will be safe for the visitors to breath. The dryness of the atmosphere is the purpose of the domes. These domes allow the Zaxins to control their environments by retaining the moisture inside the domes.

The Zaxin people are a docile race of beings who are considered to be the barristers of the galaxy. When a system has disputes over their territories, or contract disputes, the Zaxins are brought in to mediate the problem. As the Zaxin race is absolutely incapable of deception, they are trusted by all throughout the galaxy.

The shuttle now winds its way through a unique collection of domes. They are all shaped different to represent the different clans, as well as their different uses. Some of the domes are strictly used as housing, while others contain beautiful gardens filled with exotic plant and animal life. Gene truly hopes they have time for a tour.

The shuttle nears what they assume is the capitol dome. It is strictly used for the administration of the planet, but is also filled with the beautiful vegetation to add color to the Capitol City.

"Would you look at that," Allen said. "They travel by cars like we do."

The city had dozens of roads that wound throughout the city, as well as between all of the domes connecting them. It looked like little bugs crawling everywhere in organized lines much like ants.

"The Zaxin hate to fly, and from what I understand they only leave their planet when they are absolutely needed," Gene said.

The shuttle passed through an opening at the bottom of the large dome which seemed to be protected by some kind of force field to contain the environment. They traveled between the buildings until they came to what must be the ambassador's building and landed on a large extended balcony. As they exited the shuttle, they were met by the Zaxin ambassador and his aid.

"Ambassador Furgison, it is very good to see you again. What do you think of our planet so far?" Tronext asked him as he shook the two men's hands. "It' truly amazing.

It is much like we would like our planet Mars to be in one hundred years."

"I see you didn't bring your friend John Alistair along on the voyage."

"You have a very good memory, Ambassador. This is my assistant Mr. Whitt. John is very busy working on our problem on the Torani planet, so he wasn't able to make the trip."

"Shall we go to my office? We have much to discuss." He turned and walked toward the building in silence, expecting them to follow.

Once inside, they rode an elevator that ran up the side of the building, giving them an incredible view of the city around them. The two beings exited the elevator and followed Tronext down a hallway leading to his office. His aid waited in the outer office as the other three entered Tronext's large office.

"Please sit, Mr. Ambassador."

"Please call me Gene, and this is Allen."

"Very well, Gene and Allen, you may call me Tronext, gentlemen," he started with his hands folded in front of him. "The Zaxin race is a race which is incapable of deceit. We are also a race incapable of being deceived," he added as he looked the two men over carefully.

The two men looked at each other in shame. "I apologize, Ambassador. Allen has taken the appearance as my aid for his protection on the Torani planet. He is actually one of the finest intelligence operatives on my planet, and I brought him with me to help us in our quest for allies. I simply could not permit a repeat of my first folly with the Torani, and I believe he will be helpful with our negotiations with the other members of the Alliance."

"Now that, is the truth which the Zaxin people deal in."

"Mr. Tronext I have taken the information you provided us with to all the leaders of my planet, and they are appalled by the Torani deception. We have made many choices for ways to proceed in order to protect our planet. These actions all depend on the total deception of the Torani emperor, as well as his people. Honestly, we see no other way to proceed."

"You are correct in your actions, but the Zaxins cannot lie so we cannot be a part of this deception. If I was to be questioned by the Torani I would most certainly tell the truth, so I see no other option but to step down as the Torani ambassador. I am the only one of my people who knows of this information, so my replacement will be of no danger to our plan."

"Surely if you step down Tronext there will be questions which you will be obligated to answer because of your beliefs."

"Earth," Allen said. "We could move him and his family to Earth. There are many deserts on our planet, which his species could easily adapt, if not enjoy."

"That is a remarkably good idea Mr. Whitt. I have seen research on your planet, and it does have many appealing areas on its surface. I will put the question to my family and give you an answer before you leave Zaxin. Now on to other business. What can I help you with at this time?"

"The first question I have is what systems can we rely on to supply us with weapons, as well as fleet vessels to protect our planet? We have almost unlimited supplies of already processed and pure Triomicium that we could trade for these items."

"What you ask is very difficult. The galactic laws prohibit the delivery of such technology, and I mean no insult, to a race as primitive as yours."

"No insult taken, Tronext. I fully understand the laws. I just see this as a circumstance that the law shouldn't pertain to. We have been exposed to numerous alien technologies over the last year, and our planet is now being powered by such technologies. Do any of the other systems know of the Torani deception?"

"I do not believe so, or they wouldn't have voted as they did at the trial."

"Then we must decide which systems we can trust not to do the same as the Torani for their own gain," Allen said, joining the conversation.

"There is little honor in the galaxy Mr. Whitt. The Alliance, and the threat of retaliation, is the only thing that makes the systems obey the galactic laws. The Klosk race is an honorable race and could possibly persuaded to come to our aid if necessary. If they were to discover the truth about the Torani deception as well as the murder of hundreds of Corisole citizens to hide this deception, they could possibly be persuaded to join our cause."

"The Boral are a cyborg race that are only interested in the expansion of their race. With their cloning abilities they have amassed a very large military that is capable of conquering many systems, but the only thing that keeps them under control is the threat of destruction by the Alliance, so I would not trust them."

"The Antarians are completely unpredictable and are constantly raiding vessels that stray into their system. Their insectoid mentality makes them only think of themselves and the survival, as well as the growth of their race. They are entirely too unpredictable to even consider. I'm sorry, would you, gentlemen, care for some refreshments?"

"Yes, thank you, Tronext," they both answered.

Tronext spoke in his alien language into an intercom on his desk, and his assistant soon entered with a pitcher of what appeared to be juice. Tronext poured them both a glass of what was a wonderful tasting juice, then continued. "To continue, the Zakorian people are a peaceful people who make their way in the galaxy with their Cloning technologies and would be of no help at all. Gentlemen, that leaves us with the Velnor."

John is on his feet immediately. "The Velnor and the Corisole are the same race, and responsible for the death of five billion people of Earth. You can't seriously expect us to trust them."

Tronext raised his hand to quiet as well as calm the angry man. "Ambassador. The Velnor planet is a peaceful planet that only cares about exploration and the quest for knowledge. Their engine designs are in every galactic vessel in this galaxy and possibly many others. After the Torani destroyed the Corisole planet two hundred years ago, a large portion of the population who were tired of the corruption of the two planets, relocated to the Velnor planet to live peacefully. With their small Triomicium mine on the third planet of their system, they have no ties with either the Torani or the Corisole. They have disowned Corisole as a rogue planet, and have their entirely separate society. They could possibly be convinced to join our cause, and I would think that if they discovered the Torani deception, those odds would be tripled. They already have no respect for the Torani. Only fear as do the other systems of the galaxy."

"With all this being said, gentlemen, it comes down to one thing. We can get the supporters, but can we trust them not to want the same thing the Torani wanted—your planet. This could lead to a galactic war over your planet if we do not proceed carefully."

The Zaxin ambassador leaned back in his chair and drank his juice as he let the two men think about his words, as well as his warnings.

Allen stood and started to pace. He thinks better on his feet. "The Klosk sound like our most valuable ally because they have already assumed the role of peacekeepers of the galaxy. When a warrior race such as the Klosk discover the deception, as well as the dishonorable dealings of the Torani leaders that led to the deaths of what they will consider to be five billion honorable people, they will certainly rise to our aid. The size of their fleet will also be a welcome addition to our Allied forces."

"The Velnor, I would assume will want justice for the deaths of their people as well as the damage done to their planet in the past. Their vessels are designed for exploration, but after almost being annihilated by the Torani, you can also guarantee that they can protect themselves against aggressive races, which would also help our cause. All other systems we shouldn't even consider because of their unpredictability, or their submissiveness. That is my opinion."

"Your man is wise, Gene. I see now why you enlisted him for this cause. Gentlemen, I say we take a recess until the day after tomorrow, as I have business to attend to tomorrow. I will supply you with a driver to show you our planet. He will take you from here to your accommodations and retrieve you in the morning for your tour. Feel free to explore anywhere you like. My people are quite pleasant and enjoy visitors."

Tronext spoke into his intercom again using the Zaxin language, and his aid appeared to escort the earthlings to their accommodations.

"There's only one problem with your plan, Ambassador. We don't speak your language," Gene replied.

"Of course," Tronext said apologetically. "I overlooked that part." He reached into a cabinet behind his desk and retrieved two items that looked like medals. "These translators will allow you to both speak and understand the Zaxin language. Many of our people do speak your language. It's like a fad to our young. Good day, gentlemen, and enjoy your visit. I will see you again in forty-eight hours from now."

John checked his watch to mark the time, then shook the ambassador's hand and followed the aid out the door. They would indeed get their wish to explore the incredible planet and meet its people.

Chapter 46

———•◉❋◉•———

Area 51, Nevada
January 10, 2022

The Area 51 team has spent the last ten weeks enlarging the Corisole ship and now has a completed fighter. Hundreds of scientists from around the world have been working on the project so they can all return to their facilities with the knowledge to repeat the process.

The fuel sample from the lunar base was used to reproduce the fuel, which eased Brad's mind for almost ruining the entire plan. Mortisk will be arriving soon to supervise the fueling process and do the power tests. The ship's cannon is only one tenth the size of the lunar cannons, but Mortisk has assured them that they will easily cut a hole through the hull of a vessel. Horace and his men have practiced loading the fuel orbs for the past week with dummy orbs to insure the proper procedures and are ready for the task.

The fuel orbs which are a mixture of gold, beryllium, and diamond dust were completed only twenty-four hours ago and are ready for Mortisk's trial. They all hope it is correct.

An hour later their fuel technician arrived from Colorado for the tests. As he entered the lab, he was met by the applause of the scientists who couldn't have done it without his help. He appeared to be very tired, but he was ready.

"We have been waiting an hour for you to arrive, did you have problems?" Horace asked.

"It was my night," Mortisk answered shortly.

"Your night?" Horace asked curiously.

"New baby. And when a Torani woman tells you it's your night to take care of the baby, you do it," he replied, which caused Horace to laugh quite loudly.

"Congratulations, my friend, and I do feel your pain. I raised three myself, and there's nothing more lethal than an overtired mother," he said as they walked to the fighter. "How does she look?" Horace commented as they approached the craft.

Mortisk looked the fighter over closely. He started with the engine reactor, then checked all the control units and decided that it was safe to test the power. He loaded the fuel as the scientists all moved to the other side of a blast proof wall, at a remote starting unit. Mortisk sat in front of the panel with Horace and hit the start switch. The fighter began to hum with the power from its incredible engine that was designed by Olga and her team. They watched the readouts which were being displayed for all to see as they started to rise.

"Everything looks good. Let's increase the power," Mortisk said as he reached for the power controls.

They powered it up until it started to strain the restraining clamps.

"Still in the green," Horace said. "Let's test the avionics."

They put the fighter through every test they could, and the ship passed them all. They powered down the fighter and reentered the lab. Mortisk removed the plating from the engine compartment to check the engine as well as the fuel chamber. He replaced the plating, then turned to Horace and gave him two thumbs-up. The lab erupted in cheers and pats on the back. They had done it. Now for a test flight.

The fighter was released from the clamps and moved out onto the tarmac. Mortisk removed a flight suit from the shuttle and put it on. This would be the big test. The Corisole attack ships were all unmanned so they copied the avionics from the shuttle to simplify the design process.

"Are you sure about this?" Horace asked his golden pilot. "I don't want you to risk your life. We can't afford to lose the only fuel technician on the planet."

"My friend that is the least of your problems. If anything happens to me, you will have a very pissed off seven foot Torani woman to deal with. And believe me, I wouldn't wish that on any species," he replied with a smile and patted Horace on the back.

"Be careful," Horace returned with a laugh.

Mortisk climbed into the fighter and hooked all his restraints, then fired it up. After a few minutes of warm up time and preflight checks, Mortisk closed the canopy and sealed it.

"How's everything look?" Horace asked him over the radio.

"Everything's green," he answered. "I'm going to take a ride around the block."

The fighter rose gracefully from the tarmac. Keeping it only a few feet off the tarmac, Mortisk began putting it through a series of test maneuvers. After a few minutes of tests Mortisk came over the radio.

"I'm going for a spin, my friend."

"Are you sure it's safe?" Horace asked.

"We're about to find out."

The fighter sprung to life and was out of sight over the mountain in a split second. The scientists all watched with pride as their creation disappeared.

Mortisk watched the ever changing terrain below him disappear behind him, and within minutes was flying over the Pacific Ocean. He decided that that was far enough for their first flight, since they couldn't risk the new ship being discovered by Torani sensors that could be present without their knowledge. Mortisk checked the instruments, that were all still registering optimal performance of the craft and turned the craft to return to the Nevada base.

Ten minutes later the ship reappeared over the base flying at unbelievable speeds. The fighter then circled back and landed gently on the tarmac in front of them. Mortisk then rose again and skillfully flew the fighter into the lab and rested it on its locking clamps and shut it down. The huge pilot opened the canopy and climbed down from the ship.

"How does it handle?" Horace asked.

"Just like my Camaro," he said as he put on his hat and patted the little man on the back. "Now we need a simulator to train the pilots."

"Brad is almost finished with them. He only needs your input to program the computers. You'll have to go to Houston and test it."

"Let me know when they're ready and I'll be there."

"So can we go into production."

"I see no reason why we should wait. I would like to take it for an orbital test, so I will come next week and take it up again."

"You sure you don't want to do it today?"

"Like I said, it was my night with the baby," he answered, looking very tired.

"See ya next week then. Go get some rest," Horace said with a pat on the back.

Mortisk left the lab and entered the shuttle to leave. He waved at the other men as he lifted off. The first part of their plan was a success, and next week he would go for the orbital test flight and test fire the cannon. *The Torani pilot is amazed at the creative abilities of the earthlings. It is evident that there is nothing that these beings cannot achieve when they are faced with a challenge.*

Gene and Allen are waiting at the ambassador's office when Tronext arrives. The ambassador takes his seat and offers the men some of the incredible Zaxin juice.

"So what did you think of my planet, my friends," he asked as he filled their glasses.

"Incredible," Gene replied. "The gardens were magnificent, the people were all quite friendly, and the food was very interesting to say the least."

"Yes, I'm sure the food was shocking. We are reptilian after all," he said smiling.

"I have contacted the Klosk ambassador and asked him to meet with us. He gladly agreed to meet with us in one week, which means we must leave today to be there in time."

"Our vessel is ready to leave at any time," Gene replied.

"I would rather take my vessel in order to keep unwanted eyes and ears from our travels."

"How do we explain it to the Torani captain?"

"We simply tell him that you wish to sample the flight of a Zaxin vessel. If you would like you can send him back to Torani, which will allow us to visit Velnor on our return trip."

"I thought you were incapable of lying, Ambassador?"

"Not a lie. Just withholding certain information. I am a Lawyer remember?" He winked with both eyelids.

They all chuckled and drank the juice. Tronext made a toast.

"To future Allies."

"Here, here," Gene replied as they drank.

"Return to your vessel and gather your things. I will contact the captain for you, and inform him of your change of plans and dismiss him. My pilot will wait for you to take you to my vessel. We must leave in two hours. I will meet you on board my vessel.

The earthlings left the office and followed the aid to the shuttle. The next leg of their journey was now under way, and Gene hopes the journey won't create too much suspicion with the already suspicious emperor.

A lab has been created in the lower levels of the Space Center to protect its secret. This lab holds the first two simulators for the new fighters, and Brad has received the flight data from the test flight Mortisk made two days ago and is now in the process of loading the data into the simulators. A light flashed on the comm center. He answers the call discovering Horace on the other end of the line.

"Horace, what can I do for you?"

"I just wanted to see if you received the data from the flight."

"Yes, I did. I'm downloading it into the simulator now. How are we doing on your end?"

"The scientists have all returned to their countries and are going into production as soon as possible. We'll have ten facilities in four countries so we should be able to produce the fighters in great quantities," Horace replied.

"The telemetry was incredible. From the readings, he was traveling at over thirty-five thousand miles per hour, and that was at half throttle. He was halfway across the Pacific in less than five minutes. The speed created by Olga's engine is amazing."

"I couldn't believe the readouts either, they were mind boggling. Mortisk will be at Johnson on the nineteenth to give your simulator a test run. Are you going to be ready?"

"I don't see any reason why not."

"Brad we need to look for the youngest pilots we can find. The handeye coordination at those speeds is going to require a next generation pilot. We need gamers. It's like walking for today's generation to use their hands without even thinking about it, so they need to be young."

"Our experienced pilots aren't going to like that Horace. I have guys that have thousands of hours of flight time under their belts and are itching to fly these things."

"We will let anyone qualified try the simulators. I'm just saying that I don't think they will grasp the flight controls. These controls are exactly like the shuttles and you know how challenging they are to fly. Now add five times the speed and battle conditions to that equation, and you've got a monster at your fingertips."

"Okay, Horace. We'll let Mortisk make his test flights in a week and get the bugs out of the systems, then I'm going to let our pilots try their hand at it and we'll go from there."

"Okay, Brad. You're the pilot and it's your show, so I'll have to agree with you. I have to go Brad, good luck."

"You too Horace."

Brad thought about Horace's suggestion as he hung up the phone. He has learned to fly the shuttles and it wasn't easy. They might just need a new generation at the controls of these things.

Chapter 47

---•●✳●•---

The Valley
January 18, 2022, 08:00

Bill and Sassy are coming in from their very cold morning walk, when they spot Mortisk and Willis heading toward the shuttle for work. With more towns getting rebuilt, they have been setting up new collector stations to keep up with the demand.

"Hey, it's my turn to drive," Willis said as they walked toward the shuttle.

Bill couldn't believe what he has heard. "Hey, wait!" he yelled and walked over to his son. "What do you mean it's my turn to drive. You've been flying these things?"

"I've been flying this can for months. Nothing to it."

"He is actually a very good pilot," Mortisk said.

"You've been flying these things for months, and I haven't even gotten a ride yet," he said, shaking his head. "Not fair."

"Would you like to come with us. We're just making a few quick stops on our new locations to check the collectors. We shouldn't be gone all that long, I must be in Houston this afternoon to test the new simulators," Mortisk asked his friend, feeling bad for forgetting his fascination with space flight.

"Let me grab some coffee and my bowl and we'll be right back. Come on girl, let's go for a cruise."

A few minutes later they all loaded into the shuttle and rose into the cold Colorado sky for a short day of work. He has to be the first hippy to fly in one of these things, and she will defiantly be the first dog to do so, he thinks to himself as they cruise silently through the sky.

The testing continues in the lower lab of Johnson to make sure the simulator is ready for Mortisk's arrival. The techs are certain that it is ready for his first test flight. The elevator opens and their golden test pilot enters the lab.

"Mortisk, how are you?" Brad asked as the large alien entered the lab.

"I am well Brad."

"We're ready for your test of the flight simulator. We've double checked all the systems and think it's ready to go."

The simulator is an exact replica of the fighter's cockpit. Mortisk walked around it examining it carefully.

"You've done a very good job. Are we ready?"

"Climb in and we'll fire up the computers."

Mortisk climbed into the simulated cockpit and closed the black canopy putting him into a virtual fighter. As Brad watched the simulator moved slowly at first making easy turns and altitude changes. Brad motioned to the operator to start the virtual battle program.

The simulator sprung to life like a mechanical bull turned up to ten. It began to tilt and spin, then climb all at the same time to the scenario created by the computer. After a five-minute run of the battle program, the simulator came to a rest and the canopy opened. A very excited alien climbed from the cockpit, and with a slap on the back of its creator and a small adjustment of his hat, he then said the words they were all were waiting for.

"That was fun," Mortisk said with a big smile. "I would say that you have completed your task, my friends," he added, looking around the room. "Very good job. Most realistic indeed," he added, congratulating the men.

"Then we can produce more just like this one?" Brad asked.

"Don't change a thing. It's perfect."

"Now all we need is more pilots," Brad said.

Mortisk is quiet for a minute as he contemplates the consequences of his next suggestion. He knows the person's abilities, but is concerned with what could be the end results of his actions.

"I will return shortly," was all he said, and he left the lab.

Brad waited curiously, wondering what Mortisk was up to. A few minutes later Mortisk entered the lab with a very young man and his dog, which was wearing of all things a very small cape with S D printed on it. Brad had to laugh at the sight.

"Okay, I give. What's up Mortisk?"

"I want you to let my friend Willis try the simulator," he replied.

"Sure, why not."

Mortisk holds Sassy's leash while Willis climbs up into the cockpit. Willis looked at him with a big grin.

"The controls are the same as the shuttle, but you will be traveling fifty times faster so you will have to anticipate your corrections. Keep the throttle at 25 percent to start." Mortisk instructed him. "It will start out in the sky, then travel into space where you will enter into battle with similar craft. You will see the targeting cursor and this is the weapons button. Do you understand?"

"Sure, it's just like a lot of my games. Let's go for it."

"The start switch for the engine will start the simulation," Brad explained as he showed him the button as well as the belts. "You'll need these. Make sure they're real tight."

Brad then closed the canopy and looked at Mortisk with an expression that said, "What the hell are you doing."

The simulator started with its usual slow movements then after a few seconds the nose rose and went into action. As with Mortisk it spun wildly in all directions for about five minutes, then slowly came to a rest. The canopy opened a few seconds later and Willis climbed from the cockpit grinning from ear to ear.

"I have to get one of these. How did I do?"

Brad looked at the readouts, then answered his question. "Mortisk killed twenty more enemy ships than you did."

"Show off," Willis said.

"I've had more practice," Mortisk replied with a grin.

Brad scratched his head as he looked at the data from the flights. "Horace was right. He told me we needed young pilots," Brad said as he looked at the data again.

"This is child's play compared to some of the games today," Willis said as he took Sassy's leash from Mortisk.

"We start flying these things for real in six months. If you're interested, I would like to put you in charge of the second squadron of fighters. Anyone that you think is capable of this kind of challenge and responsibility can try out for the program," Brad explained to the young man. "Mortisk. Does he know?" he asked covertly.

"No. I will have to talk with his father first."

"Very well. Talk to his father and have Ben let me know what's up. Willis, is it? It was my pleasure to meet you today," he said, offering his hand.

"Thanks for letting me play with your brand-new toy," Willis said with a smile.

Brad walked the three of them to the elevator. "Keep in touch," he said to Mortisk.

"Good-bye, Brad."

As they were riding the elevator to the surface, Willis turned to his friend. "What did he mean when he asked you, if I knew. Knew about what?"

"Later, my friend. That is a secret."

They crossed the tarmac and loaded into the shuttle. The shuttle rose and flew off for the safety of the valley. Mortisk is wondering if he should have involved Willis in this, but it is his planet too and should be able to defend it. Mortisk hopes that his actions will not anger his dearest friend and ruin their friendship.

After leaving Zaxin one week ago, the ambassador's large shuttle is entering Klosk space for their meeting with the Klosk ambassador. They are hopeful that their story holds up to the emperor's scrutiny or all is lost. Gene has been making himself ready for the emperor's questions upon their return, with the help of Allen's expert advice.

The inhabitants of Klosk are now a peaceful race after many centuries of war. They have evolved from their society of fierce warriors, to the now peaceful but also still fierce race of galactic peacekeepers. As tall as the Torani and twice as fierce, the hairy Sasquatch like beings make it easy to believe their image of fearless warriors. With their skills at weapons design added to the second largest battle fleet in the galaxy, they are a force to be reckoned with.

The Zaxin shuttle entered the orbit of the planet Klosk and was immediately met by two fighters to escort them to the spaceport. As the three visitors exit the shuttle, they are met by the Klosk ambassador and two guards. Ambassador Tronext leads the group and shakes the ambassador's hand in the style of the Klosk where you grab the arm at the elbow. Tronext then introduced his companions to Ambassador Gowlisk.

"Ambassador Gowlisk, I would like to introduce you to the ambassador from the planet Earth. This is Ambassador Furgison, and this is his advisor Mr. Whitt."

Gowlisk grasped Gene's arm firmly. "I remember the ambassador from the trial of the Corisole criminals. It is a privilege to meet you again, Ambassador. And, Mr. Whitt, I am pleased to meet you also," he said with the same greeting. "I am sorry for the senseless death on your planet, gentlemen, the Corisole murders received a just punishment for their crimes."

"Thank you, Ambassador," Gene replied.

"Shall we go to my office? It is on the other side of the city, so you will enjoy a short tour of our planet."

The ambassador led them to a vehicle that sat hovering just off the ground, then proceeded to drive through the large city. The city was incredibly primitive looking in appearance. The small Klosk planet was covered with trees a hundred feet in diameter and a thousand feet tall. They have surely existed as long as the planet.

The inhabitants lived in harmony with these giants, with their homes constructed inside the trees themselves in closely spaced dwellings, which led Gene to believe that they were a very close society. It had a very natural and untechnological appearance, much like a jungle movie.

They arrived at the planet's headquarters, and unlike the rest of the cities dwellings, it was created from stone and glass. It had a Regal appearance like most ruling palaces of the galaxy. They made their way to the ambassador's office, which was quite modern as most government offices are.

The Zaxin, as well as the Earth ambassador, began to tell the story of the Torani's secret plot for the control of the Earth planet and what is left of its people. Tronext explained how the Corisole fleet as well as everyone who had knowledge of the Torani's future plans were executed not for their crimes against Earth but to hide the Torani deception.

Ambassador Furgison then explained how his people had been led to believe that the Torani were their saviors, then willingly stripped of all their defensive capabilities. Gene then explained their ongoing efforts to rearm their defenses, but also the great need for allies explaining their presence on his planet today.

Gowlisk listened to the two ambassadors' stories of deceit and dishonor with an ever-hardening demeanor. When they were finished he sat silently for a time, then the large warrior slammed his fists on his desk in anger and leaned forward to speak.

"This act of deceit and cowardice will not be tolerated. I will speak with Leader Crowath and insist that the Torani leaders, as well as their military commanders, be held responsible for their actions. We are no longer a warrior race that believes in only conquest. We are now a race that firmly believes in the ideals of honor and peace at any cost. I assure you, Ambassador, that you will receive the justice due to you."

After the ambassador finished, Gene interrupted him to speak. "Ambassador Gowlisk, we understand your anger as well as desire to punish the Torani for their crimes and deception, but that will have to wait. We ask for a five-year period to strengthen our defenses. If we move against the Torani now and fail, it will mean the destruction of our planet. Also, if we were to move against the Torani today and succeed, it will leave our planet defenseless for at least the next five years, and leave us defenseless against the possible attack of other hostile races for our resources. The Triomicium ore will now always be a goal of future attacks."

"We understand that we simply cannot be given a fleet of warships to protect our planet because it is against galactic law. What we would like to introduce is a plan to create an Alliance of systems loyal to our cause, and base this Alliance on our planet. We will construct an Alliance headquarters on our planet to house the representatives of this Alliance, as well as an orbital station for its fleet with the help of its members. We wish to be brought into the Galactic Alliance and are prepared to live in harmony with this Alliance as one."

The three visitors to Klosk await a response from their host.

"Ambassadors. With all that I have heard today I understand your need for secrecy for the time being. I also see the great need for the time to restore your defenses and the need to show strength through Allies on your planet. The Torani cannot object to this plan of action because it will perk the curiosity of the Alliance toward them, and they will not want that at this time. Therefore, I think we should begin immediately with the construction of this Alliance headquarters on your planet, and proceed with the other parts of your plan from there."

"Ambassadors, I think we have a good plan of action. You should now proceed to the Velnor planet to speak with their leaders. The Velnor are an honest and peaceful race, but once they discover the deception of the Torani as well as their past history with them, they will certainly join our Alliance. They have a large fleet, which would be a welcome addition to our own, and this fleet could easily repel any attack against your planet. I will expect to hear from Ambassador Tronext in three months' time to finalize our plans."

"Thank you, Ambassador," Tronext said. "Together we will create one of the most peaceful, as well as resilient galaxies in the universe. You will not regret your decision today."

Gene then spoke. "Ambassador, my people will show a great deal of respect to the Klosk planet for this Alliance. I will convince them to begin construction of the headquarters immediately. We will also enlist the help of other systems in the construction. Many systems working on the station will be a deterrent to further action at this time from the Torani. Thank you, Ambassador Gowlisk. Earth is in your debt."

"It was my pleasure to meet you and your assistant, Ambassador. Have a safe journey, gentlemen. My assistant will take you to your vessel."

The four beings shook hands and parted ways. Once on board the Jaxor they agreed to bypass the Boral and Antarian systems as they could only do harm their cause. Their next stop would be the planet Velnor which will be a very long journey as it is on the other side of the galaxy.

CHAPTER 48

————— •●✿●• —————

Planet Torani Learning Center
February 20, 2022

Jack has been working on the chips for the Torani force field software. They have been able to replicate the chips for the fighter's systems on Earth, but the force field science is much more difficult. After six weeks of study of the manufacturing and programming, Jack thinks he has finally succeeded. As a wise man once told him, the whole trick to mastering a technology was simply knowing how it works, and once you know that, any dammed fool can do it. And he was right. Now that he knows how it works he can return to Earth with his prize.

John has been quite busy at the Torani library researching the last three-hundred years of spaceflight. The libraries are well kept and have a complete catalogue of every vessel produced in that period. With this knowledge they will be able to produce any type of vessel they wish for the future journeys of Earth.

The men have now reached their threshold of knowledge and are eager to return to Earth. The Torani vessel Tarkon has been requisitioned to return them to their planet, so they will soon be on their way home. The new planet was an exciting adventure for Jack, but John has gotten to where he prefers his own planet Earth.

The passengers of the Jaxor have spent the last thirty days in transit to the planet Velnor. On the twentieth day of February they have finally arrived in orbit, and after a short security check they are now cleared to land on the planet's surface. The Velnor ambassador Prowlex is waiting for them on the landing pad as they arrive. The two ambassadors, along with Allen, Greet the ambassador as they exit their shuttle.

"Ambassador Prowlex. It's indeed a pleasure to meet with you on your planet," Tronext said politely. "I would like to introduce the ambassador from Earth and his assistant. This is Ambassador Furgison, and this is his assistant Mr. Whitt."

"It is an honor, Ambassador Prowlex," Gene said. "This is my assistant Allen Whitt."

The ambassador bowed to them and they all returned the greeting.

"It is an honor, gentlemen. Now if you would follow me to our transport, we will proceed to my office."

They all entered a type of ground shuttle which proceeded to take them through an all to normal city for the humans. The buildings were thousands of feet tall and reminded them of New York City. Parts of the city are actually built rising out of the water on the shallow shorelines. The planet's civilization is two hundred years old and are all inhabiting the sparse landmasses of the planet.

The Earth men have a certain amount of animosity against the Velnor because of their relation to the Corisole. It will be a great challenge to place their trust in the Velnor, but they know they must for the greater good of Earth.

The shuttle stopped at a large building constructed over the water. The ambassadors walked over a long bridge to the main building, then were taken on a short tour of the Velnor capitol building, eventually ending at the ambassador's office.

"Please sit, gentlemen. The small gray being instructed. "What brings you to our planet, Ambassador Tronext?" he asked.

The ambassadors once again disclosed the information that they have discovered about the invasion, as well as the Torani deception. When they were finished, Ambassador Prowlex began asking his questions.

"Ambassador, if you knew of this deception, why wasn't it brought out at the trial?"

"Unfortunately I discovered this information after the trial, Ambassador. One of the Supreme Leader's assistants overheard a conversation between the leader and Fleet Commander Salick. He was afraid to come forward for the fear of retribution. After the trial and the execution of Leader Mirosh, he came to me with the information. He said that he knew I could be trusted to do the right thing. I thought it best to contact the Earth ambassador first as it was his planet at the center of the plot. We have only met with the Klosk ambassador on this matter, thinking that the other systems would be either no help, or too dangerous to trust with this information."

"With all due respect, Ambassador," Gene broke in, "we were not sure if we could trust the Velnor with the information because of your relationship with the Corisole, but after much discussion it was decided that not only could you be trusted with the information, but also your right to know the truth about the events."

"Ambassador, my planet is in possession of most likely the largest Triomicium deposits in the galaxy, and possibly many others. We are worried that the greed that destroyed five-billion people on my planet, as well as what was once your planet Corisole, would once again unleashed on my planet. We come to you today with the hope of your desire to not only avenge the deaths of your people, but to put a stop to the Torani tyranny in this galaxy." Gene then bowed and took his seat.

They knew deep down that they had the Velnor support, as you could almost feel the anger emanating from him. After a moment of awkward silence Prowlex stood and leaned over his desk toward the other three men.

"We will no longer stand by and let the Torani act as gods in this galaxy. They have led our Corisole brothers astray with promises of wealth and power, only to be sucked dry and tossed away as one would an empty vessel. What is your plan to bring the Torani leaders to justice?"

The two men looked at each other and Gene rose to speak. "Ambassador Prowlex, we have estimated that the Torani will not act against our planet for at least ten years. The Corisole people are still producing Triomicium at an acceptable rate and are happy to do so as long as the Torani care for their needs. Their leaders have reduced themselves to drones over the last one hundred years and know little different."

Gene knew his next words could help or hinder the planet's rebirth. Allen put his hand on Gene's shoulder which makes him yield to his trusted friend.

"Ambassador Prowlex, on my planet I have the responsibility of gathering information as well as the decision as what to do with that information. In my opinion we cannot afford to have this information become known." Allen begins to pace as he chooses his words carefully. "First, we should establish a galactic station on our planet. This will indeed keep the Torani at bay for an extended period of time. The only downside I can see to the plan is that they may attack before the Station can be completed, but I do not think that would happen because of the galactic consequences. The Station's construction would be multisystem project, and if they did attack it would bring the wrath of the Alliance down on them."

"Second. We could think about creating a covert base on our fourth planet, which we could disguise as a mining colony. We could man it with our new fighter craft in support of the planet Earth."

"Our last stage we have already began because of the extreme secrecy along with its sheer magnitude, is the creation of a defensive Earth force. The Corisole base in our moon is currently being brought back online with the help of the Torani. They are under the impression that we will be their partner in the future of both our planets. We had to continue this ruse until its completion. This base will contain multiple laser cannons as well as our new fighters when it is finished."

"If the Torani discover that we know of their overall plan they will certainly destroy the rest of our people and seize the planet for themselves. And with the strength of their fleet combined with the Lunar Station, they could easily repel any retaliation sent by the Alliance. They would then double their hold on the galaxy by controlling all the Triomicium in the galaxy bringing all other systems to their knees, which is what I personally believe is their intention anyway."

"These are our plans so far, and we are open to additional options." Allen then sat back in his seat. "Thank you, Ambassador, for listening."

The Zaxin ambassador rose to make one last point. "Ambassador, we trust you see the wisdom of this plan. As a member of the Alliance and my friend, you know I cannot lie about such things. We have brought you the truth, and will leave it to you to make your decision based on that truth."

"Ambassadors, I will speak with our Supreme Leader and inform him of what you have just told me. I will contact you on the Jaxor in three days to inform you of his decision. This should be enough time for our leaders to come to an agreement to your proposal." The ambassador rose and bowed to his longtime friend, as well as his new ones. "Where will you go from here," he asked curiously.

"We are going to visit the Earth planet," Gene replied. "Tronext wishes to see the beauty of our planet, as well as meet its people which he has worked so hard to protect."

"I would also like to visit Earth," Prowlex said enthusiastically.

"You are very welcome to join us but you would need a return vessel. We are returning to Torani after our visit. I must keep up my appearance as an ignorant earthling that has no clue of the Torani's true intentions," Gene said.

"I believe I will do this. I have always wished to visit your planet one day, and my negotiations with the Supreme Leader do not have to be done face to face, so I will accompany you top Earth. Also, your input may increase our chances of convincing the Supreme Council to join your cause. I will supply you with accommodations for this day and we can leave in the morning on our journey. My aid will take to your room and see to your needs until then. I will retrieve you in the morning."

They all stood and bowed respectfully. Then the three men were then led to the waiting shuttle and taken to their room for the night. In the morning they would set course for Earth on board the Jaxor, which will be a ten-day journey from Velnor. Gene hopes the Velnor leaders can be persuaded to join their cause, rather than seek revenge for the Torani's deception, which would derail their plans.

CHAPTER 49

———•●✳●•———

The Valley
March 2, 2022, 10:00

Spring will be arriving soon and the temperatures are already starting to stay above freezing at night, and the residents of the town are grateful. The winter snows have put a halt to the excavation work on the homes, but the interiors of them all have been finished with the residents now living comfortably within them. They are all eager to once again work on the valley community.

This year will be quite busy. A stable and barn for horses is to be constructed from the trees that will be cut to create farming and grazing land for the town to grow their own food. The people want to create a self-sustained ecosystem in the valley, which is very welcome to Bill and his family. Gardens and a sizeable pond for fish, are also to be created for the community. A large structure will also be sunk into the mountain, to create a recreation area and meeting hall for the winter months. Bill had lost his garage and studio this winter, and he expects to not let that happen in the future.

Bill has taken up the task of creating the stone appearance of the mountain on the front of the homes, so when they are landscaped to match the natural terrain they will be as invisible as his home. Monica has been helping him with this task to keep her occupied, as well as to learn Bill's skill.

Weekly flights to NASA and Nevada have been cleverly disguised as normal workweek activities in order to keep the world's secret from the others, as well as the Torani workers still present on the planet. There are five people in the valley that know the truth and they have to keep it that way.

Tonight will be the first barbeque of the year, and the ladies are all preparing for the evening. Everyone loves the barbeques and has missed them during the cold winter months. Each one of them is helping in their own way to make it a success.

The Zaxin shuttle landed on the street in front of the new White House. The area has been cleared for shuttles and helicopters since the rebuilding began. The three ambassadors exit the Jaxor and walk to the front entrance, where Elsa and her staff are waiting to greet the newcomers. Gene is curious to see their faces when they see the strange new aliens. He is sure Elsa will be her diplomatic self when she greets them.

"Gentlemen, it is my pleasure to meet such distinguished members of the Galactic Alliance." She bowed respectfully as Gene had informed her earlier.

"It is our pleasure to visit your beautiful planet," Tronext replied politely. "We have inspected the sight for the new Galactic Station and are quite pleased."

The ambassadors were given a tour of the World Headquarters when they arrived on the planet. They both insisted on first meeting with Earth Leader Rowland as a political courtesy before any further contact on the planet.

"We have met your Leader Rowland and have been given permission to tour your planet," Tronext added.

"Let me assure you that my friend Gene is the best person to lead such a tour. Would you all please follow me and we will all get to know each other much better." Elsa then guided them all to her office.

"Ambassador Furgison has informed me about the situation with the Torani, and let me assure you that I, as well as the people of this planet, will stand behind you no matter what your final decision will be," she added as they entered her office and were seated. Ambassador Prowlex rose to address the group. "Leader Ault, my leaders have been informed of the events leading up to the invasion of your planet by the Corisole. They wish me to voice their sorrow for your loss of life and have pledged their total support of your plan to protect the planet Earth, as well as punish the Torani for their deception when the time comes."

"Our Alliance with the Zaxin, Earth, and the Klosk, should be sufficient to protect your planet until the time comes to deal with these criminals." The Velnor ambassador bowed again and sat quietly.

"We thank you for your support in our time of great need," she replied gratefully.

The Zaxin ambassador was next to speak. "Leader Ault. When I informed your ambassador of the plot against your world, I knew it was the correct thing to do. However, I was not sure how to go about the task. Without these two gentlemen, I fear the other leaders would have taken another path on this problem, and would have certainly taken revenge on the Torani for their deception. Ambassador Furgison has shown the face of honesty for your race which has certainly led to this alliance. You should be quite grateful." He offered with respect.

"Gentlemen, you don't need to convince me of Gene's diplomatic skills. He was once the most powerful leader on this planet for eight years. I have never doubted his character as well as his honor, which is why the leaders of this world chose him for this position. Gentlemen, we trust this man with the very fate of this planet." Gene stood and took control of the discussion. "Elsa I am going to take these men on a minor tour of this planet. There are a few more people they need to meet."

"It was my pleasure to meet you, gentlemen, and I expect to see you at the galactic headquarters when they are completed," Elsa said and bowed respectfully.

"I will speak for my friend Prowlex when I say thank you, and it was our pleasure as well."

The four men rose and Elsa escorted them to the shuttle, then wished them farewell. Their next stop would be the Nevada test site to see how Horace was coming with the new fighters.

The Jaxor landed at the Area 51 lab to examine the new fighters that Horace and his teams have produced. Gene, along with the Zaxin and Velnor ambassadors, are all very excited to see Earth's newest defenses, created from the Corisole attack ship. Horace is waiting on the tarmac when they arrive to greet his friend and the ambassadors.

"Horace, how are you, old friend?" Gene asked as he welcomed his friend with a warm handshake and a hug. The aliens watch them curiously.

"Great, Gene, how are you two holding out," he asked as he shook Allen's hand also.

"We're hanging in there Horace. I would like to introduce you to Ambassador Tronext of the planet Zaxin, and Ambassador Prowlex from the Velnor planet."

"Very nice to meet new friends," he said as the ambassadors held out their hands awkwardly, which Horace shook vigorously.

"You seem excited, Horace."

"Come see what we did," he said eagerly, leading them to the truck. "Gentlemen, climb in and I'll show you our lab."

The truck carried the group to the underground labs where they all unloaded and Horace led them into the building. Once inside Horace pulled the tarp from the attack ship.

"This one we've all seen before. With Mortisk's help, we created this," he added as he pulled the tarp from their new ship.

The two alien ambassadors examined the fighter, amazed with the earthling's creation.

"You built this ship?" Prowlex asked.

"With Mortisk's help," Horace replied.

"Who is Mortisk?" the small gray alien asked Horace.

"He is our Torani fuel technician."

"Torani!" Prowlex exclaimed.

Gene came forward to explain. "Ambassadors. On a stroke of extreme luck, we were able to enlist the help of a very honest, as well as very smart, Torani to our cause. He was brought to the planet to work on the fuel tower project as a technician, and after being befriended by an Earth family, he learned to enjoy the comforts and rituals of our planet and its people. When he was informed of the deception of his leaders, as well as the plan to take control of his new friend's world, he volunteered himself to our cause. He supervised the creation of the fighter as well as the simulators that now sit at our NASA base in Houston."

"Could we meet this Torani?" Tronext asked.

"I believe we can arrange that. But I must warn you, this is a very unusual group of humans," he replied, not exactly sure how the ambassadors would react to Bill's, shall he say, relaxed lifestyle.

Horace continued the tour of his lab, and the aliens were quite impressed by the extent of the advancements they have made in their technology. Gene and Allen stayed at the rear, allowing Horace his moment in the sun, so to speak.

"Are we going to take them to meet the Torani?" Allen asked quietly.

"I think we are going to have to. I just hope we don't catch them deep into one of their favorite rituals when we arrive," Gene said with a smile.

"What do you mean by that?"

"You'll see when we get there."

The tour was at its end and time for the group to move on to its next stop. Horace thanked the ambassadors for their patience and led them back to the truck. When they were at the shuttle, they said their farewells.

"Horace, keep up the good work. You guys have truly impressed me, as well as our guests, with your work. I am going back to Torani, but hope to be back in a month to start construction of the new galactic headquarters in Dubai."

"Then I'll see you in one month, my friend," Horace said, shaking Gene's hand.

They all then climbed aboard the shuttle to continue their journey.

"You have accomplished much in the last year, Ambassador," Tronext said as they took their seats.

"I have very smart people to help me, Ambassador."

"That is very evident. I am amazed by the progress that you have made in such a short period of time," Tronext added.

The group will make a stop at Johnson before Gene takes the ambassadors to meet the Torani. Brad would never forgive him if he didn't pay him a visit. They took to the sky and would arrive at Johnson in less than an hour.

Johnson Space Center is back to full readiness after a year of repairs. They have been in constant contact with the Lunar Station while they set up a new long-range sensor array on the moon's surface. The array will be capable of detecting anything that enters the solar system. Dr. Lee's insight into the Torani technology has helped bring it to its final stage. John and Jack arrived on Earth only four days ago, and with the Information they brought with them they were able to download the final software to bring the long overdue project to its completion.

Brad and his crew have had a difficult time with the integration of the two alien technologies. With the data from the last Torani visit, he was able to set up the auto tracking for the laser cannons, which will make the Station a very formidable defense system. They are now in the process of some final programming when two very familiar and unexpected faces entered the control room, followed by two unbelievable beings. The entire room came to a halt as they entered.

"John, Jack. What the hell are you two doing here? I thought you were still on Torani."

His friends were still speechless as they waited for him to explain the very odd-looking beings. Especially the one that looked identical to the invaders. "We came home early. Are you going to introduce us to your companions?" John asked with very wide eyes.

"I'm sorry. I've just become so accustomed to them I forgot my manners. Ambassadors Tronext and Prowlex, I would like to introduce you to my dear friend John Alistair, as well as our new head of NASA Brad Meyer. And I believe this is Jack Lee who has spent time on Torani with John to study the Torani technologies. Gentlemen, the Zaxin ambassador Tronext, and the Velnor ambassador Prowlex."

The group all exchanged handshakes and very curious expressions.

"It's good to see you again, Ambassador Tronext, but I haven't yet met the Velnor ambassador," he said, still wondering why a Corisole alien was standing in his main control room. "It's a pleasure to meet you, Ambassador Prowlex. Velnor, is that the same as Corisole?" he asked.

"We are the same race," Prowlex answered. "I sense your distrust, Mr. Alistair, but let me assure you that the Velnor and Corisole planets are connected only by race and very distant history. The Velnor people have no desire for wealth or power. We exist only to explore this galaxy in our quest for knowledge," Prowlex explained, hoping to ease the human's distrust.

"John, the ambassador is here to help us in any way he can, so let's cut him a little slack, shall we," Gene said firmly.

"My apologies, gentlemen, but the last eighteen months have been a very unnerving experience."

"So I understand you have a new toy?" Gene asked to change the subject.

"Yes, we do. You wanna play with it?" John said with a smile. "Follow me and I'll show you Brad and Mortisk's creation."

They all loaded into the elevator and went to the lower lab, which now contains two of the new simulators set up to either be piloted on solo missions or against each other in battle. John has spent a few days in one but hasn't progressed very much yet.

"These as you can see, gentlemen, are flight simulators for our new fighters. We are currently training young pilots for the program," Brad explained.

"Why young pilots. Why not use the ones we've got?" Gene asked.

"John is a veteran pilot as well as a space shuttle pilot. He has spent three days in the simulators and hasn't come anywhere near either Mortisk or Willis's scores," Brad said.

"Willis? Isn't that the kid we met in Colorado? Bill's son, right," Gene asked.

"That's right. The kid had flown a shuttle for a month or so, then jumped into the simulator and almost did as good as Mortisk, who has been flying these types of ships his whole life. It's the games these kids have been playing their whole lives. They can think ten different directions at once, not to mention the eye-hand coordination they have is incredible. It's based on one of your designs, Ambassador, would you care to try?" Brad asked Prowlex.

"I think I would enjoy the challenge," he replied.

"Let me get it ready. John, would you help the ambassador. Care to join him, Ambassador Tronext?"

"No, thank you. We are a peaceful race and have never needed such machines. I'm afraid I would not do well."

"Very well then. Ambassador Prowlex, you will be going into orbit to attempt to destroy a large cruiser. There will be a computer-simulated battle group assisting you. Are you ready?" Brad asked.

"Yes, I am ready."

The canopy closed on the simulator, and the ambassador was set to run the same program the others had run. The simulator sprung to life, and after a few minutes the simulated battle was over. After the cowling rose, Prowlex exited the simulated fighter.

"So what do you think, Ambassador?" Brad asked.

"Very interesting. The simulator is extremely lifelike," Prowlex declared excitedly. "How did I do?" he asked with a smile.

Brad checked the data, then smiled. "Actually quite impressive, Ambassador. One of our highest scores."

"I had an advantage. It is our design. It should be very efficient at training your pilots."

"All right, gentlemen, we have another stop to make today. John you may want to join us."

"Why?" he asked.

"We're going to see Mortisk. The ambassadors want to meet the Torani that is willing to help us stop his own leaders."

"I think I know the real reason you're asking me. You need a chaperone," John said smiling. "I'm game. Let's roll," he added happily.

"Roll?" Tronext asked, puzzled by the statement.

"Never mind. Follow me, gentlemen," Gene said.

The expanding group of men entered the elevator and rose to the main control room, then out to the shuttle for their next leg of their world tour. "Nice ship," John said as he admired the large shuttle.

"Thank you," Tronext replied.

They all loaded into the shuttle, then left for Colorado on a journey that was sure to end in an interesting evening. John and Gene hope the two ambassadors are up to it.

The workday has come to an end, the equipment has been shut down, and the chain saws have stopped cutting the trees for the new barn. The valley will now be quiet till the next morning.

Bill sits at the now somewhat larger fire pit that was built to accommodate the growing population. The first logs are now burning since it will be getting dark in a few hours, also allowing the coals to build up.

Ben and Allen are making the barbeques ready for the night's meal by using the smaller wood cut from the trees. Everything is used in the valley one way or another. Bill is watching the children, which includes little Lilly who is almost three now, play with the dog in the extremely large hole dug to accommodate the pond. Sassy is there to play with them as well as protect them from danger, and she takes both jobs quite seriously. Actually she leans more toward the playing, but I guess we all do.

Monica comes out of the house with Bill's first after work B and B (Bucket and Bowl.) and sits on his lap. Life on the Mountain brings out the best in people, and they soon forget the hustle and bustle of city life and learn to slow down and enjoy life after a few months.

"Here you go, baby," she said as she handed a cold Corona and kissed him lovingly.

"You're too good to me. You know that, don't you?"

"Yea I know, but you're learning to deserve me," she replied cockily.

He looked around the growing valley as he drank his beer. "We've got the room for six more families, so we're going to get an early start this year and hopefully get them finished and replanted by winter," he said.

"Now that's a lot of work, Bill. You've got three houses to finish the landscaping on, not to mention a barn and a rec center, which are already started, and a pond to finish. So how do you intend to do the other six houses?"

"I have a new rule this year. I will help with all the excavating and concrete work, then they're on your own from there."

"That's a good idea. You're getting to old for this shit," she said, knowing it would get a rise out of him.

"Too old my ass. I'm just ready to start enjoying this valley again. Unfortunately for you, it will mean I'll be around the house more."

"Well, I guess we better restock the bar, and you better replant your garden," she said laughing.

"You do love me don't you." He hugged her and gave her a kiss.

They sat watching the group playing in the pond. Sassy's head was covered in mud as she did her part of the digging. Bill threw another round of logs on the fire as Ben and Alex walked over.

"How are the barbeques coming?" Bill asked.

"Ready in an hour," Ben replied.

"Cold one." Bill offered.

"Thought you'd never ask," Ben replied with his usual wit.

The two men joined the circle, each receiving their gifts as they sat, and began to watch the kids play in the hole. The rest of the family should be arriving soon, and Willis and Mortisk should also be flying in at any time. The first barbeque of spring is about to begin.

The Jaxor cruises slowly through the mountain valleys of Colorado. Tronext and Prowlex are at the controls, both enjoying the incredible view. Tronext who comes from a desert planet, and Prowlex who's planet is mostly water, rarely see such beauty. The only planets in the galaxy that even come close to Earth's beauty are planet Torani and the Klosk planet.

As they come in over the Vail valley and head west toward Parachute, John joins them at the controls to lead them to their destination. A few minutes later John spots the fuel tower and searches the lower valley for the road that leads into the valley. He finally spots the valley which was actually hard to miss with all the construction going on, and points them toward a large lot that has been cleared at the mouth of the valley for parking the trucks. A small shuttle sits off to one side leaving plenty of room for the large Jaxor which is six times its size. As they landed the shuttle John spotted the ever-present fire, as well as the familiar group sitting around it.

"I hope these two are up to this," John said to Gene.

"I hope we are up for this. I remember the last time," Gene said with a smile.

"What's that supposed to mean?" Allen asked, still curious about Gene's statements.

"You'll see soon enough," Gene said as he and John laughed to themselves.

"You keep telling me that."

"Let's go for a little hike, gentlemen," Gene said as he headed for the door of the vessel.

The three men and two aliens left the ship and walked up the driveway toward the fire, Tronext and Prowlex enjoying the view as they walked.

Mortisk is on his feet along with the other men of the valley. Mortisk recognizes the shuttle as being of Zaxin design and curious as to its appearance on Earth. Sassy barks as the group rounds the last corner of the driveway, and Bill grabbed her collar to hold her back. As the group closes on the fire pit, Bill and Ben recognize two of the men. They are the president and John Alistair, along with three guests. One human, and two who are something else entirely.

"Is that the new Air Force One?" Ben asked with a smile.

"That is a Zaxin vessel," Mortisk said in a curious tone. "But they are not both Zaxin. One of them is Corisole," he added.

"Corisole, what's he doing here?" Willis asked angrily.

"I don't think he's from Corisole. I think he is from Velnor by the way he is dressed. They are the same race, but live their lives by much different principles. They are a peaceful and curious race." The three men and one alien went out to greet them.

"That's one big dammed cowboy," Allen said. "He makes John Wayne look like a wimp."

John and Gene laugh as they approach the valleys residents.

"What's so funny?" Bill asked.

"John Wayne joke," Gene said, pointing at Mortisk. "How are you Bill?" he asked, offering his hand.

"Confused," Bill replied, motioning to the two aliens at Gene's side.

"Gentlemen, this is the Zaxin ambassador Tronext," he said, introducing the reptilian to his four friends. "And this is Ambassador Prowlex of Velnor," he explained as they all shook hands. "Ambassadors, I would like to introduce you to our host Bill, and his son Willis," John explained. "This is my old friend Ben Murphy, and this is our Torani friend Mortisk."

"Welcome to our mountain, gentlemen. Follow me," Bill said.

The group walked the short distance to the fire as the residents of the valley watched with a look of wonder at the two new aliens. The children peeked out from behind the legs of their parents in wonder of the oddlooking creatures standing before them. Tronext noticed their fear and approached the children and went to his knees to make himself appear smaller to them.

"Hello, my name is Tronext," he said to the small humans. "It is my pleasure to meet you," he said, holding out his reptilian hand. The older children looked on, not knowing what to do as little Lilly walked out and took hold of the reptilian man's hand, then smiled and giggled. After seeing such a brave act by the smallest of them, the others all came over and shook Tronext's hand. "Pleased to meet you," he repeated. "This is my friend Prowlex," he said, motioning the small alien over. Prowlex walked over to the children, who all greeted him politely. Lilly giggled again as she touched the little gray man's hand.

"Gentlemen, please join us," Bill said.

They all seated themselves at the fire. After the rest of the introductions were made, the tension soon left the group.

"Cold one?" Bill asked.

"Absolutely," Gene replied and served his guests. "This, Ambassadors, is what makes Earth great. A fire, good friends to share it with, and cold beer."

They all watched as the ambassadors took their first drink of Earth beer. They each drank and nodded with approval.

"Very good," Tronext said, looking at the bottle. "Much like our Markor."

Prowlex drank the whole bottle, then burped loudly. "Another?" he asked. The crowd rolled with laughter, and the evening was off to a wonderful start.

The evening was unbelievably enjoyable. Good music filled the air, and the food was enjoyed by all. The ambassadors had never eaten barbequed food but enjoyed it immensely. Tronext was fascinated by the creature that basically lived to chase the stick without tiring, that he threw at least a hundred times. It was a perfect night.

"So Gene what brought you to our valley?" Bill asked.

"The ambassadors wanted to meet the Torani who is willing to go against his leaders to help an alien race which he has known for such a short time," he replied, pointing toward Mortisk, who was currently sitting next to Prowlex, along with Hyal and their not-so-little baby. "And I would like to meet the first Torani born on our planet," he added as he held out his arms to Hyal, who handed him the child. "They don't do anything small, do they," Gene commented as he held up the large child and looked at the others.

"Nothing," Bill replied with a chuckle.

The night passed quickly as they all enjoyed themselves with the people they loved, as well as their new friends. Gene is relaxing and talking with John and Allen. Ben is sitting with Tashike talking with Hyal and Mortisk, as well as the ambassadors. Gene leaned over to Bill and asked him a quiet question.

"You wouldn't happen to have one of those joints, would you?"

Bill just smiled and pulled two out of his shirt pocket and handed one to him, then lit it for him.

"I actually knew better than to ask," he said as he blew out the smoke.

Bill lit the other one, and on the other side of the fire, the three aliens rose and came over to where the two men were sitting. "Bogart," Mortisk said with a smile as the three aliens joined the two Earth men.

Gene looked at Bill. "Are we the last ones in the galaxy to discover this stuff."

"Evidently we are," he replied, laughing at the sight of the six-foot lizard man and a four-foot gray alien smoking a joint like it was nothing new to them. Monica came out of the house and looked curiously at the group. "I swear I had nothing to do with it," Bill said, as she shook her head at him. Gene couldn't help but to laugh.

"I think I'll bring my family up here someday," Gene said.

"You are all welcome here any time. In a few months we will have the stables finished, and there's a great little lake for Trout fishing about two hours ride up the mountain. We'll make a day of it."

"You got a deal," Gene replied, shaking his hand.

"You guys do have a place to sleep on that ship?" Bill asked.

"Yea, why?" Gene asked curiously.

"Because those aliens are going to be too wasted to fly that thing," Bill said, pointing at the newcomers and laughing.

The evening wound down and the towns people slowly disappeared into their homes. It was late and time for bed. Bill made sure his guests would stay for breakfast, then escorted them to the shuttle and bid them farewell till morning. As he walked back up the driveway with Sassy he thought to himself. Two years ago if he had told anyone that he was partying with aliens, they would have locked him up in the loony bin. "Life Is Strange."

After a wonderful breakfast and a short flight from Colorado, the Jaxor has landed at Johnson to drop John off before their journey continues. It was decided before they left Velnor that they would return the ambassador to his planet, so the Jaxor has a long journey ahead of it.

"I hope you can explain my absence on Torani, Gene," John said. "We've accumulated as much information as we need for now. The data that Dr. Lee acquired on our last trip was the weak link we had with the Corisole and Torani technology. And with Mortisk and the Velnor to help from here on out, I see no need to return. You'll just have to explain to the emperor that I am needed here for the time being and we'll send another team to work at the Learning Center."

"I'll play it by ear John, but I'm sure all eyes and ears will be on me from here on out. The emperor feels something is up and is going to try his best to find out what it is. Plus, I'm used to the cloak and dagger stuff from the Presidency, so I can deal with him. You guys just need to keep your heads down."

"We will Gene, but we really need to get their scientists out of our hair and corralled up somewhere. With them working around us, the danger of them discovering what we're up to is very high. We don't need any of them in the labs, or on the Station anymore."

"I'll see if we can get them put to work in Dubai. That should keep them out of the way for at least two years. By the time the Galactic Center is completed we should have our defenses finished, which will put us five years ahead of schedule. The funny thing is that we have a Torani to thank for our gain. Mortisk really saved our asses."

"All right, my friend, you have a good journey and be careful on Torani. I'd hate to see anything happen to you," John said to his friend with a handshake and a manly one-armed hug.

"I will see you in six months John, and tell Brad good-bye and to keep up the good work."

"Will do Gene. Take care."

Gene climbed aboard the Jaxor as John walked his way back across the tarmac. The ship rose into the sky headed for Velnor, then on to Torani. The plan is in motion, and the allies all know their part.

CHAPTER 50

---•●✦●•---

Planet Torani Emperor's Chambers
April 15, 2022

Gene is back on the planet Torani, but has spent most of his time on board the Galactic Station to open his office. He needs to be able to communicate with the ambassadors without being detected, but even on the station they have to deal with Torani security and must be extra careful when and where they meet.

The emperor has called Gene to his chambers to talk with his friend from Earth, but Gene knows that the emperor is suspicious about his connection to the Zaxin ambassador, as the Zaxins are known throughout the galaxy for their deep knowledge of all that takes place.

Gene also knows that the emperor must be nervous about his secret of the gold reserves on Earth being discovered by another of the galaxies' systems. Gene enters the emperor's chambers and is instantly greeted by his false affection. "Ambassador Furgison, please sit, my friend. I have missed your company. So how was your trip with the Zaxin ambassador? I was surprised at the Tarkon's return without you on board."

"The Zaxin ambassador felt that his vessel was better suited for the journey, especially through the Boral and Antarian systems. We also thought it would better for its landing abilities," John said, keeping to the story that he and Tronext had already set up.

"So what is your opinion of the galaxy on your first trip through it? You must have witnessed many wondrous, as well as strange, things."

"Well, Emperor, I thought that I had seen a lot of beautiful and also strange things as a leader on my planet, but when you see the pyramid shaped domes of Zaxin, or the magnificent trees of Klosk it leaves you in

---

310

awe. We didn't dare stop over on the Boral or Antarian planets because of the risks involved. But besides that, I thoroughly enjoyed the trip."

"I am glad that you had the opportunity. As a new member of the Alliance it is advisable to know just who you are dealing with, as well as their beliefs and customs. I understand you did not visit the Corisole planet."

"I thought it was best that I leave that visit for a time in the future. There are still tensions between our planets."

"You are probably correct, considering the outcome of the trial. What feelings did you get from the other ambassadors concerning the verdict?" he asked curiously.

"They all agreed the ruling was fair and gave me their sorrow for our loss of life," Gene said, knowing that it was a question he would be asked. "The other systems are all quite willing to lend any assistance they can in the rebuilding of our planet, but I explained to them that we have it under control. On another matter, they are all in favor of creating a galactic outpost on my planet. I agreed that it would be beneficial to all, and suggested the Dubai location as its location."

"Galactic Station, interesting. When are you scheduled to start the construction?"

"It is scheduled to begin in five months' time. I hate to be rude, Emperor, but the computer techs are scheduled at my new office on the station and I would really like to be there when they install everything to assure that I can operate all the systems properly," Gene explained, trying to end the very uncomfortable meeting.

"Very well, Ambassador, I won't keep you from your work any longer. I'm sure you will enjoy your new office. The view is spectacular. I will expect an update on the new Galactic Station."

"Absolutely, my friend, have a good day," Gene replied as he rose to excuse himself from the emperor's chambers.

"Good day, my friend," the emperor replied.

Gene left the leader's chambers and breathed a big sigh of relief. As far as he can tell, the emperor knows nothing of their plot, but they must continue to be extra careful with their meetings.

Horace is in the Nevada lab supervising the assembly of Earth's defense ships, or EDS as they have come to be known. The work is coming along at a respectable rate, and they are currently completing five EDS a week, and hope to increase that number to ten once Olga's Siberian lab starts their assembly.

Evan Moore has now been put in charge of the Nevada labs to free Horace to relocate to the Lunar Station to continue his work there.

"How are the Japanese coming along on the cannon assemblies, Evan?" Horace asked.

"At this time they are a little behind, but we are expecting them to increase production after the lines are adjusted. The optic feed is giving them some trouble at the present time but they assure that the problem will be corrected shortly."

"And is the Siberian plant supplying the fuselage parts we need?"

"Yes, they are. Olga is quite the slave driver and has that place humming like a Ferrari motor. Actually we need her to pay a visit to our Reactor plant to boost the production. They are running a little behind and she is the expert on the reactor construction."

"I'll give her a ring and set it up. How's the fuel team doing?"

"They have created the fuel to match the sample, all they need is the molds which are being forged as we speak. They had to get Mortisk's okay on the exact size, and he's been a very busy alien with all he has on his plate."

"All right then, it sounds like you've got things under control. Let me know if anything else comes up. I'll be on the Lunar Station working on the laser targeting systems."

Now that the EDS construction is on schedule, Horace is free to continue his work with the targeting systems for the laser cannons. The Torani technicians will soon be transferred to Dubai to begin work on the new Galactic Station, which will allow the humans to complete their work on their defensive systems, without the threat of discovery.

John and Brad are in what used to be the hangar for the space shuttles. Inside this hangar are the first four EDS along with the first six of the twenty planned simulators. The two men are now busy inspecting the computer systems that will control the simulators.

"Quite a sight, isn't it," John said. "I never expected to see orbital fighters in this hangar."

"We never expected to be invaded and have a need for these fighters. Welcome to the new space race, right," Brad replied.

The two pilots make a good team because they both know the importance of good training when it comes to flying. Excessive training prepares the pilots for a wider variety of situations during battle. The rest depends on the gut instincts of the pilots. Brad has the advantage of also being a scientist and makes sure that NASA has always had the very best equipment to train and operate with. That has always been NASA's number one priority.

"So how's the pilot recruitment coming along?" John asked.

"We have taken the game that Willis and Mortisk designed and tweaked it a little to improve it, then sent off hundreds of copies around the world to test applicants. The game judge's basic skills as well as well as common sense flying abilities. We've also sent the schematics for the simulators to Russia, Japan, and the U K for manufacturing their own simulators to train the applicants that pass the tests.

"All hands on training will be done at Area 51 and Siberia right? We have to keep a low profile on this Brad. We are taking a chance by simply storing these four EDS here."

"You know it will be a miracle if we pull this off right?"

"Then we'll have to think like magicians won't we," John replied. "Misdirection is the key to the whole plan. We have to keep the Torani looking at the other hand."

"So what do we do next?"

"We go to the Persian Gulf and pull a rabbit out of our hat," John replied with a smile.

They finished the checks on the simulator systems and everything checked out.

"Care for a little battle?" John asked, tilting his head toward the simulators.

"Why, so you can kick my ass again?" Brad replied.

"Oh come on, you're getting better," he said with a smile.

"What the hell, let's go, flyboy."

The two friends jumped into the simulators to have a little fun. It's nice to have the best toys to play with.

The valley is in a celebratory mood today with the birth of the family's newest member. Alice gave birth to an eight-pound baby boy this morning bringing the valley's population to eighteen, and of those eighteen four are aliens.

The mood is joyous, and the proud father has been hovering over Alice and their first born like they were both made of crystal. Hyal is sitting with Alice for the new mother support. Dove and Alice's mother, Mary Anne, have kidnapped the infant and will probably not give him back—until he gets hungry, that is.

Bill sits back enjoying the happy mood they are all in, as well as his own joy of having another grandchild. He rose from his personal chair at the pit and quiets the small crowd.

"I would like to say how happy I am to have another addition to our family. It has been a pleasure to have Alice in our family, and to now have this new little life added, makes us appreciate life even more. So I would like to make a toast to Willis, Alice, and little Clifford William. May they all enjoy this mountain long after I am gone from this Earth. They all raised their glasses in salute to the toast and drank.

Willis kissed his soon-to-be new wife and recaptured son. "Thank you, everyone. I never thought I would be sitting here in this valley with all of my family, and especially my own after all that happened in the last few years. This is the greatest day of my life so far and I have this lady right here to thank for it. Well, I did help a little," he joked as he gently grabbed his son and held him up. "From the newest member of this family, we thank you for all your love and support."

He sat down with his new son, a very proud father. Mortisk came over and patted him on the back and shakes his hand. Then Willis stood back up.

"Oh, and by the way, as soon as all this work is finished in September there will be a wedding to attend. You are all Invited."

Ben Murphy then stood and quieted everyone to add his own words to the speech. He looks at Tashike who nods approvingly at him.

"Willis and Alice. If you would allow it, Tashike and I would like to make it a double wedding."

"It would be our pleasure to have you join us, Ben and Tashike," Willis said, shaking his hand and then giving his golden bride-to-be a hug.

The whole group was all up now hugging and shaking hands. Bill sat back in his chair with Monica and hugged her gently with one arm as they enjoyed the beautiful evening, and the most excellent company any man could wish for.

"Wanna beer, Grandpa?" Monica asked with a smile.

"Yea, and a bowl too."

Life just keeps getting better and better as he watches his friends enjoy each other's company, as well as his new Grandson.

Gene has been extremely busy for the last two months aboard the Galactic Station, with the preparations for the new Galactic Station in the Persian Gulf. It is the largest project to be constructed by the Alliance since the building of the Alliance Station in the Torani System over fifty years ago.

The allied ambassadors of Earth, Zaxin, Velnor, and Klosk, will be the overseers of the project, in order to ensure that all systems will be involved in the construction. They hope it will draw more systems to their cause, and once the other systems put a face to the victims of the invasion by working side by side with them, it will create a stronger Alliance.

The Antarians have volunteered to undertake the task of transporting all of the technology that will be need for the station from the many systems. They are hindered by the atmosphere on all planets but their own, so they won't be able to work on the surface.

The Boral cyborgs will build all control systems for the Station, as they are the masters of the galaxy at creating systems from the technology of other races and integrating them together to work efficiently as one. Their very race is confirmation of this fact.

As Master Cloners, the Zakorian people will create the medical labs, medical systems, and install them in the station. On their planet that is isolated on the outer edge of the galaxy, they care nothing for the problems of the galaxy, but the ambassadors have stroked their huge egos to convince them to participate in the construction of the Station.

The Torani have been enlisted to oversee the construction, and have the responsibility of all power systems and production. The ambassadors hope that this responsibility will draw all the remaining Torani in the Sol System away from their clandestine projects being created to defend the planet, leaving the Earth men to complete the implementation of all defensive systems.

Gene, with the help of the other members of his Alliance, has spent the last few days tying up all the loose ends for the project so he can return to Earth. Tronext has offered him passage and they will be leaving Torani space this very day. The Torani emperor has come to the Station to speak with Gene, and has just entered his office.

"Ambassador Furgison," he said as he entered and shook Gene's hand, "you have done a fine job with the other systems to get the new station under construction."

"Thank you, Emperor Ardesnal. I have been extremely busy working with all of them to put this project together."

"Well, my friend, as I have stated, you have done a very good job."

"Emperor, we would like to transfer all of your people to Dubai to watch over the construction, until they are needed to begin their tasks with the power systems. There are many races involved in the construction, and with the Torani's experience in dealing with these races, I feel they would be the best qualified for the job," he said, working on the emperor's arrogance. "I'm sure that the excess technicians would like nothing more than to return to Torani and be with their families. They have been on Earth for a very long time and must miss their loved ones," he said again, trying to reduce the Torani presence on the planet.

"That is a very good idea, Ambassador. After almost two years and very few short trips home, they would certainly enjoy going home to their families. I understand that you are leaving today to witness the start of the project."

"Yes. Ambassador Tronext has offered me passage on his vessel."

"You and the Zaxin ambassador have become close friends I see."

"He is a pleasant creature to work with."

"Yes, the Zaxin people are known very well for that fact. You will be returning soon I hope?"

"Yes, I will need the use of the Tarkon in four months if it's possible."

"It will be no problem. I think I will join the crew on the trip to see how the Galactic Station is progressing, as well as visit your beautiful planet once again."

"I'm sure the Earth leaders would welcome a visit from you, Emperor," he lied, knowing that every person who is aware of the deception would like nothing more than to get their hands around his golden neck. The emperor has just created more work for him.

"Then I will leave you to your business, my friend. I know you have a ship to catch and I wouldn't want to keep you from your journey. Have a safe trip."

The emperor left as quickly as he arrived, and Gene was happy that he was able to once again stem the emperor's curiosity. The first, as well as the second parts of the plan are working as hoped. The ambassador then gathered his things, and is off to join Tronext on board the Jaxor for their journey to Earth.

CHAPTER 51

---•◦❀◦•---

Dubai, Galactic Station 3 Construction Site
September 10, 2022

The Gulf is extremely busy with the efforts of every type of vessel imaginable. The shoreline is a mass of steel beams which are to be used for the structure of the station, and more materials are arriving every day for the next stages of the project. The humans have created concrete facilities on huge sea vessels for pouring the pilings to support the structure, and are working around the clock to stay ahead of the steel crews. Shuttles are being used to transport and set the steel for the huge structure that will be the backbone of the elaborate Station.

The designers, which were mostly from Earth, have decided on the shape of a huge crab standing in the Gulfs waters. The shell will provide the stations many offices and labs, as well as the central chamber for the galactic leaders' meetings, and the claws will serve as the landing areas for the shuttles that will arrive at the station as well as outdoor viewing areas for its visitors. It will be an awesome sight resting one half mile off the coast of Dubai and the World Headquarters.

Workers from Earth have been integrated into the workforce to add a sense of unity, as well as familiarity with the inhabitants of the recovering planet. The Arabian coast has been dotted with several compounds to house the many races of beings, to help ease the burden of the vessels now orbiting the planet. This gathering of species occurs only during galactic projects, and has never occurred on Earth. This has created a very diverse city that the Arab people are not accustomed to. They have had had the hardest time of all the planet's many societies at melding with the rest of the planet because of their beliefs, and they have an even harder time accepting the galaxy's new visitors on their soils.

Gene and Tronext are standing on the shoreline along with Prince Azeere and Leader Rowland at the World Headquarters, watching the ongoing construction of the new Station.

"So what do you think of our beautiful gulf, Ambassador Tronext?" the prince asked.

"I have not seen such beauty since I stood on the shores of Sorlock on the Velnor planet. And I must add how wonderful your temperatures are. My people would love to be in this climate."

"Now that you mention it I do see the resemblance," Gene said. "The same sandy beaches and coastline as Velnor."

"So Gene, you truly believe that the creation of this Station is necessary to save Earth?" the leader asked. "I truthfully don't see the reasoning."

"Marta, I'm sure that you understand the political value of this station. Once this station is inhabited by the numerous diplomats from around the galaxy, if the Torani dare attack this planet, the repercussions will be severe for endangering other systems' leaders. But the Torani are the most powerful entity in this galaxy and may see the risk worthwhile, which leads to the second part of our plan. By creating this station, we will gain at least two more years to complete our Earth defense systems. Once our cannon batteries are in place, along with the hundreds of fighters, we will have assembled. It will take a fleet ten times the size of the Torani's to invade this planet," Gene explained, as the other two present nodded with agreement. "Once our planetary defenses are in place, we can begin to branch out into space and build shipyards to build our own galactic vessels to join the galactic family as an equal."

The leader listened with newfound interest but had a hard time grasping the sheer magnitude of the overall plan. The planet must transform itself into a galactic entity?

"It is a sublime idea, Gene, but it seems so large a task."

"The galaxy is a large place, Leader Rowland," Tronext said. "We all have learned to protect each other, not only from ourselves, but from the incursion of other galaxies. We have been very fortunate that has not yet happened, but it is inevitable that it will happen in our future. You must think of our galaxy as one grain of sand on this beach full of other galaxies. We are a young galaxy that hasn't breached the barrier of traveling beyond our borders because of our engine designs, but we have to assume that there are other beings that have breached that barrier and travel the universe at will. I will also assure you that eventually they will come and we have no idea of their intentions," Tronext added cautiously.

"Marta, if you truly want to grasp the vastness of this galaxy, wait until the station is completed and book yourself a flight to another system.

All it will cost you is time, and believe me the experience you will gain is unimaginable," Gene added to his friend's comments.

The two leaders stood looking at the beach and soaking in the unbelievable truth, when Gene had to put an end to their visit.

"Leader Rowland, Prince Azeere. We don't mean to be rude, but we have a wedding to attend in the Colorado mountains. We have two friends who are both getting married today, and I wouldn't miss it for the world," Gene said respectfully. "Ambassador Tronext and I must be leaving. It was a pleasure to see the two of you again."

"It has also been my pleasure to meet two of Earth's distinguished leaders," Tronext said as he shook their hands.

"Have fun, you two," Marta replied, as she and the prince turned to return to the headquarters.

The two travelers still have two stops to make before the wedding. They have to go to Johnson to retrieve John, then on to the ranch to gather his family on their way to Colorado.

"Let's roll, my friend. We've got a lot of planet to cover," Gene said to his reptilian friend as he slapped him on the back. They then returned to the Jaxor and headed for Johnson, the first stop on their journey.

As the ambassadors are busy making their last-minute stops across the district, the residents of the mountain town, which they have yet to put a name to, are all preparing for the arrival of the many guests, as well as the wedding.

The ladies are busy with the brides-to-be, running from one location to the other, making sure everything is absolutely perfect, which is what they have been doing for the past week—and will surely continue up until the last minute. Bill and the other men have been preparing for the reception afterward as men always do.

The valley is now back to its original state with the additions of a large pond surrounded by lush grasses where the wedding will take place. The stables and log barn have been completed and stocked with six horses donated by a few of the grateful ranchers. The valley is absolutely perfect, like something out of a Norman Rockwell painting.

There is now only three hours left before the wedding so they are expecting the Jaxor at any time. The family and most of the surrounding towns are already there and have started the festivities. Bill and Alex have put the finishing touches on the barbeques to go along with the pig they put in a pit of coals late last night, and are now stacking the logs for the fire later that evening. The townspeople have brought a dozen picnic tables to aid with the day's events, and Willis has of course set up his sound system for the music.

"I think we're finally ready Alex. We've got the pig ready, one hundred pounds of steaks, deserts coming out of our buts from the ladies in town, and three troughs full of ice cold beer," Bill said, digging into the ice. "Want one?"

"After all the work we've done, I think we deserve it," he replied.

Mortisk came wandering up dressed quite nicely, and sporting a brandnew Stetson.

"Where the hell did you get that?" Bill asked, looking at the hat.

"Grand Junction," he replied. "Here, I brought you one also," he said as he pulled his hand from behind his large back. "I'll trade you," he added, motioning to the ice-cold beers.

"Deal," Bill said, handing him a cold one. "Thank you, my big friend."

"You are most welcome, my crazy Earth friend," he replied with a smile.

They all laughed and drank their beers as Bill tried on his new hat. About that time, they spotted the Jaxor coming over the mountain and landing in the new hay field.

"Looks like our other guests have finally arrived," Alex said.

The three men walked through the crowd that has gathered to see who was in the fancy spaceship, then out into the field to greet the new arrivals. Most of them had never seen a Zaxin before and were in for quite a surprise. Sassy took the lead as always. The door opened on the shuttle, and in she went to greet her guests.

"She always has to be first," Bill said with a chuckle.

Gene and his family exited the Jaxor, followed by John, Tronext and a very excited dog. They all walked over to meet their host.

"How the hell are you Bill?" Gene asked.

"Absolutely wonderful Gene. Glad you all could make it."

"I would like to introduce you three to my better half Marsha, and these two are Matty and John."

"It's a pleasure to meet all of you," Bill said politely. "John, Tronext, how the hell are ya?" Bill asked as he shook the two men's hands. "Follow me, the party has already started."

"Not yet," Gene said then went back into the Jaxor, followed by Tronext and John, who all returned also wearing new Stetson hats. Gene had two more for the grooms.

"Nice touch," Bill said.

"We did come from Texas," Gene said smiling.

"That you did. Come with me, everyone. Kids, go have fun. Sassy will show you the way. Marsha, I'm going to throw you to the wolves in that pack of women, and, guys, follow Mortisk. The cold beer is over there."

The two children followed the dog back to where the other children were all playing, Bill took Marsha to the house and introduced her to all the ladies, and the three men followed Mortisk and Alex through a very curious crowd to the beer where Bill joined them soon after.

The wedding went as planned. Bill walked Alice down the aisle, as he is the closest thing she has to a father now. Mortisk walked Tashike down the aisle and gave her to Ben, which he didn't totally understand, but he did it nonetheless. They all traded vows, then each pair kissed their new mates and the wedding was complete. Complete with two bawling mothers, and Hyal to join them.

The evening went just as well. An excellent meal was served, followed by music and dancing, along with good conversation with friends. The tables were gathered and set on the lawn that surrounded the fire pit, and everyone sat talking among themselves. Gene Furgison stood and everyone quieted as their ex-president began to speak.

"Willis and Alice, I want to toast to your long life and good health. Marriage isn't always perfect, but as long as you marry the one you love, it's worth it," he said, hugging his wife. "Cheers," he added, then drank to the couple. "Now to continue. I know we already got you a gift, but your dad told me about your love for music, so I have to give you one more. John," he said to his new son, and then he came through the crowd carrying a guitar. "This guitar was given to me a long time ago by my dear friend B.B. King, and I can't think of anyone that would appreciate it more. I would like you to have it," he said as he handed the guitar to Willis.

"Thank you, Mr. President."

"That's Gene."

"Sorry, Gene." Willis shook Gene's hand and sat back down with his new bride.

"Ben and Tashike," Gene continued. "I hope you enjoyed our gift, and I personally want to toast to your good health and a long happy life on this planet." Gene again raised his glass and drank to the new couple.

"Ben, I didn't get you a dammed thing. You're the one going home with this beautiful golden bride," he said, laughing as he sat.

Everyone laughed, and the party continued. Willis couldn't help but plug in his gift and began to play a few songs for the guests. As the night progressed the townspeople all left for their homes leaving the family and their friends by the fire. Bill walked over to the young couple and gave Alice a hug and a kiss, and shook his sons hand. He is very proud of the young man. The rest of the family is tired from the long day, so he hugged his daughters and grandchildren on their way to their homes.

"Bill I've got to tell ya, you've got it made up here," Gene said. "It goes to prove that no matter what happens in this crazy world, that as long as you're surrounded by family and a few good friends, you'll always be happy." They all agreed with him.

Tronext walked over and sat by Bill and Monica. "You are a lucky man to have such a wonderful family," he said with a wave at the people sitting around them. "And a wonderful world to live in with them," he added as he looked around the valley.

"Thank you Tronext. Tomorrow, my friends, I will show you how truly beautiful this part of the world is. Tomorrow we will ride up to the top of the mountain and do a little Fly fishing. And no eating the flies," he said, slapping Tronext on the back as everyone laughed. Tronext looked at him curiously, not understanding the joke.

"Now I get it," Tronext said. "Not funny." Then he also laughed.

Tomorrow would be another day to enjoy with his friends. Bill couldn't wait to take his friends to the top of the mountain and do a little fishing. Actually he couldn't wait to get pictures of the aliens on horseback. Those will be priceless.

CHAPTER 52

━━━━━━━•●✺●•━━━━━━━

Planetwide Summary 5
October 14–December 1, 2022

The two ambassadors have spent the last month flying around the planet from one base to another surveying the progress of their defense efforts. After a week in Dubai where they have watched the skeleton of a huge crab rise from the water, they were flying into the American district to take a short rest stop at the Dallas ranch when Gene decided to make a small detour and show Tronext what has to be the biggest secret they are hiding from the Torani. They are now landing in the heavily guarded Fort Knox Gold Depository, with the permission of the World Council.

The Jaxor lands inside the facility that is now guarded by three class 1 laser cannons. The ambassadors exit the shuttle and walk toward the armed guards at the entrance to the facility. The guards sprung to attention and saluted their former commander out of respect.

"This facility is guarded quite well Gene. I would think that this level of security would no longer be needed on this planet," Tronext stated. "You have eliminated the need for currency, therefore you should have eliminated greed."

"Tronext what I am about to show you might just be one of the biggest secrets in this galaxy."

They traveled through the halls which contained many more guards, as well as many locked doors. At the end of the long corridor they came to an elevator that led to the Depository below. When the exited the elevator they were met by two more guards protecting huge vault door. The guards opened the door for them and they walked into the massive vault that held a good majority of the world's gold reserves.

"Was I telling the truth?" Gene asked his very stunned reptilian friend. "This vault contains over forty-two million pounds of pure gold bullion. Each district has stored their gold in this vault as well as others like it for over a hundred years."

As they walked through the massive vault, the Zaxin was speechless as they moved through the never-ending piles of gold bars. Tronext stopped and picked up one of the bars examining it closely, then returning it to its place.

"I now understand the Torani's reason for their deception," he said as he continued to stare at the massive amount of gold. "This one room contains more Triomicium than all of this galaxy's mines combined."

"Our planet, and possibly other planets in this system, contain a hundred times more than what is in this vault," Gene explained.

Tronext looked at his friend then picked the gold bar up again. "This one bar of gold as you call it, would fuel a large cruiser for at least five years. You have enough in this room to power the galaxy for a thousand years," he said, pointing around the vault. "And you say you have more."

"Much more. Our mines pull gold out of the planet every day. They are all shut down now since the attack. The planet has more important things to worry about right now."

"You don't understand the significance of my statement Gene. The gold in this room alone makes your planet the most important, if not powerful planet in this galaxy and possibly thousands of others as well." He stopped to contain himself. "If the Antarians or the Boral were to discover the existence of this, they would put every vessel they had in Earth orbit and treat you the same as the Corisole did, if not worse. The only difference would be that they wouldn't care about the extent of the damage they would cause."

"Now you know why I brought you here today, Ambassador."

"I wish you had not. I cannot keep this from my people, you know that. Once the news of this gets out it will certainly bring war to this galaxy." He was quite upset with what could come from this information.

"What do we do then? What if we were to guarantee each system an equal share of our gold. We could call it a 'galactic stockpile.' It would certainly counteract the Torani's control over the galaxy."

"I do not know, my friend. We must tell no one at this time. I need to consider the effects this will certainly cause before we proceed any further on this matter."

The ambassadors left the vault and returned to the Jaxor. They are both now more uncertain of Earth's future, as well as the future of the entire galaxy than before.

The station has risen out of the Gulf at an incredible rate because of the building capabilities of the aliens, which are far ahead of their Earth counterparts. The initial phase of the construction has been completed, and the technical part of the project is now beginning.

Several of the tower crews have been enlisted to begin the power distribution systems, and Mortisk and Willis's crew has been called in for the job. They will spend the next two months living at the seaside work camp while they complete their portion of the system. Today they are running the huge optic cables that run throughout the structure.

"Hey, Bret. We need more P-ten-fifty cable from the storage yard," Willis said.

"I think we have around three thousand yards left. How much do we need?" Bret asked.

"At a thousand a roll, two will probably do it for now. We're also gonna need three rolls of F-thirty-five-sixty cable, and about five hundred splicers. Take the shuttle and have the yard hands load it for you," he replied.

"I'll be back in an hour."

As Bret headed for the shuttle Willis walked across the huge superstructure to where Mortisk was working on the core connections at the center of the structure. A small reactor is being constructed to supply the Station's energy needs.

"Need any help. I've got an hour to kill until Bret gets back from the yard," Willis asked.

"Yes, I need to finish these primary circuits so they can finish the core assembly, then we can continue with the secondary coupling stations," Mortisk replied.

"No problem, I'll start on the other side and work my way back around to you."

After almost two years of working with the alien power systems, Willis has become one of only a handful of humans who truly understand the how the alien systems function, which has made him very valuable to this project.

The Zakorian and Boral technicians are right on their tails working, so to say the least, the pace is a little hectic. The Boral, with their Cybernetic metabolisms, almost never stop working so they have easily turned Mortisk's crews one-week head start into now being behind with their progress. The power team is trying their best to keep up with the pace.

"Don't these guys ever sleep?" Willis asked Mortisk. "I never see them stop."

"The Boral only rest for a two-hour sleep period, where they feed as the rest. They know only to work, and improve their races technology as they work," Mortisk answered the tired human.

"What's with the Zakorians? They seem to be waiting for us."

"They only connect the laboratory and medical systems, and yes they are waiting for us to get the lines run for their power."

"All right, next question. Who are the big hairy guys over there?"

"They are the Klosk. They are in charge of all security and defense systems on the Station."

"Furry cops then."

"You could say that, but I wouldn't let them hear you say it."

"I'll remember that," he said with a smile. "I think we might actually finish by the end of next week. That would be a week ahead of schedule," Willis said as he looked around the structure.

"That will be fine with me, I've had enough sun and sand for a while. Hyal is ready for me to return home also."

"Yea' the ladies hate it when we're away too long. Toss me a couple of those splicers will ya."

They returned to their jobs working as fast as they possibly can. The Boral set one heck of a pace to compete with, but they are trying to keep up.

With all of the Torani techs either in the Gulf or back home on Torani, the humans have finally been able to do the work needed to convert the moon into the defense system it should be. The teams on the Station have been preparing the bays as well as the elevators to handle the much larger EDS. With the new ships being larger, much of the structure has to be renovated to accommodate them.

Horace and Brad are currently working on a long range satellite surveillance system, which once it is completed and they set a booster station on Mars, they will be able to detect any vessel entering the system long before they reach the orbit of Pluto. Jack Lee has been added to the staff to find a glitch in the firing systems for the laser cannons. The cannons have been made technically ready, but the human scientists suspect a Torani code is blocking the targeting and firing systems. Jacks knowledge of Torani computer code should enable him to find and repair the problem.

"It sure is nice to be able to work around here without the Torani looking over your shoulder all the time," Brad commented

"The trick is going to be keeping them away," Horace replied.

"Well, Horace, I say it's our Station and if we don't want them here we should be able to deny them permission to return. We have our own core techs now, so there's no reason for them to be here."

"That's the way it should be Brad, but it has everything to do with the fuel supply."

"Then have it removed from the Station and the problem is solved."

"That's a good idea, I'll get John on it as soon as I talk to him again," Horace said.

The proximity alarm started to wail indicating that a vessel was nearing the Station's outer force field of the landing bay. Horace and Brad watched as the outer shield lowered and the Jaxor entered to main entry corridor, then proceeded through the inner shield after the outer was sealed.

"We have guests," Brad said.

The Jaxor set down gently on the hangar deck and John and Tronext exited the ship.

"Well, speak of the devil," Horace said as he spotted his friend and walked across the empty hangar to where the Jaxor was resting.

"John, what a pleasant surprise," Brad said, shaking his hand. "We were just talking about you. Welcome to the Lunar Station, Ambassador Tronext."

"We thought we would pay you a little visit since we had some time on our hands."

"The Corisole created an impressive station from a small research station," Tronext noted.

"A bit too impressive I think," Horace replied. "They managed to murder five billion humans from this base. We are currently refitting the station to accommodate the EDS. When it's finished we'll be able to fit three hundred of them on the station."

"How's Jack holding up?" John asked.

"He's down in the control room trying to get the Torani locks off the targeting and firing controls," Brad answered. "We have all the defenses ready and we can't bring them online. Jack's making great progress though, he expects to make a trial run within the week."

"That's good because we may need this Station sooner than we thought."

"John we were talking about having the fuel removed from the Station so the Torani have no reason to return. Could you arrange it?" Brad asked.

"I'll see what I can do Brad. I see no reason to keep it here any longer either. So how about a short tour for our guest, we have to be back at Johnson in four hours."

"Well, come on then and I'll give you the grand tour."

The four men headed for the main control room to begin their tour. Jack Lee should be happy to have a little company, since he has been in the control room for days by himself.

At this time only Gene, John, and Tronext, know just how important this Station could possibly be in the not too distant future of the planet, as well as the galaxy.

The Jaxor landed outside the entrance of the Siberian research lab where Olga is the current chief of operations. Olga met her three guests on the tarmac of the frozen base. Two of the men she is quite familiar with, but the third, which is a reptilian alien, she has never met.

"John, Gene, how are you? To what do I owe this surprise visit?" she asked as she studied Tronext. "And who have you brought to my secret lab?"

Tronext stepped forward to introduce himself. "I am Tronext. Ambassador of the planet Zaxin."

"Oh yes. From what I understand this planet owes you and your people a great debt."

"We were fortunate to learn the truth when we did Dr. Krishkoff," he replied.

"All of you come in out of the cold," she said, then led them into the base. Once inside she led them to her lab.

"So what can I do for you, gentlemen, I'm sure you didn't come to this frozen wasteland just to say hello," she asked curiously.

"Tronext wanted to visit your lab. Actually it's just an excuse for Tronext to tour more of the planet, he's a hopeless tourist," Gene said with a big smile.

"A whole planet and you want to see Siberia?"

"I have seen most of the galaxy, Doctor, but little of this planet."

"So I understand you have an operational land-based laser cannon?" John said.

"It isn't operational yet, but we expect to have it operational within the month. There are fifty other stationed around the planet currently under construction. Once they are online, no fleet will ever again invade our planet. We are considering remote operated bases on Mars, Saturn, and Pluto also to protect the whole system."

"That is a very good plan Doctor." Tronext declared.

"With no fleet to protect our planet we have no choice but to use landbased units," she explained. "My sources tell me that you have seen our gold reserves, Ambassador."

"Yes, Doctor. Gene took me to view the vault."

"Ambassador, there is that much gold if not more under this frozen wasteland. It has been kept secret for twenty years for the same reason. If the other nations had found out about these reserves, it could have led to world war."

Gene looked at her with a surprised expression. "We never knew about these reserves. We knew about the oil reserves, but not the gold." Gene thought he knew everything about these things when he was president, but he was mistaken.

"It was kept secret from everyone, even our own people. But enough of that. Follow me, gentlemen, and I will show you my cannon."

The three men followed Olga through a series of tunnels, which eventually led to a large control room that contained a reactor the size of the one on the EDS. A small reactor such as this one has the capability of putting a hole through the surface of the moon, even with its distance from Earth. On the other side of a thick sheet of bulletproof glass stood the twenty-foot laser cannon exactly like the ones on the Lunar Station.

"This is an incredible setup," Gene said

"Also completely self-contained," Olga added. "The lunar cannons are all run from a central control station and if anything were to happen to that control room the entire system would be affected. All of the cannons would be incapacitated, so we decided on individually operated cannons on the surface."

"This is very impressive, my friends. It should be very effective in the protection of your planet," Tronext said. "I am truly amazed by your progress since the invasion."

"We aren't taking any more chances, Ambassador. As you made it quite clear, if the news of our gold reserves escapes this planet or the Torani, we had better be able to protect ourselves," John said. "That's why we are already constructing cannons for the other bodies of this system. All we will lack at this time is the vehicles to transport them, and the bases to house them."

"Well, gentlemen, I'm afraid there is nothing else to show you that you have not already seen, so I really must return to my work," Olga said as she herded them toward the passageway. "Oh, and, John, I have fifty EDS ready for delivery and I'm a little pressed for space. If you could arrange for them to be transported to their bases, I would be truly grateful."

"I will personally round up some pilots to move them. Give me one week and I'll be back."

The three men bid farewell to the good doctor and left her to her work. They flew off on board the Jaxor for Johnson. Fifty fighters to move would be quite a project to complete without detection.

Chapter 53

---•●✸●•---

John has assembled twenty-five of the newly trained pilots in the old shuttle hangar. Among these pilots are the first five to train for the EDS. The others are the newly trained recruits, and some of them have never had actual flight time in the fighters. Their mission today is to fly to Siberia and move the new EDS from the secret base to their new home in the Lunar Station. Along with the twenty at Houston, they will now have a fleet of seventy fighters. With only twenty-five trained pilots, the priority will now be focused on training the new recruits.

John now addresses the young men before their mission. "Gentlemen, today we will be flying to one of our bases to transfer our new fighters to their new home on the Lunar Station. This will be the first orbital flight for most of you, and for others your first actual flight time period. For those of you who haven't flown outside the simulators, remember your training and you will be just fine. The simulators are exactly like the real thing, if not even more challenging. Let's climb aboard the Jaxor and take a little journey, then we'll all get a little more flight time under our belts."

The new pilots all entered the Jaxor for their short trip to Siberia. In one hour some of them would be making their first flights, and they would all be making their first trip to the moon. Either way the anxiety among the men was high.

The emperor is in the Torani Council chambers meeting with his military leaders. Ambassador Skyton has called an emergency meeting of the council. He has disturbing news to tell them all.

"Ambassador, you have important information for this council?" Ardesnal asked.

"Yes, Emperor. I have just returned from planet Corisole with news that is of the most importance to Torani. The Corisole people have learned the truth about the trial of the conspirators, as well as our ties to the Kabult Station and the Earth invasion. They have reached an extreme state of anger over our role in these events. The new rulers of the planet are threatening to cut all Triomicium and steel production of their mines, as well as shipments to Torani facilities. They have been in contact with the Velnor planet, to arrange for protection and supplies which they know quite well we will cut once we discover their plans to retaliate for our deception."

The ambassador took his seat indicating that he was finished. Then Fleet Commander Brydon rose to speak. "We should destroy the planet and take the mines for ourselves," the commander said angrily. "They have no fleet to repel an invasion at this time since we destroyed all but two of their cruisers two years ago during the Earth battle."

"If we invade the Corisole, we will bring the wrath of the Alliance down on us," the emperor's advisor Marteck said. "It would also put us into an all-out war with the Velnor planet, which we cannot afford at this time."

"We must do something. There is no way we will now escape the wrath of the Alliance with the truth about the invasion of Earth known. The Corisole will certainly inform the galactic leaders if they have not already done so." Brydon asserted. "I say we strike first and destroy what remains of Corisole, and deal with the Alliance as they come to us. We have the most powerful fleet in the galaxy and control all Triomicium production in the galaxy. They wouldn't dare attack. We would bring them to their knees. The only real threat to us is the Klosk warriors who have a large fleet, but if we were to enlist the Boral and Antarians to our cause with the promise of wealth and continued fuel supplies, we could easily deal with them."

The emperor has sat quietly as his council argued among themselves. They are all correct in their own way but also quite wrong. He rose and quieted the members so he could speak.

"Gentlemen, I understand your worries. We have known since the Corisole attacked the Earth planet prematurely, that our plan for galactic domination had been altered. We had hoped to stop the downfall of our plan with the execution of all who had knowledge, but somehow we missed an informant in their ranks. I have a feeling that the Zaxin and Klosk, as well as the Velnor ambassadors, were informed of our deceit after the trial. It was a risky ploy to try to mislead all of the members, but it was necessary at the time." He paused to think. "With this knowledge in the hands of the Zaxin, we can be sure that the Klosk, as well as the Zakorians, are also aware. The Zakorian people will be of no threat to us, so the logical starting point is the Klosk System. We will send our ambassadors to the Boral and Antarian systems to seek allies in this battle, and if they choose not to join us, we will cut all Triomicium supplies to their planet."

"What of the Zaxin fleet? They have many vessels," the commander stated in warning. "They are all designed for commerce and diplomatic missions, but combined with the Klosk fleet, they could be quite troublesome."

"We will not give them the time to combine, Commander. We must pounce on the Zaxin vessels to start with. Then we will attack the unsuspecting Klosk. Once the Klosk are reduced to an insignificant force, we will return and deal with the Velnor and Corisole planets. This will leave the wealth of Earth to Torani, and will make us the rulers of this galaxy and soon many others. We will become the most powerful galaxy in the universe."

The emperor sat back in his large chair and allowed his advisors to rejoice in what they all assume will be a certain victory. The conquest of the 420 Galaxy is about to begin.

On the planet Velnor, Ambassador Prowlex and the members of the Velnor Senate are all in the main council chamber awaiting the arrival of the Supreme Leader. The ambassador has called an emergency meeting concerning the Corisole planet. Leader Irkan entered the chamber and sat at his seat of honor.

"Ambassador Prowlex, why have you called us all here today?" Irkan inquired.

"Leader Irkan, I thought I should inform all of you of the information I have received regarding the planet Corisole, and allow you to decide whether an Alliance meeting should be called."

"Very well, Ambassador, let's hear this information."

"Council members, the inhabitants of Corisole are quite enraged with the actions of the Torani concerning the trial and execution of their people under false pretenses. We have tried to keep this information from them, but they have somehow discovered the truth. We have been attempting to buy time for the Earth planet to build its defenses to a point of self-reliance, but at this time I cannot expose the reason why. You will be informed of the facts at a later date. You must trust me that this is necessary at this time."

"How are their defenses progressing?" the leader asked.

"Their Lunar Station is under full Earth control, with a full complement of laser cannons. These cannons destroyed three Torani cruisers quite easily by themselves before they were destroyed by a well-organized attack on the Station," Prowlex explained.

"Then what is going to deter them from simply destroying the cannon batteries once again, Ambassador?" Irkan asked.

"The humans have also deployed these cannons on the planet's surface, as well as designed and constructed a very large number of defensive fighters that are capable of aiding in the defense of the planet's space. I believe that they have already produced at least one hundred of these fighters with the help of a Torani ally. They have approximately fifty trained pilots at this time, but we are hopeful that the construction of the Alliance Station on the surface of the planet will deter any action by the Torani in the near future to enable them to complete their training program. An attack on the planet at this time, with many of the galaxy's systems on the planet, would most certainly lead to war with the Alliance."

"The big question then is will the Torani risk a galactic war for the possession of Earth. They have already proven that they are capable of murder and deception in the name of greed," the leader expressed. "We will call a meeting of the Galactic Council to discuss this matter further. Thank you, Ambassador, for your perseverance on this matter. I will inform you all of the time for the meeting. Thank you all."

The leader rose and left the chamber to pursue this matter with his galactic allies. Prowlex hopes that they all take his warnings seriously for the sake of Earth and the entire galaxy.

Bill is taking Sassy out for her nightly walk when they both see the landing lights of the shuttle. Sassy runs to meet them as Bill walks behind. He is surprised to see them back from Dubai so soon as they weren't scheduled to return for two more weeks. The three men exited the shuttle and slowly walked up the driveway.

"You guys are back early," he said. Then greeted them all with a handshake and a man hug.

"I'm glad to be back. I've had enough sun and sand for a lifetime," Willis said. And there wasn't one stinking bikini in the whole country. A total waste of a good beach," he added with a smile.

"Are you finished on the Station? I didn't expect you back for at least two weeks."

"Our team did very well," Mortisk said. "When you have the Boral working behind you, you have to work twice as hard to stay ahead of them."

"I'm dead tired, guys, I'll see you all in the morning," Bret said as he left for the comfort of his bed—and a good long rest.

"Maggie and Lilly will be glad to see you. All of the ladies have been a little restless for the last few days with you all gone."

"I'm gonna hit the sack too, Dad, I'll see you tomorrow." The two young men headed for their homes to be with their families, and get some much needed rest. Mortisk walked slowly with Bill and the dog up the long driveway.

"So what was it like working on the Station with all the other aliens?" Bill asked.

"I am used to working with other species which is why I was chosen for the job on your planet. Willis and Brad had a harder time adjusting, as some of the other races can be difficult to work with. The Boral are one race which is very unfriendly and think only of the task at hand. We did have a two-day break that was interesting though. We went to the Siberian base and transferred the EDS to the Lunar Station. John and Tronext were there to help."

"You guys went to the moon! I miss out on all the fun stuff. I would really love to see that Lunar Station. I watched Neil Armstrong walk on the moon when I was in Elementary School and now my son flies there twice in the same day. That's just not fair."

"Actually we made several trips. There were a lot of fighters to move to the station's hangars," Mortisk replied, making matters worse.

They reached Mortisk's house, where Hyal and the baby were very excited to see their big cowboy, whom they missed terribly. Bill and Sassy finished their short walk and went home, where Monica was waiting for them. It's good to have them all home safe again.

Chapter 54

——•◉•——

Planet Zaxin
May 30, 2023

The Zaxin sensors have detected a fleet of unknown vessels entering its system. The vessels have not answered any of their hails, so the Zaxin fleet has been put on alert.

The Zaxin fleet consists of six cruiser-sized vessels used mainly for transporting goods, but they are also armed for planetary defense. These vessels may be freighters, but they are heavily armed, and have better shields to protect themselves from raids attempted by the more aggressive species of the galaxy. The Command vessel Lutan has taken the lead of the fleet, and their orders are to stop the intruders at the orbit of the fifth planet in their system.

Commander Jolan is now preparing to defend his planet. "Have you been able to contact the inbound fleet, Mr. Rotak?

"I have tried all channels, sir, there has been no response."

"Inform the commanders of the Tolnak and Jokor to flank the enemy fleet on the starboard side, and the Rozak and Toloran to the port side. The Extron is to stay with us at the point and we will attempt to contain them at this point."

"Yes, Commander," Rotak replied.

Commander Jolan's second-in-command Takor is monitoring the sensors, when he suddenly makes an ominous discovery. "Sir," he said as he looked up from his scanners. "That is the Torani fleet!"

"Torani?" Jolan went to the science station and checked the sensors himself. "Ambassador Tronext warned us of their treachery, but I did not think they would go this far. They have yet to answer any of our hails, Mr. Rotak?"

"No, sir. I have tried all frequencies."

"Then we have to assume that they are hostile. Inform all vessels to prepare to defend themselves."

"Yes, sir," Rotak replied, then transmitted the orders to the other vessels.

"How many vessels are there, Takor?"

"I count ten, sir."

Commander Jolan sits in his Command chair ready for battle, but knows as all of the other commanders do, that they don't stand a chance against ten Torani battle cruisers.

"Rotak inform the Zaxin ground defenses of our situation and have them prepare to defend the planet, then order the fleet to pull back inside the cannons' defense perimeter or we're all soon be dead."

"Yes, sir."

The Zaxin fleet turned and sailed for the safety of their planetary defenses, discarding their previous plan to try to even the odds against them. The Torani fleet is bearing down on them and will soon be in firing range.

"Sir, they are set up in groups of three vessels, with the Command vessel hanging back out of range," Takor noted.

"Have all vessels target the first three vessels until they pass. We will let the planetary cannons deal with them, and we'll continue with the next wave. We can't fight them all at once."

"Yes, sir," Rotak replied and relayed the orders.

The Zaxin knows his foe well. He knows that Commander Brydon will stay behind with the Empress Commanding his fleet, and Commander Skoby will be leading the attack on board the Jayden.

"All vessels fire at will. We must protect Zaxin from the Torani invaders."

Jolan was correct. At the center of the first group was the Jayden, along with the Tory and Haldeck on her flanks. The three cruisers approached at attack speed with their cannons blazing.

"Open the channels Mr. Rotak."

"Channels open, sir."

"Rozak, Tolnak, target the Jayden and let the others target the remaining vessels."

The Jayden and her two support vessels blew through the Zaxin lines with their cannons blazing, and headed for the planet. As the first wave of Torani vessels approached the planet, they took heavy fire from the cannons. They targeted the planetary cannons but the Tory is taking heavy damage. Skoby and his group sweep the planet's surface then return for another run on the Zaxin fleet.

"Report, Takor."

"Our vessels report minor damage, and it appears that the Tory has taken several hits from our planetary cannons, sir."

"Prepare for the attack from the rear. Aft gunners target the Tory, I want that vessel destroyed while it's damaged."

The second wave hits the Zaxin fleet from the front as Skoby comes in from the rear. The Torani aren't here to win a battle, they are here to destroy the Zaxin fleet.

"Jokor, Rozak, watch our rear. All other vessels attack the incoming vessels."

The Zaxins are caught in the center of a bombardment of cannon fire, and the Jayden is concentrating her fire on the Extron in an effort to destroy her. The second wave is tightly in sync with the first and concentrates their fire on the Extron on their way to the planet also.

"Extron report."

"Commander, our weapons are down and our shields." At that moment the Extron exploded in a brilliant flash of light.

"She's gone, sir." Takor informed his commander.

"Pull back closer to the planet, we need the support from those cannons."

"Sir, the Tory is adrift."

"All vessels target the Tory," Jolan ordered.

The Zaxin fleet retreats closer to the planet, raining fire on the now helpless Tory as they pass. As they close in on the planet there is an explosion behind them.

"The Tory is destroyed, sir." Takor reports.

The battle continued with the five remaining Zaxin vessels in a death match with the more powerful Torani cruisers. As the battle continued, the planetary cannons destroyed the Torani cruiser Mayden.

"Report, Mr. Takor."

"It's not good, sir. Our shields are down to 50 percent, and the commanders of the Rozak and Jokor report that they are adrift."

Suddenly the Jokor exploded and was gone with a flash of light. The Torani fleet, which are simply overpowering the Zaxin fleet, are taking their time and picking their targets at will. The planet's cannons have been effective, but 30 percent of them have now been destroyed by the powerful Torani cruisers.

In a flash the Torani cruiser Valstar fell prey to the cannon fire from the surface. The Jayden has pulled back alongside the Empress to watch the battle from a distance, as the five remaining vessels set up for their attack run on the dwindling Zaxin fleet.

Reports of heavy damage as well as casualties are coming in from the planet and the cities are taking heavy damage. The Torani aren't only targeting the defense systems, they are targeting the cities killing thousands of civilians. Jolan contemplates his next strategies carefully.

"All vessels concentrate fire on the two center vessels, and hit the others as they pass."

The Torani fleet hurtled itself at the weakened Zaxin vessels. The Toloran and Rozak are now adrift and the Lutan and Tolnak are at 50 percent. The two outer Torani cruisers broke from formation and headed for the crippled Rozak, engulfing it in a rain of laser fire.

"Report, Mr. Takor."

"Sir, two vessels are adrift, and us and the Tolnak are at 50 percent. The Torani fleet still has seven fighting cruisers, and two of them have broken formation and are attacking our crippled vessels."

"Target the Haldeck with all available weapons."

"Sir, the Rozak is gone," Takor reported as the flash from the explosion faded.

The two vessels hit the Haldeck with everything they had as she passed.

"Haldeck is adrift, sir."

"Now target the Brightstar and let the cannons deal with the Haldeck."

The cannons destroyed the Haldeck as she slowly passed the planet, leaving the other four cruisers bearing down on the crippled Zaxin fleet planning to destroy them. The Toloran and her crew suddenly disappeared in a flash of light, leaving only the heavily damaged Tolnak and Lutan to fight this battle.

"Mr. Rotak signal our surrender."

"Sir?"

"Now, Mr. Rotak."

Rotak sent out a surrender message to the Torani fleet as they gathered into formation for another attack run.

"Any reply, Mr. Rotak?"

"I think that is our answer, sir."

The four Torani cruisers came in with all weapons firing on the two remaining vessels. The Lutan and Tolnak were easily, as well as ruthlessly, destroyed by the cruisers, which then proceeded to the planet to finish with the remaining cannon batteries. After they had destroyed all Zaxin defenses, they simply turned and set course out of the system for their next target. The Zaxin fleet did leave their mark on the superior Torani fleet by destroying four of their valuable cruisers, but their planet has suffered dearly with the total loss of their fleet and thousands of lives on the surface of the planet.

The Torani fleet gathered after the battle and set course for the Klosk planet. The Zaxins dealt them a severe blow by destroying four of their cruisers, but the remaining six heavy cruisers should be enough to deal with the Klosk. On board the Empress, Commander Brydon prepares for the next part of their plan. "Major Arden, what is the status of the fleet."

"We've lost Four of our vessels, but the rest of the vessels have suffered minor damage."

"How long will it take us to reach the Klosk planet?"

"Ten days, sir."

"Very well. Get all available hands making any repairs necessary. I want us back to 100 percent before we arrive at the Klosk System."

"Yes, sir."

"Are we picking up any communications from the planet?" Brydon asked.

"None, sir. Their communications systems have been destroyed," Arden replied.

"Set course for Klosk. We can't let news of the attack on Zaxin arrive before we do or the Klosk fleet will escape before we can execute the rest of our plan."

"Yes, sir," Arden replied. "Helm, set a course for the Klosk System at maximum speed."

The commander sits comfortably in his chair, safe on the bridge of the Empress. Now they sail for Klosk where the Empress will surely be brought into play because of the losses the suffered at the hands of the valiant Zaxins. The Klosk are a formidable race of warriors, but Brydon expects to overpower them with his massive cruisers, as well as the element of surprise.

The Galactic Station is entering its final stages of construction, and is now a year ahead of schedule. The Earth allies will have to deal with this setback in their plan. The structure and landing pads are completed, all power and technical work is finished, and all that remains is for the interior crews to finish with the leader's offices. The final stage will be the completion of the main conference chamber.

Gene and his three friends are gathered in the dining area of the Station for a lunch meeting. They must be careful as the emperor and many other galactic leaders are on the station to ensure that their offices are completed to their specifications.

"Gentlemen, I have taken the liberty of ordering lunch for all of us. They say when in Rome do as the Roman's do. So when you're on Earth you eat hamburgers and french-fries for lunch," Gene said, smiling at his friends as their food is delivered.

"What is it with you humans and your craving for roasted meat?" Prowlex asked.

"I have learned to quite enjoy it," Tronext said.

"Ambassador Gowlisk, I know you will appreciate this meal, it's an Earth delicacy," Gene said, smiling at Tronext.

The group all enjoyed their lunch while they talked quietly among themselves. After the meal, the ambassadors all returned to their offices to supervise the completion of the work. Gene was about to enter his office when he heard an all too familiar voice behind him.

"How are you, my friend?"

He turned and faced the Torani emperor. "I am doing very well, Emperor," he said, greeting him with a handshake.

"I expected to see you on Torani before now."

"We have quite busy here on Earth. The Galactic Station has become a bit of an obsession for me."

"It is a splendid design. It is a crustacean, is it not?"

"We call this one a crab, but yes, it is a crustacean. Have you been to your chambers?"

"Yes, and they have been finished exactly to my specifications."

"I'm glad you are happy with them. When are you returning to Torani?"

"I am scheduled to return tomorrow. My work here is finished and I have important matters to attend to on Torani."

"Well, it's too bad you couldn't stay longer," he lied. "I have at least another month of work to do here. Then I will be free to roam the galaxy again."

"Then I shall see you next month, my friend. I am sorry we didn't have more time together, but I have many details to finish before I return to the Tarkon."

"You didn't travel here on the Empress?"

"The Empress is taking care of other matters at this time."

"Well, it was a pleasure to see you, Emperor, and I will speak with you again in one month on Torani. Have a safe trip, Emperor."

"You also, my friend," the emperor said as he left en route to his new office.

Why would the Empress be away from Torani? Gene thought to himself. He dropped the thought for now and returned to his office to ensure that it was completed to his specifications. The Station is almost finished now, and most of the ambassadors are already living on the Station. The Torani wouldn't dare attack Earth now, he hoped.

The Torani fleet rests just outside Klosk space preparing for their attack on the Klosk planet. They are extremely lucky, as they have discovered through the monitoring of the Klosk transmissions that a majority of the Klosk fleet is currently busy in the Malor System, chasing a pirate fleet that has been raiding vessels in between the Boral and Antarian home worlds. They have caught the remaining three vessels unguarded and sitting in a space dock, unaware of the Torani fleet's presence. They will be no match for the power contained in the six Torani cruisers. Commander Brydon is getting them ready for the attack.

"Commander Skoby," he ordered over the open comm channel. "I want this fleet and that space dock destroyed on the first pass. We have three unaware vessels sitting in space dock, so the victory should be short and sweet," Brydon said. "All vessels form in a three-by-three attack formation. Engage now, Commanders."

The Torani fleet sprang into action and were quickly passing the fourth planet before the Klosk fleet was aware of their presence. The first Klosk vessel didn't even clear space dock before the first three Torani vessels reached their prey. The three Klosk vessels, as well as the space dock, have engaged the attackers with defensive fire, but it was like shooting fish in a barrel for the Torani fleet.

The first pass has destroyed two of the Klosk vessels, and left the third as well as the Station in flames and without weapons. The attackers then continued on to the planet to destroy the planetary defenses, which were light compared to the Zaxin planet's defenses. In a matter of ten minutes, the battle for Klosk was over, and the commanders awaited orders from Commander Brydon.

"This is the Empress. Destroy that ship as well as the space dock, then set course for the Malor System," Brydon ordered. "The remainder of their fleet is somewhere near the Antarian planets."

"Yes, sir," Skoby replied. "Brightstar, you're with me. Let's finish this."

The Jayden and the Brightstar attacked the helpless vessel as well as the Station. They made quick work of the task, which ended in a very bright flash of light as the space dock exploded, taking the remaining Klosk cruiser with it. They returned to formation and set course for the Malor System, and the rest of the Klosk fleet.

"All vessels engage at full speed for the Malor System," Brydon ordered. "Engage engines now."

The Torani fleet left the scene of their latest crime with all vessels unaffected. They know that if they don't destroy the last of the Klosk fleet, it will haunt them later, as the Klosk are the only thing standing in their way of galactic domination.

The Earth ambassador is in his office putting the last of his books on the shelves behind his desk. Pictures of his family, along with one of him with Bill, Tronext, Mortisk, and Prowlex all sitting on horses by the barn, are sitting on his desk. The Zaxin ambassador along with the Klosk ambassador burst into his office. Startled by their entrance Gene turns to them with an expression of concern.

"What is it, my friends?"

"The planet Zaxin as well as the Klosk planet have been attacked," Tronext said, slightly out of breath. "We just received a message from Klosk, and I cannot make contact with my planet, so I am assuming that it suffered the same fate."

"Torani?" Gene asked.

"It must be. They are the only fleet capable of such an act," the Klosk ambassador said angrily. "They caught my planet as our fleet was engaged in the Malor System chasing a pirate fleet. Three vessels as well as our Space Station was destroyed."

"Where is your fleet now, Gowlisk?" Gene asked. "They are on their way back to Klosk. The Torani fleet must have known the location of our fleet as they are now headed for the Malor System. Our fleet is aware of their current course and will be ready for them when they make contact. The cowards won't have such an easy battle this time," he said angrily.

"You have absolutely no word from Zaxin?" Gene asked Tronext.

"The new Zaxin ambassador has informed me that a planetary distress message was picked up twenty days ago, but no further communications have been received. I have asked the Zakorians to check on the planet's condition."

"Twenty days. Why haven't we heard of this sooner?"

"The message was picked up by a passing freighter, and it has taken this long for my ambassador to receive it here on Earth."

"We have to see Prowlex. His fleet is the only thing that stands between the Malor System and Earth," Gene said as he walked toward the hallway. "Then we need to call a meeting of the Galactic Council."

The three men exited Gene's office on their way to the Velnor ambassador's office. The Torani have undoubtedly learned of their knowledge about the Corisole attack, and are making a well-planned series of attacks before the galaxy learns of Earth's supply of Triomicium.

As the three men arrive at Prowlex's office, they entered without prior notice causing Prowlex to rise from his seat surprised by their unannounced arrival. "What is it, my friends?" he asked, aware that there was something wrong by their expressions.

The three men joined him at his desk and explained the events of the prior twenty days. When they finished, the Velnor ambassador sat heavily in his seat, deep in thought.

"What do you think the odds are of your fleet being able to stop the Torani, Ambassador Gowlisk?" Gene asked.

"My people are great warriors, and as long as the Torani fleet is not too large, I believe we would do well," he replied.

"It would do no good to send the Velnor fleet. They wouldn't arrive in time to be of assistance," Prowlex said sadly. "Also, our fleet only consists of three cruisers for defense and three research vessels, which are heavily armed, but their crews are not warriors."

"All right then, what do we do, gentlemen?" Gene asked. "There has to be a way to stop them."

They all sat quietly thinking about what a bad predicament the galaxy was in, and none of them have an idea how to prevent the Torani from achieving their goal. The Klosk ambassador is the first to speak.

"In my opinion, gentlemen. If the Torani are defeated by my fleet, we of course have nothing to worry about. They obviously didn't expect to be chasing the Klosk fleet across the galaxy, so their plan has already been altered." Gowlisk then paused to think, then continued. "If my fleet is unable to stop them, they will most certainly be very damaged and will have to return to Torani to repair their vessels and regroup for an attack on the Velnor and Corisole planets. This will buy us time to prepare, but if we cannot stop them, there will be no other systems to help you defend this planet. The Boral and Antarians will certainly join them and then there will be no way I can think of to stop them."

They all thought about Gowlisk's word. Then Gene leaned forward to speak.

"Ambassadors, we need to first call a meeting of the Alliance to measure our strength. Then we need to see just how busy our friends have been on this planet with our defenses. With the cannons and fighters, we just may be able to defeat them. We make a stand here, gentlemen. Let's finish this where it started," Gene said rebelliously. "Ambassador Prowlex, if your fleet is not at Velnor, what reason will they have to attack your planet?"

"You may be right, my friend," Tronext said. "Gowlisk is it too late to reroute your fleet to Earth?"

"I can try, but I must hurry."

"I think this is our best chance, gentlemen," Gene said.

"I hate to bring more suffering on my people, but we never run from a fight," Gene added firmly. "I like your attitude, Gene," Gowlisk said. "I will go right away and see if I can get our fleet turned toward Earth. Prowlex, you should do the same thing. Let's gather our forces and ready for battle."

"Then let's get busy, my friends, we have a galaxy to save," Gene said, ending the conversation.

The men rose from their seats, and all of them went in their own directions to proceed with their tasks. Prowlex and Gowlisk have gone to call their fleets, which leaves Gene and Tronext to gather the council.

PART 4

CHAPTER 55

---•●✳●•---

Independence Valley
July 4, 2023, 10:00

The inhabitants of the valley have finally decided on a name. After a vote it was named, finally, Independence Valley. It is a warm Fourth of July day and the valleys as well as the surrounding towns populations have gathered together to celebrate.

The valley is in full bloom with the fields tall with the hay for the livestock, and the gardens are multicolored with a wide variety of flowers and vegetables growing in them. The tall pines mixed with the aspens also create both added color and shade for the assembled masses.

The town is finally completed. All thirteen homes are concealed in the hillside with no visible signs of habitation with the skill of Bill and Willis's craft. It now looks like one of the best campsites you could ever come across. They have all succeeded in keeping the valley pure, except for the barn and corrals, which were necessary to house the livestock. They have created a Utopia and are proud of it.

As usual, the valley is once again ready for a huge party. Music is playing, and the food and drinks are flowing freely to a whole lot of good friends. Bill has already claimed his new "Stone Throne," as he calls it, along with Monica at the fire pit. He has always been, and always will be the King of this valley, surrounded by his family and friends. "Life is good."

The Earth leader and her ambassador have come to the Earth Station for a very important meeting of the Galactic Council concerning the now unfolding galactic dilemma.

Gene is standing outside the chamber with his three friends, going over the events of the past few weeks. After the attacks on Zaxin and Klosk, they are very concerned about the future of all their planets. The Klosk fleet has been turned back for Earth in time to avoid the Torani fleet, which will save their vessels for a combined resistance against the Torani.

The Klosk and Velnor fleets are now in orbit of the planet, and their crews have been allowed to tour the planet that they are protecting. A base has been established at the now deserted work camp in Dubai to house the visitors while they tour Earth. The ambassadors have seen to it that their people have taken advantage of these tours.

"How are your people enjoying our planet, my friends?" Gene asked.

"This region of your planet is much like Velnor," Prowlex replied. "My people are actually enjoying the tours of your mountains and tropical zones much more."

"I have noticed that your crewmen have been enjoying the sand and surf of the gulf Gowlisk. The beaches are new to them I take it."

"Yes. It is a rare adventure for them and they are enjoying it very much. We have no oceans on our planet. We have only lakes and rivers, so they are quite intrigued by such a sight."

"I'm glad they are enjoying themselves. Do we have any new information on the Torani fleet?" he asked, changing the subject back to the task at hand.

"After the news of the attacks reached the Alliance Station, it was quickly abandoned by all but the Antarian and Boral leaders, which brings our worst fears to reality," Tronext said. "The two races will certainly join the Torani in the inevitable battle, and will add to the power of their fleet considerably. As the Diplomats were leaving the Station, the Torani fleet was spotted on the long-range sensor array returning to Torani space from their attacks. They still have six heavy cruisers in their fleet, and from the information that has been provided to me, there is another in the shipyard that is only three months from completion. We are not expecting any further action from the Torani before then. They will need the new cruiser in their inventory."

"What was the extent of the damage to your planet Tronext?" Gene asked sympathetically.

"The cannon batteries were well outside the cities, but the Torani gunners did not employ marksmanship during their attacks on the batteries, and many of the cities received heavy damage. We estimate somewhere around ten thousand killed, but that isn't a final number. There are still rescue teams going through the damaged areas, and once the finish we will have a final count of the dead."

"I'm sorry to hear that, my friend. After the attack on Earth I have a new insight to just how destructive these attacks can be," Gene said sympathetically.

"Thank you Gene. I appreciate your sympathy."

"I understand that Klosk wasn't too badly affected by the attacks. Just how bad is it Gowlisk?"

"The Klosk planet was fortunate. The Torani destroyed three of our battle cruisers as well as the spaceport they were moored to, but the attacks on our cannons only caused few deaths and created several fires, which have been dealt with. Our death toll was low, maybe two thousand. I haven't received a final number as of yet."

The crowd began to file into the main chamber, so the four ambassadors joined them for the session that is about to begin. This meeting will be led by Leader Rowland, as the Torani emperor has been removed from his post as leader because of his actions.

As the members all start taking their seats, the temporary leader Rowland of Earth entered the chamber and the members all quieted out of respect for their new leader. Although she is in a very new environment, she is still a very qualified leader and brings the meeting quickly to order.

"Members of the Galactic Council," she began. "I am honored to be chosen to lead this council until a permanent leader can be appointed." She then paused. "We are called here today for several reasons, the most important being the attacks on the Zaxin and Klosk worlds. These acts show the lack of respect for the lives of our citizens by the Torani leadership, however, we should not hold the Torani people responsible for the acts of their leadership. I have met and worked with the Torani people for these past two and a half years, and find it hard to believe that these people could have anything to do with such evil acts. The respect due to all life forms is the main goal of this Alliance, so we cannot judge their race by the acts of its leadership."

"I would now turn the floor over to the Leader Enxnor from the Zaxin planet. Thank you." She bowed respectfully, then sat.

The Zaxin leader Enxnor rose and took his place at the large speaking podium.

"Members of the Galactic Alliance. Over the past few months the Zaxin investigators have been reviewing the facts concerning the invasion of the planet Earth. We have withheld the disclosure of this information until we were certain of the validity of our information, and it has now been fully proven that the Torani leadership was indeed involved with the Corisole invaders. Unknown to the Torani, the Corisole took advantage of this partnership and staged an assault on the planet Earth years ahead of the scheduled time, hoping to gain control of the Sol System and all its riches, making them the most powerful force in the galaxy." Enxnor paused to choose his next words carefully. "I must now explain the true reason for this invasion. The Sol System contains the largest deposits of Triomicium in the known universe."

The chamber came alive with uncontrollable conversation as the members heard the unbelievable news.

"Members, please. This information has been known by a select few in this room for several months, but we have had to keep this information concealed for obvious reasons. The Torani and Corisole leaders on the other hand, have known about these deposits for decades, and have been planning the annexation of this planet throughout that time."

"Leaders of Galaxy 420, we have now been thrust into the position as the most powerful galaxy in the known universe. Earth has volunteered to share these vast deposits with all systems in this galaxy in exchange for our help with the undeniable attack that the Torani and their Allies will certainly launch on their system. They also ask that we help them to achieve galactic travel, to exist as an equal in this galaxy as well as protect their system from invading races that will certainly come when the news of these deposits spread to other galaxies. Thank you all."

The membership once again began talking among themselves with the new scenario of not having to worry only about the systems of their galaxy, but the new worries of threats from surrounding galaxies.

Leader Enxnor, having completed his statements, returned to his seat, and Leader Rowland once again rose to speak.

"Council members, as the elected leader of this planet I have been in contact with a great many of our scientists, as well as military leaders brought to me by our ambassador, whom I believe you all know and trust. I want to assure you that we are working on defensive measures to protect this planet, but they may not be enough to repel a Torani attack. With the help of our new friends the Klosk and Velnor planets, we may be able to defeat the Torani when they attack."

"We must now look toward the future of this galaxy. The Sol System has much to offer in the way of Tera formable planets, as well as mining opportunities, and we welcome our new neighbors to our system to pursue both options. My friends, as long as there have been humans on this planet they have looked to the stars and yearned to visit them. All we ask in return for your share of our wealth, is that you all help us achieve this dream of living in peace, and discovering what is beyond the next star. Thank you all." Leader Rowland returned to her seat, hoping that her pleas, as well as offers, hadn't been in vain.

The Zaxin leader once again rose to speak. "Members of the Alliance, and I stress the word Alliance. As one force in this galaxy, we will not only put an end to the Torani tyranny, but we have the opportunity to make this galaxy the galaxy it deserves to be. We all strive to be a peaceful and technologically advanced galaxy, which will finally breach its boundaries and explore the universe around us, plus make new alliances in the process. Thank you all." The Zaxin leader retired from his position at the podium and headed for the exit of the chamber. The other leaders all then rose and followed suit.

Gene waited in the outer corridor for his friends to appear. After a few minutes the ambassadors entered the corridor and Gene gathered them all together because he has a suggestion for them. "Ambassadors. Oh screw the titles. My friends I have a suggestion and I think we should include Gowlisk in this. In my district this is a very important day in history, and there's only one thing to do on this day." He looked at his very attentive friends. "Barbeque," he said with a smile.

Tronext and Prowlex both smiled widely. Gowlisk looked at them curiously.

"What is a . . . barbeque?" he asked curiously.

"You'll find out," Gene said, giving the other two ambassadors a wink.

"Colorado," Tronext said happily.

"Stetsons," Prowlex added.

"Absolutely," Gene answered.

They all surrounded the large wooly alien, and escorted him out of the Station and onto the waiting Jaxor.

"We've got to make one stop on the way Tronext," Gene said.

"Dallas?" Tronext asked.

"Yes, I've got to pick up the wife and kids."

They all boarded the Jaxor and took to the sky. After months of hard traveling and preparation, the group needed to relax and prepare for the months to come, and there was no better way to relax than one of Bill's barbeques in their opinion.

The Empress was entering Torani space after spending two weeks hunting the illusive Klosk fleet. The Torani fleet had given up the search and returned to their system to regroup.

"Major!" Brydon barked. "How long before we reach Torani?"

"Six hours, sir," he replied. "Sir, the emperor is on the comm."

"Put it through to my ready room, Major."

Brydon exited the bridge to his ready room and activated the video, where the emperor was waiting.

"Commander, I take it there was no sign of the Klosk fleet."

"We searched the entire galaxy between the Malor System and here, sir, and found no sign of them," Brydon replied.

"I was afraid of that, Commander. The Alliance Station has been evacuating for days, so I'm afraid our plans have been discovered and the Klosk fleet is most likely headed for Earth."

"Have we had any contact with our people on Earth?" the commander asked.

"No, we haven't. I'm assuming that they have blocked all communication from the planet."

"We will be in orbit in six hours. We need to rethink our options on this attack, sir."

"I will see you in my office in seven hours, Commander."

The screen went blank, and the commander sat wondering if the communication blackout does indeed mean that the Klosk fleet is in Earth space. It can be the only explanation and puts a new degree of difficulty in their plans to invade Earth.

The men have all gathered at their favorite meeting place at the pit. The townspeople are all dancing and eating, and the children are either petting the animals at the barn or swimming in the pond. It couldn't have been a nicer day for a barbeque.

As the beers are being passed out, babies are being bounced on knees and thank god old men being hugged and kissed by their loved ones. All of a sudden a familiar sight comes over the mountain and lands in the hay field.

"The Jaxor?" Willis asked, surprise by the unusual visit.

"I believe so," Bill replied.

"What did they do, smell it from Saudi Arabia?" Willis joked.

"Must have," Bill said. "Let's go greet our guests."

The group walked into the hay field to meet their guests with the dog leading the way. The door opened and Gene and his family were the first to greeted by the tongue of the very happy animal.

"Sorry Bill, but we just couldn't resist. I brought a few old friends, along with a few new ones. This is my father Al, and my mother Cathy."

"It's a pleasure to have you in our valley," Bill said, shaking their hands. "This is my better half Monica."

"You are a lucky man," Al replied, as he shook her hand.

"Independence Valley?" Gene asked, pointing at the sign over the entrance to the driveway.

"We had a vote and that was what we all decided on."

The rest of the shuttles occupants began coming out of the ship. Tronext and Prowlex, both wearing their hats, along with a newcomer, who is also wearing a hat on his hairy head, but not quite sure why.

"Tronext, Prowlex, nice to have you back. Who's this outlaw?" he asked, pointing at the hairy alien.

"This is Gowlisk, the Klosk ambassador," Mortisk said as he walked over and shook his arm in the Klosk way. "How are you, my old friend."

"Small galaxy," Bill said.

"Getting smaller all the time," Gene replied.

"Starting to look like a freak show around here," Bill said, smiling.

"We'll charge extra for them to see you," Willis said with a smile.

They all made their way back across the pasture to the ongoing party.

"Gentlemen, have a seat and a beer. Ladies, I wouldn't dream of telling you what to do," he said with a big smile. "You just couldn't resist, could you?" he asked Gene.

"I like to show our galactic friends the best time possible, and if it's not snowing, chances are that there's a barbeque going on," Gene said. "Gentlemen," he said, standing for a toast, "to Independence Valley and the best dammed barbeque on the planet."

They all agreed, then drank their beers. Gowlisk drank his down, then looked at the small bottle in his large hand.

"Another?" he asked. Then looked at them all as they all laughed. Mortisk and Gowlisk sat talking to each other for some time. The old friends had not seen each other in many years.

Mortisk showed off his child with pride, as well as his wife, whom Gowlisk had not met before today. All the problems in the galaxy were left behind to enjoy the day at hand.

They all ate, drank, and danced with the aliens well into the night. As usual nobody was leaving till morning, so they all made room for their guests. They may even teach Gowlisk to ride a horse tomorrow. Another picture for the wall.

CHAPTER 56

---•●✹●•---

The four ambassadors have traveled to the White House to meet with Elsa and her cabinet. With eminent war on the horizon the need for NORAD and its tracking and targeting systems is great. The colonel has decided that he wants the systems all integrated into the worldwide tracking systems for a higher efficiency during battle. Unlike the Lunar Station, which has its own systems, the planet's batteries are yet to be linked together and are operated by individual systems that affect that efficiency. John has made the trip to Washington to make it happen.

"All right, gentlemen, let's get started," Elsa said as she entered the new briefing room. "We are all here today to come up with a plan to coordinate our cannon batteries. We now have fifty operational cannons around the planet and the colonel wants them to be controlled from NORAD, since it is the most sophisticated and secure tracking facility on the planet. What ideas have your men come up with, Lance?"

"For the last week, my men along with John's guys at NASA have been working on a few ideas. By using NASA's tracking systems along with the lunar systems, we will be able to control all ground-based systems from Cheyenne Mountain. We will leave the lunar cannons on their own systems, since these systems destroyed three Torani cruisers during their last encounter in a matter of minutes. We have John's man Brad Meyer, along with our own Captain Rice, who helped with the design of the Star Wars systems, working on the problem now. Unfortunately, these systems are out of date and badly damaged during the Corisole attack."

354

"But you are saying that we can still use those systems, right?" Jack Law asked.

"Absolutely Jack. We're downloading the new software now, and Brad is tying us in with the lunar tracking array. We should be operational in twenty days. We are planning tests on some of our dead satellites as soon as we're finished."

"That's great, Lance," Elsa said. "John, how's your fighter fleet progressing?"

"Our force is at full strength. We have two hundred ships ready to launch, with one hundred in reserve. We have been short of qualified pilots but our last batch of fifty will be completing their training within the week. They just need some more flight time and more target practice and they'll be ready."

"How many do you have fully trained John?" Jack asked.

"We have one hundred and fifty fully trained at this time with fifty more within the week. There are seventy-five others engaged in training for reserves which should be ready in thirty days. Our main problem right now is all the fleet vessels in orbit, which is hampering our flight training. We've got to have them move to a higher orbit so they are out of harm's way. I would hate to have one of them accidently damaged by one of our new pilots."

"That's in the works now John. I've asked them to pull back to Mars orbit for our cannon tests. Also we've been going over some defense strategies that we would like to run by Ambassador Gowlisk. He is experienced in galactic warfare and would be of great help to us."

"I will gladly help in any way I can," Gowlisk replied.

"Thank you, Ambassador. We are assuming that the Torani fleet will come in expecting all of our vessels in orbit to protect the planet. What if we were to hide them behind the other planets, and hit them from behind as they engage Earth's defenses. If we were to put the Velnor research vessels in our orbit, and hide two of their vessels in the shadow of the moon to protect them, they may think that the Klosk fleet has left for their home planet."

"If we were to hide the remaining fleet vessels behind the planets, which can easily hide two vessels each, we simply let the Torani fleet pass through the system, then come in from behind and box them in catching them by surprise. The planetary defenses combined with the Lunar Station will be able to help protect the Velnor vessels until the other vessels arrive."

Gowlisk listened and visualized the plan in his head, and after a minute of patient silence he spoke. "Colonel, your plan sounds like a good one in my opinion, but I will take this plan and present it to our commanders for their approval, and possible alteration."

The Torani have the most powerful cruisers in the galaxy since they are the primary builders. They don't allow any of the other systems to purchase their models insuring this fact. Our commanders are well aware of their own vessels capabilities, and will certainly be more qualified to answer your question than I am. I'm sorry I can't help more."

"Thank you, Ambassador," Elsa said. "How long are we estimating before the attack?" she asked.

"Their newest cruiser is still in the shipyard, and will be finished in two, possibly three months. We don't expect them to come without it," John explained.

"Well, that should leave us plenty of time to accomplish our preparation. Let's get on it, gentlemen. That will be all for today, and thank you all for coming," Elsa replied and closed the meeting.

Jack Law walked over to John and his three comrades. "John I'll stay in close contact with you at Johnson and Lance at NORAD. The key to this battle in my opinion is them not expecting so many cannons, and they have no idea that we now have fighter squadrons. We could possibly handle this problem on our own, but I'm definitely not going to refuse the added help."

"You're right, Jack. The galaxy has already suffered enough at the hands of the Torani on our account. It's time for us to kick some ass ourselves for a change," John said. "Plus I'm always up for a little payback," he added as he shook the colonel's hand.

"Spoken like a true fighter pilot, John," Jack replied.

The four men returned to the Jaxor, to return to Dubai so Gowlisk can pass on the colonel's plan to his commanders. The Torani fleet will arrive within the next nine to thirteen weeks and they need to be ready. The fate of the galaxy depends on their preparation, as well as the outcome of this battle.

The fleet vessels have been pulled back to Mars orbit to clear the way for maneuvers. Earth's warriors have two months minimum to hone their skills.

Willis and his squadron have been on the lunar base for the last five days putting themselves through several training scenarios. The very green pilots need all the practice they can get, so the dead satellites in orbit are being used for the fighter pilots training.

The Corisole have created a magnificent base. The only improvements the Earth men have made is the expansion for the fighter squadrons support. Earth's lunar base is now the most powerful defense system in the galaxy, and will certainly be a model for other systems in the future. After the Torani's quite simple destruction of two of the galaxy's systems, it has become evident for the need of these types of defenses.

The commanders of the new fighter fleet are the first trained and most experienced of the pilots. This exalted group is made up of Mortisk, Willis, Bret, Willis's two brother in laws, and John for the reserve squadron if needed. Each of the men have a squadron of fifty fighters with four squad leaders below them in charge of ten fighters each. With each group of ten having the ability to destroy one of the large cruisers if properly utilized. The firepower of the fighter is overwhelming, but they do have a weakness which is the pilot's inexperience in battle.

Mortisk has been set as the leader of the fleet because of his experience. He has been very busy at scheduling and running the training drills for the pilots. He has called a meeting of four of the other commanders.

"How are the squad leaders progressing in their lessons?" he asked his commanders.

"I would say that we are at about 90 percent. What do you think, Bret?" Willis asked.

"I would have to agree. Even our backup squads which have the greenest pilots are doing quite well," Bret replied. "All pilots are scoring the 90 percent or better range on targeting and maneuvering. With a few more weeks we should be at our best without actual combat experience."

The other commanders all agreed with Bret's appraisal. Then Willis spoke up with an unforeseen problem.

"There is one thing that we really don't know. We have been so busy learning to fly that we really don't know exactly what to shoot at besides their engines. We need detailed schematics on the different vessels laser ports. I would rather go in knowing what I'm firing at, instead of waiting to be shot at to discover where the ports are."

"I am sorry, my friends, I have so busy with this entire program that I overlooked this problem," Mortisk said.

"How many different types of vessels are there?" Brad asked. "I thought the Torani were the only builders."

"The Torani are the largest builders of galactic vessels, but the Boral as well as the Antarians build quite dangerous fighting vessels. The Antarian pirate vessels are heavily armed and very fast, which makes them very dangerous. The Boral vessels are not as heavily armed, but with their cybernetic abilities they literally become part of the vessel which gives them incredible maneuvering and targeting speeds."

"Can you get us schematics on the different vessels?" Willis asked.

"They should be in the galactic data banks at the Dubai Station. I will get them for us."

"All right, then for now we just keep up the training until we can get the schematics and down load the vessels into the simulators. Once that is done we will have each commander take his squadron to Johnson for Sim time," Willis ordered.

"It will take at least two weeks to get the simulators ready because we will have to write the software for the programs," Mortisk added.

"Then we need to go to Dubai today, Mortisk."

"Agreed, my friend."

"You two take care of that and I'll keep the pressure on the squads from here," Bret suggested.

The commanders all agree with the plan and continue with their training duties. Mortisk and Willis have a very important task in front of them and must start immediately to complete it.

Brad Meyer and Captain Rice have been quite busy with the groundbased cannon arrays. By connecting the NORAD computers with the lunar-based systems, they have been able to utilize the lunar tracking systems to tie it all together. Olga is at the Siberian site which will be a perfect test of the system because of its location from NORAD. They are only minutes from making their first live fire test of the cannons.

Two targets have been put in lunar orbit to attempt a true test of the cannons abilities. If this test is successful they will next try multiple targets. Olga is in the control room at the facility currently in contact with NORAD for the test.

"Olga this is Brad, are you ready for the test?"

"NORAD we are at full power and ready to fire."

"All right, we have the target acquired and will fire in thirty seconds."

"Confirmed NORAD, in thirty."

The cannon began to move as it acquired its targeting data. They watched the countdown at both locations. Five, four, three, two, one. The cannon erupted with a laser beam at least a foot in diameter. A fraction of a second later and two and thirty thousand miles away the target exploded in a ball of fire.

"We have a confirmed hit," Rice said.

"Did you hear that, Olga?" Brad asked.

"I sure did," she replied. "Good job, guys."

They all enjoyed a moment of great victory after the successful test. Olga returned to the comm station to talk to NORAD.

"So when is the next test, Brad?"

"How about a week from today. It will take that long to set up the targets."

"One week then. Siberia out."

The team at NORAD is quite pleased with their progress and congratulations go out to all involved in the test. They will have a test of the entire cannon array in one week and hope for the same results as today.

Mortisk and Willis are landing on the pad at the Galactic Station in Dubai. They need the information from the Station's data banks to write the new programs for the simulators. As they exited the shuttle they watched a streak of very bright light reach for the moon.

"I take it that was the laser cannon they are testing."

"Your guess would be right. The cannons are the only thing capable of that kind of power," Mortisk replied.

"I'm glad it's on our side. Why don't we put a system of those things, on Mars or Pluto?"

"I believe that plan has already been set in motion, but it can't be completed in time to help us with the Torani."

"That's too bad, those things are bad to the bone."

"Bad? They are incredible weapons," Mortisk replied. Puzzled by Willis's remark.

"Just an Earth expression."

"I should have guessed."

"Come on, let's go download the information we need and get out of this place. I've had enough sand for a lifetime."

Mortisk is still looking at him, puzzled by the expression. When is bad, good, he thinks to himself as they walked toward the main entrance to the incredible building.

They recovered the data, then flew home for a rest. After five days on the moon, they were both eager to be with their families.

Elsewhere in the station, Gene is in Gowlisk's office with Tronext, and Prowlex. Gowlisk is hanging up a picture of the new "Wild Bunch." Four aliens and two humans on horseback next to the lake at the top of the mesa.

"That was quite a day wasn't it?" Gene said.

"That valley is one of the wonders of the galaxy," Gowlisk said as he stood back and looked at the picture. "You humans put a lot of effort into enjoying yourselves, don't you."

"That's why we're still stuck on the same planet. We would rather fish and drink beer, than fly to other planets," Gene said, joking with his friends.

"There is a certain logic to it, isn't there," Prowlex replied.

Tronext changed the subject back to the matter they are currently dealing with. "I understand you are had a successful test of the Siberian cannon today."

"Yes, they contacted me only fifteen minutes ago and gave me the good news. They tied the cannon systems together between NORAD and the Lunar Station. The test was a success. They hit an old satellite that was only about a cubic yard, and almost a quarter of a million miles away. I would call that dead on," John said proudly. "We're going for a fifty cannon test in a week."

"Wonderful news," Gowlisk said. He is becoming aware of the human's ingenuity and drive. "With that kind of fire power the Torani will not know what hit them. They are aware of the lunar cannons, but when we cram one of these up their asses they'll know we mean business."

The ambassadors all looked at him, surprised by his expression.

"Have the last of the Torani been removed from the planet?" Gowlisk asked.

"They have no long range vessels available for the journey. I am assuming that the emperor doesn't care if he kills his own people also," Gene replied.

"I suggest that we gather them at this station and tell them of the emperor's plans. From what Mortisk has told me, no Torani would go along with such a plan. It will have no effect on our plans, because they have no knowledge of our defenses." "I agree," Tronext said. "We should at least inform them of the emperor's deception, and let them choose their own fate."

"You know, my friends, I think we should send the three Velnor research vessels along with a two-cruiser escort to Zaxin and Klosk to aid with the damage control on your planets," John suggested. "With our cannons and fighters, we should be just fine with five warships to repel the Torani fleet."

"That would be a blessing to both planets. With both fleets destroyed, we have no way to transport the needed supplies. The Zakorians have been lending aid, but it is a great distance between the two systems, which is making the shipments very slow," Tronext said.

"I will contact the commanders of our explorers and notify them immediately to join with your cruisers, Gowlisk. They can leave immediately."

"I will inform the cruisers commanders. They can decide which will accompany them."

With his time spent as president, Gene still has the habit of taking charge of a situation and dealing with it as quickly as possible. The last few years has compounded that habit.

CHAPTER 57

---•●✹●•---

Elsa and Gene have met with Leader Rowland to inform her of the timeline for the assured attack by the Torani fleet. The three alien ambassadors have also accompanied them to the World Headquarters to give testimony at this meeting. They are now entering the main chamber that is now filled with all the world's leaders, who have been informed of the importance of the meeting, and the fate of the world is once more at risk.

Leader Rowland rises to address the assembled members. "Ladies and gentlemen, I would like to start this meeting today with a statement from the American leader, Elsa Ault." The leader yielded the podium to Elsa.

"My friends, as well as leaders of the world districts. I would first like to thank you for showing up at such short notice. My friends it has been two years since we discovered the Torani treachery, and during the past two years I am glad to say that we have been working together as one planet. We have gathered our best scientists, in order to set them to the task of protecting us from another invasion such as the Corisole unleashed on our world."

"Over the period of the last two years our scientists have not only supplied us with the power we need to survive, but they have also been working on several Top Secret projects to prepare us for the future. This future."

"Because of their efforts our world is now in possession of threehundred orbital attack fighters. These fighters are currently based on board the newly refit and fully operational Lunar Station."

"Our scientists have also repaired the laser cannons on the Station, as well as created fifty ground-based cannon installations on the planet's surface for our protection. This cannon array is capable of destroying large vessels as far away as the moon accurately. The hard working teams involved in this two-year project would like to assure you that we can and will protect our planet in the future. I would now like to turn the floor over to Ambassador Furgison. Thank you."

Elsa sat as Gene made his way to the podium. He is joined at the podium by his fellow ambassadors of the Galactic Alliance.

"Thank you, Elsa," he said with a polite bow in her direction. "Leaders of the planet Earth. We have called this meeting today out of respect. We respect your right to know what is happening on this planet as well as the rest of the galaxy that we are now all a part of."

The ambassador proceeded to tell the leaders of the destruction of the Zaxin fleet as well as the damage done to their planet. He then told them of the destruction of the Klosk Space Station and the destruction of three of their cruisers, as well as the attack on the planet as well. He then explained how the Klosk and Velnor fleets had come to our aid while the other two planets lay in ruins, in order to help with the forthcoming battle that was about to take place.

Gene finished the speech with the news of the importance of the Sol System in the future of the entire galaxy, as well as the universe. After releasing all of this information on the unsuspecting members, he paused and studied the faces of the members. He looked at his friends standing next to him and once again spoke.

"My friends—and I call you my friends because I know almost every person in this chamber personally—we, with the help of the men standing next to me, will win this battle. But I will also assure you that after this battle is won, the real battle will most certainly begin, since this galaxy will take a new standing in this universe. We have become unwillingly one of the most powerful galaxies in the universe, and we had better prepare for that truth by using our wealth in the valuable gold we possess. Along with the vast knowledge of our friends in the galaxy we will protect ourselves from the greed that we can be sure exists not only in this galaxy, but most certainly in others.

"Now, my friends, for our last piece of business for the day. In approximately sixty days from today, and this is by no means a hard date. The Torani fleet is going to try to take our planet from us as the Corisole planet did. We have our defenses I described earlier, as well as six cruisers from the Klosk and Velnor planets. We are certain we can win this battle, because unknown to the Torani, we are the ones with the element of surprise. Believe me when I say that we do have a large surprise waiting for them when they arrive. We have informed you of their coming and we will inform you again when the time is near. This will give you approximately two months to prepare your people to take deep cover when this battle occurs.

"Ladies and gentlemen, this is absolutely everything we know at this time. If any more information comes to us, we will surely notify you all. Are there any questions?" Gene watched a very stunned, but not afraid group of leaders. "I take that as a no. If you do have any questions later feel free to contact any of the men standing before you, and they will gladly answer them as best they can. Thank you all, and good luck."

Gene and the other ambassadors all bowed respectfully then left the podium for their seats as Leader Rowland came to speak before the meeting is adjourned.

"My friends as Gene has made it perfectly clear, and like you I am at a loss for words at this time. I suggest that we all heed Gene's warnings and prepare our districts for the battle that is upon us. Thank you all for attending today."

The leader adjourned the meeting, gathered her things as the rest of the members did, and left the chambers for her office. Gene and his friends gathered in the hallway.

"Well, I think we managed to scare them all to death, but at least they are prepared for what is coming."

They all headed for the Jaxor, then to the Lunar Station. They all still had a lot of work to do to defend the planet Earth.

The emperor and his advisors are going over their plans for the impending invasion of Earth. His advisors are all sitting around the table arguing among themselves about the best way to proceed. The emperor has had enough of their bickering and quiets the room.

"Gentlemen, that will be enough." The room quieted at his outburst. "Commander, let's start with your thoughts on the invasion."

"Thank you, Emperor. My main concern, Emperor, is the fact that we have absolutely no idea where the Klosk and Velnor fleets are located. Our Boral scouts have not reported any fleet traveling into Klosk space, which leads me to believe that they have been informed of our attack on Klosk as well as the Zaxin system, and have deduced that we are about to attack the Earth planet," Brydon explained.

"Emperor, why would they risk their remaining fleet to protect a planet they care nothing about?" Skoby asked.

"It is quite simple, Commander. They know," Brydon answered for the emperor.

"Know what?" Skoby asked, finally realizing that he has been kept from very vital information.

The emperor leaned forward to speak to the commander, who is in way over his head at this point. "Commander, the reason the Corisole idiots attacked Earth was to try to get their hands on its reserves before we did. We have been working together for thirty years to take possession of the Earth planet. They got greedy and thought they could defeat us in battle, which they may have if we hadn't discovered their fleet headed for Earth when we did."

"What reserves are we talking about, Emperor?" Skoby asked.

"Commander, the Earth planet, as well as many of the planets in the Sol System, contain the largest Triomicium reserves in the known universe. The Corisole leaders attempted to cheat us out of our rightful share of these reserves. We tried them for their crimes, then altered the verdict to put them all to death to keep our secret, but someone, and I'm assuming the Zaxin ambassador, discovered this fact and informed Furgison of the wealth of his planet as well as our deception. So now the Zaxin, Klosk, and Velnor are aware of this fact as well and are now combining their forces to protect the planet."

The commander cannot believe what he is hearing. To be part of such an evil plan sickens him. He is a warrior. Those men aboard the Corisole vessels were warriors also, and probably knew as much about what they were fighting for as he did, and dying for the greed of their leaders.

"Do you have a problem, Commander?" Brydon asked the now angry Skoby.

"No, sir," he replied, knowing it was the only answer.

"Emperor, the Klosk fleet is only five vessels. If the Velnor join them they will have eight vessels. They are no match for our fleet," Brydon said confidently.

What about the Kabult Station? It destroyed two of our vessels quite easily during the last battle," Sub-commander Dorin stated.

"We can deal with the Station as we did last time. There's also the fact that our scientists have locked out the fire control systems on the station, and even if they have overridden the lockouts, we will destroy it as we did last time." Brydon bragged, very sure of himself.

The emperor again stops the arguing between the men. "We have no choice, Commanders, with our actions. We could ask for help from the Boral and Antarians, but they are pirates and would end up stabbing us in the back to take the planet for themselves. How long until the new cruiser is completed?"

"Thirty days, Emperor."

"Then we sail for the Sol System in thirty days, Commanders. I suggest you make the fleet ready for battle. That will be all for today," he said and then left the room.

The commanders are all still in disagreement about the plan. Skoby is sickened by the fact that he was tricked into such an evil plan, but has no idea what course to take from here.

The fighter squadrons have been flying in and out of Johnson freely for the last two weeks. Mortisk and Willis completed the new programs for the simulators, and the pilots are all spending as much time as they can on them during the time they have left before the battle with the Torani.

The station is prepared for battle, and the planetary defenses are also standing at ready. Olga, as well as everyone at NORAD, can breathe a lot easier these days. Gene and Tronext have been invited to Houston by their friend John to witness the fighters in flight as they fly in and out of the base as they no longer have to worry about security.

Willis and Mortisk are there assessing the pilots on their progress with the new program. Their men are doing extremely well so they now can breathe much easier also, along with everyone involved in the last two years of preparation.

John is giving Tronext and Gene a tour of the hangar that contains the simulators, when Gene spots the two pilots. "Mortisk, Willis. How the hell are ya?" Gene asked with a slap on the back.

"Great, how are you guys holding up?" Willis asked.

"We're hanging in there. It's been crazy the last few weeks. We have barely had a chance to sleep," Gene said.

"How are you, Mortisk?" John asked his friend. "How's the family?"

"They are well. My daughter gets bigger every day and Hyal gets more tired," he said laughing.

"How's your little one Willis?" he asked.

"Always hungry, and crawling all over the place. But you can see for yourself on Sunday."

"What's Sunday?" John asked, now confused, thinking he has forgotten something.

"Dad's birthday party. He would be upset if all of you guys didn't show up."

"I can't believe I forgot. We've been so busy the last few weeks, I forget who I am sometimes," John said.

"Hey, guys!" John yelled to Tronext and Gene. Bill's birthday is this Sunday."

"No shit. Well, we all know what that means," Gene said.

"Barbeque," Tronext replied with a smile.

They all laughed at the Zaxin's excitement.

"You're all invited," Willis said. "You know Dad. He doesn't judge anyone by their scales or how hairy they are," Willis said with a smile.

"We'll be there with beer mugs in hand. I'll bring a couple of big ones for Prowlex and Gowlisk. Those little bottles aren't big enough for those two," Gene said. "To be honest. I can see where the hairy Klosk puts it all, but I still can't see how a four-and-a-half-foot gray alien can drink so much beer."

They all laughed heartily at the thought.

"Well, we better let you two get back to work. We're just passing through. See you Sunday," Gene said.

"We better," Willis replied.

John led his small group out of the simulator room and on to other parts of the base. It has changed a lot in the last three years. The area around Johnson now has a population of over ten-thousand people.

The new town of Independence Valley is alive with the sound of music and laughter. It has been six weeks since the last barbeque, but for the people of the three towns, that's too long.

The valley is filled with at least one hundred and fifty people who all came here today for one reason, to show their respect for the man who helped bring most of them back from the brink of disaster. Without his resolve to rebuild what the Corisole had destroyed, the towns would have turned to dust as many others did. The new town that has been created is proof that if people pull together as a family, they can accomplish anything. This new collection of thirteen homes and nine different families, has become one family of thirty-eight members and still growing.

The other members of this family are just arriving as Gene and his family arrived in the helicopter Elsa gave to him for his use. John and the ambassadors, along with Brad, Horace, and Allen, have all come by way of the Jaxor. There isn't a person in the galaxy that would miss this party.

A very nice, as well as very large gazebo has been constructed next to the pond where the fire pit is now located. The old stones for sitting have been replaced by comfortable benches with tables. Bill was forced by his higher power, Monica, to build the structure. They are now all sitting in the shade of the structure and watching the people enjoying themselves.

"Beautiful day," Gene said as he watched. "Happy birthday, old man. So this makes you what? Older than dirt." He smiled as he said it.

"Pretty dammed close," Bill replied. "But I guess we all know the value of a little dirt nowadays, don't we."

The group all laughed at the men's jokes, knowing that after a few more hours and more beers, the jokes would only get more plentiful.

Bill's son came over him with a mysterious look about him. "Dad, me and the guys want to give you a very special gift this year. We know how you feel about space, so we've all figured out the perfect present. Let's grab a case of beer and your bowl and go for a ride."

"I've already got the beer," Ben said, patting the Coronas tucked under his arm.

"Where are we going?"

"Up there," Willis replied, pointing at the moon that was bright in the midday sky. "We can be back by five if we leave now."

"What about all these people?"

"They already know. This is a gift from all of us."

"Come on, baby," Monica said, pulling him from his seat.

"You're going along?"

"Wouldn't miss it for the world."

Bill and his dear friends, along with the second dog in space, followed by the grandchildren that were old enough, all loaded into the Jaxor for a tour of the Lunar Station. It would be a journey none of them would ever forget, and the first unofficial party on the moon. Leave it to Bill to pull that one off.

At five-thirty that afternoon, the Jaxor returned to the valley with a very happy crew aboard. It was a once in a lifetime trip for some of them, and for the young ones probably only their first time in space.

"Thank you all," the birthday boy said. "I've dreamed of going into space my whole life, but to be the first one to party on the moon, that will go down in history," Bill said with a huge grin.

"We knew you would jump at the chance," Ben said.

The grandchildren ran to tell their mothers about the incredible journey, and Monica had to tell the other ladies about the flight through space. Gene and the others knew that they had chosen the perfect gift.

The evening progressed as planned with Willis and his new band playing as the people all danced. The Men from NASA, outer space, Kitt

Peak, and wherever else they came from, are all now in the friendliest place in the galaxy. They all know what the next few months have in store for the planet and intend to forget about it for a few hours. They are going to enjoy every minute they have left until life gets real serious again.

"Who's up for some fishing tomorrow?" Mortisk asked.

"Count us all in," Bill answered for all of them.

"I wouldn't miss it for anything," Tronext replied. He is the newest alien to be addicted to the hobby.

They toasted to good fishing tomorrow, but at this point they would toast the grass for growing. They were all here to relax, and that's exactly what they did.

CHAPTER 58

Galactic Summary 2, M-420 Galaxy
September 15–October 30, 2023

Planet Zaxin
September 15, 2023

The ambassadors have traveled across the galaxy to assess how the rescue work is progressing on the now rebuilding Klosk and Zaxin planets. With the Zaxin planet hit the hardest, the Klosk and Velnor vessels are still in Zaxin orbit helping with the relief efforts. It has been three months since the Torani attacked the peaceful planet and the efforts are going well.

The Jaxor is entering the planet's atmosphere and assessing the damage. Gene is amazed as they tour the planet, at the randomness of the attacks. The once magnificent forest dome as well as the Capital city domes have been destroyed senselessly, along with the innocent lives of the inhabitants that they contained.

"Why?" Gene asked. "There were no cannons around the cities."

"They did not come as ambassadors. They came as conquerors," Tronext replied. "They did not care where their weapons landed after the cannons were destroyed."

"The Torani have no honor, and to expect any less of them has been a mistake," Gowlisk added. "True warriors have honor and do not attack the innocent."

"We should leave the research vessels here and send the other two vessels to Klosk," Prowlex recommended.

"Yes, I agree. The Zaxin leaders have everything well in hand here, and the Velnor vessels can assist them in whatever they need now," Tronext replied.

The Jaxor made one final sweep of the Zaxin planet and proceeded to Klosk, along with the two Klosk cruisers. With the Zaxins having everything under control, it is now time to help the people of Klosk.

After a seven-day journey, the three vessels are entering the orbit of the Klosk planet and the Jaxor proceeds to the planet's surface. The main targets on the surface were the cannons, along with the capitol city and the planet's communication center. With the planet's defenses centered at the orbital station, there were few batteries on the planet's surface, which kept the damage to a minimum.

The immenseness of the trees is what saved the people of Klosk. The charred areas of timber are the only telltale signs of the attack, their immense size protecting the inhabitants below from the Torani lasers. There was needless loss of life, but not to the extent of the Zaxin planet.

"It appears my planet was much more fortunate than yours, Tronext," Gowlisk said as he viewed the damage. "We will set down in the capital city and see if we can help in any way."

"How many of your people were on that station?" Gene asked.

"The station plus three cruisers puts the number at over seven hundred Klosk warriors," Gowlisk replied.

"I'm sorry, Gowlisk," Gene said.

"We will make all responsible for this pay with their lives, then make sure this kind of destruction is never again unleashed on any system of this galaxy. The destruction of the Torani fleet will be the first step." Gowlisk is enraged as he says it.

The Jaxor landed in the capitol, and the ambassadors met with the leaders of the planet to explain their missing fleet. They have not yet discovered the Torani's overall goal, and after the ambassadors filled them in on the details of the Torani plans, as well as their own plan, they were back on the Jaxor and headed for Earth with the Klosk leaders' hopes for a great victory. The group has only thirty days before the expected attack, and it is a twenty-one-day journey to Earth, so they hope they will be there in time.

John and Brad are in the Main hangar of the station. The fighters are all ready for battle with a full complement of pilots waiting in their quarters for the call. The Station has been refit to launch ten fighters at a time at two-minute intervals, enabling them to launch fifty fighters every ten minutes.

The entire cannon arsenal of the station, as well as planet, are on high alert status with the men of Cheyenne Mountain up to the task of managing them when the time comes. The Klosk have installed sensor arrays on the Mars planet that will allow the defenders to have a six-hour warning on the approach of the Torani fleet. It's all a very painful waiting game now.

Willis and Mortisk have joined John and Brad on the hangar floor. They walked among the fighters, making sure they are all ready for battle.

"This waiting is absolutely killing me," Willis said.

"We have no choice but be in a constant state of readiness at this point," John replied. "We don't expect them for another thirty days, but since when does a bully make an appointment to kick your ass."

"The Torani have already showed their skill at deception so we have to be ready at all times," Brad added. "No insult intended, Mortisk."

"None taken, my friend, and you are both correct. Any warrior either depends on the element of surprise, or overwhelming firepower. There are no substitutes for victory."

"I don't think they can finish that cruiser before the middle of next month, but what we have accomplished in the last two years should have taken five," John explained. "So it just goes to show you that the impossible can be done." They all nodded in agreement.

"How about some lunch? I'm hungry," John said, as he tried to take their minds off the waiting.

"I'm not really hungry, but I've started eating out of boredom lately," Willis said.

They all took the lift to the cafeteria to try to relax and get a bite to eat. They've been on the station for a week now and it's hard to just sit and wait. They are all ready for battle, and wait for the chance to get a little payback for the destruction to all their worlds.

Bill is at the gazebo drinking his morning coffee and throwing the stick in the pond for the dog. It is helping him not to worry about the boys on the station, and the dog needed a bath. Monica came out to sit with him knowing just how worried he really is.

"Hey, baby," he said as she sat down beside him.

"Here I thought you might want this," she said as she handed him his bowl.

"Thank you, I can use it."

"Worried about the boys?"

"Well, considering that we've got five of them from this valley on that station right now waiting to go to war, yes I am."

They sat quietly as he smoked and played with Sassy. Ben wandered over and sat with them.

"Mornin," he said shortly.

"Hey, Ben, how's Tashike?" Monica asked.

"She's with Hyal. They're not taking all of this very well."

"None of us are, Ben," Bill said. "But those two have a totally different problem than we do. Mortisk is up there right now getting ready to destroy his own people. It's different for our guys, they have a reason to fight. The Torani haven't fought their own people in over three-hundred years from what Mortisk told me. There isn't a person on this planet right now that isn't affected by this, but I've got the only other three men in this family up there right now ready to go to war, and if even one of them dies it will affect this family greatly."

That's what happens in war Bill, people die defending what they believe to be important to them," Ben said.

"I know Ben and I've been lucky enough in my lifetime to never have to fight in one until now."

They all sat quietly sharing the contents of Bill's bowl and watching the dog, all silently praying for the safe return of all the men from the valley.

The Jaxor touched down at Johnson after a short stop at the Lunar Station. They are at Johnson to return Brad to his post in the command center. John has stayed on the station to prepare his reserve squadron for battle if they are needed.

The deep space sensors are working perfectly as Brad watches the screen which now shows the positions of the Velnor and Klosk vessels. The five cruisers are lying in their ambush positions waiting for the Torani fleet. They have decided upon putting three vessels behind Jupiter, and the other two behind the Mars planet. They are confident that the Torani won't detect the cruisers on their approach to Earth and hope they are right. Their plan absolutely depends on their ability to catch them by surprise from behind.

John has stationed fifty of the fighters at the Nevada base. By doing so he hopes to create a stronger attack. With the lunar and Earth-based cannons, along with the two-sided fighter attack, the Torani should be so overwhelmed that they won't even notice the cruisers coming in for the kill.

It appears that they will be able to easily destroy the Torani fleet, but they are still concerned about the unknown. Have the Torani enlisted the Boral and Antarians? This is one very dangerous unknown to them.

The emperor and his commanders are in his chamber making the final preparations for the launch of the battle group. The commanders of each of the vessels are making absolutely sure their vessel is repaired and ready for battle.

The emperor has elected to lead his battle group personally, from the command chair of the Empress. His advisors have warned him against this action, but his arrogance has convinced him that this will be an easy victory.

"Commander Brydon. When will the fleet be ready to launch?"

"The vessel Solstar has been released from space dock, and is now ready for battle. The remaining vessels have completed all repairs and are also stand ready, sir."

"Then at the start of the new day we will set sail for the Sol System. I will command the Empress, and Commander Brydon will command the Solstar. At O-six-hundred-hours tomorrow we will sail into the future of the Torani race. I will meet with you in the morning by video on board your vessels. Good day, gentlemen."

The chamber empties as the commanders are returning to their vessels. Commander Skoby has one stop to make before he returns to the Jayden. Skoby has elected to reveal the truth to the Corisole trials to a friend who belongs to an underground antigovernment group. Before the events of the last few months, the commander has been a faithful member of the Torani military, but after the information he has gained during these months, he can no longer allow the emperor to rule the Torani people. They are a good and peaceful race that have been deceived by their rulers into believing that the Corisole were the evil threat, and the last few months have shown the commander just exactly who the evil ones really are. Now he has unwillingly become one of the evil ones and cannot live with this on his conscience. Skoby will tell his friend the information, hopeful that this knowledge will lead to new leadership for the Torani people. The emperor must answer for his deception.

After their three week trip from the Klosk planet, the ambassadors have insisted on a meeting of the Alliance members that are present on the station. They have all now gathered in the chamber to hear the most recent news on the Torani fleet's movements.

The Alliance leader calls the meeting to order as the ambassadors wait to speak. "Leaders of the Galactic Alliance, I have called you all to this emergency meeting at the request of the Zaxin ambassador Tronext. I have not been informed of the nature of this meeting, but I believe we all have a very good idea. Ambassador, you have the podium."

Tronext made his way to the podium with his friends at his side. They have all decided that he was the best one to relay the news to the council members.

"Leaders of the Galactic Alliance. This morning I received a message from our informant on the Torani planet. According to him, the Torani fleet left the system five days ago with their course set for the Sol System. The fleet has sailed with a complement of seven heavily armed vessels, one of them being the new Solstar, which is the most powerful battle cruiser ever constructed. We had hoped that the building of this station would deter the Torani from attacking this planet, but we were mistaken. Their greed for the resources in this system has blinded their leaders of anything other than total domination of our galaxy."

"The Earth leaders have recommended an evacuation of this station. The Torani fleet is expected to reach the system in the next forty-eight hours, and they cannot guarantee your safety. The Velnor planet is offering refuge on their planet for all Alliance members until this situation comes to whatever end it may."

"Our Earth friends intend to do all that is in their power to repel the invasion, and as you know, the Velnor as well as the Klosk fleets, have left five of their cruisers to assist with this battle. The new Earth defenses are expected to be powerful enough to defeat the Torani, but we all know that battle is unpredictable. Thank you all for your attendance today, and good luck."

The three men left the podium to return to their seats as leader Rowland again takes the podium. "My friends as leader of the planet Earth I would like to thank you for your support these last three years during this tremendously difficult time. I am now offering any of you who would like to remain on Earth a safe haven until the battle is over. We have created a reinforced bunker deep within the Alps after the first attack, and any of you who would like to join me there are welcome. If you would like to rely on the safety of this station, or the safety of Velnor, that is of course your choice. Thank you all, and we will hopefully be meeting again at the conclusion of this battle."

Leader Rowland made her way out of the chamber. The Earth leaders are all vacating the World Headquarters for safer locations, which the galactic leader will now do also. She will travel to the Alp bunker to ride out the storm that is now headed for their world.

Gene and the others have come to Washington to help Elsa prepare for the attack. The people of the district need to be informed of the coming attack and they have joined Elsa and her staff in the briefing room.

"Thank you all for coming, gentlemen," she said to the distinguished group.

"We can't stay long, but I wanted to help you prepare the emergency message, and I do have lots of practice," Gene said.

"I appreciate all the help I can get. So what's the time frame? I heard through the grapevine that we're looking at forty-eight hours."

"The grapevine was correct. We expect them anywhere from twelve to forty-eight hours, but we're betting on forty-eight."

"Leader Ault," Gowlisk broke in. "Their main objective will certainly be the Lunar Station, and any fleet vessels they encounter. The ground Installations as well as the fighters will be a surprise to them if they have not learned of their existence, and we cannot say what their reaction will be toward them."

"Aren't the cannons all in remote locations?"

"They are, Elsa," Gene said. "But when the shooting starts from beyond the moon, and at so many targets, we expect the collateral damage to be high. We have recommended that everyone get as deep as they possibly can until it's over. The emergency broadcast system is still active so all you have to do is record a message and feed it into the system."

"Unfortunately I remember the last time we used it Gene."

"Sorry. Just trying to help."

"I know, Gene, and thank you."

"Elsa, I just wanted to stop and make sure you were okay, but I see that you have everything under control without me, so I really need to run. My family is still in Dallas and we are going to get them to a safe place. We are all going to Colorado Springs and ride this thing out at NORAD. I figure it's the safest place to watch this from."

"Thank you all for your help during the past few years, gentlemen," she said as she shook all their hands.

"Take care, Elsa," Gene said. Then they headed back to the Jaxor.

Elsa began to record her message to the people of the American District. It has been two years since anyone listened to their emergency radios, and she hoped they all had them still turned on.

Bill and Monica are outside enjoying the last few warm nights before winter arrives, but they are both worried about their loved ones on the station. They know the attack is coming soon, but not exactly when. The emergency radios have all been turned on to wait for the certain message to come. With the new satellites, they have been told that they will have a six to ten-hour warning, but they are still ready and waiting to head for cover.

The valley has been chosen to shelter the people of the surrounding inhabitants, and they are ready for their arrival. They estimate that they can handle three-hundred easily, and four-hundred if they have to for a short period of time. They are all hoping it will be a short battle and not a war.

Sassy is taking one of her last swims of the year, when Dove and Tiffany come running out of the house with one of the radios.

"There's a message," they both said as they ran to the gazebo.

The radio is playing a message from the American leader. They all waited for it to start from the beginning so they can listen to it fully.

"This is a message from the emergency broadcast system. The leader of the American district Elsa Ault will now speak." There was a short pause. Then Elsa started to speak.

"People of the American District, we are again at a time of great danger to our planet. The Torani leaders have deceived the people of Earth, and are now on their way to this planet. The news of their deception is not new, but the news of the impending attack is."

"We expect the Torani fleet to enter Earth space within the next twelve to forty-eight hours. We are well prepared for this attack, but are going to ask you all to find the safest place you can to protect your families from possible harm. Stay under cover until you hear from me again on this frequency. Again, we do not know exactly when they will attack, or how long the battle will last, so take enough supplies to last at least four to five days."

"We have a great deal of faith in our defenses and have prepared for this battle for the last two years, but we don't want any undue loss of life, so please take shelter and be prepared for at least four days in that location. Thank you all, and pray for our forces fighting this battle for our planet. Until the next broadcast, good night and god bless you." This has been a message . . .

Bill turned off the radio and looked at the still-gathering crowd. "Someone needs to go down to the city hall and tell the sheriff to get the people moving our way," Bill said.

"I'll jump in the Jeep and go now," Alex volunteered.

"Ben, there's at least a hundred sleeping bags in the storage. Let's get them over to the rec center for starters. Everyone else start making room, we're gonna have a lot of visitors."

They started with gathering the gear out of the garage storage, and spread to the houses for all the blankets they could spare.

"We can fit at least fifty in the garage and the studio," Bill said to Ben as they gathered the gear. "Maybe a hundred in the rec center if we squeeze them in, and another hundred in the houses with the families. That is going to leave anywhere from fifty to a hundred. What are we gonna do with them?" Bill thought out loud.

"What about the barn. It's not underground, but it may be big enough. What's the chance of it getting hit?" Ben asked.

"I'm not as worried about it getting hit as I am the cold Ben. It's getting cold at night, and the barn doesn't have much for heat."

"Like always Bill, we'll figure something out," Ben replied with a pat on the back.

Within an hour the people of the area started rolling in. The valley filled with people that knew they would be protected as best as they could. After they were all housed, they gathered at the gazebo and talked among themselves. They all knew there was no need to worry until it started, but with the thought of the imminent battle upon them, they were all worried nonetheless.

CHAPTER 59

————•●✹●•————

Torani Vessel Empress
October 21, 2023, 06:00

The emperor is on the bridge of the Empress as his fleet hurtles toward the Sol System and the Earth planet. They travel with the vision of an easy victory, and the extreme riches of Earth within their grasp.

"Major Arden!" he roared.

"Yes, Emperor."

"What is our estimated arrival at the Sol System?"

"We should reach the system in twelve hours, sir."

"Are we within sensor range yet?"

"Not for another six hours, sir."

"Very well Alert me when we are in sensor range. I will be in my quarters. And, Major. Inform the other commanders that I want a meeting of all commanders in six hours."

"Yes, sir."

The Torani fleet is only twelve hours from history, and the emperor is quite confident of an easy victory. The Earth forces hope to change that history and prove him wrong.

The Torani capital of Carista wakes to a new day of confusion. The Torani Freedom Movement has been broadcasting over a private radio system for days, and the Torani security forces have yet to find the source of the broadcasts. The broadcasts talk of deception and death at the hands of the Torani leadership, based on the information passed by Skoby. This information has been put to good use.

The people of Torani are now all hearing of the deaths of tens of thousands of innocent victims from their neighboring Corisole, to the other side of the galaxy on the Klosk and Zaxin planets. The most incredible rumor of all is that the emperor not only had a hand in the deaths of five billion people on Earth but is now en route to the Sol System to finish the job started by the Corisole. This news is an insult to the integrity of every Torani citizen.

Its early on the third day of the broadcasts and the masses are beginning to gather outside the Torani Leadership Plaza. The mood is turning for the worst as each day progresses, and the people want answers, but none are being given. It's eight o'clock in the morning, and already several thousand Torani are gathered. After three days of silence from the leaders, the crowds are becoming more agitated. The broadcasts continue hour after hour, insuring that the leaders will answer for their deception one way or another.

The Jaxor rests on the road that leads into the Cheyenne Mountain complex. The two monstrous doors are closed, and the facility is ready for the Torani attack.

The ambassadors, and Gene's family, have been given quarters deep inside the mountain. The alien ambassadors are quite impressed by the NORAD facility, and are currently in the control room watching the action as it unfolds.

"So what do you think of our facility, Ambassadors?" the colonel asked.

"Absolutely impressive," the Klosk ambassador said. "Those are my vessels?" he asked, pointing at the very large screen containing a map of the solar system.

"The Kryton, Otheum, and Kastin are here in the shadow of Jupiter. Here in the shadow of Mars is the Densor and Sardon. We hope to come up from behind as they pass Mars orbit, catching them as they begin to target the Lunar Station. When they see no vessels in orbit we hope they will drop their guard just enough for us to bring our fighters along with your five cruisers into action," Lance explained. "We are counting on the planets to hide the cruisers from the Torani sensors."

"The planets should shield them quite well, Colonel," Gowlisk said.

"Glad to hear you say that. That is the weakest spot in our plan. If the Torani discover your cruisers, the whole plan goes to hell."

"Gentlemen, let's get some lunch while we can. Once this starts we'll be here for the duration," Gene said. "The colonel will let us know when the Torani fleet enters sensor range."

Gene led his friends through the bowels of the mountain. He knows this mountain well from his time as president and hopes for the day when it's no longer needed.

The first wing of the defensive fighter forces is on the Ground at Area 51. Willis is in the control room with Horace, waiting for news on the Torani fleet. The telemetry from the satellites is now being sent to all vital links on the planet. Mortisk and the other five wings await deep inside the moon for their time to pounce on the Torani vessels.

The plan calls for Willis and Mortisk's wings to be deployed first, with two more waiting if needed, and two more in reserve. They don't want more than a hundred fighters in space at once because they expect a tight battleground. After three weeks of waiting, they are all ready for battle and making last-minute checks of their equipment.

"Men, I know we've been over this a thousand times, but we're gonna do it again," Willis said over the radio. "When we break to engage, I want one group of ten to attack each cruiser. I will take the first one, with each group peeling off as you go. Hit them hard and get the hell out, then circle around for another run. Don't stay any closer than you have to because of the cannons. It's gonna be a zoo up there. Just remember your training and we'll all be all right."

"Mortisk's wing will launch at the same time as we do, and we'll have two wings loaded and ready, with two in reserve. Stay on them and make them pay for the five billion that died in the first attack. Good luck, gentlemen."

He sat thinking of all the people in the valley that he was fighting for, as well as the unfortunate people he watched disappear right before his eyes during the first attack, which helped give him the courage as well as anger he needed to continue with his mission.

On the Lunar Station, Mortisk is giving his men the same advice and hopes the inexperienced Earth men will come back alive. They are all well trained, but inexperienced in real orbital battle conditions.

CHAPTER 60

---•●✲●•---

Sol System, Battle for Earth
October 21, 2023, 18:00

As the warriors of Earth wait silently to ambush the Torani fleet upon their arrival, the sensor array on the Mars planet's surface has just picked up the image of the seven Torani cruisers on the outer edge of the solar system. The Torani are also watching their sensors, and with no sign of any other fleet vessels in the system, they see only victory. Their course is set directly for Earth and the wealth that awaits them with their victory.

The warning sirens are wailing in the NORAD control room as the Torani fleet enters the Sol System, and is on a direct course for Earth. The colonel readies his men as the alert goes out to all cannon batteries and fighter wings. Total radio silence is being observed to suppress the chance of the Torani discovering the hidden fleet. The ambassadors have heard the wail of the sirens, and are now on their way to the control room to witness the coming battle. They are all hopeful that their preparation has not been in vain, and the galaxy will soon be free of the tyrannical Torani emperor.

The Lunar Station is now on high alert status as the enemy fleet has just been discovered on the sensors. John and Mortisk have been notified and are now getting their men ready for battle. The pilots of the second attack wing are now heading for their fighters and preparing for the upcoming battle. They have less than six hours for the arrival of the invaders, and they will be ready for them.

Mortisk's wing sets ready in the large launching bay of the station, with Bret's wing on the main hangar floor ready to take their place after they launch. They have trained hard for this day, but are all anxious about the mission they are about to undertake. Every man fears death, but sometimes there are things that are just worth the risk.

Horace and Willis are watching the satellite feed from the Mars sensors in the control room at Area 51, which is now showing a fleet of seven cruisers less than six hours from Earth space.

Willis, and the men of the first fighter wing, will soon be preparing to fly off to protect the inhabitants of Earth from certain destruction. They have less than six hours until the enemy fleet's arrival, and tensions are now at their highest point since they will all soon be heading for war. After eighteen months of training for most of the group, the pilots now wait to join their comrades in the battle for the planet Earth, and are prepared to do whatever it takes to win.

The commanders of the Klosk and Velnor cruisers are hidden in their attack positions. The Klosk vessels, now waiting behind the massive Jupiter planet, will be the first to face the Torani sensors. If the cruisers are detected the Torani fleet will turn and destroy them before the Earth defenses are able to be put into action and do their part to protect their new brothers in this war. So far they have not been detected. The invaders are still sailing directly for Earth, reinforcing their hopes of finally putting a stop to the emperor's evil plan for galactic domination.

The people of the valley have been informed by way of the emergency broadcast system, of the inbound fleet heading for the planet. The Torani fleet is expected to arrive at midnight, and Bill and some of the other men are now watching the skies, knowing there's nothing they can do but pray to help their loved ones during the battle to come.

They all feel safe in the small valley town, but are still cautious and have withdrawn all of the women and children to the safety of the mountain. Most of the men are still outside waiting for the fireworks to begin, hoping for a much different outcome than the last time they were attacked by the Corisole.

The Torani fleet is still on a direct course for Earth, and within the next sixty minutes the lunar cannons will open fire on the invaders. The fire from the lunar cannons will be the first piece of bait dangled before the Torani's noses, and once they set their sights on the station, the Earth batteries will open fire signaling the Earth fleet, as well as the fighters, to spring into action.

The three Klosk vessels are already beginning to fall in behind the advancing cruisers, hoping that the Torani have all of their sensors scanning the path ahead of them so they won't be detected. The Velnor vessels will fall in behind them as they pass the Mars planet in thirty minutes and assume their attack positions alongside the Klosk. Their plan is holding together so far and they all are hopeful that their luck will hold.

The Torani fleet is at battle stations and on a direct course for Earth. The emperor is in command of the fleet on board the Empress, with the Solstar and Commander Brydon on his wing for protection. They have traveled halfway through the Sol System with no signs of another fleet. This is a good sign, but Commander Brydon knows better and has a strange feeling about the ease of their mission. Something just doesn't feel right to him.

"Major Arden. Open a channel to all vessels and keep it open," Ardesnal ordered.

"Yes, Emperor."

"Attention all vessels. We have finally reached our objective, and all vessels will now fall into attack formation. Commander Skoby, your formation will attack the Kabult station and put it out of commission."

"We will do as ordered, sir," Skoby replied. "Mardeck, Oran, fall in behind me for our attack run, and remember to keep tight as we did the last time. Those cannons are deadly and we have to start with a small group of cannons to begin with and work our way out."

"Yes, sir," the commanders of the two vessels answered.

The three vessels began their first run on the Lunar Station, confident that they could repeat their performance from the previous battle.

"Mornstar, Brightstar, you are to proceed to the planet and destroy those fuel towers. I want that planet in the dark," the emperor ordered.

"Yes, sir," they replied and headed for Earth's orbit.

"Solstar you will remain with the Empress until we are needed. I don't see a need for more than five vessels at this time."

"Yes, Emperor, but I don't like this at all. It is too easy. They had to have learned of our fleet's movements." Brydon warned.

"The Velnor are cowards, and the Klosk fleet evidently returned to their own system when they discovered our attack on their planet. You had to of missed them in your search. All vessels will remain on their course and attack, Commander."

"Yes, Emperor," Brydon replied, knowing deep down that there was much more than there appeared to be protecting this planet.

The Torani fleet plunged forward of its mission of destruction, totally unaware of the five vessels in their shadow as they pass through the system. Their arrogance has made them careless and they will pay for that mistake dearly.

John and Brad are now in the control room of the Lunar Station. Nobody knows this station better than Brad since he rebuilt it from the ground up. The telemetry on the large screen has the trajectories of all twelve incoming vessels on their way toward Earth.

Brad activated the hangars intercom. "Attack wing two, launch all fighters and target the incoming vessels. We show three bogies on a direct course to the Lunar Station." The battle for the Sol System has now begun.

"Acknowledged control. Launching second wing now," Mortisk replied.

"Third wing to launch positions as soon as they are clear."

"Yes, sir," Bret replied.

"Cannon control, target all inbound vessels and open fire," John ordered.

"Yes, sir. Targeting all Torani vessels." The Lunar Station came to life in a big way.

The fighters are exiting the launch bay as the cannons open fire on the advancing fleet and the Torani cruisers are right on top of them before they see the small fighters.

Skoby is approaching the station as the cannons open fire on his group, then he sees an unbelievable sight. "Oran, Mardeck, evasive action. Where the hell did those fighters come from?" he said as he watched the fighters swarm out of the station. "Attention all fleet vessels, we've got bogies coming from the station, all vessels converge on the station."

"Yes, sir," the commanders replied.

The Earthbound cruisers diverted from their original course, and made way for the Lunar Station to engage the fighters. They have just run into the first glitch in their plan which has put them at a higher state of awareness.

At the Nevada base, Horace is watching the telemetry and sees that the Torani have swallowed the bait they dangled in front of them, and are all now converging on the station.

"First fighter wing. Launch all fighters," he said into the comms.

"Yes, sir," Willis replied to the order. "All right men, let's go kick some ass. Remember your orders, ten fighters to a vessel. Let's roll gentlemen."

The first wing left the Nevada base on its way to engage the Torani fleet. In fifteen minutes they will all be doing exactly what they have trained the last eighteen months to do. They are all afraid, but that's a good thing as fear only makes you fight harder to survive.

The NORAD screens are filled with the telemetry of the one hundred and twelve vessels that now inhabit Earth space. The first wing from Nevada has now entered space and is on an intercept course with the Torani cruisers. The ground-based cannons are all ready for action and wait for firing solutions from the computers. Ambassadors all watch the battle unfolding before them, as Colonel Law waits for the right moment to open fire.

"Captain Rice, put all cannons on auto fire and let them rip."

"You got it, Colonel."

The twenty cannons currently facing the Lunar Station, as well as the Torani fleet, began to fire carefully distinguishing friend or foe targets as they fired. The Torani fleet is caught totally by surprise by the fire from the planet's surface.

The emperor can't believe what he is witnessing. How could the earthlings not only have created a fighter squadron but have planetary cannons as well. They have been busy, and they evidently had help. These fighters are of Corisole design, with Torani engines. There is no way they did this on their own he thinks to himself.

"Commander Brydon, follow me. We've got to destroy those planetary cannons or they will tear our fleet to pieces.

"Yes, Emperor."

The Empress and the Solstar set course for the planet in an attempt to locate and destroy the cannon batteries. With all that is going on around them they have missed another very important fact. There is a fleet of five cruisers bearing down them that will be in firing range in minutes to close the lid on the kill box. The Earth Alliance plan has worked perfectly so far.

The men of the valley were all sitting outside watching the sky as the battle began, and can now only hope for the best. The ground cannons have begun to fire as the massive beams reach from the planet for their targets in the space above. The moon is once again doing its impression of a disco ball, as the lasers fire in all direction seeking their targets.

With the epic battle going on over the planet the valley is lit up with a glow like there is a full moon. As they all stand there pointing at different areas of the night sky, the laser blasts start to hit the planet's surface, either from missed shots or the hunt for the cannons. They all decided it was time to take cover and headed for the safety of the mountain. They must now trust in the defenses their friends and family have worked so hard to create, to do their job and protect them from further harm by invading alien forces.

Willis's wing is engaging the cruisers, when he spots the two cruisers heading for the planet and firing on the cannons. Being that he is the commander of his wing, he makes a judgement call that he hopes is right.

"First wing. Squads 1 and 2, with me, and the rest of you stay and cripple those cruisers. Squad 1, you take the Solstar, and we'll get the Empress. Move quick and think quicker, gentlemen. Let's get 'em."

"Yes, sir," they all replied and headed for two cruisers that were now headed for the planet below.

The battle is absolutely under way. The Torani fleet is concentrating their attention on the Lunar Station, but with the large amount of fighters attacking their vessels, they have had to change their plan of attack in order to keep from being destroyed. The third wing of fighters has been deployed against them now to join the fight, making their task seem even more impossible.

The first Torani group led by the Jayden, is concentrating on the lunar cannons, while the second group is busy dealing with the fighters. It was like they had hit a hive with a stick the way they were swarmed by the angry fighters. The fighters are having a hard time penetrating the large cruisers' shields, but they are inflicting damage on the vessels by targeting their weapon systems and engines.

Commander Skoby and his group are coming around for another pass on the Station when he sees the one thing he has been deeply concerned about. A fleet of five cruisers has suddenly has appeared out of nowhere, and are concentrating their fire on the unsuspecting second group that is engaged with the fighters. The Brightstar is automatically destroyed as it takes the full force of the attack from all five vessels. The Mornstar takes evasive action and heads for the planet to join with the Empress and the

Solstar. The Jayden's group turned from the station to intercept the fleet with a hail of fire that splits the defending fleet into two, making two small groups to fight instead of one massive wave of concentrated fire.

"Emperor, the Klosk fleet has appeared from open space and destroyed the Brightstar." Skoby informed his leader, then turned to make another run on the advancing fleet.

"All ships concentrate on that fleet. Get in close in order to make it more difficult for those cannons to target our vessels," the emperor ordered.

The Klosk commander came over the fleet's communications channel. "This is Commander Hilldar, split into three formations. Kastin with the Densor, and the Sardon with the Otheum, I'll go it alone. Work around those cruisers and draw them toward the planet, we need the cover fire from those cannons. Watch the fighters, I don't want them hit by mistake."

"Yes, sir," they answered.

The vessels joined their counterparts and headed for the planet with their lasers blazing, drawing the Torani cruisers with them as they went.

"First and second wings, you heard the commander, let's give them some cover fire," Willis ordered.

The fighters of the first and second squads turned to engage the two cruisers with all the skills they have obtained from their training.

"Lunar Station, this is Mortisk. We need another wing launched to protect the station. We've already lost thirty craft and with another wing headed for the planet we need more help."

"You got it, buddy," John replied. "Wing four, launch and stay in lunar orbit for defense

"Yes, sir," the wing commander replied.

Meanwhile on the Solstar, Commander Brydon is occupied with the fire from the cannons as well as the fighter threat. "Where did all these fighters come from? They are taking a toll on our vessels," he said. "Commander Skoby, what's your status?"

"Besides being quite busy, Commander, the Jaydon is down to 80 percent, and the Mardeck has taken heavy damage from the cannons. The Oran reports." At that moment the Oran exploded in a brilliant flash of light, and the shockwave shook the other vessels. "The Oran's gone, sir," Skoby informed him.

"Emperor, this is Commander Brydon. Acknowledge."

At that moment the Klosk vessel Kryton joined the fighters and opened up on the Mornstar which has already taken heavy damage, and destroyed her in a single pass.

"Empress come in, this is Brydon."

The Empress takes a direct hit from one of the cannons and turns to run for the safety of space. The Densor followed her into open space firing as she went. They weren't going to let the emperor escape so easily.

"Commander Brydon this is the Empress. All vessels pull back to the fourth planet to escape the fire from those cannons," the emperor ordered.

"Yes, sir. All vessels pull back," Brydon ordered.

As the Torani fleet turned to escape, the Haldeck was hit by a three cannon salvo that turned it into a cloud of space dust. The Jayden was then suddenly disabled by several of the fighters concentrating on her engines and set adrift in space, helpless to support his retreating forces.

"This is the Empress. All remaining vessels retreat from the Sol System. I repeat, retreat to galactic space."

"Yes, sir," Brydon replied, being the only other vessel currently under its own power.

"This is lunar control. All units, cease fire," John ordered. "Commander Hilldar. Can you pursue the remaining two fleet vessels?"

"Lunar command. We could pursue, but even in their state they are much too fast for us to apprehend them."

"Then return to the station and hold the Jayden where she lies."

"Yes, command," Hilldar replied, then set a course for the crippled Jayden.

The two remaining Torani vessels slunk off into open space on what they all assume to be a course for Torani. The Jayden has now been captured, as she lies powerless in Earth orbit from the damage done by the valiant fighters. The Klosk and Velnor fleets suffered no losses, but three of their vessels will need extensive repair before returning to their home planets.

The Alliance plan has worked like clockwork with the help of the Klosk and Velnor fleets, and the invaluable help of a single Torani man. The planet that was the most technologically retarded planet in the galaxy today defeated the most advanced fleet in the galaxy with the help of their new friends from the Klosk and Velnor planets. It has always been well known on this planet, and is now known across the galaxy, that you don't piss off the human race because we will fight back and never give up until every last one of us is dead.

The control room at NORAD is on its feet and celebrating. It is a great victory for the people of Earth as well as the rest of the galaxy. The cannon arrays suffered minor losses and will stay active to protect the planet in the future. But hopefully in the future it will only be from stray asteroids or comets and not invading forces. But if they are necessary again, the warriors of the planet Earth know exactly what they are capable of.

The ambassadors are all quite proud of their accomplishments during the last two years, as well as their combined fleets' mettle in battle. They all know that this has been the last day of Torani rule in this galaxy, and a new alliance led by a just leader will rule from this moment further.

"Lance, dammed good job, my friend," Gene said as he excitedly shook his hand and patted him on the back vigorously.

"I can't take the credit. It belongs to Captain Rice and Brad Meyer at NASA. And let's not forget Jack Lee. Without his software improvements we would have never cracked the Torani locks. We all owe a great deal of thanks to them all," Colonel Polaski replied.

The NORAD team has done what it has trained to do for the last sixty years. They have done their part to save Earth from destruction. They have finally been rewarded for their many decades of training.

John and Brad watch from the Lunar Station's control room as the fighters funnel back into the station after a great victory. Wave after wave waits patiently to take their place in the station to celebrate this great victory.

"How many did we lose?" John asked.

"Thirty-eight," Brad replied.

"What about our wing, Commanders?"

"All accounted for."

"Thank god. Every one of them was from the valley."

"They were the best trained," Brad replied.

"Thank god for that. Where's our commanders?"

"They want to be the last ones in. They won't come in until all of their men are in safely."

They continued to watch as wave after wave of fighters entered the bays and were returned to their resting places. When the last four fighters entered the hangar and the shields were closed, the commanders exited their ships and were met by the two men with a respectful salute.

"Congratulations, gentlemen," John said as he shook all of their hands in turn. "You did a hell of a job out there today."

"Thanks, John," Willis said as he wiped the sweat from his face.

"Mortisk we couldn't have done any of this without your help. Thank you my dear friend."

"You are very welcome, my friend."

"You guys gonna park those?" he asked, pointing at their ships.

"No, we figured we would borrow them in the morning," Willis said with a smile. "We'll have some very worried people waiting for us."

"I saw nothing, how about you, Brad?" John said.

"Saw what?" Brad replied smiling.

The six men headed for the main hall for a well-deserved drink to celebrate their victory, as well as a toast to the ones that didn't make it back. The worst part of war, is the knowledge that men will die, no matter how well you are prepared.

On board the Jayden, Commander Skoby has surrendered his vessel as requested by the Galactic Alliance, to the Klosk Commander Hilldar. The prisoners will all be taken to a secure location on Earth until they can be tried for their crimes.

The Jayden has been claimed by Earth and will be used as a model for future cruisers, as well as being the first vessel in their fleet after a crew is trained for her. The commander has informed his crew of the emperor's deception, and apologized for putting them in harm's way under such dishonorable pretenses. He hopes that the Galactic Alliance, as well as Earth's leaders, will go easy on them under the circumstances. A detachment of Klosk warriors are now on board the vessel to oversee the transfer of the prisoners to a detention facility on the planet.

The residents of the valley, along with the townspeople, have left the safely of the mountain to gather at the gazebo and look to the now dark and quiet sky. They know the battle is over, but now the question remains of just how many lives were lost.

It's late at night and they don't expect any news till morning, so they all slowly return to their shelters for a restless night's sleep. Hyal came over to Bill and Monica and gave them both a big hug. She looked at them both, then at the sky. "They will all be home tomorrow," she said with a reassuring smile. They felt much better with her assurance and went to get some much needed rest.

After a restless night, it's now eight o'clock in the morning and the people of the towns rise and began to return to their homes. Bill has been sitting in the gazebo with a fire going since five this morning. There was no sleep for him, as his son, stepsons, and two friends, were still unaccounted for. Hyal's sixth sense said they were all okay, but he wouldn't sleep until he was sure they were all okay.

Monica came out in a blanket with a fresh cup of coffee and curled up with him at the fire. As the townspeople all returned the things to the storage and thanked him for his generosity, he bid them a safe trip home and reassured them that all will be okay.

As they watched the last of the cars leave, Sassy rolled her ears to the sky. She knows that sound. "Jaxor?" Bill asked.

"Too loud for the Jaxor," Monica said.

They stood and watched the five fighters come in over the mountain. The families all came out of the houses as Sassy barked continuously at the strange vehicles. They landed in the hayfield, the canopies opened, and their family was finally home. All five of them. The tears began to roll down the cheeks of the wives and children as they ran to meet their loved ones. Bill sat back down and dumped his coffee cup on the grass. Monica rose without a word and went into the house returning a few minutes later with a case of beer and Bill's bowl. It was time to celebrate. His son was home from war.

"How was it up there?" he asked his son.

"Dangerous," he replied as he grabbed a beer and sat with Alice and his son.

"He did good," Mortisk said, patting him on the back.

"I knew he would," Bill replied. "Beer?" he asked his big friend.

His big friend gladly took the beer and sat. His wife and child sat next to him, happy for his safe return. Alice and little Clifford also sat wrapped in a warm blanket next to her husband. The rest of the family all sat with their loved ones, quiet at first, but after they relaxed for a while they began to enjoy themselves. They all made it back. "Life is good."

Chapter 61

---•●✵●•---

Torani Space, Space Dock
October 30, 2023

The remaining two vessels of the once great Torani fleet limped into the space dock after a bitter defeat and long journey home. The emperor and the commander, having relived the incredible defeat handed to them by the Earth forces for the last eight days, slowly left their vessels. As they entered the inner sanctum of the station, where their shuttle was docked for their return to the planet, they were met not by cheers from their people but by armed guards who have orders to arrest the commanders and crews of the vessels.

"What is the meaning of this disrespect?" the emperor demanded to know.

"We have orders from the temporary ruling council to detain everyone on the vessels," the guard replied.

"I am the emperor of Torani. You have no right," he said.

The two men along with their crews were escorted to a secure location to wait until they can be brought before the Galactic Council for their crimes. The people of Torani have spoken, and no claim to power can overrule their decision. The council members have been notified of their capture, and the people of the galaxy now wait for justice to be served.

After the news of the emperor's capture reached Earth, the ambassadors have all come together to discuss their upcoming trip to Torani for the trial of the emperor and his council. It has been decided that the crewmembers will not be severely punished for their unwilling participation in these crimes.

The galactic leaders are all now on their home worlds, as they left the station before the attack. Leader Rowland will make her first galactic trip, along with her trusted Ambassador Furgison, to present testimony at the upcoming trial.

"Well, my friends, I guess we will be parting company for a short while," Gene said.

"Yes, I must travel to Velnor to join the leaders of my planet for the trip to Torani. They expect a full report on the events that have occurred over the last three years before the trial," Prowlex explained to his friends.

"That will take a great deal of time. Lucky for you it's a long journey," Gene said with a smile. "Gowlisk, are you traveling all the way to Klosk to join your leaders?"

"No, I would like to join your group if you would allow it."

"We would be honored to have you with us on the Jaxor, Gowlisk," Tronext said. "The Zaxin leader is already in transit to Torani as we speak, so there is no reason for me to return to Zaxin."

"Not to mention the fact that you have to shuttle the earthlings around the galaxy," John replied jokingly.

"It can be a never-ending task. Had I known how much work it would be to be your friend, I would have thought twice," Tronext replied with a smile on his reptilian face.

"Was that humor?" Gene asked sarcastically.

They all laughed together, and the ambassadors can now relax since the crisis is now over and start to plan rebuilding the galaxy's new alliance.

"I must be leaving, my friends. My shuttle is waiting on the pad for my return to Velnor," Prowlex said as he shook all of his friends' hands in turn.

"We will see you on the Torani Galactic Station in two weeks," Gene said as he shook his friend's hand.

They watched as their friend left for his shuttle, then started making plans for their own departure in one week's time. Gene has to schedule the trip with Leader Rowland, who is very nervous about the two-week trip on board the Jaxor. The Earth leader has never left the planet's surface before and is quite nervous about the trip to Torani.

All of the leaders of the Galactic Council have been summoned to the Torani station for the proceedings that will decide not only the future of their galaxy but the fate of the emperor and all of his conspirators.

The Zaxin leader Enxnor has been elected as the temporary leader of the council. The first meeting has been called to install the new Torani leader Akalind. Akalind was the leader of the secret organization that came forward with the information provided to him by Commander Skoby. He has pulled the Torani back together after the great disappointment in the previous leadership and hopes to usher in a new era of peace for his planet. The leader has also acknowledged the injustice done to the people of Corisole and has offered them citizenship on their planet. The Torani planet is quite large and has hundreds of islands that they can easily settle their society. The new Torani leadership has taken responsibility for the damage done to Corisole and will commence immediately with the terraforming of the planet, with an offer by Earth to supply all the fuel needed to complete the project.

To add to their long list of debts, they have sent thousands of workers to Zaxin and Klosk to aid in the rebuilding of their planets. They no longer want to be known as an evil, deceptive empire. The council has been ordered to the main chamber to begin the hearing.

The leaders, along with their ambassadors, are all now taking their seats as the new leader Enxnor calls the council to order.

"Leaders of the Galactic Alliance. We are here once again to resolve an extremely evil and deceptive matter. We will call witnesses before this council who will testify not only of the premeditated destruction of four planets, but the plan to deceive this council, and control all Triomicium production in the known universe."

"Ambassador Tronext will serve as the prosecution for the Alliance, and Councilor Mernox has been appointed as defense for the accused. The trial will commence at the start of tomorrow's session. The Torani leaders, along with all other conspirators, will be present at that time to present their defense against the evidence that will be presented by the prosecution. Until tomorrow I will now adjourn this council. Thank you all."

The ambassadors gathered outside the chamber along with the Earth leader. Gene has gathered the group with plans for a nice evening before the trial starts. The new Torani emperor approaches the group and introduces himself.

"Gentlemen, and dear lady, I am Emperor Akalind. It would please me if you would all allow me to treat you to dinner, to show my deepest regrets for all that has happened to your planets at the hand of our previous leaders," he asked humbly.

"As long as I get to pick the place, you're on," Gene replied.

The emperor looked at Gene curiously, then laughed. "Now I know why the galactic leaders like you so much. Where would you like to dine?"

"Ocean Mist Café in Carista," Gene replied.

"Very good choice, Ambassador. That is also one of my favorites. Leader Rowland, if I may?" the emperor asked as he offered her his very large arm.

"I would be delighted," she replied and hooked her tiny arm around his.

The very diverse group left the station for the Torani capital of Carista and spent the next several hours touring the capitol and enjoying the fine food of the seaside café. Tomorrow would bring on a new day, and there is very serious business to attend to.

The council is called to order at the beginning of the new session. The leader ordered the accused brought into the chamber. The emperor and his advisors, ambassadors, and military leaders are all in the chamber to answer to the charges against them. The vessels' crews will not have charges brought against them, but they have been ordered to help with the rebuilding of the damaged planets as their punishment for their involvement in the attacks.

The defense started with a statement asking for leniency from the council in their punishments. With the evidence all being so incriminating, there is no real defense to be presented, so the defense waited to hear the testimony of the witnesses.

The prosecution proceeded as Tronext called the numerous witnesses, who testified to the facts of the three-decade-long conspiracy of the Torani leaders to gain control of the galaxy's Triomicium and the decades of murder carried out in the name of that cause.

Commander Skoby testified against his fleet commanders who willingly took part in the Zaxin, Klosk, and Earth attacks. He then told of how he discovered the information of the galactic domination plan and informed the new leader Akalind of these plans, as well as the deception of the last three decades, which led to Ardesnal's removal from office.

The Earth, Velnor, and Klosk ambassadors gave testimony covering the previous two years of preparation before the truth could be brought forth, and eventually their plan to defeat the Torani fleet in order to save the entire galaxy.

When all of the evidence had been heard, the defense was again given an opportunity to disprove the evidence against them. With no defense to the charges, the defense rested.

The leaders all retired to the galactic leader's chamber to consider their options. The prisoners were returned to their cells to await the verdict against them.

After what was actually a short deliberation, the council was called back to the main chamber. The prisoners were then once again brought into the chamber to face their fates, and leader Enxnor then stood to read the verdict.

"Members of the Galactic Alliance. Once again we are called to this hall to pass judgement on these defendants for the crimes committed by them, upon the many races and systems in this galaxy."

"The defendants are being accused of the deaths of billions of inhabitants of this galaxy, and the sentences will be handed out as follows. The crews of the fleet vessels will be sentenced to hard labor for the entirety of the rebuilding of the damaged planets. Upon their completion of these sentences they will then be allowed to rejoin our society as freed citizens of our planet, with only their consciences to punish them. Commander Skoby will be sentenced to supervise this rebuilding until its completion, and has only been granted leniency because of his actions that indicated his remorse for what the Torani fleet had done to its neighbors in this galaxy. We value his honesty as well as his actions during the final days.

"The remaining defendants, which include the emperor and his council, and the military commanders involved, are all sentenced to death for the billions of lives that they have affected. Now with all that being said, as the leaders of a new galaxy, we do not want to follow in the footsteps of the prior leadership, so the death penalty will be suspended."

The members of the Galactic Alliance rose with strong disagreement to the verdict.

"Hold on, council members. This suspension of the death penalty will be replaced with a life sentence in the Triomicium mines of Harken. I will not follow in the footsteps of the previous leadership and start this new future with more death. This session of the Galactic Alliance is now adjourned."

The council members all then cheered the fact that the members of these crimes would spend the rest of their lives at hard labor, digging the hard rock of the prison planet Harken, instead of a quick death.

The prisoners were all then escorted from the chamber and led to the shuttle to take them immediately to the Harken planet. They would spend at least as many years at the prison planet before their deaths as they have created tyranny in this galaxy.

The galaxy has now been restored to a galaxy that treats all systems with respect. This respect will reach out to help those in need as well as protect those who cannot protect themselves.

Epilogue

————•●✸●•————

2030

The 420 Galaxy has healed its wounds over the past seven years, and after three long decades of Torani tyranny, the galaxy has put its attention on what has been the most productive seven years in the galaxy's history.

The systems of the galaxy have all pulled together to spread out into the universe. With the discovery of the vast fuel reserves, the inhabitants of the 420 Galaxy have prospered since the reserves were far more than anticipated. Throughout the Sol System the reserves were spread from one end to the other. They discovered five additional planets, as well as the asteroid fields that were rich with ore and other metals for the production of starships.

With such riches in the galaxy, it created the need for more protection from invaders, which has led to the creation of five more Galactic Stations. These stations are manned at all times with five heavy cruisers and a squadron of fighters to deter unfriendly galaxies' advances. We hope this deterrent won't be needed, but with such great wealth in this galaxy, there will always be those who'll try to take advantage of it.

Other galaxies of this sector of the universe have begun to visit our galaxy, offering new engine designs that would finally give us the ability to travel to other galaxies. With this ability we can be the explorers that we all crave to be and explore the universe at will.

The Zakorian and Boral systems have managed to advance medical sciences at least a hundred years with the unlimited resources on their sides. Soon all races will be able to live hundreds of years, which will aid in the exploration of the never-ending universe. Technology, however, has grown at a much slower pace than medicine, as other galaxies think much as we do. They hold back the technologies that they feel we are not ready for.

Within one decade the 420 Galaxy has come out of the ashes and risen like the phoenix into the future. We have grown from a nonexistent dust cloud in the universe to a very powerful entity. This is a very dangerous position we now sit in. With the offers from other galaxies, we must look back in time and remember the very hard lesson on trust the Torani taught us. It was a very important and costly lesson on trust and greed, paid for with billions of innocent lives.

Sol System Summary
July 4, 2030

The Sol System has been affected more than any system in the galaxy. With the discovery of the Triomicium in our system, the colonization of the system has been great.

We have opened our system to our neighbors to create a less scattered galactic population, and the wealth has created new systems in the galaxy that were never even considered before. With us all working together, those systems that were once considered too extensive of a task to inhabit are now being created by using the unlimited power of the Sol System.

The Sol System now has cannon batteries on every planet in the system, which give security from rogue species from other galaxies that might be tempted by greed to invade our now peaceful system. These planets are now inhabited by our neighboring systems, who are working diligently to terraform the planets for their use. The Boral as well as the Zaxins, who are quite happy living inside the domes, now inhabit the planet Mars. The Antarians, who no longer have the need to be pirates because of the distribution of the Triomicium, have inhabited the planet Jupiter, which contains an atmosphere much like their home planet. They have constructed domes that float in the atmosphere of the huge world.

Shipyards have been constructed along the asteroid belt because of the massive amount of metals contained within them, which has also enabled the galaxy to become a large manufacturer of freighters and starships for other galaxies. Many of these freighters are now in use in the mining of the galaxies' ice worlds, to help with the regeneration of the Corisole planet's ecosystem. It is estimated that the planet may be inhabitable again in as few as twenty years. The Sol System is now an integral part of the 420 Galaxy family, as well as the universe.

Earth Summary
July 4, 2030

Earth is returning to normal after ten years of hard work. The major cities have all been cleared and are now being rebuilt with the help of any species that wishes to live on our planet, which we have come to find is a great many. With only two billion remaining earthlings on the planet, it leaves a lot of room for other systems to create new settlements on our world.

New technologies now power cargo vessels on land and at sea, although most of them will soon go the way of the dinosaur as large shuttles are much better at the task. Cars are slowly being replaced by flying vehicles with engines based on fighter technology, but thankfully for the people on planet Earth, they don't travel at the same speeds. With people like Bill and Mortisk, the classic vehicles of the past will never be totally replaced. The minimal effect on the atmosphere has been deemed immeasurable with new atmospheric purifiers that were constructed to clean the old air, so the planet has allowed the limited use of fossil fuels.

With the advancements in medicine by the Boral and Zakorians, almost all diseases have been eradicated on the planet, and humans now have an estimated lifespan of two hundred years and rising. With this extended lifespan, the people of Earth now foresee the ability to travel to other galaxies with the new starships currently being created.

The use of technologies from other systems has allowed the deserts to be transformed into fertile regions capable of feeding their people, as well as growing things that have become delicacies on other systems, and even in other galaxies. Earth has become the source of many items thought to be normal and plentiful on our planet but which are rare delicacies on other worlds.

The people of Earth can no longer imagine coming from a planet plagued by war, famine, and disease. A planet that had a hard time planning to inhabit our moon or Mars on even a temporary basis, then becoming one of the most diverse, with its many species of inhabitants, along with its grand-scale involvement in the universe. It took only ten years to go from a crawl to traveling the universe. But was it worth five billion lives to do it?

Independence Valley
July 4, 2030

Independence Valley, Colorado, is now the home of over eighty citizens from all parts of the galaxy. After the original forty-eight people and thirteen homes, the valley started attracting interest from the rest of the galaxy and is now one of the most diverse towns for its size.

Ambassador—or should we say Earth Leader Furgison now resides in the valley with his family. The Zaxin ambassador as well as Galactic Leader Enxnor have both moved into the valley—seasonally, that is—since they both have jobs to do now that the galaxy is creating new worlds to inhabit.

Prowlex and Tronext both retired from politics and now spend their days riding horses and fishing with Mortisk. They are absolutely dedicated to the two sports. They have also discovered classic cars as the Torani did when they arrived. Of course the barely four-and-a-half-foot Prowlex does look a little ridiculous in a '54 Cadillac. The valley wouldn't be complete without the hairy Klosk and his family living there also, joining all the rest in the fun.

You can surely imagine the school—with Torani children, Zaxin children, Klosk children, and Velnor children, playing along with our own. The children of this galaxy are what will make it great in the future.

The family has grown also. Mortisk and Hyal have added two more golden babies to the mix. Ben and Tashike have had two children, which are a mix of the beautiful Tashike and Ben, but we won't hold that against them. Willis has added another grandchild to the family for his father, and Fawn and her husband have finally decided to start the process and added one more.

Then we move on to the next generation, who are his grandchildren. They are now twenty and twenty-two and surely will make him a greatgrandfather soon. What a wonderful place for Bill to be, surrounded by such a large family and the greatest friends in the universe.

As usual on the Fourth of July, there is a huge party going on in the valley. It has almost become a galactic ritual. "Bill's barbeque." Where the beer is cold and plentiful, the food is always barbequed, and everyone has the best weed in the galaxy. No wonder they call it the 420 Galaxy.

The guys are all sitting around the even bigger fire pit as usual, watching the many races of children play in the water. Sassy is getting old like her master and doesn't play as much anymore, so she is simply lying there watching them now.

"Nice crowd, Bill," Gene said, looking around the valley.

"Sure is, isn't it. Keeps getting bigger every year," he replied as he lit the pipe and handed it to Gene. "I didn't realize how much lizards liked to swim," he said as Tronext did a cannonball into the pond.

"Wait till the Wookie jumps in," Ben said, pointing at Gowlisk. "Where's the camera? We've got to get a picture of this." He was now pointing at the large golden man sitting in an inner tube with a beer in one hand and a joint in the other.

"Here, I've started to always keep it close," Bill said. "He's really come to like that tube. You'll catch him out there almost every day."

Willis and his band are entertaining the crowd with their music. Dove and Allen are on the grass dancing along with his sisters and their husbands. Bill never dances in public since the dog started laughing at him many years ago while he worked.

For ten years now they have had this barbeque, and everyone from all over the galaxy has enjoyed it. The ambassadors have spread the tradition to their home worlds also. They are the same as on Earth; they just have better weed. The night goes on with all of the families sitting at the tables talking and laughing with each other. Monica came over and snuggled up with the man she loves, and they watched the small children taking some of their first steps.

"You think they'll grow up here?" she asked as she watched them.

"I sure hope so," Bill answered and gave her a kiss.

Earth is now like that small child taking her first steps into the universe. Bill wonders to himself where those steps will lead her in the future. Well, he's got at least another hundred years ahead of him, so he'll just sit in his valley by the fire, drink his beer, and enjoy all of the wonders of the 420 Galaxy. "Life is good."

THE END?

CPSIA information can be obtained
at www.ICGtesting.com
Printed in the USA
BVHW031951170520
579828BV00001B/11/J

9 781648 716768